I0606674

THE THREE

FORSAKEN SONS: BOOK 1
CHRISTA KINDE

YAHAVIM

ALSO BY
ℭHRISTA KINDE

THRESHOLD SERIES

The Blue Door (Book 1)
The Hidden Deep (Book 2)
The Broken Window (Book 3)
The Garden Gate (Book 4)

THRESHOLD COMPANION STORIES

Angels All Around
Angels in Harmony
Angels on Guard
Angel on High
Angel Unaware
Rough and Tumble
Tried and True
Sage and Song

POMEROY FAMILY LEGACY COLLECTION

Pursuing Prissie
Sweets for the Sweet
College Bound

*Angels: A 90-Day Devotional
about God's Messengers*

Forsaken Sons, Book 1
The Three

Cover Art and Interior Illustrations by Hannah Christenson
    HannahChristenson.com

Jacket Design by Bumble Bess
    BumbleBess.com

⨯HRISTAKINDE.COM

For the chosen ones.

TABLE OF CONTENTS

THE THREE

People don't know
much about us,
but that's okay.
We were important
for a while. We even
made history. It's
right there in the Bible,
assuming you know about
stuff like that. Most don't.
Crud, even scholars
probably couldn't
dredge up our names.
But they're there.
And so were we.

1

Burying the dead is hungry work.

With every strike of Benaiah's pick, dry soil crumbled away from the trench's edge, piling around his feet, getting between his toes. He swiped at the sweat trickling from under his head covering—a sloppy turban of knotted linen scarves in fading shades of brown, green, and yellow.

Time to switch.

Tossing aside his pick, Ben winced when it clunked dully against some guy's head. Not that the dead man could feel it. Judging by the snarl on the corpse's rigid face, the last two things *he'd* felt were rage and a Philistine javelin through the chest.

What kind of fool goes into battle without armor?

Benaiah shook his head and adjusted the damp cloth tied over the lower half of his face. It helped a little. As in *very* little. The stench seeped into everything—heavy with copper, sweet with decay. If his stomach hadn't already been pinched by hunger, he probably would have retched it dry.

Aleff's gonna be disappointed again. But he doesn't get it. He can't understand.

Reaching for the jagged-edged board that was his shovel, Ben made do. Anyone who could afford better wouldn't be caught in a place like this. *Not unless they're caught dead.* He scraped up dirt and pitched it. The king's men were halfway across the valley, stripping bodies and collecting weapons from the slain. *Picked as clean as if the carrion birds were on 'em.*

Benaiah waved away a buzzing fly and focused on clearing the loosened soil. What did it matter to him if the proud sons of proud families marched to their deaths? He thrust his makeshift shovel at the earth with too much force, and the end snapped. *Crud.*

"You there. Aren't you done yet?"

He didn't even look up. "If you're in a hurry, feel free to lend a hand."

"Don't get ahead of us, boy. We need to reclaim their armaments before the earth reclaims them."

Hurry up. Don't rush. Make up your mind. Ben rolled his eyes at the haughtiness in the man's tone. "You think I'm stupid?"

"I think you're an insolent son of a camel!"

Ben stilled. *Camel. Why's it always gotta be a camel?*

Letting the broken board fall from his hands, he slowly straightened. This wasn't the first time he'd resorted to this kind of work, and it wasn't the first time someone had looked down on him for it. Pulling down his face cloth, he smiled up at the man. "And you croak like a carrion bird."

Usually, he avoided eye contact with people. Hiding his hair wasn't too hard, but eyes were another matter; icy green irises marked him as different. Not a son of Israel. Not one of God's chosen.

Benaiah narrowed his eyes at the soldier, whose bravado slipped a notch. *I know his type—prissy about the polish on his sword, proud of the shield he hides behind. This guy probably spent the entire battle shaking his weapon and yelling a lot ... from a safe distance.* To Ben's amusement, the man made a quick hand gesture for warding off evil. *Way too late for that, idiot.*

"You're *not* one of us," he accused.

"Nope. I'm not one of you." This guy was definitely a local. The Benjamites were a small tribe with a big chip on their shoulder. They'd been favored by God because Israel's first king was a Benjamite, and Saul's hometown now ranked as a royal city. Chances were, this officer could claim to be one of the king's many cousins. *Like I care.*

Nervousness seeped into the man's posture, but he held on to his bluster. "Name yourself, boy! Who are you?"

Planting his palm on the hard-packed ground he'd been hired to break, Benaiah swung smoothly out of the trench and stood to his full height. Leggy as the young camels Aleff was forever comparing him to, Ben had always been overly tall. At sixteen, he loomed over the soldier. *Not such big stuff, are ya, little man?*

"I'm called Benaiah."

"*What* are you?"

So much for hospitality toward strangers. As the soldier's lip curled in disdain, Ben's smile twisted bitterly. "Busy. So if you're done wasting my time, I'll get back to work." He dropped into the trench and checked to see if he could salvage his board. Out of the corner of his eye, he saw the man's hand drop away from his sword hilt. *Good. Now, go away.*

Instead, the idiot persisted. "How do I know you're not a Canaanite spy?"

"Would a spy be scuffing in ditches with the dead?"

"Which tribe claims you?"

Benaiah looked up and honestly said, "Not sure you'd call it a claim, but there's someone who'll vouch for me. He's a Levite. Lives in Ramah. But he gets around some."

"Are you a servant in his house?"

"Nothing like that. He's kinda a friend."

Skepticism sharpened the soldier's voice. "You claim friendship with one who serves the priests?"

"He's more of a prophet."

It was funny to watch the pieces click together. The Benjamites might boast a king, but Benaiah knew the man who'd anointed Saul—the king-maker. God's prophet was both feared and revered, and this guy wasn't taking any chances. Backing up fast, he snapped, "I should have you cast out for your lies."

"I'm not lying."

With an oath, the pest retreated, leaving Benaiah to his toil. Pushing the facecloth firmly across his nose, he grabbed his pick and returned to battering the earth. He didn't have much, but he had what it took to survive. All a foreman cared about was a strong back. All the motivation Ben needed came from his empty stomach. A steady glare usually took care of any trouble, but in a pinch, it definitely helped to know a bushy-bearded old-timer who could hear the voice of God.

The facecloth hid a crooked smile as Benaiah the Forsaken muttered, "Thanks, Samuel."

Not many knew what I was,
and that suited me fine.
There's a shame in my past
that twists my gut. But it's not
something I can change.
More humiliation's the
last thing I want. Pity's the
last thing I need. So I hide
one truth and hang onto another.
I hate where I came from,
but that doesn't mean
I hate myself.

2

Grilled goat is an acquired taste.

Benaiah heard them talking, guessing where he came from. A barbarian from the north. A leper's whelp. A runaway slave. That one was partly true. Not the slave bit, but he'd left without a word. *Living with Aleff isn't so bad.* Their hut amidst a sea of reeds was probably as close to heaven as Ben could ever hope to get. No one stared into his eyes with fear. No one asked uncomfortable questions. No one hurled insults. Or stones.

Rolling his shoulders, he made his way to the foreman's tent. With the setting of the sun, his long day in the trenches was over, and he joined the line of diggers and pickers looking for their reward. *'Bout time. Better be worth it.* Keeping his head down and slouching, Ben rubbed at his empty stomach. *Aleff's food is good—tastes nice, keeps you going. But it doesn't satisfy every part of me.*

Benaiah's earliest memories were mostly bad, but he remembered the smell and savor of grilled meat. And he craved it. With a vengeance. So he found ways to get it.

He'd tried hunting. *Tried and failed.* Fast as he was, Ben couldn't outrun a rabbit, and birds were no better. *It's not like I have wings.* He drew the line at poaching sheep and goats from the many flocks that wandered the hillsides.

Pretty sad that drudge work with maggot-infested bodies is the quickest, safest route to a decent meal. Every so often, he found something he could trade. A pocketful of salt or some wild figs were often enough to coax a few skewers off the cook-fire of a kindly woman. And a fresh egg was as good as coin. Unless someone decided you stole it.

"Next in line," droned the man seated on a low platform inside the tent. The grizzled foreman gazed up at Benaiah without interest. "I remember you. Started just after sunup."

"Yep. Full day." Men who labored in the field all day could expect to feed their family with a share of the crop. Battlefields were a little different. The pay was better, but you couldn't just pick up and leave. According to the Law, if you touched something dead, you were unclean, and getting clean again wasn't a matter of scrubbing off the crud in the closest river.

The man nodded at a jumble stacked along the far side of the tent. "We have permission to divide the spoils. Choose from what's left."

Benaiah angled over to see if there was anything worth taking. There were some dinged up weapons, a stack of roughly-woven cloaks, and a battered pile of farm implements. Not much to look at, but not a bad deal. A poor man might be glad to trade a day's labor for a coat. *Wash out the blood. Mend the tears. Almost good as new.* A farmer might have his eye out for a decent hoe. Or even an ax. Ben had earned his pick under similar circumstances. Glancing over his shoulder, he asked, "If I leave this stuff for the others, can I eat more?"

A bland smile appeared on the foreman's face. "Hungry?"

"Usually."

The man shook his head. "You earned your share along with a full belly." Gesturing to the pick propped on Ben's shoulder, he remarked, "A shovel would serve you well. Even in times of peace, there's dung to clear."

With a bit of rummaging, Benaiah located one with a long enough handle. "This one'll work. Thanks."

The foreman nodded and pointed to the east. "The priests and Levites are already in the encampment beyond this hill." In warning tones, he added, "Follow their instructions without fail."

"I know the routine."

Nodding dismissively, the foreman called, "Next in line."

Benaiah ducked outside and joined the trickle of men aiming for a column of smoke drifting into the twilit sky. He followed his nose toward the smell of char and meat, his stomach gurgling in anticipation. Before he'd rounded the last bend, Ben already knew what was for dinner. *Goat. That'll do.*

Dealing with people was kinda tricky. It wasn't like he could make a good impression. Dirt in his teeth, sweat in his eyes, blood under his nails—he reeked as much as the rest of the rabble. *But they'll overlook the filth so long as you stay downwind.* Doing his best to seem harmless, he stopped to hear the instructions of the farmer standing guard over his well. "Welcome, all you who tilled my field! Eat, drink, and by all means … wash! There's a stream yonder!"

Field, huh? Benaiah gazed out over the battlefield, which moved like a thing alive. Wild dogs skulked, disturbing the bolder, black-winged birds hopping from body to body. They'd left the dead Philistines to them. In the fading light, Ben could still make out faint lines beyond the churned up earth. And the far slope bristled with scrawny sticks. Vineyard? Grove? It was hard to tell. *That guy's got a strange sense of humor. Bet he didn't volunteer his field for this stand-off. War ruined his crop.* Ben looked back at the man who laughed so freely, the gap between his front teeth showed. *If it was me, I wouldn't be smiling.*

Fires kept the cold and the critters away, and men wrapped their cloaks tightly around fresh-washed bodies. The food was good, and there was plenty of it. No one complained when Benaiah went back for seconds, then thirds. Or maybe it was too dark for them to tell he was gorging himself on the spitted meat. *Or they're too drunk to care.* Some of the soldiers had found wine, and cups of fermented milk were passed from hand to hand. Ben drained his canteen and drifted back to the well.

The farmer was still there, picking his teeth with a thorn. "Back for more? Hungry as a bear, thirsty as a camel!"

There was no sting to the remarks, especially coming from a man who was drawing water like a woman. "Yeah, I'm empty." Benaiah held out the limp skin. *Can't blame the guy from protecting his well. In this land, water's life.*

"You'll rival the king himself once you're done growing into those feet!"

"He's taller'n me?" Ben asked in surprise. Few were. Especially among the tribes of Israel.

"I've seen for myself," confirmed the farmer. "He's head-and-shoulders taller than any man among us. Tall and proud, with armor that gleams in the sun."

"He's here?"

"He was. My lord the king drove the Philistines from this place. It was a great victory!"

Since Benaiah had spent all day covering up the cost of that victory, he only offered a shrug.

As the farmer topped off the canteen, he slyly said, "This well will quench your thirst, but it'd do you good to taste from the cups! Might put some hair on your chin!"

Ben scruffed self-consciously at his baby face. Yet another thing that set him apart. "Water's fine," he grumbled.

"The finest!" countered the man, returning the full, sloshing skin.

When's the last time someone talked to me like this? Ben found himself liking the farmer. Maybe some men still embraced God's command to be kind to strangers. Lingering a little longer, he asked, "What was planted down there?"

"Nothing worth mentioning!" At the teen's skeptical look,

the farmer's smile faded away. In a low voice, he said, "'Though He slay me, yet I will hope in Him. Indeed, this will turn out for my deliverance.' Better the field than my family."

"You know the lessons of Job?" Benaiah asked in surprise.

Smiling anew, the man retorted, "As do you! Not bad for a stranger."

Lifting the canteen, Benaiah said, "Thanks," and faded back into the milling crowd. A few of the men called out to him as he strode past. Drunken jests and raucous laughter. Benaiah was used to the ribbing. *Let them question my parentage. I do.*

He silently gathered his things and trudged in the direction of the stream. Aleff liked for him to stay out of remote places, but Benaiah didn't want the protection the gathered men offered. Not when the speculations turned to his mother's tastes and his father's species. It would have been easier to laugh off their crude jokes if they weren't so close to the truth.

He needed us. Bad.
But before we could
be there for him,
we had to be born,
and that's no easy thing
when your mother's human
and your father's not.
People like us aren't
welcome in the world.
Sons of the sons of God.
Our fathers were angels.
Fallen angels.
But for his sake,
we were spared.

3

Some questions don't need answers.

Ben had dodged a full bath earlier, but he wanted it now. He didn't like undressing by daylight. At home, it was different, but here, his skin was sensitive to sunlight. *And I hate the gawkers.* With a furtive glance toward the encampment atop the hill, he undid the necessary knots to unwind his turban and loosen his hair. The stuff wasn't as ridiculously long as Aleff's, but Benaiah's waist-length hair was the soft brown of a baby camel's and straight as a sheaf of grain. Odd to the extreme in a land where browned skin and dark curls were the norm.

He sat in the stream. The sluggish water was chest deep and chilly, but he'd never minded the cold. Other things bothered him, though. Like being alone.

Wherever he went, he saw people who were part of something—a family, a village, a tribe, a people. *I'm part of nothing. No one claims me. Except maybe Aleff, and I don't think he counts.*

If he thought back, Benaiah could recall the first time he'd met the person who'd become his whole world. *It was raining. The skies opened up, and water fell in sheets.* He could remember it hissing on roof tiles, pounding on paving stones. Everyone had run screaming to hide from the strange water, but Aleff had come for him. *He didn't look frightened.* Benaiah had reached out to grab hold of the stranger's ankle-length hair, yanking hard to see if it was real. Every strand had glittered like threads of copper, fine as spider's silk.

He didn't scold. Just smiled and opened his arms. Ben lay back in the water to wet his hair, staring up at the stars. Now that he was old enough to understand, he knew he'd been snatched. Kidnapped. *But when Aleff carried me away, he saved my life.*

Those rains were scary for a reason. That had been the earth's first storm. A judgment that plunged the entire world into the depths of the sea. *Those were the days of Noah. Probably.*

Sitting up and splashing water on his face, Benaiah wondered if Aleff was teasing. *I only have his word for it.* Then again, he doubted his caretaker *could* lie. Even though Ben had been very small when Aleff came for him, he'd known that his rescuer was different. Aleff's ears came to points, his clothes shimmered, and their new home stood alone in an ocean of reeds where it was always summer and never night.

Are all angels as weird as Aleff, or is he a special case? It wasn't as if Benaiah had any basis for comparison. *But really ... he's gotta be cracked. Why else would an angel be willing to raise the son of a demon?*

There weren't many places he could go where Aleff wouldn't follow, so Ben wasn't surprised when his caretaker appeared on the stream's opposite bank. "Little Ben Peep's been gnawing on sheep," Aleff said in a sing-song voice.

Benaiah despaired of understanding half the nonsense Aleff spouted. He burped loudly and replied, "Goat, actually."

"Sounds ... delectable." The slender angel tossed him a waxy lump and took a seat.

"People are gonna notice if I smell pretty." But Ben worked the soap between his hands and slicked the thick, honey-scented lather into his hair. Suds soon drifted on top of the water around him. Carrying away the stench of death.

"Did you wilt in the heat, little flower?"

"I kept covered," Benaiah replied tersely. "No sunburn."

"And did my gangling camel find better water than this to drink?"

"Yeah. There's a well up top. Got accused of trying to drink it dry."

"At least you show *some* sense." The angel gazed around their vicinity with a grave expression. "But you're not making it easy for us to hide you, out here by yourself."

The soap slipped from Ben's hands and he had to fish around for it. Aleff never lost his temper—assuming he had one—but there were times when his tongue was as sharp as a pike. "You said I'm safe when you're around."

"True."

Ben shrugged. "You're here."

Aleff's smiles always came and went quickly, but he didn't ever hide them. And even though the angel mostly let Ben do as he pleased, he never pretended he didn't care what happened to him. Aleff always came to bring Benaiah home. *Those first few times, I ran to see if he'd chase me. I'd hide. He'd seek.* And time and again, the angel had found him, dispelling his doubts and washing away his worries.

"Any signs of trouble?" Aleff inquired lightly.

"Just the usual junk," Benaiah replied. "Got picked on for having big feet. Knobby knees. Eerie eyes."

"Looks aren't everything." Aleff spread his hands wide and soothed, "You're just an ugly duckling."

Ben stared at him in disbelief. "Did you just call me ugly?"

"No, I called you a swan."

He narrowed his eyes. "I'm not deaf, Aleff. And I can't help how I look. My father was probably …."

"Fair as springtime, cheerful as summer," the angel glibly interrupted.

Benaiah held very still, his fingers tangled in his hair. In a low voice, he asked, "You knew him?"

"I did."

"You *knew* my father."

Aleff's expression didn't change. "Quite well."

"B-but why didn't you ever tell me?"

"You never asked."

Benaiah didn't like that answer, but it was true. *I never*

asked. I was afraid to ask. And the only reason they were talking about him now was because Aleff had volunteered something new. But this didn't make sense. Angels and demons didn't mix. Shaking his head, he argued, "But my father's a …"

"Once upon a time, your father was a Messenger. I knew him *before* he Fell."

Ben stared at the angel who was his companion, teacher, friend, and maybe even the father he'd rather have. Questions filled his mind. *Were you friends? What was he like? Can you see him in me?* But Ben shut his mouth tight and ducked underwater to rinse away the soap. *What's the use? The answers make no difference.* No matter what his father used to be, he'd Fallen. Only a demon remained. And if there was any resemblance between father and son, Benaiah was afraid of it.

Wringing out his hair, Ben asked, "Are you here to take me home?"

"Mmm … not quite." Aleff tapped the ground on which he sat. "Meet me back here after the priests finish their sacrifices. We're going on a little journey."

"Where to this time?"

"Ramah."

Benaiah feigned indifference. "I'm okay with that."

Aleff's brown eyes shone with amusement. "What a surprise."

I'm not sure you could
call us destined. We were
caught up, set aside,
reserved for one purpose.
But that didn't mean
we had no choice.
Everyone has a choice.
Sometimes it's hard to make.
Other times, it's impossible.
But most people would have
called us impossible, and that
made it easier to be fools.

4

The prophet and the angel are in cahoots.

Ben followed Aleff along the dusty road, head down, gaze unfocused. *My father used to be an angel. Started out with heaven for a home. But where you begin isn't always where you end.* Benaiah had seen enough to know that brave men could end up in a shallow grave. When bright angels messed up in big ways, their fate was even worse than death. Their piece of forever was snatched away, and whatever was left rotted out, leaving nothing but a hollow existence. *And a stench.*

No matter how hard Benaiah tried, he couldn't remember his father's face. Just a bad smell and worse feelings. They set his teeth on edge and left the pit of his stomach queasy and uneasy. *Damned as a traitor. Cast out of heaven. Thrown into a world where he preyed on humans.* Ben's brows drew together as a new thought occurred to him. *If he hadn't Fallen, I'd never have been born.*

How was he supposed to feel about *that*?

Aleff stopped so suddenly, Ben nearly collided with him. "What?" he grumbled.

"Words on the wind."

That was Aleff's way of saying another angel was nearby. Benaiah glanced around, then dropped his gaze. *I may not fit in with humans, but I'm blind as one.* His eyes were useless when it came to heavenly things. From time to time, Aleff entertained other angels, but Ben never saw them. *Only in dreams. And those fade as soon as I wake up.*

Men avoided him. Angels eluded him. Either way, he was left out. *Being both is being neither.*

Lurking thoughts reared up—unwelcome, yet unanswered. Was it possible that he belonged with demons? Given the chance, would the Fallen accept him as one of their own? Did his father even know he'd survived that ancient Flood? Benaiah hadn't seen the Fallen any more than he'd seen the Faithful, so how could he know for sure? *I've always known we're hiding, but it's not like I'm being chased. Shunned is more like it.*

Benaiah stared hard at Aleff, who'd moved a short distance along the road. He was disguised as a human. And with his hair hidden under a turban that covered his ears, he looked ordinary enough. Their clothes were nothing special and well-coated in dust since they were walking to Ramah. *Just to get grubby.* Aleff said it lent them an air of authenticity. Which was just a fancy word for sweat, grit, and sunburn.

Aleff turned and caught him staring. Crooking his finger, he called, "Time to take a shortcut!"

Squinting warily at stuff he wished he could see for himself, Benaiah demanded, "How come?"

"The rumor mill is grinding," Aleff replied, all smiles. "And the grist is unusually fine."

Ben scowled in annoyance at the odd terms, but he caught on enough to guess. "Was there a Messenger?"

"How astute!"

"So there was a message. A Sending? A warning?" he pried.

"A little of each, with a cherry on top!"

Benaiah tugged his turban further down over his eyebrows. Aleff kind of made him want to tear his hair out. Dumb jokes. Silly riddles. *But at least he never lies. Push hard enough, and the truth's there.* "Did something happen?"

Aleff rubbed his hands together. "No, but it's about to. And we mustn't be late."

With that, the angel reached out and took hold of nothing. He pulled, and the space in front of him bent and broke, opening like a doorway. From where they stood, Ben could see past the opening, along the road that stretched on toward a distant smudge—Ramah. The city where Samuel lived. But if Ben looked *through* the opening, there was spiky grass and tall trees. Between their branches, he thought he could see a city wall. Their destination was much closer, but the time of day was off. A breath of cool air drifted through the door, soft as an evening breeze. Aleff could open doors to anywhere … and any*when.*

"Is that later or earlier?" Ben asked curiously.

"Does it matter?"

"Nope." The shortcut would save hours of walking. *And probably keep me from burning the rest of the skin off my nose.* "Could be a year ago, for all I know."

Aleff's lips quirked, but the only answer he gave was to wave him through. Benaiah knew his way around Ramah pretty well, so he cut through the cluster of trees that covered their approach. In a matter of minutes, they reached the gate. A winding alley led them into the part of the city set apart for the Levites. Samuel stood at the entrance to his family's courtyard, gazing up at the emerging stars.

When the old man turned and saw who approached, there was no surprise on his face. Only outstretched arms and a genuine smile. "My good friends! How is it you always arrive in time for the evening meal?"

"The true mystery is how you are always waiting for us at the gate!" rejoined Aleff, who embraced the man.

Samuel's chuckle was a whispery thing. "Can there be any mystery when a prophet is involved?"

"Then you know why we've come?"

The old man held out his hands to Benaiah, who hesitantly bent to accept Samuel's embrace. He'd always worried that he was impure by birth, breaking some unwritten law by his very existence. *I'd rather not mess things up for him. Make him unclean or something.*

But before Benaiah could waste more time worrying, Samuel set him at arm's length and said, "You are here, and you are welcome. Eat your fill. Rest in peace. Cater to an old woman's whims. And on the morrow, we'll set before you a choice. One that will forever change the future."

It took several heartbeats for Ben to replay that last part. The old guy said it in such a normal voice. Like how you'd say that there was mutton for dinner or the wind was heavy with tomorrow's dew. "Say what now?" Ben demanded, looking between the two. "I've gotta make a choice?"

"Once, for all," Aleff confirmed.

Samuel smiled pleasantly. "And I shall bear witness. But first we will eat and drink, talk and laugh, sing and sleep."

As their host led them into the house, which really did smell like mutton, Benaiah yanked on Aleff's sleeve. "About this choice-thingie …"

In warning tones, his caretaker said, "Tomorrow."

The oldest story tells about
the First of the Fallen
turning on a man,
ripping his life to shreds.
Not sure why I like it so much.
There's a lot of ugly.
It's hard to say Job wins.
I'm not even sure that
the demon loses. But I
can't ignore the parts
where God puts
everyone in their place.
In those sections, I can
almost hear His voice. And
His words are just for me.

5

They knew what my answer would be.

The next morning, Benaiah quickly found himself in Huldah's clutches. Which wasn't such a bad place to be. Huldah was Samuel's older half-sister, and she'd put Ben to work crushing ingredients for her dye pots. The linen cloths that made up his turban were her handiwork. *The first gift I ever got.* Being the old woman's favorite was embarrassing, but Benaiah privately enjoyed her fussing. Still, he couldn't help wondering if she'd have treated him differently if she could see him. *The only people not scared of me are an angel, a prophet, and a blind woman.*

"Your voice has changed," she said, lisping slightly in her toothlessness.

"Maybe. It's been a while."

"And your hair smells sweet."

Ben shot a dark look at Aleff, who only smiled indulgently. "Don't flatter him over-much, Huldah. He's already blushing!"

She chortled and went right on playing with Benaiah's hair, reminding him uncomfortably of when he was a little boy. Brushing Aleff's unusual hair had been his favorite pastime. *He better not bring* that *up.*

Thankfully, Huldah urged, "Continue, my boy. I like this part."

"Sorry. Sure." Benaiah cleared his throat and picked up his recitation. "Have you given the horse strength? Have you clothed his neck with thunder?" Between the slow grind of herbs under his rolling stone and the steady flow of familiar words, he fell into a relaxing rhythm. "His majestic snorting strikes terror. He paws in the valley, and rejoices in his strength."

Words came easily to Benaiah, maybe because of Aleff. While they walked, when they ate, whenever it was time to sleep, the angel shifted into story mode. *He stuffed me full of words and manna, manna and words.* The lives of Noah, Abraham, and Joseph from the Book of the Beginning were so familiar, Ben could quote whole sections. Back when he was twelve, his knowledge of the Law had brought him to Samuel's attention. *Guess it was a good thing those scribes tried to put me in my place. Otherwise, I wouldn't have found* this *place.*

But Job's lessons were Benaiah's favorite. He could reel off any part of it. "He gallops into the clash of arms. He mocks fear, and is not frightened."

Samuel and Aleff listened with silent respect, but the household was far from quiet. The old prophet's kin were weavers, and the clatter of looms filtered down from their upper room. Huldah's hands were too bent with age for her to manage the weaving any longer, so she ground herbs and stirred dye pots in a little alcove off the courtyard. Children ran past. Chickens wandered through. Someone was milking a goat. But none of that bothered Ben. He was wrapped up in the world God's words created in his mind. "Have you entered the treasury of snow, or have you seen the treasury of hail, which I have reserved for the time of trouble, For the day of battle and war?"

Eventually, Benaiah reached the end, and Huldah sighed happily. "Such a good boy. Even our Samuel cannot do half so well!"

Benaiah protested, "It's nothing much. I'm just saying stuff everyone knows. Samuel can prophesy."

"A prophet receives no special treatment in his own home. Here, I am nothing more than an old uncle, with too many sisters to boss me around."

Aleff chuckled. "It's nice to see Benaiah so meek and mild. You bring out the best in him, Huldah."

"But …?" she asked, ever quick to sense a shift in mood.

The disguised angel kindly said, "Your brother and I need to borrow him for a little while." Catching Ben's eye, Aleff arched his brows. "It's time."

Aleff left so swiftly, Benaiah was still tugging his turban back into place when he caught up. Samuel's relatives scattered as politely as possible, and Ben kept his eyes lowered as he crossed the courtyard. *Don't blame them. I'd hide from me, too, if I was normal.* Which was sad, really.

"The roof, I think," Aleff said.

Samuel led the way up one flight of stairs, then a second. Like most homes in the Levite district, additions rose upward to accommodate four generations. Privacy was scarce, but the prophet had been given his own space up top. It wasn't much. Little more than a lean-to with a mat inside. *At least it's quieter here. This is probably where he comes to pray.*

As soon as they were all seated, Aleff cheerfully began, "About this choice-thingie …"

Benaiah tensed. Thanks to Huldah's plea for a story, he'd stopped worrying about the all-important decision that was supposed to "forever change the future."

Aleff didn't keep him in suspense. "Do you want to continue as you are, living as a man among men? Or will you embrace your angelic inheritance and be counted among the Faithful?"

"What's the difference?"

Samuel spoke. "You will know the voice of God."

"Like you?" Ben asked, sitting taller and looking to his keeper. "Would I be a prophet like Samuel?"

"No, you're set apart for a different task," Aleff replied.

"But our purposes are bound together," Samuel said, stroking his bushy beard. "It would bring me great joy to share the role of king-maker with you, Benaiah."

Living as a man probably meant a lonely lifetime of ditch-digging and body-burying just to satisfy a growling stomach. *Do they really think I'd refuse this?* Maybe the alternative came with a catch. Snatches of phrases circled through Ben's mind. *Set apart. Change the future. Shared purpose. A task. A king.* Everything pointed to two things he wanted badly—a place and a purpose.

Some part of Benaiah rebelled. Was he supposed to bow down and thank God for noticing him after years of being ignored? Couldn't someone have told him there was a plan? Why had he been left to struggle in ignorance? But Benaiah's indignation quickly cooled. Hadn't he been steeped in the lessons of Job? *That guy didn't know what the crud was going on. Why should I be any different? God answers to no one, least of all to a demon's whelp.*

He'd have been grateful for any scrap, but this sounded like a feast. And it was hard to take in. Slowly shaking his head, Ben asked, "God wants to talk to *me*?"

Samuel grasped his arm, giving him a little shake. "To hear is to obey." There was a hint of warning in the prophet's tone. "You will be stretched. You will be stained."

"But you will be woven in," said Aleff.

You will, you will, you will. They're talking like I've already made up my mind. And maybe he had. Benaiah swallowed hard. "Yeah."

Aleff's expression was deadly serious. "Is that your answer?"

"You need me to say it fancier?" he grumbled. "I want to be like you."

"Very well. Stand up," the angel commanded, rising smoothly to his feet and leading him into the open. "Samuel, bear witness to Benaiah's choice. He belongs to God."

"He shall be counted among the Faithful," agreed the prophet.

Then without any warning, Aleff tugged at Benaiah's tipsy turban, uncovering his head. Used to concealing anything that made him stand out, Ben felt exposed to the sun and sky. At first, he wanted to hide, but then he realized something was going on inside his head. There was a strange buzzing, and his vision wavered. *Did Aleff do something?* Benaiah blinked several times, trying to focus.

"Calm down, Benaiah, and listen well." And Aleff started to sing. Hardly strange, since the angel was often singing, but this song was about him, his childhood, and even his father. Ben stilled, not wanting to miss anything Aleff might reveal about his past. But with a new stanza, the song changed. "Where is the way to the dwelling of light? And darkness, where is its place, that you may take it to its territory, that you may know the paths to its home? Do you know it, because you were born there?"

Benaiah recognized the passage from Job's lessons, with its questions like riddles. *The dwelling of light. A dark territory.* Wasn't he caught between the two? Born from both, belonging to neither. But Aleff's song seemed to offer a path home.

The clamor in Benaiah's head strengthened, and he reached for the angel, catching handfuls of rough robes. Aleff drew him closer, steadying him on his feet. And the song changed again. This time, the lyrics were about eyes to see, ears to hear, and a heart that followed only after God.

Ben trembled in the familiar shelter of his caretaker's embrace. *No. Not just my caretaker. He is a Caretaker, one of heaven's samayim.* This angel was much more dangerous than he appeared, capable of unmaking him with a touch. But Benaiah couldn't bring himself to fear the only person he'd ever trusted, so he tightened his hold.

Suddenly, he realized that Aleff wasn't singing alone. There were others. Many others. Strong, deep voices rang out on every side, and Benaiah's eyes darted wildly. *Where? Who?* Tilting his head back, he stared straight into the sky, which whirled with colors that didn't belong there.

Gradually, his focus sharpened, and he could make out individuals—tall, fierce, and terrifying. They wheeled overhead, their eyes fixed on him. *Angels.* Once again, Ben's mind supplied the correct term. *Cherubim.*

Awe ripped through him, from the top of his head to the soles of his feet, and he did the only thing that made any sense to his addled brain. He hid his face on Aleff's shoulder and bawled his eyes out.

The Caretaker's hand settled on his head, patting him affectionately.

Samuel's voice boomed over the rooftops as he proclaimed, "Let it be known that this one is no longer Benaiah the

Forsaken. From this day forward, he shall be called Benaiah the First!"

Too much. Too fast. Ben shuddered under a burden he couldn't fathom, let alone carry. The last thing he remembered before slipping into unconsciousness was Aleff's voice, low with emotion, rich with approval. "Welcome to the ranks of heaven."

Of course I'd want
what they had.
To be like them.
To finally fit in.
Right then, the
consequences of
my choice didn't
mean anything,
because if I didn't
fall in line,
I wouldn't mean
anything. To anyone.
But by saying yes,
I'd matter to one man.
And that was enough.
Or so I thought.

6

If you ask me, the heifer's suspicious.

Benaiah woke later in the lean-to on the roof of the house. Several hours had passed, for the sun was now setting.

Aleff asked, "Feeling better?"

"No."

"Thank heaven itself that you've always been honest." Leaning closer, he asked, "Where does it hurt?"

Ben placed his hand over his heart, which was hammering hard. "What happened to me?"

"You made your choice. Picked sides. Joined the team." Aleff touched his shoulder, sending a wash of calm over him. "You'll find that membership has its privileges … and its obligations."

Holding his hands in front of his face, Benaiah frowned deeply. "Am I supposed to be an angel now?"

"Not precisely. You *are* a Messenger, but you're still half human. And that still makes for tricky business."

"Tricky, huh?" With a push and groan, Benaiah sat up and clumsily gathered his hair, glancing around for his turban. "Can you be more specific?"

Aleff handed him the neatly folded linen. "In one sense, nothing happened. You're still the same, lovable guy with delicate skin who craves meat. And you're *by far* the surliest malakim I've ever met."

Ben scowled, but it was comforting not to have lost any sense of self. "I'm me. Guess that works. I'm used to being me."

"Did you think your personality would vanish?"

He shrugged. "I figured angels were perfect."

Aleff's eyes sparkled. "You've lived with me for years, Benaiah. Did you think *I* was perfect?"

"Mostly."

He laughed. "I'll introduce you to a few friends, now that you can *see* them. Once you have a basis for comparison, you'll realize that I'm not near—"

Benaiah caught at Aleff's sleeve and demanded, "What are you not telling me?"

The angel glanced away, then solidly met his gaze. "Humans aren't perfect."

"And half-humans?"

"Equally flawed, but you're counted among the ranks of heaven now."

"Which means …?" prompted Ben.

Aleff quietly replied, "The consequences of disobedience are no longer on the disappointed looks and guilt trip end of the spectrum."

The truth hit Benaiah hard, and his voice cracked. "I'll Fall."

"I can't deny that you *could* Fall, but I have every reason to believe that you won't."

An oily slick of horror worked its way up Ben's throat. By taking a step closer to heaven, he'd made it possible to follow in his father's footsteps. "Crud," he whispered.

"There's something else," Aleff admitted. "I need to leave."

"Where are we going this time?"

Aleff shook his head. "You're not coming with me, my gangling camel."

Panic washed over Ben. "But you're supposed to stay with me."

"As much as I enjoy being joined at the hip—at least until your stomach growls and you obey its call—I have an errand to run."

He tried to smile at Aleff's attempt to break the tension, but this wasn't funny. Benaiah said, "You're not a Messenger."

"True. But I go where I'm Sent. As will you."

Hurt and angry, Ben growled, "I thought joining this team of yours meant we'd be together."

"I'll miss you, too!" In more serious tones, Aleff said, "Calm yourself. You don't need me as much as you once did, but you're still very much *my* responsibility. I'm only loaning you to Samuel for a little while. He needs someone to watch over his cow."

Benaiah limped along the road, his mouth set in a grim line. Traveling with Samuel wasn't so bad. The old man was quieter than Ben was used to, but maybe the prophet was listening to the voice in his head. *Words on the wind, and me still not hearing them.*

So far, God hadn't bothered to say hello. Ben could live with being out of the loop, but the heifer Samuel had purchased was getting on his nerves. Twice, she'd stepped on his foot, and thanks to her constant balking and head-tossing, rope burns reddened his palms. Judging by the baleful expression in the cow's big, brown eyes, some bovine intuition told her that this road led to an altar where she'd meet a bloody end.

All Ben really knew about this trip was their destination— Bethlehem. He was tagging along as cowherd, body guard, and guide. Thanks to Aleff, he'd spent his childhood running wild through the Promised Land. This stretch of Judean hill country had been his playground, and he knew every wadi and goat trail, river and den, walled city and well.

Except the view's changed. Angels everywhere.

He gave up keeping count of the Messengers that zipped by, and wherever there were people, there were Guardians. From a hilltop, Benaiah had looked out over an empty plain and seen row upon row of tents made from gleaming cloth. *An enclave of angelic warriors. Cherubim.*

With so many new things to take in, Benaiah was grateful that the old prophet set a slow pace for the journey south. When they finally reached the gates of Bethlehem, the men of the city greeted Samuel's arrival with fear.

"Do you come in peace?" they demanded.

Huh. Guess I'm not the only one who gets glared at. Benaiah kept a close eye on the men, but then Jesse was called for, and everyone was smiling again. Probably because they hadn't been singled out. *Why don't they want to be chosen?*

'For the same reason you question your choice.'

Benaiah tripped over his own feet and landed hard on his knees. As someone who was used to being alone with his thoughts, he really hadn't expected anyone to answer. Sitting there in the dust of the road, Ben grappled with a rush of emotions—confusion, elation, dismay, delight. He was still trying to steady his breathing when some helpful citizen remarked, "There goes your cow."

Crud.

By the time Ben dragged the heifer back into line, Samuel had been welcomed into to the courtyard of a prosperous household. The place was filled with enough women and children to count as a village unto itself. Benaiah didn't make it past the gate. He was already getting nervous glances and thought it wise to remain with the ill-tempered cow. Sitting against a wall, he gave the heifer some slack so she could reach a tuft of dry stubble.

A man exited the house and spotted him. "You're the prophet's servant?"

"Yeah." Benaiah slowly rose to his feet and did his best to look unassuming. "I'm with Samuel."

He strode off, calling back. "I'll show you where to water

your animal."

The guy wasn't completely rude, but he was far from welcoming. *Same junk, no matter where I go. Aleff was right when he said some stuff wouldn't change.* Benaiah made sure the idiotic she-cow slaked her thirst, then grabbed a quick mouthful for himself. *Guess my host figured what's good enough for her is good enough for me.*

Benaiah did his best to remain inconspicuous. Being the servant of God's prophet clearly didn't ensure his welcome into the house, but Ben slipped into the courtyard and sat outside a wide doorway. If Samuel called for him, he'd be ready.

Through the entrance, he spied a wall hung with instruments of all shapes and sizes—harps, drums, pipes, tambourines, and even a pair of trumpets. Not many households were this rich in the musical arts, and he hoped there'd be singing later. *It's been a long time since Aleff snuck us close enough to a festival to hear the music.*

With a pang of homesickness, he sat back, pulling his knees to his chest.

Benaiah could hear Messengers calling to one another and looked up. The rooftops and skies overhead were just as busy as the courtyard, with angels leaping and whirling. *No swords drawn. Guess it's peaceful. And they don't consider me a threat.* Self-consciously tugging his turban lower, he hunkered down some more.

Samuel's voice reached him then. The old man was able to make himself heard if he wanted, especially on formal occasions. "Bring your sons before me!" he commanded.

Peeping through the doorway, Benaiah watched to see what would happen. Jesse waved one of the men forward and said, "My firstborn, Eliab."

The household's heir was a middle-aged man with a large nose, full beard, and lustrous curls. Eliab bowed low, then stood tall as he offered a personal welcome to their guest. When several children giggled loudly from the opposite doorway, the man's sharp glance was enough to scatter them.

He's the boss, and everyone knows it.

Samuel accepted his greeting with pleasure, but to Ben's surprise, a voice echoed through his mind. *'Do not look on his outward appearance. He may be tall. He may seem respectable. But what I see and what you see are two different things.'* The old prophet's expression grew solemn, then thoughtful as the voice of the Lord continued, *'You see the outside, but I know the heart. He does not please Me. This is not the man.'*

Shaking his head, Samuel asked, "And your next son?"

Benaiah was a little rattled … and a lot curious. *Can't help eavesdropping if God wants me to hear.* All he could do was duck his head a little lower and keep watching. Jesse was introducing his second son.

Abinadab greeted the prophet of God with less reserve than his older brother, curiosity alight in the quick gaze that darted from face to face. *Another proud son of a proud family. And definitely one who's come back from battle. Wonder how he got that scar.* He, too, was rejected, and a third son was summoned.

One thing was obvious to Benaiah. Samuel was searching for someone that God had chosen. The next son was the one who'd escorted him to the cattle shed and left him there. Ben was privately glad that God rejected him. And they repeated the process over and over.

How many sons does the old guy have?

After seeing seven of them, Benaiah was picking out family traits. The resemblance was mostly in the eyes, though the sons of Jesse all had the same thick, black curls. Most of them were married, but it was hard to tell which of the women hovering in corners and doorways were their wives and which were Jesse's unwed daughters.

The women laid out a meal while one of the older grandchildren hurried off to locate Jesse's youngest boy, who was apparently out in the fields. The food smelled good, but Benaiah wasn't sent for, nor was food sent out. He was beginning to think that God had somehow rendered him invisible since people were passing to and fro without showing any signs of recognition, concern, or fear. *Maybe this was one of those privileges Aleff was talking about. Lurking.*

However, that theory was destroyed when a hand slapped his arm. Benaiah started guiltily and turned to find another teenager crouched directly in front of him. Loose, damp curls framed a face still pink from scrubbing. He smelled distinctly of sheep, and he clutched a lumpy bundle to his chest.

"Who's the guy?" he asked in a low voice, his gaze fixed on the crowded room.

"Samuel, a Levite from Ramah. He's the prophet of God."

"No kidding?" The newcomer pursed his lips. "What's he want with me?"

Benaiah shook his head. "I couldn't say."

"At *least* tell me if I'm in trouble!" he whispered, his gaze finally switching to Ben's face.

This must be son number eight. The resemblance was unmistakable, but the baby of the family had been spared Abinadab's hook nose and Eliab's sour expression. A direct gaze, an easy smile, a casual confidence—Benaiah wasn't used to being on the receiving end of any of them. He blurted, "You're not afraid of me?"

His companion laughed. "I know a predator when I see one. And you're not." Shoving the bundle of soft leather into Ben's chest, he added, "Hold this for me."

Then he strolled through the door, an apology ready on his lips. Greetings were called all around, and several children ran forward to hang from the teen's arms.

And the voice of God came to Samuel, loud and clear. *'This is the man.'*

Ben wanted to protest. *The man's a boy. No older than me.*

Jesse's voice rang over the noise of the meal as he announced, "Forgive the delay. My youngest son has finally arrived. Here is David."

"This is the one," Samuel decreed. "God has chosen him."

Scattered pieces fell into place inside Benaiah's head as he stared at the other young man. With an awed expression, he whispered, "He's the one."

God spoke again, confirming it. *'This is your king.'*

People assume that
being chosen is wonderful,
but they're not thinking straight.
If God chooses you, it doesn't
mean you're more loved.
There's no guarantee of
a smooth road ahead.
And it won't ensure your
happiness. Being set apart
put us on a lonely path
twisting through deadly
territory. But at least
we were together.

7

No one mentioned the part about treason.

Jesse ordered the men of his household into their grove of olive trees, which was located on a slope outside the city walls. Benaiah was invited along this time, mostly because someone had to bring the heifer. He quickly stashed the bundle David had left with him, then struggled along as best he could. To his relief, Shelah and Jubal stepped in to lend a hand. They were the two brothers closest in age to David.

Slapping the cow's flank to hustle her along, Shelah remarked, "Pity we can't add her to the herd. She's a fine animal."

Jubal scoffed, "As if God's prophet would bring a second-rate sacrifice."

"Only the best will do," Shelah agreed, with a sidelong glance in his youngest brother's direction. "And in *our* case, that's little David."

"Chosen cows die. What's in store for chosen sons?" Jubal

lowered his voice and asked, "Say, stranger, do you know what Samuel's up to?"

Benaiah had a pretty good idea, but he shrugged and shook his head. *Let the prophet speak. That's his job.* "I'm just the cowherd."

"Then you'll soon be without work," said Shelah, pointing to the altar Samuel was inspecting.

They caught up to Jesse, who was clearly proud of his family's holdings. He was gesturing broadly as he rambled on. "… as far as the forest along the third stream."

"Good pastures," Samuel politely replied. "And a fine vineyard."

With a pleased smile, Jesse promised, "Tonight, we shall feast from both. Peace and plenty, with cups running over. And music!"

Ben's heart beat a little faster, and not because of the promise of meat. Something was happening near the base of the slope. Dark shapes slipped out from amidst the olive trees, brushing aside their silvery leaves as they slunk closer. *There's something wrong with them.* He could tell they weren't animals, but they didn't really move like men. The bent creatures prowled from shadow to shadow like … *like the predators I'm not.*

All around their group, angelic warriors drew their weapons. That's when it hit him. *Demons.*

With a hair-raising screech, two of the Fallen surged forward, baring their teeth and brandishing dark blades. The attack completely unnerved Ben, so he missed most of what

Samuel was saying. The old prophet's words flowed past—a prayer, something about preparation, and then one word repeating. "Benaiah … Benaiah …? *Benaiah*!"

"Huh?" Snapping to attention, Ben realized that Samuel had removed his coat and tunic. So had Shelah and Jubal. The former rolled his eyes, and the latter took the heifer's rope from his hands. Samuel quietly urged him to follow suit.

"Sorry," Benaiah mumbled, obeying with extreme reluctance. And not because he was worried about sunburn or stares. He was much more concerned about the possibility of demons tearing the life from his body.

Warriors met the attackers, their swords gleaming. Soon, the grove rang with the clash of battle, but none of the men in Jesse's household showed any sign of noticing. Even Samuel appeared oblivious to a scene that turned Ben's knees to water. While he watched, two of the Fallen swarmed one of the burly angels, dragging him down. The warrior was bitten and stabbed several times before his cohorts could drive off the attackers.

Benaiah had been curious about demons. Not anymore. If he never saw another of his father's ilk again, he'd be grateful. With only half a mind on the task at hand, Ben wasn't much help in wresting the heifer into position. He hardly noticed the flash of Samuel's blade. But then there was blood on his hands and a voice in his mind. *'For his sake, you will be stained.'*

For David? That sounded ominous.

'For his sake, you will be scarred.'

On some level, Benaiah thought that was unfair. *I barely know the guy, but I'll be bloodied and battered so he can keep smiling?* But this was God talking, and Ben would just as soon stay on His good side. His mouth thinned into a grim line. *I don't care about any of that, so long as I don't Fall.*

By the time the sacrifice had been offered, the sun was sagging lower in the sky and the angels had established a perimeter around the olive grove. Benaiah was beginning to think the show was over when suddenly, Samuel's voice boomed. "Bring me David, son of Jesse, of the city of Bethlehem, in the land belonging to the tribe of Judah, son of Israel."

David had been all smiles earlier, but not anymore. His brown eyes were wide as a child's.

Can't hardly blame him. This is comin' out of nowhere, and he can't fend it off. It's his turn to make the choice. Benaiah stood off to one side, trying to fade into the background but not wanting to miss a moment. *What'll it be, David? Will you trust God, even if it rips your life to shreds?*

Samuel's gaze swept the crowd of murmuring onlookers, and he announced, "This is the man God has chosen. He is set apart. Kneel, David."

The young man dropped to his knees before the prophet, and a hush fell over everyone in the grove.

Removing the stopper from the flask at his belt, Samuel poured out its contents, spilling scented oil over David's head. Its spicy-sweet aroma quickly spread, and several of the men traded panicked glances. This was the sacred oil that belonged in the Tabernacle. In lower tones, the prophet declared, "You belong to God."

"I do," David replied in a clear voice. More softly, he added, "I always have."

Samuel patted the young man's shoulder, then addressed the rest. "You, his father … you, his brothers … you, his friends. Let it be known among you that David will be king over all Israel."

Silence.

Every face registered disbelief, and no wonder. They couldn't have expected this. To be chosen by God might sound enviable. But to oppose God's first choice for king? There were no cheers. No one in their right mind would welcome this news … except one person.

Bunch of idiots, standing around like stumps. With a scowl for anyone who'd challenge his right, Benaiah shouldered his way to the front of the crowd. David stared up at him, oil dribbling down the sides of his face, hands fisted on his thighs. Holding that stricken gaze, Benaiah sank to his knees in the dirt and delivered his first message. "Don't be afraid. I'm here."

"You?" David asked, not sounding terribly impressed.

"I belong with you," Benaiah explained, his voice too quiet to carry far. "I always have."

The newly anointed successor to the throne of Israel blinked, then smiled crookedly. "Are you sure? Because I don't even know your name."

"It's Benaiah. And yeah, I'm sure." Now that he'd found

his purpose, there was no way he was letting it out of his sight. "You're my king."

Swiping his chin with the back of his sleeve, David's smile evened out. "Well, Benaiah. Looks like you're the first. Let's hope you're not the last."

Back then, I was willing
to do anything for him.
By serving this king,
I'd prove my faithfulness.
Putting him on the throne
would justify my existence.
To waver was to fail ...
and to Fall.
So I grit my teeth
and barged into his life,
all serious and determined.
And he laughed at me.

8

He smiled for their sake.

From what Benaiah could see after reclaiming his spot in the courtyard, Jesse's family was very good at living in the moment. *David best of all.* Fears for tomorrow were drowned out by food and drink, music and laughter. Uncles, sisters, and cousins formed a band, and their bright tunes closed the day on a celebratory note. Samuel's foot was tapping, and David whirled through an exaggerated dance, laughing as he taught his young nieces and nephews the steps.

"He doesn't act like a king," Ben murmured.

"And how should a king behave?" challenged a deep voice.

Benaiah started when a mountainous angel drew his sword. But the newcomer only propped his weapon within easy reach and joined him on the ground. "I am called Rei," he said stiffly. "I am Sent to offer my greetings. And to rest."

Guardian, Ben's mind supplied. And one he recognized.

This was the guy the Fallen had dragged to the ground earlier. Bandages swathed his dark skin. Doubts lurked in deep blue eyes. Ben said, "I saw what happened. You okay?"

The warrior's gaze shifted to David. "He is, and that is all that matters. Where did you put his things?"

Recalling the bundle pressed on him earlier, Benaiah quickly checked the niche where he'd stashed it. *Safe and sound.* Hauling it out of hiding, he returned to the angel's side. "It's fine."

"When something is placed in your hands, keep it close."

That felt like a reprimand. "Sorry. I'm Benaiah, by the way."

"I know."

Ben might have been able to dredge up random facts, but he didn't really know much about the different orders of angels. Ignorance made him self-conscious. "So … you're a Guardian?"

Rei nodded, but his attention remained fixed on the future king.

It took several moments for Benaiah to catch on. "Are you *David's* guardian angel?"

"Wherever he goes, I will be there," acknowledged the big, broad-chested swordsman. "And if you are by his side, I will defend you."

Again, Benaiah sensed reluctance. Still, he was grateful. "Then that's where I'll be."

Their meager conversation ended as Rei fixed his full attention on his charge. Which made it easier for Ben to steal curious glances at the warrior's armor and raiment. *Scars everywhere. Muscles everywhere. Makes me look scrawny.*

Kinda feel scrawny, actually. Ben rubbed idly at his empty gut and watched David steal sips of wine, play pranks, and sing loudly. His antics brought a smile to Jesse's face, and with a jolt, Benaiah realized what was going on. "David's usually like this."

"He is."

"So he's doing it on purpose. Pretending nothing's changed."

Rei repeated, "He is."

Just then, Abinadab pulled his older brother aside, right in front of Benaiah's hiding place. Either the shadows were deep enough to hide him, or the men were too deep in their cups to notice their audience.

"Did Father decide?" Abinadab asked.

Eliab waved aside his brother's worries. "We won't put a price on our sister. Father will refuse Nabal's marriage offer in the morning."

"Good!" Abinadab exclaimed. His quick eyes sought someone in the crowd, and he lowered his voice. "The fool's not worthy of our women, no matter how rich the offer."

Eliab the eldest asked, "Was he there during the sacrifice?"

"No. Family only."

"At least we won't have to buy his silence. I wouldn't want word of David's anointing to reach the royal city. And I wouldn't put it past Nabal to try to turn a profit at our expense."

Abinadab tugged at his beard. "What happens if the king finds out?"

"You know as well as I do." With a grim shake of his head, Eliab said, "We'll die."

"Are you lying in wait?" David asked, dropping to one knee in front of Benaiah and waving a couple of meat skewers in his face. "I've been looking for you, but no one's seen you. Now I understand why."

"We're … I'm here." Ben glanced at Rei, who was giving him a flat look. "Sorry."

David said, "I'm hoping you still have that thing I gave you earlier. Father wants me up front."

I do, thanks to Rei. Benaiah held out the leather-wrapped bundle. "It's safe."

"I can see that," David replied, giving the grilled meat an insistent jiggle. "Trade you for these. Once I'm done, I'll thank you more properly."

Benaiah relinquished the bundle and sniffed lightly at the meat. He'd expected mutton since the courtyard was heavy with the scent of cooked sheep, but this wasn't that. *Why does this smell familiar …?*

"Filched those off the prophet's plate," David confided. "You're okay with beef?"

"Never had it," Benaiah admitted, sliding a chunk off the

skewer and popping it into his mouth.

David watched his face with a half-smile as he unwrapped a harp. It wasn't very big, but it looked valuable. Firelight glinted off wood that had been richly carved and lovingly kept. "Hello, old friend," David murmured, touching the head of a lion decorating its base.

Benaiah gulped and coughed. *He left something that valuable with a complete stranger?* "I didn't mess it up or anything, did I?"

Propping the instrument on his thigh, David spread his fingers across the strings, then plucked a chord. Fiddling with one of the knobs, he tilted his head to one side, listening to the light notes, then flashed a smile. "All good. I'll find you later!"

And he was up and gone, jogging to the head table. Sitting at Jesse's feet, David waited until the other instruments reached the end of a dance. Into the lull that followed, he began to play.

Silence.

But this hush was very different from the last. Traded glances. Soft smiles. And pride. David may have been the youngest of his brothers, but he was beloved. *He's their darling.* Benaiah leaned forward, but the children ran forward, crowding around David like a little flock. And he encouraged the impression by singing a silly rollick about lambs in springtime.

Next, the harpist modulated into a song with more somber tones.

> Have you given the horse strength?
> Have you clothed his neck with thunder?
> His majestic snorting strikes terror.
> He paws in the valley, and rejoices in his strength.

Benaiah had never heard Job's lessons set to music before. By the song's end he was humming the tune under his breath. David performed one more ballad before the other instrumentalists returned to the front. Dance music resumed, and in the rush to form circles, Ben lost sight of his king. "Where'd he go?"

Rei answered, "Out."

"No kidding," Benaiah grumbled, getting to his feet. "Then I'm out of here."

The guardian angel didn't try to stop him, so Ben headed for the gate, pausing just outside to get his bearings. A tug, barely more than an impulse, sent him toward the sprawling cowshed where the cantankerous—but admittedly tasty— heifer had spent her last hours.

Away from the smoke and noise, Benaiah breathed easier. Until he remembered what had happened earlier. *How the crud am I supposed to know if there's a demon close by?* He quickened his pace, scrutinizing every shadow until he made it inside. Breathing a sigh of relief, he listened to the soft rustle of animals in their pens and the soft flutter of chickens roosting in the rafters. That's when he spotted David. And the girl he was kissing.

Clearly, Ben had stumbled into the middle of a moment,

and he wasn't sure how to get out gracefully. He had very little experience where girls were concerned. *Okay. Experience I've got, but it's all bad.* When he was small, they'd whispered and worried, skittering away as if hair color was catching. As soon as he grew tall enough to look down on them, he morphed from diseased oddity to heathen pillager. *They act like I'm some kind of monster who preys on innocents.*

Ben eased backward, but David turned and saw him. With a small smirk, he whispered something to his companion, a pretty girl with plentiful curves and a saucy tilt to her chin. She left without any hint of hurry, her hips swaying provocatively.

David ambled over. "Ben-something, wasn't it?"

"Benaiah. Who's she?"

"A girl." With a casual shrug, David said, "She heard about earlier. Wanted to congratulate me … and offer to be my queen. It was a very generous offer."

"So is she your betrothed or something?"

"Her? No." He laughed and explained, "Hino's the daughter of our family's third wife, if you catch my meaning."

Ben didn't. "She's a cousin?"

"Maybe. She could even be my niece. Not sure anyone knows for certain."

"I don't follow."

David's brow furrowed, but he shrugged again and explained, "Back before I was born, my oldest brother brought back Hino's mother from one of the mountain villages. Jezreel, I think. At that time, Eliab already had his first wife, and father had arranged for his second. So Eliab built Betah a house and provided for her, but I guess she got tired of waiting around. She started keeping company with my other brothers, my uncles, and my cousins. She has two daughters, and they mostly take after their mother."

Benaiah understood then. "She's a harlot."

"Don't let Hino or her mother hear you say that!" David shook his head. "Betah will tell you she's generous to those who are generous with her. As Abinadab likes to say, when a man's first wife is squabbling with his second, the only place he's welcome is in the third wife's embrace."

"But to go to a harlot is to commit adultery."

"I don't need to *go* to anyone." Arching his brows, David said, "They come to me!"

Benaiah couldn't bring himself to laugh.

David rolled his eyes. "Look, all I did was kiss Hino back. In her own way, she was trying to cheer me up." Grabbing Ben's hand, he dragged him back toward the light and noise of his party. "She and I grew up together. It's Jubal she really wants."

And that makes it all right? Although it had never come up before, Benaiah hoped Aleff was prepared to answer several blunt questions about girls.

"I haven't seen you at any of the meals. Have you eaten?" David asked.

"You gave me food a little while ago," Ben replied awkwardly. "Thanks for that."

"Is that all?" David protested. "Let's check in the back.

Abi's probably still there, and she's good about sharing."

They cut right through the middle of the courtyard, with David half pushing, half pulling Benaiah along. He felt like a camel wading through a flock of black goats. He hunched his shoulders and lowered his eyes, but it wasn't any use. Even though he was with their precious son, they scattered at the sight of him.

"You're useful," David said, peering up at his long-legged companion. "They part like the sea, so I can get where I want to go!"

"They're *afraid* of me," he muttered.

"And that bothers you." David chuckled. "Further proof that you're mostly harmless."

Ben grit his teeth. "I'm not going to hurt your family."

"Nope," the future king agreed. "But *I* might. In here."

David yanked Benaiah through a doorway so low, he had to duck to get through. Several earthen mounds lined one wall, the ovens for baking bread. A mill for grinding meal occupied one corner, and there were jars for water and oil beside crocks for pickled vegetables. Stacks of baskets, wine skins, bundles of herbs, and a churn. The only person still working was a young woman mixing leaven into the meal for tomorrow's bread. She turned with a smile, which flickered out at the sight of Benaiah.

If David noticed her nervousness, he chose to ignore it. "We're *hungry*, Abi! What's left over?"

She frowned. "You were served a double portion at dinner!"

He laughed and offered an introduction to a slender girl who was his own height. "Benaiah, this is Abigail. She's … huh." Looking to the young woman, he asked, "How are we related again?"

"We're not," she sighed. "I'm your brother's second wife's sister's daughter."

"Like she said," David laughed. "No relation. But we grew up together."

Which counts for something with him. Benaiah ducked his head and gruffly said, "Sorry to bother you."

She stared, but the wariness faded from her manner. Abigail wasn't as pretty as the last girl, but intelligence shone in her dark eyes. "Jesse welcomes strangers to his table. I apologize for our neglect. Please sit, and I'll serve you both."

"See!" David exclaimed. "I told you Abi would come through!"

Without a word, she piled flat loaves of bread into a basket and set it on the edge of a low platform in the corner of the room. David stepped up and sat down, patting the mats at his side. While Benaiah joined him, Abi kept busy, adding bowls and plates until a feast was set before them. Her movements were quick and efficient, and Ben found himself relaxing. *She's not so bad for a girl.*

When she pulled the covering off a tray of leftover meat, David urged, "Don't be stingy!"

Abigail smiled serenely. "If a tiny glutton like you has room for more, do you think I'd stint a man twice your size?"

"Twice?" David's voice cracked in his indignation. "Ben's not *that* much taller!"

"He has a cubit on you. Easy," she replied smoothly.

Instead of offering them a sampling of the mutton, Abi set the whole tray between them. David crowed victoriously. "This is why I love you!"

She icily replied, "Is the future king's favor so easily bought?"

David winced. "Don't tease, Abi. Not about that."

"I'll stop if you'll stop," she retorted, returning to her kneading.

He pouted. "Too serious!"

"And you're too much."

Benaiah helped himself to bread while he watched the squabblers interact. Their banter made him miss Aleff, who always frustrated him with his carefree manner. Maybe that's why Ben could easily see past Abi's front. *The way she looks at David ... that steady, unswerving gaze. It's different from that Hino girl, but it's just as greedy.*

Most of my early self-confidence
came from how I looked.
Tall, different, frightening—
no one challenged me. I could
straighten my back and scowl,
and grown men whimpered.
With one glare, victory was mine.
But any real fighter would see
through my camouflage.
My strength had no substance.
I was easy prey.

9

Entertaining angels can be humiliating.

Benaiah woke before sunrise and stared at the sharp angle of the woven mat offering him and Samuel shelter. When he sat up, the old prophet murmured, "What is it, young man?"

How am I supposed to describe this feeling? A sense of urgency swamped his whole being, and he knew exactly where he needed to be. Even though this was the first time it had happened, Benaiah could tell what it meant. "I'm Sent."

"Then go." And Samuel closed his eyes, a peaceful smile on his face.

Just like that. Well, fine. Not like I have a choice in the matter. Ben shook out the bundle of cloth he'd been using as a pillow and grabbed his loose hair, twisting and knotting as he walked. He stopped briefly beside the cowshed to splash water from the animal trough on his face, then set off at a jog toward the trees at the head of the nearest wadi. *David must be returning to his flock.*

The predawn sky was pearly gray, but shadows were heavy. *I'm breaking every rule Aleff ever gave me. Don't go out alone. Don't leave the company of people.* Which made sense now that Ben could see how many guardian angels crowded into populated places. Their secondhand protection vanished whenever he sought isolation.

Dropping into a shallow valley whose grasses were already cropped short by goats, he kept moving. *I've explored plenty of these hills and valleys, but never like this.* Ben knew where to go. And it wasn't just a gut instinct. He could *see* the way. Bright and clear, the path ahead was illuminated with the same soft light that always filled the hut where he and Aleff lived. Pushing down a fresh pang of homesickness, Ben skirted a thicket and wove his way to the top of the rise. In the wide open pasture beyond, a flock of goats milled.

"You, there!" called the gruff voice of a shepherd. Benaiah recognized him as one of David's many relatives, a cousin, or perhaps a nephew. "You're the prophet's servant."

"Yeah. Did David come through here?"

The fellow leaned against his shepherd's crook. "What do you want with my uncle the king?"

"I want to go with him … to speak to him."

"As long as you're speaking *with* him … and not *of* him."

Benaiah wasn't often menaced by grown men who barely came up to his shoulder, but David's family must have decided to rally around their chosen son. Holding up both hands, Ben swore, "I'm no talebearer." At an inner prompting, he quietly added, "I'll be his friend and his support."

The shepherd grunted. "He could use a friend. His sheep are pastured along the banks of a stream in that direction." Turning to point, the man added, "He's barely an hour ahead of you, but he's a swift runner. Even with those legs, you'll be hard-pressed to catch up."

With mumbled thanks, Ben strode off, confident of his course.

He heard him before he spotted him, walking along, swinging his staff and singing one of the songs they'd been playing the night before.

"David!" he called, lengthening his stride.

The shepherd boy turned and lifted a hand in greeting. "Ben, wasn't it?"

"Benaiah."

"That was it! Did you lose your way to the trenches? My aunties may be fussy, but even the goats don't have to go this far to relieve themselves."

"I was looking for you."

"And you found me. Why?"

Ben admitted, "Not sure."

David laughed and started walking again. "Do you sing?"

"Not sure," he repeated.

"How can you not know if you can sing? Are you tone deaf? One of my uncles couldn't find the right note if he was sitting on it, but none of us can keep him quiet."

"I don't think that's it." Aleff had never made a big deal of it, but Ben didn't join in when the angel would sing. He loved listening. *Listening was allowed.*

David's tone was incredulous. "You've never tried?"

Benaiah tried to explain. "I was told not to sing when I was little. It made problems for my mother. I think. I don't remember everything."

"Well your mom's not here."

"Nope."

"So sing with me!" David wheedled.

"I don't know any songs."

"No problem. I'll teach you an easy one," he offered. "We use it with the little ones, so dad gave it a catchy melody."

"Your father writes songs?"

David grinned. "Do lambs drop in springtime? We *all* write and play some. Me most of all."

He wasn't boasting. Just telling it like it was. After David's demonstration, Benaiah cautiously joined him on the melody line. Words had always been his. Songs had always been forbidden. But even though he sang through the song two, three, and four times, nothing bad happened. No blows. No pain. No tears. Only pleas for more.

Something unknotted in Benaiah's soul, and he shed caution. It was surprisingly easy to sing loud when you were someplace where no one could overhear. Open sky. Empty hillsides. And David, who was giddy with delight. "Don't know why you were holding back. You were *made* for this!"

Angels, maybe. But me? Benaiah wasn't so sure. *I'm only half.*

The voice of God echoed through his mind with a gentle reminder. *'All creation sings.'*

By mid-morning, they reached David's flock and relieved the nephew who'd been standing in for him. After stashing his things inside a squat hut built around the entrance to a shallow cave, David hung a sling from his belt, shouldered a sturdy club, and scanned the hillside. Under his breath, he sang a little song about green pastures and still waters.

Benaiah didn't recognize the words, but they reminded him a little of Job's lessons. "Whose song is that one?"

"Mine." David strolled along, eyes on the ground.

"Your own words?" Ben followed. "How do you do that?"

"How?" he echoed, taking the question seriously. Pressing his hand to his heart, David said, "Put the feelings that are here into words, and make them sound nice. When it's right, you can hear it." He bent to pick up a rock, which he slipped inside the pouch at his waist. "It can take a while until I'm satisfied. Especially since some songs change with the day. Depends on the weather. How I slept. How I feel. Where I've been. Where I'm going."

Suddenly, God weighed in. *'David is a man after My own heart.'*

Benaiah's breath caught at the depth of feeling in those few words—love, pleasure, anticipation. Noticing David's quizzical gaze, he asked a question he probably should have saved for Aleff. "Can God look forward to something? Doesn't He know everything?"

Mercifully, David didn't laugh. He gazed off over his flock and said, "I know my songs, but that doesn't mean I don't look forward to performing them." In lilting tones, he listed, "To hit every note, to share lyrics you labored over, to dance to a familiar beat, to repeat a song because it's one of your favorites."

"You sure say embarrassing things."

"Didn't *you* bring it up because it was on your mind?"

"Well, yeah."

"That's the same thing, even if you don't say it outright." Jabbing Benaiah in the chest, David said, "It's still right there."

Benaiah remembered what God had said on the day Samuel sifted through Jesse's sons and came up with a king. *He doesn't look at outsides. It's the heart that matters.* Rubbing at his chest, Benaiah thought to wonder what God saw in him. *Is there such a thing as a half-man after God's own heart? Crud. That just sounds dumb.* Benaiah didn't realize he was staring into space until David tackled him. He yelped in surprise as the guy he'd been sent to serve pinned him down.

David laughed, "What's the matter?"

"Why'd you do that?"

"You don't have brothers, do you?" David guessed.

"There was just me."

"Fight back."

Benaiah stared in disbelief. "Huh?"

"You look strong," David said. "I want to see how strong you are."

Giving the other teen a funny look, Benaiah clamped his hands around David's ribs and thrust upward.

He dangled there, his face a picture of surprise, but then he planted his feet on Ben's chest and smirked. "Not bad, but you're still flat on your back."

Narrowing his eyes, Benaiah lunged upward, easily displacing David and sending him sprawling across the grass. The shorter boy was on his feet in a heartbeat, charging Ben, who stopped him with a hand on top of his head. "Guess that extra cubit comes in handy."

"You've got reach, I'll give you that," David replied, a gleam in his eyes. Quick and confident, he ducked out from under Benaiah's hand and slapped his opponent's thigh, ribs, and collar bone. Stepping back, he boasted, "But if I had my knife out, you'd be dead."

"You have a knife?"

"Doesn't everyone?" David rolled his eyes. "You're big,

but you'd never survive a real fight."

"Nope. I mostly concentrate on avoiding people. Saves them from having to avoid me."

"What happens if someone turns on you?" the shepherd challenged. "I can't be the only one who's ever wanted to see if I could knock you down."

Benaiah couldn't very well admit that he relied on Aleff to get him out and patch him up if things got ugly. Pushing at his turban, which had been knocked sideways in the scuffle, he said, "Guess I'll have to depend on you to protect me."

"If you needed me, I'd be there. But what a waste." David beckoned to him with both hands. "Come on, Ben. I'll teach you!"

"To fight?"

"It's simple. All I have to do is keep knocking you down until you figure out how to stop me!"

Scowling, Benaiah said, "That *doesn't* sound like learning."

David raised his fists and began to circle. "I'm the youngest of eight, and I have six nephews bigger than me. Trust me, you'll learn in no time!"

Before Ben could react, David swung upward, his fist connecting solidly with Ben's jaw. His head snapped back, and he saw stars … and the bemused stares of a pair of angels. *Betcha Rei's enjoying this way more than I am.* Landing on his back, he glowered at David, who stood over him, eyes sparkling, hand extended.

"You'll be sorry for that," Benaiah growled.

"No regrets so far!"

The scuffle didn't last long, and Ben hurt in brand new ways. Probing his split lip with the tip of his tongue, he asked, "Is this all you do out here? Wrestle the sheep?"

"Usually, I play," David replied, taking a long drink from his waterskin.

Benaiah snorted. "This isn't playing?"

"I meant my harp." Flexing his fingers, he nodded. "These seem to be intact. Go fetch my harp from the hut."

"Get it yourself."

"One tussle and your loyalty's gone? That was a short-lived alliance."

With an injured look, Ben levered himself up off the ground.

David was beside him right away, pushing the canteen into his hands. "That joke left a sour taste in my mouth. I'll bring bread as well as my harp. Sit."

Sitting heavily, Benaiah scowled. *Was that pity or an apology?* Rubbing the back of his neck, he winced and adjusted the folds of his clothing and glanced around. When David returned, Ben asked, "Is there shade?"

"Over here." He led the way around the hilltop to where an outcropping of rock shaded a spot the shepherds must have used regularly. Stones had been arranged in a half-circle. They were too low to be comfortable for Benaiah, but it was a relief to be out of the blistering sun. Stretching out on the cool ground, he accepted both bread and cheese from his host.

David took a seat and tested his harp strings. The song he played had no words, but it was pleasant and peaceful. Ben propped his hands behind his head and closed his eyes. *Wonder if he's making it up.* Like a cradle song from another lifetime, the notes wove their way around the reclining teen. *Maybe it's not such a bad thing, going where God wants.*

Benaiah's respite was short-lived. The harp was some kind of signal, and he and David were swiftly surrounded by—and practically buried under—sheep. Shoving a wooly butt out of his face, Ben complained, "They stink!"

"You get used to it."

Wrinkling his nose, he argued, "Only because *we'll* stink."

"You're learning fast." David kept right on playing. "I'll make a shepherd of you long before anyone makes a king of me."

Days passed.
People's speculations
came to nothing.
Worries died down.
Everyone seemed glad
to forget about
David's anointing.
But I stuck around,
a constant reminder
of the future
God had promised.

10

For a little while, I forgot myself.

Life fell into a pattern. Three days with the flocks. One day back home to rest and resupply. Whenever David was with his family, there was music after dinner. *Guess they might do it every night.* Since Benaiah was always with him, he couldn't say for sure. But everyone always seemed glad to have David back. And he was right in the middle of everything, begging for news, teasing his sisters, reporting to his father.

While some of the men in Jesse's family were wool-traders, the rest saw to the needs of family and flock. Planting and harvesting. Building and breeding. Watering and winnowing. All the while, Benaiah stuck close to David, who didn't seem to mind the constancy of his new companion. No one ever questioned why Ben had stayed behind when Samuel returned to Ramah. Maybe his oath at the anointing was reason enough.

A few times, David brought some young nephew or

cousin back into the hillsides. The kids vied for their chance at his undivided attention while he taught them the basics of shepherding. During these lessons, Benaiah mostly hung back. And eavesdropped. It seemed unlikely that God had spared the son of a demon just so he could become an assistant shepherd. *But what else am I supposed to do?*

So he sang a lot. Learned which sheep were biters. Failed more at hunting. Missed soap. Inherited several dozen fleas. And gave the slingshot a go.

"Do you *ever* miss?"

David grinned, reaching for another stone. "Not often."

"At least I'm consistent," Ben grumbled. "I've hit the ground every time."

"It's what you hit *before* the dirt that counts."

Benaiah fitted another rock into his sling's pouch. "Sheep-wrestling, song-writing, and developing a deadly aim."

"You may not have noticed, but there isn't a whole lot else to do out here," David said as he set his sling whirling. "All my brothers have deadly aim. Whenever they're called to join the army, they form ranks with other shepherds. Abinadab says the slingers are better than the archers."

David's stone hit one of their targets with a *crack* that echoed in the sudden silence. Mention of the army brought thoughts of the king. "Aren't you worried?" Benaiah asked.

"About what?"

"You were anointed king by Samuel."

"Oh, that," David replied, a faraway look in his eyes. "Not especially. I don't know why God picked a wool-gatherer like me."

"But He did. And that means you're going to be the king."

"Yep."

"Aren't you worried?" he repeated.

David sighed and shrugged. "When I was seven, my father entrusted me with my first flock. There were eight old ewes who couldn't keep up with the rest of the flocks. My older brothers laughed at me, but I didn't care. I found the easiest trails, the gentlest slopes, the best grasses. Those old ewes made a shepherd of me." With a small smile, he said, "My father knew what he was doing. My God is surely more wise. If He puts His people in my keeping, I'll do everything I can for them. And they'll make a king of me."

Benaiah watched Rei fly in lazy circles over the stream where David's flock watered. *Must be nice. Get above the smell of sheep. All that fresh air in your face.* Suddenly, the guardian angel changed course, sunlight glinting on his drawn sword. He swung low near the edge of the woods, and Ben sat up for a better look. *Something's moving.* "That can't be good," he muttered.

David heard him and followed his line of sight. In the next instant, he was running for the spot, whistling and calling out to his sheep.

Crud! Benaiah grabbed his staff, jumped to his feet, and raced after him. "That's a lion, you idiot!"

David slowed enough to scoop up a rock and set his sling whirling. The first stone hit the ground at the predator's feet, spraying grit in her face. Tawny ears lay back, but the big cat slunk forward, intent on her prey.

Benaiah's longer legs quickly conquered David's head start, and he exclaimed, "What are you doing?"

"Protecting my sheep!"

Another rock went flying, proving that David *could* miss. The flock panicked, scattering in every direction. Several ran their way, inadvertently slowing down their shepherd.

Stepping over the pesky obstacles, Benaiah cut toward the river, planting himself between the lion and David's stragglers. "Git!" he ordered, brandishing his stick. But the cat wasn't impressed by his eerie eyes or unusual height. Her low growl rose to a scream. And when she leapt, Benaiah went down.

David shouted, but Ben was too occupied with staying alive to hear what he said. Claws raked his chest, spattering the cat's fur with blood, and sharp teeth snapped at his throat. Ben's hands scrabbled for a hold, then closed around her neck, and he brought up his knees, trying to dislodge his hissing, spitting attacker. He felt cold. He smelled death.

And then David landed on the lion's back. His added weight pushed Ben's attacker down, forcing those deadly jaws closer. He shot a panicky look at David, whose expression was as fierce as the lion's.

Suddenly, a voice filled Benaiah's mind. *'Lion of Judah, shepherd My people.'*

Seizing the lioness by her chin, David wrenched her head upward and cut her throat. The cat's scream ended in a gurgle that sprayed blood all over Benaiah, whose arms fell to the sides. He lay there, spread-eagled on the ground, shaking.

David swiped his nose with the back of his arm, grinning down at his friend. "Thanks for helping me deal with this mooch. She's been picking off sheep in this area for a while now, but my brothers haven't had any luck trapping her."

Ben blinked.

"Shelah's going to be all cranky that we claimed his prize," David went on. "He and Jubal have been planning a hunting trip."

Ben shuddered.

Swinging his leg over the dead lioness, David stood and kicked the warm carcass off Benaiah. Kneeling down, he demanded, "What were you thinking, going after a lion with your bare hands?"

"You went first," Benaiah muttered, trying to sit up. David helped him to his knees, but that's as far as his woozy head would let him go. "That was a lion!"

"Yeah, I noticed. How much of this blood is yours?"

Benaiah looked down at ruined tunic—torn to shreds and soaked in blood. The lioness's claws had ripped across his chest, leaving seeping wounds. "Not sure."

"If Abi saw you like this, she'd think you were mauled instead of scratched." David pressed one of his scarves against Benaiah's chest. "Let's get you to the stream before you keel over. I can take care of you, but I can't carry you."

With David's help, Ben made it to a patch of shade beside the stream, then numbly surrendered his shirt. In the process his turban knocked loose, and David's hands stilled. "Are you under some kind of vow?"

"Huh?"

"You don't cut your hair."

There was really only one reason Benaiah kept his hair long, and that was Aleff. Shaking his head, he replied, "It's nothing like that. But I'll keep my promise to you."

"You know what I think?" David said, probably to distract him while he tried to stop the bleeding. "It would only take a handful of men like you to make a king of me."

"Then I'll bring more like me." As soon as the words were out of his mouth, Benaiah knew they were true.

"And where will you find these loyal subjects?"

"I'm not sure yet, but that's how it'll be."

David's hands were gentle and sure. "Are you a prophet like your master?"

"My master's a shepherd who's going to be a king." With a defensive glare, Benaiah added, "I might not be a prophet, but just the same, I'll do it."

"If possible, make sure they're better warriors than you," David teased.

"That won't be hard," Ben conceded, tensing as the numbness began to wear off. Pain tightened his voice. "If I can find them, will you lead them?"

In careless tones, David replied, "Better yet, if you can bring them to me, I'll let *you* lead them."

"But *you're* the king."

"A king needs his captain. This is my first royal promise, so cherish it."

Ben grit his teeth and asked, "Can I keel over now?"

"Not until I get you back up to the hut. My cousin should be here in the morning to relieve us. Can you live that long?"

Ears ringing, focus wavering, Benaiah muttered, "So far, so good."

I didn't know much
about Messengers,
other than the obvious.
They carry messages.
On the whole, the order of
malakim is filled with
friendly guys—chatty, cheerful,
and a bunch of other things
I'm not. But being with David
loosened my tongue. He wanted
to know what I thought. And
he listened to my answers.

11

Old memories make for strange dreams.

Benaiah had survived various injuries over the years—scrapes and breaks, burns and bruises. Always, Aleff had been there to soothe away the pain. But Ben's caretaker was someplace else, and the pain of his injuries lingered. Sometime in the chill of the night, he slipped into a fevered dream.

He stood on a glossy floor flecked with colors. Columns, cushions, curtains of silk—just like he remembered. *I'm home?* There was no joy in the knowledge. He automatically glanced around for a hiding place and noticed something out of place.

It was raining.

The skies were emptying their stores upon the earth. *Is this how it was?* Past nightmares had never been this vivid, nor had he been able to think clearly. Only impressions of feelings, all fuzzy around the edges. Someone ran past, one of Mother's servants, and with a start, Benaiah realized that he was small again. Three years old, but only in size. Feeling vulnerable, he trotted to one of the cool, stone columns and hid.

This is when Aleff came. Any minute now. That knowledge sustained him, even though thunder cracked and boomed overhead, and wind tore at the filmy curtains. Frightened people cried out for rescue, prayers to an absent god. *Father isn't here. Father doesn't care.*

Only one person remained calm in the midst of the confusion. A man. He sat on a low bench, and he was watching Benaiah. It seemed the most natural thing in the world to go to him. Slipping into the open, Ben scampered over.

"What do you want, little one?"

"Aleff," he replied, embarrassed that the answer came out in a baby's voice.

"Who is Aleff?"

Benaiah struggled to put his answer into words. As a three-year-old, he had so few. Holding up his first finger, he replied, "My one."

"*Is* he your only one?"

No, that wasn't right. Adding the first finger on his other hand, Ben said, "David, too."

The stranger smiled. "Yes, David is on your heart and in your hands. However, two is not enough to keep your hands full. Look what I have planned."

And in this strange dream, the man touched each of Benaiah's fingers, and letters flowed from his hand onto Ben's. Letters shone against his skin, spelling out names. He could read them, and each filled him with a blend of eagerness and urgency. "This many?"

"Yes. You'll need to bring them together, like this." He helped the little boy fold his hands together, fingers entwined in a firm clasp. Then, he surrounded Ben's hands with his own. It felt safe.

That's when Benaiah noticed how many names were written on the man's hands. Small and delicate, in many languages, the words twined across his fingertips, wrapped over his knuckles, and continued right up his arms, disappearing under his sleeves. "Is my name there?"

"Yes."

Ben asked, "Are we friends?"

"That would make me very happy."

A steady hand rested lightly atop Benaiah's head, whose heart ached with the enormity of his joy. *A new friend.* He'd always wanted friends. It was lonely without Aleff.

The ground shook, and a fresh gust of wind sent hailstones rolling into the room. The noise startled Benaiah, and he crowded closer to the man. He asked, "Do you want Aleff to come for you?"

"Miss him," Benaiah admitted.

"Then I will Send him."

"Can you?"

"Yes. And when the time is right, I will Send you." With a kind smile, the man murmured, "Trust Me, Benaiah."

He woke with a gasp and stared confusedly into the face of the second angel he'd seen hanging out with Rei. This warrior's skin was just as dark as his partner's, but instead of rows of tiny braids, his hair was shaved in patterns that zigzagged around his head.

"Your face is shining," the Guardian informed him.

The dream was already fading. Benaiah could feel it slipping away. He rubbed his forehead, then stared at hands that felt empty. "I need to find … someone."

"He is here," said this new angel, easing away from Ben's mat on the floor of the shepherd's hut.

Benaiah turned his head in time to be blinded by the opening of a door. And then Aleff was on his knees beside him, his face creased with concern. "Look at this mess! What, were you chased by villagers with pitchforks?"

"Lion."

"Well, I have shocking news." Bandages vanished, and Aleff prodded tender skin. "Taming oversized kittens is not your area of giftedness."

As his pain faded, Ben stared into the face of the one he knew better than anybody. *He's worried.*

"And your swimsuit modeling career is over before it began. This'll scar."

More nonsense. *Whatever it is, it's bad.* Catching at the shining sleeve of the Caretaker's raiment, he asked, "What's going on?"

Aleff met his gaze, but he didn't answer. Maybe he couldn't. That would explain his pained expression. Shaking his head, the angel urged, "Sleep. I'll turn up at Jesse's tomorrow; we can talk then."

Benaiah couldn't disobey Aleff. Eyelids grew heavy, and

drowsiness muddled his mind. "No fair," he grumbled.

Aleff cradled one of Ben's hands in both his own. Dredging up a sad smile, he whispered, "No, it's not."

When Benaiah jerked awake, the sun was already halfway to its peak. He reached for his chest, fingertips brushing neat bandages. *Doesn't hurt anymore.*

"Thought the smell of food would bring you around," David said, fanning a plate of steaming fish. "Hungry?"

"Usually."

"Good, because the stream was very cooperative this morning. Eat your fill before Elim turns up. Then we'll get you home."

They were outside, leaning against the wall of the shepherd's hut when they spotted a runner. "He's late," David remarked. Then he sat forward and frowned. "That's not my nephew."

Jubal stumbled to a stop beside their cookfire, doubling over as he tried to catch his breath. "News," he gasped. "A messenger from Gibeah."

"The royal city?" Benaiah asked.

"That's the one."

"Good news or bad news?" asked David.

"Father isn't sure, but I don't like it."

David stood up, dusting off his robes. "Last time you hurried me home from my flocks, I was anointed king. This *can't* be more upsetting."

"Don't be so sure, little brother," Jubal replied. "This time, you're being sent for by the king."

There are times when
you just have to
tighten your grip,
grit your teeth, and
follow the order to attack.
That's simple.
But there are times
when you have to
loosen your grip,
open your hand,
and follow the order
to walk away.
That's brutal.

12

Everybody has something to hide.

Eliab the eldest barely gave David time to change before taking his arm and hurrying him away, muttering advice all the while. Benaiah followed, needing to know if King Saul had learned of his friend's anointing. *The family's been tight-lipped. And I can't see Samuel blabbing.*

As expected, Jesse's household was readying a feast. The smell of roasting meat filled the courtyard, and the women were stretching dough for baking. Green olives, preserved lemons, and other pickled vegetables were mounded in shallow bowls. Ben spotted Abi with the other women, but she only had eyes for David.

Pausing just outside the alcove where David had been led, Benaiah scanned the gathered men. *Which one's the messenger?* He trusted his gut where men were concerned, but his stomach dropped when he met the gaze of Jesse's guest. *How is ...? How come ...? There's* no *possible way!*

His face must have been a treat to behold, because Aleff was laughing at him from across the room. The angel had disguised himself, and the quality of his turban and robes were finer than usual. *Not a traveling merchant this time. But why is Aleff with the king's men? God Sent him to Gibeah?*

Once Benaiah recovered from the initial shock, he realized that the Caretaker was part of a larger group. Four strangers sat with Jesse, who was introducing his youngest son. "We're little more than farmers and shepherds, but songs brighten our days. This is my youngest son, David. He's the one you seek."

The heavyset man at Jesse's right stroked his full beard. "Word of your skill has reached the king's ears, but I didn't expect one so accomplished to be so young!"

David said, "I have fifteen years."

Jesse jumped at his chance. "All of my sons and daughters are skilled musicians. Perhaps one of his elders would …?"

"No. King Saul asked for David, the harpist from Bethlehem. I will not disappoint him." He fixed the teen with a haughty look. "The king has called for you; it's your duty to answer."

David held his father's gaze. "Of course I'll go."

Concern creased the old man's face, but Jesse bowed his head. "So be it. But I beg a little time to prepare."

"The king's need is *urgent*."

Aleff jumped in then. "As you said yourself, the boy is young. Let him bid his farewells."

The messenger stroked his beard, then grudgingly replied,

"You have five days. We depart for the royal city after the Sabbath."

The next days were busy for David and boring for Benaiah. Apparently, it took a whole household to get one teenage boy ready for a road trip. *Whenever I wanted to go somewhere, I just left.* For David, there were new robes, sandals, blankets, servants, animals, and elaborate gifts to present to King Saul. Between fittings and sessions in etiquette with his father and the king's men, Ben barely saw David. Even Aleff seemed to be avoiding him, which made it easy to sulk.

Benaiah finally caught up to his friend during the heat of the day, while the house was quiet. He grumbled, "I think I liked the shepherd's hut better. It was less … I dunno. Just *less.*"

With a faint smirk, David propped his harp on his knee and plucked random notes. "How are you feeling?"

Unneeded. Unwanted. Unimportant. Ben's gaze slid sideways and he tapped his chest. "I'm healed."

"That's good. There's only two days left before we leave."

Ben felt something inside him grow still. Expectant. "We?"

David was pulling a wistful melody from his instrument, but he paused. "You're not coming along?" he asked in surprise.

This whole time, he's been planning to bring me?

Benaiah's surge of elation met a swift end as God spoke. *'No. Your path lies elsewhere.'*

Before he could think how to tell David, Abi found them. The young woman's hands were clasped tightly together, and her face was drawn. Benaiah eyed her uneasily. *She looks ready to cry. Or kill something. Hard to tell.*

David took one look and breezily said, "If this is about a missing honeycomb, it wasn't me. I haven't been near the …." When her hands balled into fists, he cut himself off. "Abi?"

"Did you meet that man who's been here for several weeks? The one who offered a brideprice for your sister."

"Sure, the one from that village in the Desert of Maon. Father turned him down flat," David replied candidly. "We think better of our women than to send them so far away and with such a fool."

Benaiah saw Abi flinch and elbowed his friend. "Idiot."

She forged on. "*My* father was not so considerate of a woman's feelings. He blesses God above for the heavy purse that has fallen in his hands."

"One of your sisters …?"

"No, David. I'm here to say goodbye."

Benaiah saw several emotions flicker through his friend's eyes—surprise, dismay, loss. *Not so oblivious after all, are you?*

Her lips pressed into a firm line. "The wedding day is set. I'm going to my aunt for a time of preparation."

David quickly stood. "Hold on. Let me talk to Father. There must be a place for you somewhere here."

Her gaze didn't waver. "You're leaving."

"You know I am, but … maybe my brother?"

She stiffened, then turned her back and walked away. "Goodbye, David."

"*Idiot*," Ben hissed.

David stared after her with a wounded expression. "She's crying. Not on the outside, but Abi's crying." Shoving his harp into Benaiah's chest, he ran after her. Taking her hands, he knelt down in front of her, tears in his eyes. "I'm sorry, Abigail! If there was anything I could do, I would. *This* is your home! You belong with us. With me."

Benaiah hovered uncertainly a short distance away. To his surprise, the young woman turned his way. "Take care of him for me."

"Yeah. I will."

Nodding once, she gently pulled free from David's grasp and walked away, head high, back straight.

David's shoulders sagged, then shook.

With a gusty sigh, Benaiah sat next to his friend and silently bore witness to the tears he shed on her behalf.

The evening before David's departure couldn't have been more awkward. Forced conversation. Hollow laughter.

Uneasy glances. With the king's men in their midst, no one could speak their mind. David sat at his father's feet and sang his farewells. If many of his songs held a mournful note, none of the guests remarked upon it. He sang for his flock, for his family, and for his childhood friends.

In the morning, a small caravan queued up outside Jesse's gate. Tension hung thick in the air. *None of them are hiding their worries very well. David least of all. He can't hide his fear from me.*

Somehow, in the chaos of leave-taking, Benaiah managed to get close to him. "I'm sorry I couldn't go with you. I would have liked to."

"You're still welcome. I'll smuggle you into one of the carts," David offered.

"Can't. There's something I need to do," Ben explained. "For you."

"And what's that?"

"I'm going to find those warriors you need, and when I come back, your strength will be threefold. We'll set you on your throne."

David laughed. "Don't say that too loud. Saul is king, and I doubt he's ready to relinquish the crown."

Benaiah stubbornly asserted, "That's how it'll be. You'll be king, and we'll follow you."

"What kind of warriors would follow a boy?"

"Ones like me." With a sudden flash of insight, he revealed, "There are more just like me."

David sighed, and for a moment, God's anointed one

looked very small. "If they have your heart, I'd welcome them. Find me, Benaiah."

"I will. I swear it."

It made no sense.
But stuff doesn't.
Maybe that's what faith means.
But right then, the last thing
I wanted to be was Faithful.
I finally had a friend.
I finally had a purpose.
And just when I was
the happiest I'd ever been,
God snatched it all back.
What the crud was He thinking,
Sending me from David's side?
Yeah, I was angry.
But mostly, I was scared.

13

If this was a test, I passed.

Benaiah didn't fit in with the weeping women or shouting men who'd gathered at the gate to bid farewell. A whole pack of children ran alongside the travelers, begging for David to come home soon and promising to be good. All Ben could do was scowl. *I'm the one left behind, but he probably thinks I'm abandoning him. And where's Aleff in all this?*

Not far from where he stood, two of David's brothers were laughing and trading jabs. Their congratulatory attitude didn't sit well with Ben. Shelah and Jubal noticed his glare and let him in on the joke. "Don't worry so much! David'll be fine!" Jubal exclaimed. "We sent him off with *all* the comforts of home."

"At great personal sacrifice," Shelah added.

Ben wasn't sure what to make of his knowing smile, nor his older brother's smirk. "What are you talking about?"

Jubal rocked forward on the balls of his feet and whispered.

"I smuggled something into that last cart for him. Won't he be surprised?"

"Ah, the delights of king and castle are nothing compared to the delights he shall know," Shelah intoned.

Focusing on the last cart, Benaiah searched for some clue what they were up to. Even with the puffs of dust kicked up by the animals, he could make out a loosely-veiled figure looking back at them—light brown curls, full lips, blue eyes. Benaiah didn't recognize her until she lifted her chin in what may have been valiance, defiance, or pride.

"That girl," Ben muttered, dredging up her name. "Is that Hino?"

"That's what he calls her," Shelah said. "Ahinoam will keep little David company while he's far from home. I'm sure she'll keep his spirits up!"

Turning his back on their raucous laughter, Ben walked away.

Benaiah was sitting under a broom tree an hour's walk out of Bethlehem when Aleff found him. Screwing up his face against the sun's glare, Ben muttered, "Since you're supposed to be halfway to Gibeah by now, you must be a mirage."

"You're not the only one with a talent for running away." Sitting down, Aleff said, "I'll catch up long before they miss me. And we need to talk."

"Why?"

"Why talk? Or why *here*? Because personally, I'm questioning the *here*." Peering around, his caretaker said, "This has to be the most inhospitable acre in kilometers, furlongs, miles, leagues, and possibly even light-years."

Ignoring the blather, Benaiah demanded, "There are more like me, aren't there?"

"Yes."

"And you failed to mention this because …?"

"You didn't ask."

Ben snapped, "I'm asking now."

"Which is why we're having this little heart-to-heart," Aleff said. "On the day we met, the world was drowning. Only eight humans were spared. They were chosen to reestablish the world's population."

"Noah and his family."

Aleff nodded. "And on that same day, eight boys were spared. Children of the Fallen, born to human mothers. They were chosen to establish an everlasting kingdom."

"Me?"

"You'll be more of an *us*, but I suppose being first allows for a brief stint of *me*." Aleff slipped the strap of a lumpy bag from his shoulder and offered a lidded basket as well. "Provisions. The fullness of time has come."

"For what?" Benaiah asked suspiciously.

"In another time and place, it would probably be called a quest."

"Uh-huh. And what would you call it in the here and now?"

Aleff added a full water skin to his stock. "A journey."

"And you're not going with me," Ben said dully.

"You catch on quick!" In slightly more serious tones, Aleff said, "If it makes you feel any better, I'll be close to David while you're away."

"Yeah." Benaiah tugged self-consciously at his turban. "Yeah, that's good. So where am I going?"

"I haven't a clue!"

"So I'm just supposed to wander aimlessly until I run into some guy who looks like he might be half-human?"

"No, no. God squirreled the eight of you away, saving you up for a rainy day."

Ben glanced at the sky. "It's the wrong season for rain."

"What I mean is … you were all hidden. And until you tell me where you're being Sent, I can't open the way." With an expectant gaze, Aleff asked, "Where would you like to go?"

Into Benaiah's mind, a solemn melody threaded. He could almost hear David's voice, singing the lessons of Job. Without really meaning to, Ben sang along. "Have you given the horse strength? Have you clothed his neck with thunder? His majestic snorting strikes terror. He paws in the valley, and rejoices in his strength. He gallops into the clash of arms. He mocks fear, and is not frightened."

Understanding flashed in Aleff's eyes. "Clever."

"You know where I'm going?"

"Without a doubt," the Caretaker assured, standing and dusting off his robes. "Shake a leg! Up and at 'em!"

Benaiah stood, but dawdled. "Will I ever be able to go back to our home again?"

Aleff's expression softened. "Missing your pick and shovel?"

He couldn't answer. His gut hurt, and not in the usual gimme-meat way.

Resting his fingertips over Ben's heart, Aleff asked, "This tells you to go?"

"Yeah."

"Then you go. Or else it will shatter beyond repair, and I will have lost another friend."

That's not happening. Ben shouldered his pack and canteen.

"Take good care of your picnic basket," Aleff warned. "Where you're going, there may not be much to eat."

Benaiah had a sneaking suspicion he knew what was in the basket. "You *shouldn't* have."

"You'll thank me later," Aleff promised in a cheerful sing-song.

Sighing, Ben tucked the basket into the crook of his arm while his companion reached into midair and opened a door. Immediately, they were hit by a stiff wind that ripped at their robes. Benaiah grabbed at his turban and raised his voice to be heard over the rush. "Where does this go?"

"Let's just say you won't be in Kansas anymore!"

Which was no answer at all. Ben scowled in the face of Aleff's smile, then strode through the door.

I didn't know what
I was looking for,
let alone what I
would find.
Someone like me.
Call me a fool,
but I think I was
hoping to find family.
This guy—whoever he
might be—was another
forsaken son of
a faithless angel.
And that could
make us brothers.
But it'd also
make us rivals.

14

He found me first.

Benaiah stood in a place of endless winds. He automatically pulled the trailing end of his turban over his nose and mouth, but then he realized. *This land doesn't spit grit.* Yanking his headgear more firmly around his ears, he took in his surroundings.

The buffeting air felt thick, as if a summer storm was gathering, and everything was green. Wading through calf-deep grasses, he scanned the sky. Light rippled overhead, with swirls and eddies that always reminded Ben of water. This same sky stretched over the tiny hut in the sea of reeds he'd come to think of as home. *Which means this is one of heaven's havens.*

Confident he was at least safe from demons, Benaiah walked up the slight incline on which Aleff had stranded him. A five-minute hike took him to the top, where the wind snatched a gasp from his lips. The land dropped at his feet, leaving him on the edge of a precipice. Below spread a wide, green valley filled with horses.

Wild and untethered, they ranged across their pasture, noses to the ground as they cropped grass. Ben found a decent spot to climb down, and once he was below the valley's rim, the wind dropped off so he could hear himself think.

I've never seen a herd so big. Counting them was out of the question, but admiring them was easy. They were large, proud beasts with muscles rippling under glossy coats.

When Benaiah finally reached the grassy lowland, he sat and rehearsed the words that had guided him here. "He paws in the valley, and rejoices in his strength. He gallops into the clash of arms." Although Ben kept his voice low, the nearest horses' ears angled in his direction. A pale stallion lifted his head and stared at their intruder for several flicks of his silky tail, but he simply returned to grazing.

Since no one looked ready to trample him, Benaiah turned his attention to Aleff's gifts. Lifting the top of the basket, he asked, "You guys okay?"

Two yahavim knelt together, arms wrapped around each other as they blinked up at him with faceted eyes. These little guys were technically angels. *Lowest order. Easiest for humans to spot.* Which was probably why Benaiah had always been able to see them. Of the six Aleff kept, these two were the Caretaker's best-beloved pets—clever, but a little clingy. *Just what I need. Someone to baby.*

"Come on out," he coaxed.

With a buzz of translucent wings, they zipped to his shoulders, pressing close to his neck and patting his face with small hands. Yahavim looked like tiny, bright people, but they weren't able to speak. The higher orders kept and cared for them because of their ability to change light into manna, the food of angels. "Not as filling as meat, but at least I won't go hungry."

Benaiah held out his hands, and they flitted to sit on his palms. The pair smiled trustingly at him, and when he smiled back, the little guys lit up even brighter. *The happier they are, the more I squint.* "Ease off, Neri. Dim it, Pazi. You know I can't handle the glare."

Their brilliance softened to a bearable glow, and Benaiah nodded his thanks. He didn't feel quite so alone with these two along. Turning the manna-makers loose, he said, "It's windy here, so let's get organized."

Removing his turban, Benaiah separated a section of hair at the front and quickly braided it into a thin rope which he knotted off. "Handhold for you, Pazi," he said to the yahavim with a tangerine bob. The only real way to tell yahavim apart was by their hair, which came in wild colors. Repeating the process on the other side, Ben created another plait to anchor Neri, whose tea green waves were tucked behind pointed ears.

While he worked, Benaiah hummed one of David's songs. *He'd have loved grazing his sheep in a place as green as this.* Snugging away the rest of his hair under his turban, he stood and started walking. Away from the cliff's shelter, the winds picked up again, swirling around him and forcing his two tiny passengers to hold on tight. The herd parted before him and closed ranks behind him, allowing him to pass through, but avoiding contact.

Riding one of these would definitely make a guy feel like a king.

A rock formation on the other side of the valley seemed to call to Ben. That was the direction in which he was Sent, and the way was bright before him. *Somewhere over there, there's someone like me.* That's where he'd find the one David needed. Not a war horse, but a warrior.

Without a sun in the sky to mark the passage of time, it was difficult to say how long it took Benaiah to cross the plain. The yahavim fed him twice, and his water skin was nearly empty when he finally put the horses behind him. He skipped across a clear stream, slowing his steps as he entered a narrow place sheltered from the winds. Right away, Pazi and Neri let go and chased their curiosity deeper into the vale.

The little manna-makers poked their arms into nooks in the mossy stone, then whirled through the overlapping branches of gnarled trees, whose roots bulged from cracks in the canyon walls. But Benaiah was more interested in the stuff scattered around. Someone had woven long grasses into mats, ropes, and nets. The screen leaning against the rock wall looked tight enough to keep off rain … or cast enough shadow to make it easier to sleep.

Whoever made this has been at it for a while. New weavings were a soft green color, while older things had dried to gold or brown. *He lives here. But why's he alone?* Maybe something had happened to this one's Caretaker. Except … no one could get the better of an angel of that order. *What could have happened? And where is he now?*

Hearing a noise somewhere above him, Benaiah backed away from the wall and peered upward. The stare he'd used as a shield all his life turned into wide-eyed surprise, then glazed over with fear. A lone figure plummeted off a ledge high above. *Idiot! Don't break your neck before I can talk to you!*

There wasn't a doubt that the person skipping from stone to stone in a reckless descent was the one Ben was looking for. For the most part, the guy didn't look much different than other men—brown skin, brown eyes, brown hair. But his size set him apart. As did his speed.

The oncoming man's gaze locked on him with startling intensity, and Benaiah's mouth snapped shut. There was murder in those eyes. *Not good. Crud. What do I say?*

Benaiah had a fraction of a second to note that his attacker was half a head taller before they collided. All the air left Ben's lungs, which made it really hard to talk his way out of dying. "Wait!" he wheezed.

"Why should I?" inquired the one pinning him down.

Ben struggled, but a hand was slowly cutting off his air

supply. "You're heavy."

Those brown eyes gleamed maliciously. "You're *dead*."

Suddenly, the two yahavim flew into the new guy's face, catching at his hair and pulling. There was no chance such tiny creatures could hold the man back, but his entire demeanor changed. "What did you bring here? Are those birds? Bugs?" Flapping his hands wildly, he swore. "Where are they?"

Benaiah did the only thing he could think of. He swung one fist upward, connecting with the guy's jaw. His attacker's head snapped back, but he didn't go down.

Ben growled, "Stop flailing! You'll hurt them!"

"If you brought bugs, I'll do more than hurt them!"

Anxious for Neri and Pazi, who were braver than anything that small had a right to be, Benaiah grabbed for his opponent's hands. "Not bugs! They're yahavim!"

"What now?"

"Angels!"

The guy went still. "You can see angels?"

"You can't?"

"Never could, but if you *can* … that's interesting." He sat back on his heels, leaning heavily into Ben's stomach.

Trying not to show how hard it was to breathe, Benaiah said, "My father was Fallen, the same as yours. And I was Sent to find you." From the depths of his mind a whisper lent him the words he needed. "Josheb the Rider, your time has come."

He was everything I wasn't.
And he was exactly
what David needed.
But how do you convince
someone that you know
their destiny? Not the
easiest thing to tell
someone you just met.
Especially when they're
wild and free. Josheb isn't
a follower, but God asked me
to lead him. Lucky me.

15

I needed to make a big impression.

How do you know my name?" The deadly intent faded from Josheb's face. "You came to find me? Then why are you *fighting* me?"

"You attacked me."

Josheb had the gall to look smug. "And you're on your back, passive as prey, ready to accept death?"

"No, we're talking."

"Wrong. You're explaining."

"Fine," grumbled Benaiah. "Let me up."

The guy rolled off and slouched beside him, leaning back on his arms—relaxed, non-threatening, and utterly confident in his superiority. Ben rubbed at his abused throat and took a closer look. Josheb's hair was wavy, and sideburns framed his jawline. Although he couldn't have been much older, the tuft of facial hair under his bottom lip made him look more adult. *And more human.*

Josheb would do a better job of fitting in than Benaiah

ever had. With his hooked nose and brown eyes, he didn't give off a *stranger* vibe. Still, he'd stand out. *Not many humans are that big. And his clothes don't make sense.* Josheb's pants were different than those worn by desert nomads, close-fitting at the waist and hips, and his big feet were encased in soft leather. The colorful, patterned scarf wrapped around Josheb's midriff had tassels that tugged at Benaiah's memory. *Father wore something similar.* The throwback fashion hinted at an earlier era.

The only other thing he wore was a short leather vest trimmed with green stitching that matched the strange marks on Josheb's forearms. His skin was overlaid with a pattern that reminded Benaiah of flames—wide at the wrist, thinning to points as they wavered and twisted toward his elbows.

"What're those for?" Benaiah asked.

"For people stare at," Josheb answered. Pointing to Ben's turban, he demanded, "What's that for?"

"To keep people from staring," At Josheb's gesture, Benaiah sighed and unwound his headgear. "Where I've been, nobody looks like this. I make them nervous."

Tugging at that small patch of hair on his chin, Josheb smirked. "Just because your hair's pretty as a mare's tail?"

That *wasn't* a compliment, and Benaiah scowled. He needed to hurry this guy along. The sooner they returned to David, the better. Who knew what his friend was facing in the royal city? Keeping a firm hold on his irritation, Benaiah asked, "Where's your Caretaker?"

Josheb shrugged. "I don't need him."

"But there's an angel here with you?"

"Angels come and go regularly, but my babysitter's the only one I can see."

Benaiah glanced around but didn't see any angels. "If they're invisible to you, how can you tell they're here?"

"The horses."

"And your … babysitter?" Ben asked.

"Him and me, we don't get along so well." Josheb's expression hardened. "I left, and he let me. That's all there is to it."

Whenever I left, Aleff came after me. But I wanted him to. "You'd rather be alone?"

"I'm not alone. And believe me, the horses are much better company than Othniel."

Benaiah was having trouble imagining one of God's Faithful being hard to get along with. Was Josheb the difficult one? Choosing his words with care, Ben asked, "Was he strict?"

"Boring. I lost interest." Josheb looked him up and down. "But when you turned up, something clicked. Death to the intruder. Nice change of pace."

"Uh-huh."

"I wanted to squeeze the life from your body with my bare hands. Or run you through with my blade. Grab a sharpened stick. Maybe even a rock to bash your brains out."

Ben didn't particularly like the direction Josheb's creativity was taking. "Excuse me for not being thrilled."

Josheb sat forward. "What kind of angel sired you?"

"One of the malakim—a Messenger."

"Well that explains a lot. You were made for words; I was made for war." Clapping a hand against his muscular upper arm, Josheb said, "My father was from the order of cherubim, a so-called Protector. So when you brought a threat, you gave me something to war against. *Very* interesting."

A bubble of hope rose inside Benaiah. *I promised David a warrior. This guy's a natural.*

"So explain why you were looking for a mongrel like me."

"There are eight of us," he said. "We were chosen, saved, and hidden away in isolated places."

"Hidden." Josheb's eyes narrowed. "From who?"

"I'm not …." The question had never occurred to Ben, but he trailed off as the answer came. "Well, crud."

"What?"

"God just told me who He hid us from."

"Answers to you, does He?" Josheb asked sarcastically. "So why was I dropped into a world with nothing but horses and a stodgy old man for company?"

Benaiah fought to keep his voice steady. "We've been hidden from our fathers."

Josheb led the way back into the valley where horses grazed. "I've been here since I was twelve. Before that … it doesn't matter. All I know is that two of my grandfather's best horses picked up their hooves and left the stable. I was sent to bring them back on pain of death."

Much older than when I was taken. Puzzled by the difference, Ben asked, "How long ago was that?"

"My favorite mare has dropped five foals," Josheb replied. "The horses still follow the pattern of seasons, so I mark time by them."

Five years have passed for him, but I was with Aleff for longer. After a brief ponder, Benaiah prompted, "Did you find your missing horses?"

"They were with some crazy old coot who was building a boat." With a shrug, Josheb continued, "He offered to take me with him, but that's when Othniel showed up on a horse twice the size of the ones I chased down. He said I needed to go with him. And here I am."

"You trusted him enough to leave your home?"

"Trust?" Josheb snorted. "I just wanted to ride his horse."

"That's all?" Benaiah stared out over the plain. *Either this guy really liked horses, or he jumped at the chance to get away.*

"Hey, that stallion could *fly*! Not every day a kid sees a flying horse." Josheb almost sounded embarrassed. "I was understandably impressed."

Ben pointed at the milling herd. "These things can fly?"

"Stick around, and you'll see for yourself. How long are you staying?"

"Probably as long as it takes for me to convince you to come with me."

"And why would I do that? Do *you* have a flying horse?"

Benaiah scowled. "No."

"Can you fly?"

"No," he muttered. "But going with me is why you're still around. When this Othniel person brought you here, he saved your life."

"How do you know?"

Ben spread his hands. "My caretaker saved my life, too. We're from the same place in time."

"How do you know?" Josheb repeated.

Rolling his eyes, Benaiah replied, "Because of the Flood."

"What flood?"

"You don't know?"

This time, Josheb rolled his eyes. "If I knew, I wouldn't be asking you to explain."

"I can tell you the whole thing if you want."

"Is it a good story?"

"Listen and see for yourself." Taking a deep breath, Ben began, "Now in the days of Noah …."

Josheb was nothing like me,
and that was good.
If I hadn't been different,
I wouldn't have been interesting.
But I was also envious.
This guy would impress David
in ways I couldn't. And ...
there was the facial hair.
I know it's dumb, but crud.
I was jealous of every whisker
on his cocksure face.

16

Grass is a poor substitute for breakfast.

When they returned to the shelter of the vale, Neri and Pazi flitted over to swing from Benaiah's trailing braids. He didn't mention their presence to Josheb. *Just in case he was serious about swatting them out of existence.*

Ben wasn't sure what to do next. The drag on his senses meant he needed to sleep, but Josheb showed no signs of drowsiness. *Guess I can tough it out a while longer.*

Small hands patted his cheeks, and green-haired Neri dove into a midair somersault that resulted in a falling wafer of condensed light. Pazi caught it and pressed it to Benaiah's lips. It melted on his tongue with a lingering sweetness.

"Thanks," he murmured, feeling markedly better. *Kinda prefer food I can chew, but these two will keep me on my feet.* He was wondering if he should offer manna to Josheb, but the guy was already chewing. "What are you eating?"

Josheb held up a blade of grass before adding it to the rope he was twisting.

"You eat grass?"

"Chew on it." Josheb must have liked to keep busy. Evidence of his handiwork was all around them. Many years' worth of weaving, knotting, and interlocking grasses.

"What are you making?"

"A halter for a foal." He paused to spit out a green wad and stick the tip of a fresh blade of grass into his mouth. "I'm going to see if I can gentle him enough to ride."

Bad sign. He's acting like he plans to stay. "Why are you doing that?"

"Not much else *to* do while you're waiting for the wind to change." Josheb nodded in the direction of the valley. "All that's here is grass, and the herd doesn't mind sharing."

Benaiah dredged up some polite interest. "You're been very … productive. It's kind of impressive, how much you've accomplished on your own."

Josheb gave him a flat look. "There's no value here. One spark of fire, and all the years I spent building this house of straw would turn to ash." Holding up the tightly-wound cord in his hands, he said, "This is grass. Turning it into a rope or a roof doesn't change what it is. It'll always be grass."

"That's a good point."

"It's a terrible point! I'm sick to death of grass! I want to do something that can't be burned away! Don't you want to make your mark?"

Benaiah shifted uncomfortably, quite certain that this young warrior didn't want his pity. *A withering legacy. An unchanging, uninteresting view. And voiceless friends. He's making the best of it, but he's restless.* A sudden certainty bolstered Ben's confidence as he asked, "What if I could promise you a better legacy?"

"Keep talking."

"You'll put a king on the throne. You'll establish a royal line that'll never end. And your name would be listed beside his for all time."

Josheb didn't exactly jump at the offer. "Some guy I never met sure is expecting a lot of me."

"David doesn't know. This is God's plan."

"To use us as a stepping stone for a king who'll forget our names as soon as his crown goes to his head?"

Benaiah scowled. "Oh, you'll stand out. And when you stand before him, he'll look up to you." *Because he's really short.* "But before you know it, you'll be looking up to him." *Because you'll be on your knees.*

"You know all the right words, Messenger. But I need more. Show me this king. I want to see for myself if he's worth more than grass."

"Yeah, I can do that. But you'll need to come with me."

"Where?"

Good question. The internal tug was back, and Benaiah stood. "For starters, back to where your caretaker is."

Josheb grumbled, "Why him?"

"I can't take you to David until I catch up to Aleff, and something tells me that's where he'll be."

He dropped the grass and rose. "It might be interesting

to meet this Aleff of yours. Assuming I can see him. I'm running shy on flakes anyhow."

"Flakes?"

"Food. I tried not eating once, to see if I could keep from going back, but after about a week, it gets hard to do much." With a shrug, Josheb explained, "Othniel leaves me these flakes in a stone basin near his tent. They're boring, but better than nothing."

Manna! Ben was about to offer Neri and Pazi's services but thought better of it. *Hunger's a strong motivator. And it'll get us one step closer to David.* With a short nod, Benaiah started walking. To his relief, Josheb fell in step at his side.

They didn't get far before the constant winds suddenly fell away. Something in the sky caught Benaiah's eye, and he stopped walking to stare. Four figures streaked past, stirring the winds from a whole new direction.

"Something's coming." All around them, horses lifted their heads, and Josheb demanded, "It's angels, right?"

"Yeah."

The Protector's son stood tall, sweeping the herd with an assessing eye. "Time to run!"

Benaiah was about to ask why, but the answer became obvious. *Stampede. Crud. I hate running in these things.*

Hopping from one foot to the other as he pulled off his sandals, Ben tore after Josheb on bare feet.

In another display of impressive speed, Josheb ran alongside the herd before veering off, aiming for a short rise where a lone horse stood looking out over the rest. The white stallion pranced in place, shaking out his silky mane. "Feeling left out?" Josheb greeted, fearlessly laying a hand on the excitable horse's neck. "I can't blame you. Seems like forever since the last time."

Catching up, Ben asked, "What's going on?"

"This one's my favorite. If I'm supposed to be Josheb the Rider, he's why." He sprang easily onto the stallion's broad back and reached down. "You don't want to miss this."

Benaiah gripped Josheb's forearm, scrambling pathetically as the muscular young man hauled him off his feet. "I've never ridden," he protested.

"This'll ruin you for any other nag," promised Josheb, who sat behind him. "Hold on. He's faster than any of them."

Hastily rearranging his clothes, Ben caught Pazi and shoved the yahavim inside his shirt. Neri followed on his own. Which was a good thing. A moment later, the stallion leapt from his vantage point, slamming Benaiah backward into Josheb, who let loose a fierce cry that made Ben's hair stand on end.

And then they were thundering across the plain.

Benaiah wasn't at all sure what might offend a horse of heavenly caliber, but with hooves thudding across turf, he was much less interested in being polite. Keen on surviving this ride, Benaiah seized two fistfuls of their steed's long mane and tried to catch his breath. Plunging into the midst of the other horses, they hammered across the plain. *Fast!* Eyes wide, Ben leaned over the horse's neck. *Faster!*

Four angels dropped from the sky, choosing their favorite mounts—white, red, black, and pale. This was the signal the herd had been waiting for. In one stomach-dropping lunge, the tromp of galloping feet vanished, and they were airborne.

When Benaiah slipped sideways, Josheb laughed in his ear. "Use your knees."

"What the crud do I use them for?"

With a smart slap to the sides of Ben's legs, he explained, "If your knees aren't water, grip his sides to keep your seat."

Realizing the rider wasn't even hanging on with his hands, Ben shot his companion a startled look, only to be met by an expression of fierce joy. *The guy lives for this. Biggest thrill of his days. Kinda like a belly full of roasted meat.*

No, this was better.

With the stallion's mane wrapped around his hands and his knees firmly clamped, Benaiah concentrated on enjoying his first flight. Wind roared in his ears as the herd soared through a wide turn. Without the jarring thud of ground underfoot, they accelerated smoothly, and he reveled in the exhilaration. What Ben didn't expect was a sudden stab of regret.

His father had once flown on wings of light. Messengers were easy to spot, what with their crazy aerobatics and insane speeds, and Benaiah was counted among them. Until this moment, his lack of wings hadn't bothered him. But now Ben knew that he'd been born for flight just as surely as he'd been born for song. The deep ache in his soul flared into anger over his father's cruelty. *He passed on the desire, but denied me the sky.*

Looking back, I wonder why
I never asked more about
angels. Maybe I was jealous.
Maybe I was angry. I dunno.
But I sure felt stupid right then.
Flights of angels. Different orders.
Varying purposes. Even though
I lived my whole life with one
of them, I didn't know anything
about my allies. Or my enemies.

17

Guardians sure don't talk much.

Benaiah managed to impress Josheb by leading him straight to Othniel's camp. He lived in a tent with sides draped in shining cloth. And he wasn't a member of the Caretaker's order. Josheb's "boring old man" turned out to be a huge, thickset Guardian with a bristling mane of red hair standing out around a broad face. And Othniel wasn't alone. When Aleff stood and opened his arms, Ben rushed into his embrace.

"Barefoot and bareback! Aren't you a wild child?" Aleff exclaimed, holding him at arms' length.

"I thought you were with David."

"I missed you, too."

"Well, yeah," Benaiah muttered. His gaze slid sideways, which was when he noticed the other teen's stunned expression. Usually, it was just him and Aleff. Having an audience was definitely embarrassing.

Josheb turned to the big warrior and demanded, "Is that

what you expected from me?"

Othniel snorted. "I am not Aleff."

Aleff added, "And you are not Benaiah."

Ben tried to explain. "He's my family … he was my only …."

"Benaiah was barely three when I carried him off, so I raised him," the Caretaker smoothly inserted. "Every situation is different. Each of you was placed with the one best suited to meet your needs."

Pointing to Othniel, Josheb demanded, "I need him? I don't think so."

Aleff gazed steadily into Josheb's face. "You were permitted to run wild. Are you weary of your empty years of independence?"

"I'm not alone. I have the horses."

"I never said you were alone," Aleff countered. "You've never been alone."

Josheb squared his shoulders. "If you're talking about those angels, I know they're there, even if I can't see them. Whenever they're here, the horses go on a rampage through the skies."

"As fascinating as that may be, you haven't answered my question. Are you tired of being pointless?"

"I'm tired of you." Josheb whirled and started to stomp off, but to Benaiah's surprise, the young man paused mid-step and exclaimed, "What did you do?"

Aleff circled around to face Josheb again. With a smile that sent a chill down Ben's spine, the Caretaker replied, "We're having a nice little intervention."

"No, really. What did you *do*?" Josheb repeated, sounding interested. "I'm stuck."

Othniel snorted again, and Ben glanced over in time to catch a flicker of amusement in the Guardian's gray eyes. *The guy's a mountain. And just as talkative.*

Aleff looked to Othniel. "Your problem child is ready to listen. Would you like the honors?"

"Tell him," the Guardian answered in a gravelly voice.

Addressing himself to Josheb, Aleff said, "First off, you're an idiot boy with a stubborn streak as wide as this plain. If you'd bothered to listen to your Guardian, you might have learned something useful."

"Listen to him? The horses say more than he does."

Aleff's eyebrows arched. "Othniel, what were you told to do about your causeless rebel?"

The Guardian replied, "Be patient."

"Let it be known that on this day, patience has met its end!" Looking the teen up and down, Aleff released him and said, "You need to make up for lost time. Welcome to cram school."

Josheb tested his arms and legs, then shot Benaiah a look. "Mine doesn't talk, and yours talks nonsense. Which is worse?"

"Six one way, half a dozen the other," Aleff said. "More to the point, Othniel *is* the one you need. Were you aware that he's a weapons master?"

"That's interesting." Josheb glanced at Othniel. "If that's so, how come all you ever gave me was this?" The teen pulled a slender dagger from inside his boot and gave it a twirl.

Othniel released the hold on his weapon and drew a double-edged sword with a tracery running partway down its blade. He said, "*That* is for cutting grass. *This* is for cutting down the enemy."

Benaiah turned his head sideways, then eased closer to Othniel. *I can read that.* Lightly touching the bared blade, he asked, "Why's my name next to Josheb's?"

Aleff butted in. "Because both of you are woefully unprepared for what's next."

"Your names are under my hand," Othniel said gruffly. "I am Sent to equip you for battle."

Ben shot a dubious look in Aleff's direction. "I'm supposed to learn how to fight?"

"I'm sure if you bash away at each other for a while, Othniel can get your skill levels up where they belong!"

Josheb tucked away his puny blade. "Are you saying I get a sword?"

The Guardian hesitated, then said, "You would excel with the spear."

"How do you know?"

Othniel replied, "I have watched you."

Folding his arms over his chest, Josheb asked, "What if I want a sword?"

"Then you shall have a sword," the big warrior replied in even tones.

Josheb looked disgusted. "Why don't you ever push back?"

"Though your father was once an angel, you're counted

among the ranks of men," Aleff explained. "You have the option to disregard wise counsel, even if it leads to your eventual demise."

"Help me out, Messenger," Josheb complained. "What's he trying to say?"

Benaiah's lips twitched dangerously close to a smile. "Aleff said, 'Take the spear, idiot.'"

Planting the tip of his sword in the grassy ground, Othniel folded powerful hands around its hilt and said his piece. "Josheb the Rider, death is in your hands. Thousands will fall before you. Do not flinch, but do not revel. Wrest victory from every foe and offer it to your king. In this, you will please God."

Josheb looked from face to face, then stubbornly said, "Maybe. If he's interesting."

Aleff smiled knowingly. "He will be your everything."

Rounding on Benaiah once more, Josheb asked, "What is it about this king that has you prancing like a yearling who's caught wind of a fresh updraft?"

"He's …." Ben hesitated, trying to put everything into words that would make sense to someone who'd never met David. *When it comes down to it, only one thing matters.* "He needs us."

"Can you use this?" Aleff asked, jabbing his finger into the green pattern on Josheb's forearm.

In guarded tones, the half-cherub replied, "I know they're all wrong."

"That's not what I asked. You've educated yourself on several aspects of your unique legacy. Did you get around to these?"

"Yes."

"And?" Aleff prompted.

"I can't fly, if that's what you mean," Josheb snapped.

What the crud are they talking about? Benaiah stared hard at the marks, which apparently had angelic significance. He checked out Othniel's forearms, which had plenty of scars, but no green tattoos. On closer inspection, Ben noticed golden splotches here and there on the Guardian's upper arms and more on his shoulders. Like dappled sunlight on his fair skin.

"That also wasn't my question." With pointed patience, the Caretaker pressed. "Can you use them?"

"Yes."

"And what do you use them for?"

With a put-upon sigh, Josheb replied. "Big jumps. They slow me down."

Benaiah would have liked to jump in with several questions of his own. The first time he'd seen Josheb, the guy had dropped down from a mostly vertical canyon wall without any problem. *I would have noticed wings. Come to think of it, where are Othniel's wings?*

Aleff wasn't done. "Do you have them anywhere else on your body?"

"Nothing worth mentioning."

"Show me."

Josheb shrugged out of his vest and turned his back. From the nape of his neck to the center of his back, flourishes of green skin rippled along his spine.

"Is that all?" Aleff asked.

Rolling his eyes skyward, Josheb muttered, "Ankles."

"Show me," the Caretaker repeated. The teen sat on the ground and hauled off his footgear.

Benaiah had no idea how Aleff could remain so patient with someone so uncooperative, but he watched carefully. *Handling Josheb is going to be my job.* Any tips or tricks he could pick up from Aleff would be great.

The Caretaker knelt to inspect the set of green blazes that began at Josheb's ankles and laced up around his calves. "You don't use these as much."

"No."

"Why not?"

"I don't like going barefoot. Feels off."

Aleff nodded. "Unfurl your wings, please."

Josheb balked. "They're not wings. I told you; I can't fly."

"Yes, you mentioned that," the Caretaker said quietly. "Neither can I, if that's any comfort."

"It's not."

"Do you wish you could?" inquired Aleff.

Josheb looked away, then said, "I can ride. That's good enough."

"But if you join Benaiah, you'll be leaving these herds behind."

"Are there horses where we're going?" Josheb asked.

Where we're going! Ben tried not to smirk. *He's already made up his mind to go back with me.*

Aleff's eyes took on a sparkle. "Not so many. None so fine. But yes, the royal stables have horses."

"Good to know."

"Unfurl your wings, please," Aleff repeated.

Benaiah's eyebrows shot up when Josheb finally obeyed.

David would have to fight
his way to the throne.
And I'd be right there with him.
I liked the sound of that,
but there was one problem.
I was worthless as a warrior.
That made it a little easier
to tough it out during
Othniel's training.
If he could turn me
into a fighter, it'd be
worth every welt and bruise.
But a part of me still
shrank away from these
voluntary beatings.
They brought back
old memories.
Stuff about my father.

18

Never mess with a Caretaker.

The green markings spun away from Josheb's skin, expanding into undulating folds. *Looks like cloth. Moves like it's alive. But if they're supposed to be wings, they're in the wrong place.* The half-Protector's legacy from his father was stuck on backwards, from wrist to elbow instead of along his back and shoulders. Ben contemplated the excess pooling on the ground around Josheb's ankles. *No wonder he can't fly.*

"Aren't you a cute little sugar glider?" Aleff murmured.

The green stuff quivered and snapped. "What's that supposed to mean?"

Ignoring the evidence of Josheb's irritation, Aleff poked and prodded, tugging at the misbegotten wings. "Have you learned to hold positions?"

Josheb's surly expression was back. The only answer he gave was to tighten his fists at his sides.

"Othniel, if you please?" urged the Caretaker.

Benaiah stared in fascination as the Guardian's pattern of spots began to glow, then spread outward in a golden billow. Overlapping layers of translucent light flowed like cloth as Othniel showed off his full wing span. "Watch." Shifting through various wing positions, Othniel said, "Glide. Arrow. Slow. Pivot. Rise."

He repeated the pattern several times, and Josheb struggled to approximate. "This isn't working," he complained. "These messed-up things are hardly worth having."

Othniel folded his arms over his chest, held his pupil's gaze, and said, "Shield." Both amber wings flashed forward, the ends overlapping to create a seamless barrier of warm light.

Josheb stepped forward to touch the obstruction, pushing against it and finally punching it. Wincing and shaking his fist, Josheb demanded, "How'd you do that?"

"Yes, this could be very useful," murmured Aleff, who was playing with the folds that had sprouted along Josheb's backbone.

"Don't *do* that!" Josheb yelped as the green stuff snapped up and out, fending off the Caretaker.

Aleff leaned over to see past Josheb as he addressed Othniel. "He'll only need a breastplate. Everything else is covered." Patting the teen's shoulder, he assured, "No one will be riddling your body with bullets anytime soon."

Josheb glanced at Benaiah, who interpreted, "You have armor." Since it was the sort of thing he'd want to know, Ben added, "All the cherubim I've seen have a breastplate and boots. Like you."

Humming thoughtfully, Aleff said, "If you can extend far

enough from wrist to ankle, creating a seamless line, I was right. You'll glide."

Othniel scratched at his bristling sideburns. "Agreed."

Aleff immediately opened a door and hustled Josheb through. The moment the young man stepped across the threshold into air, his surprised exclamation became a prolonged scream from somewhere high overhead.

Benaiah's gaze snapped upward. "What did you *do*?"

"Pushed a baby bird from the nest," Aleff replied, his eyes pinned on the plummeting dot. "He may be willing to take a coach's advice, Othniel."

The Guardian launched into the sky with a rush of wings, climbing quickly toward the flailing teen. Ben muttered, "I'm almost glad I don't have wings."

Aleff said, "Your new friend is idiotically stubborn, but a quick learner. I think he'll cooperate once he sees the personal benefits."

"He could have killed me."

"If he tried, he failed." With a sidelong glance, Aleff said, "Josheb's a warrior, born and bred. Whether or not he'll live up to his order and become a Protector ... that remains to be seen."

Benaiah caught the note of caution in his caretaker's tone. "Is he dangerous?"

"Of course. You all are. You need to be."

Benaiah flopped onto his back in the windblown grass and let his eyes slide shut. "Hurts," he groaned. Loosening his grip, he let go of the latest weapons in Othniel's never-ending arsenal. *This isn't a matter of figuring out what I'm good at. He's just looking for what I fail least at.* Ben held his hands in front of his face and squinted. *Good thing I already had calluses from digging trenches.* His pick and shovel had spared him from Josheb's bout with blisters.

Reddish mud spattered Ben's entire body, the aftermath of another round of hacking away at the clay pillars Aleff made for their practices. *How long was that? Felt like forever. Do real battles last whole days?* He tried flaking away some of the mud with his fingernail, but it was too much work. Crossing his arms over his eyes, he waited for sleep to claim him.

Aleff found him first. "What, no scowl? I barely feel welcomed!"

"Too tired," Ben sighed. "And hungry."

"Neri and Pazi were trying to feed you earlier, and you turned them away."

Ben lifted his arms just enough to glare. "I'm sick of flakes."

Aleff's lips quirked. "Is that what you're calling the bread of angels these days?"

"Calling it *bread* is a stretch. I've eaten bread. Way more filling."

"I take it you're in withdrawal? Craving something smoky and charred?"

Benaiah's stomach growled, and he whined, "Can we talk about something else? How's David?"

"Saul took a liking to him. David plays for him nearly every evening."

"How do you know? I mean … you're here a lot."

"I always return before I'm missed."

Messing with time again. Wonder if he ever bumps into himself?

"Besides," Aleff continued, sitting beside him. "You three need a doctor who makes house calls. Any wounds, sprains, or spasms to report?"

"No, but Othniel's hiding a limp."

"I'll sneak up on him later. So what are you test driving today?"

Ben replied, "Othniel figured out that thing about my hands."

"Is my ambidextrous copyist doing double duty?"

"Feels that way." Patting the grass on either side, Benaiah found the hilts of two short swords. "Training with these means I have to jab everything twice."

"Very menacing," Aleff said approvingly.

Benaiah stared at his dual blades. "How much longer will these lessons continue?"

"That's not for me to say."

"Yeah, but you must have *some* idea."

"When the time comes, you'll know. Sendings are always clear."

His answer was about as satisfying as a wafer of manna, which brought Ben's thoughts back to the empty cavern in his gut. "Can I get some real food?"

"Can you?" Aleff challenged. "Let's find out."

Josheb leaned on his spear, eyes bright with interest as Aleff asked, "What are you hungry for?"

"Meat," Benaiah answered. "Lots of it. Preferably something we can catch."

"One sitting duck, coming up!" The Caretaker smiled and opened a door. "Off you go. Just make sure you're not the ones who're caught."

Ben stepped through and found himself in a forest. Morning light angled through enormous trees, and a cool mist trickled along the ground. After so many days of stiffening his back against the wind, the stillness felt strange.

"Where are we?" Josheb asked.

"No idea."

His companion frowned. "And what are we looking for?"

Benaiah shrugged. "Aleff didn't say."

"Is that bad?"

"Can be. He likes surprises."

Josheb turned, scanning their hunting grounds. "Do you like his surprises?"

"Not really."

Suddenly, Josheb went still. "Found it." With a wolfish grin, he added, "Hope you're hungry."

I never gave much thought
to inheritances until I saw
what had been passed down to
Josheb. His father must have
been a powerful warrior. Taller,
stronger, faster—I couldn't match
him, no matter how hard I tried.
But there would be things
only I could do. And they
were all thanks to my father.

19

Fear is an excellent motivator.

From behind came a snuffle, followed by a grunt. Benaiah turned in time to see the bear rear up on its hindquarters. The towering beast's muzzle wrinkled as it sniffed and snorted, batting the air with an enormous paw. *That thing's almost as big as Othniel.* Taller than he and Josheb, it probably weighed more than both of them put together.

Ben said, "Let me rephrase that. I *hate* Aleff's surprises."

A low growl turned into an angry snarl as Josheb slowly circled the animal. "Aleff did say you were hungry enough to eat a horse," the rider said, his tone as sharp as the tip of his spear.

"He was joking." Benaiah lifted his hands and shuffled backward. "Your horses are safe. *We're* not."

"Think of this as more training." Josheb gave his weapon a twirl. "We shouldn't waste the Caretaker's generosity."

Ben's frown deepened into a scowl. "This isn't generosity. How are we supposed to kill a bear?"

"Here's a plan. You slash. I stab. It stops being alive."

Some strategy. He'd been on enough battlefields to know that life was just that easy to snuff out. But instead of looking for openings, Benaiah found excuses. *I'm not a warrior. My father was a Messenger, and they don't know crud about fighting!*

Suddenly, the bear dropped to all fours and shambled forward. Using his long legs to best advantage, Ben bolted for the nearest tree and swung up into its branches.

Arms wide, Josheb yelled, "I thought you said you were hungry!"

The noise was enough to draw the bear's attention. With a grunt, it changed direction. Josheb stood his ground, spear ready.

'Your mother knew what it meant to fight.'

Benaiah's grip on his tree branch loosened, and he had to scramble to keep his seat. "Wh-what?"

God's voice held compassion. *'She protected you from your father. Her ferocity saved you long before Aleff caught you up and carried you off.'*

"My mother?" Ben had fragmented memories—sheer silk, jingling shells, and tinted nails on both fingers and toes. He knew she'd been beautiful enough to attract the interest of a god. But a fighter?

'She loved you as much as she hated him. So he demanded a sacrifice.'

Icy dread slipped into his heart. "My father wanted to kill me?"

'Worse. He wanted her to kill you.'

"But she didn't."

'Not all warriors have wings.' The vague impressions in Benaiah's mind slowly coalesced into a woman with black hair so long, it rivaled Aleff's. There were intricate patterns painted on her face and jewels bound into her hair, but Ben didn't care about the trappings. He knew those eyes. That smile.

Benaiah had often grumbled over the unfairness of his life, cursing the father who'd made him strange. *But I have a life. I'm alive.*

War might not be a Messenger's business, but Ben wasn't so limited. Half human, he could draw on his mother's resolve. *She* was the reason he could become the warrior David needed.

The moment his king stood before his mind's eye, Benaiah was ashamed. David wouldn't have run. *David would stand his ground and protect those who belong to him.*

Once again, God's voice touched Ben's innermost thoughts. *'Defend your men. They are your flock.'*

"Crud!" Benaiah dropped from the tree. He had no business running away. Not when Josheb was in danger. Drawing both swords, he drove himself forward.

Josheb was laughing as he taunted the bear, testing its temper, dancing just out of reach.

Not giving himself time to think, Benaiah took a page from David's book. He recklessly flung himself onto the bear's back, bringing both blades around its neck. When the beast reared back, he was ready. Digging deep. Pulling outward. Ben sliced through fur and flesh, cutting their prey's throat. It bucked, trying to shake free, and Benaiah lost his balance, toppling backward in an ungainly heap.

The dying bear staggered, and Josheb quickly set his spear so that gravity drove its point through the slumping animal's heart. He strolled around the fallen beast, admiring their success. Then he turned to Benaiah, who lay on his back, staring up at the sky. Josheb offered his hand. "Not bad. You slashed. I stabbed. It stopped being alive."

With this one, you gotta earn every scrap of respect. Letting go of his weapons, Ben allowed Josheb to haul him to his feet. It was probably the closest thing to acknowledgment the guy would every give. And it felt good.

Stooping to pick up his blood-smeared swords, Benaiah asked, "Ever cook a bear before?"

"No, but when I was a kid, I cleaned fish." Josheb kicked the bulky carcass. "It's fur instead of scales, but the principle's the same. Scrape off the parts you can't eat. Skewer the parts you can. Hold them over a fire until it smells good."

"Yeah, that'd do it."

Josheb asked, "You want to take charge? It's your kill."

Benaiah did take charge, but in his own way. "You gut. I'll get a fire going. We'll eat faster that way."

With a soft grunt of agreement, Josheb drew his blade and attacked the bear again.

Two gorged teenagers sprawled on either side of dying embers, watching smoke drift toward a sky that had begun changing colors. It was evening, and Aleff still hadn't come for them. Relaxed and bored, Benaiah asked, "What do you know about your father?"

Josheb didn't answer immediately. But he *did* answer. "I know what he used to be, and I know what he became."

"What did he look like?"

"I don't know," Josheb replied, tugging at the tuft of hair under his lip. "The way I heard it, some village girls disappeared. My mother was one of them. When they found her again, she was … broken. And not long after that, they realized she was carrying me."

"Do you miss her?"

"Can't miss someone I never knew. Birthing me killed her."

Benaiah was grateful to have memories of his mother. Even if they were tainted. "I don't exactly remember my father—what he looked like or if he spoke to me. But he was around, and I know how that made me feel." Benaiah's jaw tightened. "Bad."

"You lived with a demon?"

"Sort of." Ben wasn't used to spilling secrets, so the next part was hard to say. "We lived in his temple. My father was a god."

Turns out, there were crickets in the woods.

Ben had expected all kinds of reactions—shock, awe, horror, pity. But the moment he met his companion's gaze, he realized Josheb was laughing.

"What?" Benaiah demanded.

"Did your father have a throne?"

"Yeah."

"And fancy clothes. Good food. And people to fawn over him."

Ben wasn't sure where Josheb was going, but he nodded. "All that stuff."

"Sounds like he was smarter than the skulker who sired me. But … a god?" Josheb's laugh deepened. "I'll bet it cinched up tight in his craw, watching them lose faith in him. Who wants a god that can't save them?"

Well, crud. It is funny in a way. Cracking a smile, Benaiah said, "Tough to be a god when there's no one left to fool."

"Faithless fools." Josheb shut his eyes with a smile. Several moments later, he murmured, "But didn't you say God hid us from our fathers?"

"Yeah."

Josheb hummed sleepily. "Then we'd be fools to discount them."

A good point. One Benaiah was content to file away for future consideration. Right now, he was enjoying the drowsy contentment that came with a full belly. Bear wasn't so bad.

He was half-asleep when Josheb's voice startled him. "What did you say?"

"Nothing."

Josheb's tone sharpened. "Yes, you did. I *heard* you."

"I don't know what you're …" One look at the other teen, and Benaiah trailed off. Josheb's face was screwed up in confusion. Maybe even suspicion. Slowly sitting up, Ben asked, "What do you think I said?"

"You said you'd rather eat goat."

We were taller and stronger
than mere men. Better.
And this was our destiny.
Plus, God was with us.
Didn't that mean we
couldn't lose? I thought
we were ready for
anything David's enemies
might throw at us.
But I was wrong.
I was forgetting that
not every enemy is human.

20

We failed the final exam.

Aleff peered into Benaiah's eyes and inquired, "Are you experiencing headaches?"

"No."

"Dizziness, nausea, shortness of breath," the Caretaker listed. Ben blinked. "*No.*"

"Indigestion, incontinence?"

"Did you just accuse me of bed-wetting?"

"It's been *years* since you …." Clearing his throat, Aleff rerouted his answer. "*No,* but I'm curious if you're broadcasting on all channels, or if Josheb is the only one tuning in."

"It only happened once, and I don't even remember it," grumbled Benaiah. "Maybe full-fledged Messengers can talk like God, but I don't know how it happened."

"What a lovely analogy," Aleff murmured. "Of course you would understand, since God talks to you."

"Well, yeah." Shrugging, Ben said, "Ever since you and Samuel did that thing, we've been saying stuff to each other."

The Caretaker's fussing fingers stilled. "What?"

"Look, are we done with this check-up thingie, because …"

"He hears you?" Aleff interrupted.

"Yeah."

"And you hear Him?"

Benaiah rolled his eyes. "Wasn't that the whole point of my choice?"

Aleff's expression was difficult to read. "An angel hears and obeys the voice of God, for we are His servants. But God hears the prayers of humans, for they are His children. It's one or the other, but apparently, *you* can bat from either side of the plate." Messing up Ben's hair, he added, "Aren't you a special snowflake?"

Just then, Othniel returned. "The wind has changed. That boy is useless once the herd is running."

"Are you limping?" Aleff asked.

The big Guardian grumbled, "Just fix it."

"If Josheb is landing blows on you, no man on earth stands a chance," Aleff remarked. "Is it time for … that *thing* we discussed?"

Othniel turned to Benaiah. "Go on, boy. The horses will not wait."

Tossing aside his shoes and tightening the knots on his turban, Ben left the angels to their cahoots.

Aleff was grim. "This door will lead you to a place where one of the Fallen is confined. You'll be imprisoned with him. You won't be able to avoid fighting him. But most importantly, you won't be able to hold back. If you do, he'll kill you."

"Not if we kill him first," Josheb countered.

"You cannot end him," Othniel said flatly.

Benaiah asked, "Can't because we're no match, or can't because …?"

" …we have no end," Aleff finished for him. "Death isn't an option."

Josheb frowned at Othniel. "What *are* our options?"

"Capture. Surrender. Dismemberment."

Aleff interjected, "There's one teensy thing I'd like you to bear in mind. Please."

"Yeah?" Ben asked.

"You've been flying under the radar for centuries. But if things go wrong, you'll both be blips on the enemy's map."

Josheb muttered, "Does he do this on purpose?"

Benaiah sighed. "*What* could go wrong?"

"Too many things." Aleff shook his head. "Don't let down your guard."

"If it's that bad, why the crud are you risking it?"

Shaking his head, the Caretaker said, "You need to be ready for that time when your secret is discovered. Because it will be." Aleff traded a look with Othniel before continuing. "Focus on gathering your strength quickly and quietly. Secrecy is your third-best ally."

Ben's brows shot up. "Who's first?"

"God."

"And second?"

Aleff winked. "Me."

"We need more allies," Josheb muttered.

The Caretaker continued. "Othniel agrees that this is the simplest way to see if you're ready. Young Protectors and Guardians train against Fallen."

"Not right away," Othniel quickly inserted.

"True. These aren't baby steps, boys." Aleff took hold of reality and opened a door. Darkness lay on the other side. "This is the real deal, and it's not a pretty picture."

"What'd he say?" Josheb checked.

"Don't die."

"Sounds simple enough." Shouldering his spear, Josheb sauntered through the door.

Before Benaiah could follow, Aleff gripped his shoulder. "Caution, my gangling camel. There's only one thing worse than a demon."

"What's that?"

"A cornered demon."

Benaiah drew his short swords and walked through the door. Its disappearance extinguished most of the light, leaving him and Josheb in the murk of a forest at twilight. *Woods again.* But not the same ones. Moss clung like spider webs to overhanging branches, and his ears caught the faint whine of insects.

Josheb slapped the back of his neck as he strolled in a

tight circle around Ben. "Did you notice the trees?"

This didn't look like any kind of prison. No pit. No cage. No wall. But amidst the smells of leaf and loam, a different odor reached Benaiah's nose—decay and rot, dank and sweet. Tensing at the familiar stench, he muttered, "Someone's here all right. Be careful."

"The bear was easier to find."

Ben was noticing more details—torn branches, scarred trunks, upturned stones. The damage seemed to be confined to a wide circle. *He can't get away. And neither can we.* A shadow he'd initially taken for a rock shuddered, then lengthened. Benaiah hissed, "Over there!"

Josheb's spear came around, but he scanned the woods with a blank expression. "You sure? I don't see anything."

"Right in front of you!"

"There's nothing …."

Benaiah roared, "Josheb, duck!"

The young man dropped, rolling to one side before scuttling behind him. His dark eyes registered zero recognition of their looming foe. The first obstacle in this death match was glaringly obvious. Ben's partner couldn't see their enemy. Josheb was fighting blind.

'Open his eyes.'

Benaiah relayed, "Open your eyes."

"They *are* open."

"Not good enough." Snagging the hem of Josheb's vest, Ben retreated to a safer distance. "I need you to open your eyes. Don't you want to see what you're fighting?"

Reluctance. Annoyance. Confusion. Finally, Josheb asked, "Do I have a choice?"

"Yeah, *you* do. But I don't stand a chance without you. So this time … when I say *open*, I expect more."

"That makes no sense."

"Not my fault. Now open your eyes before that thing decides to do more than stare." With as much authority as he could muster, Ben commanded, "*Open!*"

Josheb blinked, then slapped his hand over his nose. "Ugh! What did you step in?"

"Look over there," Ben whispered, pointing to the dark bulk on the far side of the circle. Intelligence glittered in watchful eyes.

With a groan, Josheb said, "Opening my eyes—useful. Opening my nostrils—nauseating. That thing reeks worse than a piss pit in summer!"

The demon's eyes narrowed, and Benaiah elbowed his companion. "Not sure you should be offending people with personal remarks. Might rile them up."

"*Is* that thing people?"

"Yeah, idiot. The kind of people *we* came from. So take a good look."

Dark limbs stretched outward with an unsettling series of creaks and pops. Except, nobody had that many arms. Josheb asked the question on both their minds. "What are those things?"

And suddenly, Benaiah knew. "Those used to be wings."

"Can it fly?"

The spines rattled, and sour notes clanged from the litter of dirty glass dangling from them. "I don't think he appreciates being referred to as an *it*."

"If his skin's that thin, this won't take long." Hefting his spear, Josheb rushed the demon.

And it was ready for him.

"Look out!" Ben shouted, but it was too late. The broken wings were far from useless. As the Fallen sidestepped Josheb's thrust, twitching spines lashed out, catching Josheb's shoulder in passing. As soon as he made it back to his partner, Benaiah muttered, "Those things are dangerous!"

"Already confirmed that, Captain."

"Use your wings, idiot."

"Yessir." Although Josheb's tone was mocking, he immediately obeyed. Green frills fanned out over his injury and flared out around his wrists. This time, he measured his steps more carefully, and when he brandished his spear at the demon, he deflected the answering jab.

With a short bark of laughter, the Fallen spoke. "They told us all the pups were drowned. Lies and more lies."

Benaiah cringed at the cackling and muttering that followed. *He doesn't sound sane. I can't quite hear ....* He had to stop himself from edging forward to hear what the demon was saying.

"What lucky rutter have you been hiding behind?" asked the demon.

"I don't have to answer that," Ben replied with a scowl.

"Don't need to. It's plain to anyone as knows, and I do.

There's always something that gives it away." Bloodshot eyes raked the boys from head to toe. "No pointy ears. No extra fingers. But no raiment, either. Were you Cast, or were you Sent?"

"We're here to fight, not talk."

The demon licked the blood-slicked tip of his ruined wing. "Tastes mortal. Which means they want you dead." Pointing to Josheb with a gnarled finger, he asked, "Have you been bad? I can make it worse."

Josheb glanced at Benaiah. "I have a plan."

"Yeah?"

"Dismemberment. And we're starting with its tongue."

In other words, stop listening to all the crud he's spewing.

"Exactly!" replied the rider.

This time, they attacked together. Metal crashed against scrapped wings, and from amidst his tattered clothes, the demon withdrew a barbed blade. More than once, he sent them sprawling, but they rallied, driving him back. *Maybe the training worked.*

"Didn't we train under a master?" Josheb exulted. "We're strong!"

Their opponent sneered, and a warning note rang through Benaiah's mind. Too late, he realized there was another possibility. *Or maybe it's a trap.*

Josheb caught on a fraction of a second too late. He'd already thrown his spear, and there was no calling it back.

"Crud."

The weapon tore past the border of their circle, slicing

through what looked like a veil. Diving for the breech, the demon scrabbled to widen the opening. Escape cost him three of the fanning appendages on his back.

Josheb stamped on one of the twitching spines as he glowered after the freed prisoner. "Should I follow him?"

"No," Benaiah whispered. "This is bad, but that would be worse."

"Halfers are a treat to break!" jeered the demon from the other side of the veil. "If you have a fleck of your fathers' courage, you'll Fall!"

"Still spouting nonsense," Josheb growled, kicking dirt. "At least let me try to chase him down! I'm fast."

"No," Ben repeated, rubbing his temple. The one thing Aleff had stressed, and they'd blown it. *Can we fix this?*

With a burst of light and wind, Aleff entered the battlefield, glanced around, and sighed. "Cat's out of the bag."

Without another word, he turned and began lifting things from the other side, piling them on the scuffled ground. Packs. Blankets. Canteens. Picnic basket. Benaiah's heart sank.

Josheb distracted him with a prod to the shoulder. "Cat?"

Ben could only shake his head. He was too ashamed to open his mouth.

"Do you have your swords? Your spear?" Aleff asked briskly. When Josheb pointed beyond the torn veil, the Caretaker waved a hand. An opening appeared, and the young warrior skulked through to reclaim his weapon.

"I have bad news," Aleff began. "Your run as heaven's best-kept secret is over, and that means you'll need to hurry along."

"Can't you just back things up?" Benaiah asked.

"I cannot."

"Why not?"

Aleff's mouth pressed into a straight line. "Evidently, that plan doesn't fall in line with God's purposes."

"I'm sorry!" Ben blurted. "This was an accident. A mistake."

"And there will be consequences." While he talked, Aleff healed the cuts and scrapes they'd earned in their skirmish. "More training would have been ideal, but there's no use crying over spilled milk. I'm sending you forward to the next location. Now."

"Where?"

The Caretaker's eyebrows arched. "You tell me."

Searching his thoughts for some clue, Benaiah ran up against the thread of a melody. David had put the lesson to music, and without even trying, his mind supplied the words to the tune.

"I *heard* that." A gentle smile spread across Aleff's face. "You really are a special snowflake."

Josheb turned sharply, gazing out into the darkness of the woods. A rough shout reached them from the direction the demon had run. Then a crash, like a falling tree. "Did you hear *that*?"

"By the pricking of my thumbs," Aleff said in weary tones. "Othniel and I will mop up here. No time for more. Ta-ta!"

This time, Aleff didn't open a door. He used a trapdoor.

It was like walking into
a world that used to be nothing
but words. I'd read about it,
and I liked the idea. But I'd
assumed it was just a story.
Not a real place. Yet there I was,
standing knee-deep in a
world of white. Squinting
against the glare.
And stupidly happy
because I knew
where I was. This was
the storehouse of snow
from the scrolls of Job.

21

Too late for cold feet.

No time for a goodbye. Or to scream. Josheb didn't even have a chance to extend his winglets before they fell face-first into something cold, white, and powdery. *At least it was a soft landing.* Benaiah peeped out of his full-body crater, then struggled to his knees. "Snow." His breath came in a puff that wisped away toward the pearly sky.

Hastily locating their tumbled basket, Ben checked on Neri and Pazi. "Sorry, guys. You okay?"

The pair of yahavim peered around the gleaming world. Clambering up the front of his robes, they latched onto the trailing end of his turban. Benaiah loosened the folds, and they crawled up underneath. *Guess that's safer.*

Josheb sat, idly brushing at his bare shoulders while he stared at the landscape. "It's so still."

"No wind."

"And this is *snow*."

"Yeah." Benaiah had never seen snow before, at least not to touch it. Aleff had pointed it out before, a smudge of white on a winter mountain, but this place was made of the stuff. The chill seeped through his clothes, turning the sweat on his back to ice. Thanks to his heritage, the cold didn't really affect him. It was a refreshing change from their last location. Ben thought to ask, "You cold?"

Josheb shouldered a pack and canteen, then propped his spear over his shoulder. "Wouldn't want to sleep in this stuff, but I'll live. Where to?"

Everywhere around them were peaks, pillows, pillars, and piles of white. Edges were softened, which was why Ben didn't see the one at his feet. When he took two steps to the side, he windmilled for a moment before plunging off a short precipice. The snow-filled gorge below broke his fall, dislodging his turban and its two small passengers. Neri and Pazi peeped out from under the tumbled linen.

"Did you survive, Captain?" called Josheb, whose voice held laughter.

"Thanks for asking." Benaiah snatched up his turban and stuffed the cloth inside his robes. While he hunted for a way back up, the little manna-makers hid under the curtain of his loosened hair.

By the time Ben made it to Josheb, the young man was inspecting a pile of what looked like glass pebbles. Clear as water, hard as stone. Josheb picked one up and popped it into his mouth. "Ice."

"Hail," Benaiah explained. "Once in a while, it falls from

clouds like rain."

There were more piles, which seemed to be sorted by size. Some of the hailstones were small as mustard seeds. Others were startlingly large. Picking up a sphere the size of his fist, Josheb said, "If these fell onto an unprotected herd, not many would survive."

"Are these big, or are we small?"

"That's an interesting question." Josheb stared at him, then at the hailstones. Tossing another chunk of ice into his mouth, he shrugged. "Does it matter?"

"No idea."

Josheb paused to lean against his spear. "So which way do we go?"

Ben turned in a slow circle, taking in arches of ice and spires of snow. *No trees. No animals. No buildings.* He was about to admit that he didn't have a clue when a dark patch in the distance caught his eye. The tug of Sending made him sure. Pointing, he said, "That way."

Josheb started walking, his boots making deep impressions in the snow as he broke a trail.

Shouldering his own share of the baggage, Benaiah hesitated, then slipped off his sandals, cramming them inside his robes along with the turban. They cut a path across an endless snowfield. The cave-ish looking thing was far off, so they had a long trudge with very little to make it interesting. *If David was here, we'd sing.*

At first, Benaiah thought his eyes were playing tricks on him. The splash of color was there and gone again. But he couldn't have imagined it. "Did you see that?"

Josheb stopped. "Where?"

He nodded in the same direction they were headed. "I saw something. Someone. Wearing bright blue."

"Blue," Josheb repeated, training his eye on the horizon line. "Shouldn't be hard to find something blue in a world that's only white. Unfortunately, we're just as easy to pick out. Good chance whoever you saw spotted us."

"Yeah."

"Was it him? The one like us?"

It wasn't as if there were long lines of candidates. "Yeah, I think so."

Josheb frowned. "Not sure what to think of someone who'd hide from intruders instead of hunting them down."

"Maybe you should be glad he's not as protective as you," Ben said. "You're a ravager of hailstones, a tromper of snow."

Grinning, Josheb picked up the pace. "Betcha he's prey. Like you."

"Hey, I can fend!"

"But can you hunt?"

The answer to that was still *no*, so he let Josheb keep the lead. When they reached the far end of the snow basin, the dark patch turned out to be nothing more than bare stone. Josheb tapped it with the butt of his spear. "So there's something here besides snow and ice. Rock."

"Your home didn't have much more variety—grass, wind, and horses."

Josheb climbed to the top of the snowy formation, poked

his head up over the rim, then quickly ducked. He waved furiously for Benaiah to join him, victory shining in his eyes. "Found him."

Ben clambered up and peeped over the edge. Just in time to see someone take a flying leap off a ledge. The jumper was airborne for several moments, arms and legs waving, before plopping into an oversized bowl of snow. "What's he doing?"

"*Playing*," Josheb whispered. "Doesn't it look fun to you?"

"Guess so."

"I gotta try it!" Before Benaiah could stop him, Josheb was up over the top. His short run ended in a long leap … and a thin whoop.

The other person froze, a puddle of blue cloth against the white snow. Then he was on the move, scurrying like a frightened rabbit.

"Wait!" Ben called, just before he vanished over the other side. "We want to talk to you!"

Josheb was already on the move, chugging through the deep snow below. Benaiah stuck to the top edge, circling around to the spot where the other guy had disappeared. Ice made the passage tricky, so Josheb was up and over first. He called, "Down here, Captain. I have him cornered."

Ben slipped along a narrow gully and found Josheb standing guard over the entrance to a cave. *Crevice might be a better word.* There wasn't much to it.

"You need to take a look," Josheb said. "I think we're chasing the wrong prey. This one's too puny to be a warrior."

"What do you mean?" Concern and confusion brought a scowl to his face. "Did you hurt him?"

"I wouldn't treat a foal harshly." Josheb sighed and explained, "He's a child. Just a runt."

Benaiah ducked through an icicle-edged opening. "Hello?" he called, his words ringing against the walls. The crevice quickly narrowed, so it didn't take long to reach its dead end. At the farthest point, someone was hunched up. *Looks like a shivering mound of hair.* "Hey, kid. Can we talk? Look, I'm not going to hurt you."

The child's trembling didn't stop.

Getting down on his hands and knees to make himself smaller, Ben inched closer. "I know this might sound crazy, but I'm looking for you. At least, I think it's you." He lightly touched a slender shoulder. "Did Josheb scare you? To be honest, he kind of scares me, too."

The child looked over his shoulder, and Benaiah caught a glimpse of wide eyes and pallid skin. And something else. "Would you look at that?" Ben murmured. "Yeah, you're the one. Not sure what God's thinking, Sending me to a little guy like you."

"God?" he asked, uncurling and turning around.

"Yeah. Long story." Benaiah held very still as the kid reached for him. The boy's hands were slim as a woman's, but his fingers were blunt-tipped. And though his features were delicate, there was a firmness to the chin and brow. *On the pretty side, but definitely a boy.*

To Benaiah's amazement, the kid grabbed a hank of his

light brown hair, giving it a tentative tug. *Well, crud. Is that how it's gonna be?* Just like Aleff had done for him, Ben opened his arms, offering shelter. "C'mere, kid. I gotcha."

The boy scooted into his embrace just as a shadow fell across them. Josheb asked, "That him?"

"Yeah."

"I don't get it."

With a small shrug, he addressed the boy. "I'm Benaiah. Are you alone?"

"You are here." Deep blue eyes swiveled, and the kid solemnly said, "And he is here."

Dropping into a crouch, Josheb muttered, "He can't be more than eight years old. Ten at the most. What use is he going to be to a king?"

Gently lifting a section of the boy's straight brown hair, Ben tucked it behind an ear that came to an elfin point.

Josheb tugged thoughtfully at his chin. "That mean what I think it means?"

Benaiah smirked. "Shammah is part Caretaker."

The runt was a shivering mess,
but he was definitely the one.
Skinny and pale. Snot dribbling
from his nose. But God had
chosen him as a gift
for my king. I probably would
have dismissed Shammah
as quickly as Josheb did ...
except for his hair and ears.
This kid was like Aleff.
And that meant one thing. Power.

22

All he needed was a lullaby.

ow what?" Josheb asked.

Benaiah set down Shammah and waited for a push or pull in any given direction. *Nothing.* Reaching inside his robes for his turban, he was met by a wriggle and several pats. *At least Neri and Pazi weren't squashed.* Ben wasn't used to having his hair flapping around his shoulders, but he hesitated over hiding it away. The barefoot boy's dark brown hair must have been knee-length. *Maybe it's good to have something in common with the kid. Make it easier for him to trust us.*

Except trust didn't seem to be their biggest problem. Shammah's hand slipped into Benaiah's as the boy gazed up at him with a solemn expression.

Looking them over, Josheb snorted. "Son of a Caretaker, meet raised-by-a-Caretaker. Let's hope the next five have more bulk, less hair."

Ben left the turban for the yahavim and gave one sandal a

turn since it was poking against his ribs. *Might not be worth much here, but who knows where we'll be next?* Assuming they could find a way out. "Now what?" he sighed.

"Just said that," grumbled Josheb before turning to the boy. "Shammah, huh? Did you sneak out to play?"

"I do not sneak."

"So is your babysitter close by?"

"I am not a baby," Shammah replied in lofty tones.

Benaiah felt like an idiot. Of course they should be looking for the angel assigned to this child. Joining the inquisition, he asked, "Who tucks you in at night? Gives you dinner?"

"I am neither tired nor hungry."

"You sure?" Ben asked worriedly. He was no expert, but Shammah looked way too thin. *Like it's been a lifetime since his last skewer of goat or loaf of bread. Maybe I should offer some manna.*

Josheb pushed for more. "Well I'm both. But I'm fresh out of flakes, and I can't sleep on a bed of hail. Where do you live?"

Shammah hesitated, then pointed.

"Lead the way," Josheb invited, making it an order.

And the kid obeyed, tugging Benaiah along by the hand. While they walked, Ben checked, "Is there someone here with you?"

"Not one. Two."

Ben muttered, "I meant *besides* us."

Shammah's hold tightened. "There are two more."

"Yeah? What are their names?"

"I do not know." His next words sounded hollow. "They will not tell me."

After a long, silent walk, the trio rounded a bend, and a tower came into view. Instead of aiming for the gleaming white structure, Shammah led them to a wide opening in the rocks behind it. "I am kept here."

Josheb was studying the tower. "Who lives there?"

"Angels."

Benaiah frowned in confusion. "The angels have a tower, but you live in a cave?"

"Yes," Shammah replied, walking into the dark passage.

"Maybe mongrels don't rate a room," Josheb said edgily.

Something's off. Ben couldn't bring himself to believe that God would allow His angels to misuse a child. Even the son of a demon. *But what about neglect? It's not like Shammah can help who his father was.* Josheb crowded close on Shammah's other side. The rider was bristling with indignation, and Benaiah was glad to see him offering protection and support. *We mongrels need to stick together.*

"Welcome."

Josheb brought around his spear, pointing it at the slight angel who stepped from the shadows. This newcomer's hair hung in knotted ropes, and his raiment glowed softly in the absence of other light.

Although their apparent host didn't smile, his manner was polite. "Benaiah the First. Josheb the Rider. Shammah's room is this way."

Ben noticed that the new guy didn't make eye contact with the boy, nor did Shammah greet him. *That's not right. No, it's* wrong. *Why would God allow something wrong?* The little boy darted ahead and yanked at a ring in the wall. Even when Shammah leaned back on his heels, he barely budged it. But a rim of light appeared, gleaming against hammered metal. Ben couldn't decide if the kid's door belonged to a prison or a palace. Set into thick stone. Covered in gold.

Josheb followed Shammah into a room filled with firelight, but Benaiah stopped on the threshold. He glared down at the angel whose dark hair glinted with purple highlights. *Caretaker*, his mind supplied. But that wasn't enough. "Do you have a name?"

"No."

"You don't?"

"Not one which is spoken," the Caretaker replied.

Makes no sense. Makes no difference. "Fine," he growled. "But about the kid."

"Yes?"

"Why do you keep him here?"

"He is free to leave this chamber."

"But he's in the dark."

The nameless angel explained, "Warmth and night relax him. This place was provided for Shammah's comfort."

Missing the point? Or dodging it? Ben's teeth went on edge. "Why has the kid been alone?"

"For his sake." The angel's gaze rested briefly on the child, who sat on a tufted pillow. "You will also need to take care."

Funny advice, coming from a Caretaker. Ben wasn't sure if the guy was trying to tell him that Shammah was now his responsibility … or if he was trying to warn him about something. This room with its high ceilings and tapestry-draped walls was bigger and grander than the little hut he'd called home. But it felt as empty as Shammah's listless gaze.

Benaiah wanted to get back to the kid, but first he asked, "Do you know a Caretaker named Aleff."

The hint of a smile appeared on his host's face. "Yes."

"He was my … he *is* my …." Ben didn't know how to finish. "He might show up."

"Thank you for the warning."

"By any chance is he …? Well, crud. I dunno." How did you go about asking an angel if your own caretaker was cracked. Clearing his throat, Benaiah asked, "Are most of the samayim like you?"

The guy stuck to evasion. But he also answered the real question. "*No one* is like Aleff."

Shammah's room was pretty comfy. *For a cave.* Most of the light came from a large brazier in the corner. Josheb dragged several cushions and blankets closer to the shallow basin with its crackling fire. Collapsing onto them, he basked in the heat, and before long, he was snoring.

"Guess he was colder than he let on," Benaiah remarked.

Shammah nodded. And pinched himself.

Ben watched in silent fascination as the boy tugged his ear, jiggled his legs, and finally got up to pace the room. "What's wrong with him?" he whispered to the lingering Caretaker.

"He needs sleep."

"So why doesn't he?"

With a vague hum, the angel said, "Shammah is fighting a battle he cannot win."

Fighting against sleep? Benaiah frowned. "Does he have bad dreams?"

"Probably. But that is not why he struggles so hard."

This guy reminds me of Aleff after all. Too many answers that mean nothing. "What's the big deal?"

Taking a backward step toward the door, the angel suggested, "Lull him, and you will understand."

"If you say so." When the door clicked shut, Ben indulged in a scowl. Tired as he was, lulling suddenly sounded like a bad idea. Except the kid yawned, and those things were contagious.

Benaiah stashed his luggage next to Josheb's, then turned loose his passengers. While Neri and Pazi spiraled to the ceiling, Ben fished out his sandals and tossed them onto the empty picnic basket. He snagged two cushions and a blanket, then crossed to Shammah. "Hey, kid. You tired?"

"No."

"Mind if I borrow some floor?"

Shammah looked down, then up, his face creased. "Will you sleep as well?"

"Relax a little. If that's okay."

He grudgingly replied, "Yes."

While Benaiah lined up the borrowed cushions, Shammah brought over a few more, making the makeshift bed longer. "Good idea. My feet won't hang out."

Apparently, a little encouragement went a long way. The kid hauled every puff and pillow in the room onto Ben's pile. It was sort of cute. Like a game. *And I win.* Falling back onto the mountain, he shut his eyes and sighed. *Gonna sleep for a week. Or at least as long as it takes Aleff to find me.*

A small hand patted his shoulder, and Benaiah opened one eye. Shammah's lower lip was jutted out in an expression of pure sulk. *Doesn't want to sleep. Doesn't want me to sleep.* But this was a battle Benaiah knew he would win. "Do you know about lambs?"

Shammah nodded.

"What about lions?"

Again, the boy nodded.

Stuffing one of the smaller pillows more comfortably behind his back, Ben did what Aleff used to do. "Would you like to hear a story about a lamb who was almost caught by a lion?"

The kid's eyes widened. "Was there blood?"

"Yeah, plenty. It's a good story, and it ends well. And it's true. See?" Benaiah loosened the ties on his tunic. "I have the scars to prove it."

"The blood was yours?" Shammah asked, scooting closer. "Did it hurt?"

"Of course it did! And I might have been eaten right along with that lamb, but I was saved by a king."

Shammah was hooked. "Does the king have a throne?"

"Not yet. Workin' on that part." Thumping a pillow to get the kid to lie down, Benaiah explained, "This king is young. Somewhere in between me and you. But even though he's short, he's brave. He stopped the lion. Stopped him dead."

"He killed the lion?"

"Yeah. Before it could kill me." The pensive expression was back on Shammah's face, so Benaiah changed the subject. "Y'know he taught me a song about sheep."

"I will listen."

Ben blinked. "You want me to sing?"

"Yes, please."

"Yeah, okay. I can do that." Benaiah folded his hands behind his head and stared up at the ceiling. Singing through the psalm reminded him of David. The place that had inspired the lyrics was worlds away, but the song brought it closer. Ben missed the sheep, the pastures, and his friend, so he sang the whole thing again.

Somewhere in the middle of his third go-around, Ben realized that Shammah was humming along. So he kept right on singing, stealing glances at the kid every now and then. The boy's frown of concentration faded, and as he relaxed, he curled closer.

Lapsing into softer tones, Benaiah's song drifted on. After a yawn, he switched to humming. Warm and safe and drowsy, he slowed to the rhythm of Josheb's snores. The lullaby ended with a sigh as Benaiah fell asleep with Shammah's small hand pressed over the ragged scars on his chest.

In the camps that
spring up around battlefields,
stories get shared. There's
never much truth in them.
Monsters from the sea.
Chariots in the sky.
Men as tall as houses.
The wilder the tale, the better.
But once, the pickers found
a shield left behind by
an enemy warrior.
It took six men to lift it.
When I found the guy's
footprints nearby,
it was suddenly easy
to believe in giants.

23

Bigger is better.

Benaiah stirred and tried to turn over, but a weight across his chest pinned him to the bed. *The kid.* He shoved, but it was no use. *Heavy for a little guy.* Opening his eyes, he blinked in the darkness. The fire in the brazier had burned down to embers, so the room had cooled. Not that he was cold. *Well, crud. Is the kid draped over me?*

Fumbling to find Shammah's shoulder, Ben ran up against a hand. A large hand that covered his entire chest. It was as if he'd shrunk. *Wait. That can't be right.* He turned his head and squinted at the boy sharing his pillow. *Too dark.* At least, it was too dark for details. But he could make out enough to send his heart skipping. "What's going on?" he whispered.

The last thing he expected was an answer.

"He is the son of a Caretaker. Our stature is variable." The soft gleam thrown off by the nameless angel's raiment drew closer, bringing more light onto the scene. "This is Shammah's natural size. He reverts whenever he falls asleep."

"He can change size?" Ben murmured, scrambling to make sense of what he was seeing.

The Caretaker didn't bother to answer. He was too busy replenishing the fire.

Shammah's face was peaceful in sleep, brows and lashes dark against skin that looked as if it'd never seen the sun. But something else had changed. *The kid isn't just bigger. He isn't a kid.* "Hey, you. Guy without a name. How old is Shammah?"

"He has been here for centuries."

"Hundreds of years?" Ben asked in disbelief. "Okay, he's older, but not *that* old."

Moving closer to tuck in his charge, the Caretaker said, "Despite his mother's humanity, Shammah's samayim nature is strong. He grew slowly. In terms of physical maturity, perhaps … nineteen."

Benaiah draped his forearm across his eyes. *Older than me, and I carried him around, held his hand, told him a bedtime story, and sang him to sleep.* He peeped at Shammah's hand, which looked big enough to crack his ribs and crush the life from his body. "Why'd he pass himself off as a kid?"

"Because he is afraid."

"Of me and Josheb?"

With a solemn shake of his head, the angel replied, "Of himself."

After that, Ben couldn't sleep. Shammah's slow breathing and Josheb's snores kept right on going. The fire burned low. And he kept remembering stupid stuff he'd said. *How come I was so chatty? I gushed like an idiot, all because I thought he was a frightened little kid.*

'He is.'

Benaiah stifled a groan and mentally argued. *Not little. Not a kid. And if he's frightened, I got no clue why. He's a brute. Grown men will run screaming from the battle lines.*

For the first time, Ben realized that he could hear God's smile.

His lips quirked in response. *Crud. Fine. This is good for David. But did You hear me talk about the lion and lamb thing? I sounded like a simpleton.*

'Simple words were enough to show Shammah his king's heart.'

Although he was glad things would work out, Ben was still embarrassed. *This is so messed up. I get why we were hidden. But why is this guy pretending?*

No answer came. But maybe he was asking the wrong person.

He held his hand over Shammah's to compare. *I thought Rei and Othniel were massive. This guy makes* me *look like a kid.* Ben really wanted to get this giant on his feet and see what he could do. *Was this how David felt when he tackled me?* That scuffle had turned into friendship, but Benaiah doubted that decking Shammah was the right course to take. *The kid was shaking the first time I touched him. Even Josheb said he wouldn't treat him harshly.* Besides, if God said Shammah was a frightened little kid, then that's how it was.

So what do I do now?

Hours later, Benaiah didn't have much of a plan. But he did have an example to follow. So when the Caretaker with no name returned to tend the fire, Ben was ready to face up to his growing responsibilities.

As the fire crackled to new life, Shammah woke with a start. Lifting his head, he stared into Benaiah's eyes. "I fell asleep," he said. His voice was a little deeper, but still light.

"You must have needed it. Feel better?"

Confusion flashed through Shammah's eyes.

Benaiah could almost hear himself asking David why he wasn't scared. *He knew I was different, but he didn't care. I can give Shammah that much.*

The giant finally noticed that he'd trapped his companion and lifted his hand. "Sorry. Did I hurt you?"

Pushing himself up on his elbows, Ben replied, "Nope. All in one piece." He rubbed his chest to prove it, then looked down in surprise. The ragged scars left behind by the lion's claws were missing. "How'd this happen?"

"Shammah is the son of a Caretaker," remarked the nameless angel, who'd finished rekindling the brazier. "Things happen from time to time. Usually to those he cares about."

Benaiah stared hard at Shammah's babysitter. *Why's that feel like another warning?*

"It was an accident. Sorry."

Although there was a pang of regret that the marks of David's rescue were gone, Ben shook his head. "Nothing to apologize for. Thanks, Shammah."

Just then, the drone of Josheb's snoring ended with a caught breath, followed by noisy yawn and scratching.

Shammah quickly reverted to the size and shape of a scrawny child. It happened too quickly to see. *One second, he's twice my size, the next he's half.* "Why'd you do that?"

The kid glanced nervously at the rousing rider, then crawled around behind Ben. "He likes to fight."

"Yeah, he does."

Shammah actually tried to hide himself in Benaiah's hair. "He will want to fight me."

"Good call." Pulling his hair together, Ben twisted it up into a knot and glanced around for his turban. "He definitely will. Don't you think you can take him?"

Catching at Benaiah's sleeve, Shammah whispered, "He would die."

When I thought Shammah
was a kid, I dreaded
all the stuff I'd need
to tell him. How do you
explain to an innocent
about demons and death
and destruction?
But I wasted those worries.
He knew. Firsthand.
Shammah lost his
innocence long ago.

24

Kids don't belong on the battlefield.

Josheb prowled every corner of the chamber, then shifted into one of Othniel's training exercises. Shammah watched silently as the rider lunged and pivoted with his spear. Benaiah mostly ignored him. Until Josheb demanded, "Trade with me."

"Huh?"

"Loan me your swords. And get over here. I need an opponent."

Ben groaned, "I fail with a spear."

"All the more reason to practice," Josheb said.

Which is probably true. With a sigh, he hauled himself off the mountain of cushions, messing up Shammah's hair on his way past.

The kid's eyes widened in surprise, but his expression quickly soured. "I am not a child."

"No?" Ben's eyebrows lifted. "Coulda fooled me. Are you going to tell Josheb?"

"No."

"Yeah, well pay attention. Because where we're going, you're going to have to fight. And a battlefield's no place for a kid."

Josheb was a decent coach, but he was also a relentless attacker. They sparred long enough to turn Benaiah's arms to jelly. *Othniel needs to show up. Preferably before I need Aleff to piece me back together.*

Thankfully, Josheb lost interest. "I'm going outside." Waving for Ben to toss back his spear. He returned the swords, saying, "You make double blades look easier than it is."

A compliment. Benaiah stared at his teammate's retreating back with a crooked smile on his face.

Shammah remarked, "He is your superior."

Returning the weapons to his belt, Benaiah strolled over and scooped up Shammah, cradling him. "And you're dead weight. So far." A quick glance showed a thunderous expression on the little boy's face. *Good. I'm not the only one who finds this embarrassing. Maybe that'll cure him.*

Whisking past the nameless Caretaker, whose bemused gaze spoke volumes, Benaiah sauntered along the dark passage leading outside. He caught himself humming and shrugged mentally. *Why not?* The words David had put to music had been on his mind ever since they arrived. He sang, "Have you entered the treasury of snow, or have you seen the treasury of hail, which I have reserved for the time of trouble, For the day of battle and war?"

Benaiah turned Shammah loose as soon as they caught up with Josheb, who asked, "Where's the best place to climb, runt? I want a high spot to jump from." Grinning at Ben, he said, "No wind."

"Better to crash into snow than hit dirt," Benaiah agreed, already scanning the icy peaks decorating the landscape.

Shammah pointed at a particularly lofty pinnacle, and they trekked out to it. All the way there, the kid lagged behind, a pout firmly in place.

At least Josheb's having fun. One look at the looming obstacle before them, and the half-cherub staked his spear in a snowbank and started to climb. This really was a good place for Josheb to practice his form. *No wind means no lift, but he won't be blown off course, either.*

A flash of green overhead pulled a soft noise of surprise from Shammah.

"He inherited scrappy wings," Benaiah explained. "And no fear."

Josheb's first plunge from the top was little more than a straight drop. Landing heavily in the snow, he stalked back to the spire, winglets fluttering behind him. His second attempt involved a running leap and a better angle. When he skidded to his knees in front of his audience, there was a gleam in his eyes. "Almost got it."

Benaiah found a likely pile of snow. After a little pushing and packing, he had a comfortable enough seat. Dropping into it, he waved Shammah over. "He'll be a while. C'mere."

The kid shuffled closer, gaze suspicious. "Why?"

With a lunge, Ben caught him and dragged him onto his lap. "Wouldn't want your toes to freeze off."

Shammah stiffened. "I am no child, and I do not wish to be coddled."

"So long as you look like a kid, I'm going to treat you like a kid." How often had Aleff cured him of a stubborn streak by giving him exactly what he wanted?

"This is mockery!" Shammah exclaimed, tearing himself away and glaring up at him.

"Nope," he replied, making himself comfortable. "Seems to me, you actually like the attention."

Benaiah quickly discovered that Shammah's size wasn't just variable. It responded to his moods. And he'd just caused a tempest in the guy's soul. Suddenly, instead of a quiet, quivering child, he was staring into the eyes of a young man who shook with outrage.

"You understand nothing!"

So he will *push back. That's a start. But how's this guy supposed to be David's strength?* Shammah might have his pride, but he was still pale, thin, and fragile-looking.

Ben spread a hand wide, saying, "Then you better explain."

Shammah let loose. His full height must have been twice Othniel's. Dropping to one knee, the giant drove his fists into the ground on either side of Benaiah's snow throne. "This is not safe!"

No kidding. Without batting an eye, he said, "But this is *you*, and you're the one I need."

"But *I* was not born without fear." And the scrawny kid was back. "I am afraid."

"Why?"

Placing his hand over his heart, Shammah said, "I was conceived by one of the samayim."

Which meant nothing to Ben. He scratched under the edge of his turban. *A little help here?*

'His carries a Caretaker's nature.'

Right. Caught that part. But didn't that make Shammah like Aleff? These guys were the most powerful angels in existence.

'And the most limited.'

Something clicked into place, and Benaiah leaned forward. "I get it! Caretakers always do as they're told."

Shammah nodded miserably.

"And you can't hear God."

The child whimpered.

Ben was as good as his word. Treating the kid like a kid, he pulled Shammah back into his arms. "Crud. No wonder you're so skittish. You're afraid to sneeze wrong."

Benaiah looked up as Josheb reached the top of his launching point and leapt. This time, he found the right arrangement of his winglets to veer into a slow spiral. Ben waited until Josheb grabbed his spear and started another climb before quietly remarking, "I get it, but crying isn't gonna fix this."

Changing size again, Shammah grabbed the front of Benaiah's tunic with huge hands. Even though he was bigger than any man, his voice cracked with adolescence. "You cannot understand!" he repeated. "You cannot know what I have done!"

Ben held up his hands in surrender. *These mood swings are something else.* "Calm down, big fella."

"I have waited so *long*."

"We all have." *Though not as long as you.* Reaching up, Benaiah yanked some of Shammah's long hair. "My size. It'll make this easier," he commanded.

Shammah hung his head and dwindled.

By the time Ben stood up, they were finally eye-to-eye. "I'm going to tell you something that maybe you should think about." He gripped Shammah's thin shoulders and gave their team's new giant a shake. "I'm here to get you. Period. I was surprised when you were just a kid, and I'm just as surprised that you're not. But that doesn't change why I'm here. And it doesn't change that you're the one I came to find."

Some of the tension left Shammah's body.

"Pick a size. Change sizes. Whatever," Benaiah said. "But that doesn't change me. And it seems to me, God put us together. So we'll stick together, talk, spar …"

"I will not fight you," Shammah interjected.

"Fine. But we can still sing and crud like that. Or just sit here and watch Josheb belly-flop into snow drifts." He cut a glance in the rider's direction. Josheb was experimenting with throwing his spear from midair. "You really should let him know what's going on with you."

"Is that what God commands?"

"Nope, that's just me, saying what I think." With a small shrug, Ben said, "We'll let Josheb get his falling fix, and maybe later I can help you explain. I swear, he'll be impressed."

An inarticulate shout sounded from overhead, and Josheb's graceful flight path wobbled off course. Losing altitude in a rush, he dropped smack into a mound of snow, sending up a plume of powder.

"Crud. He spotted you," Benaiah said, doing a double-take. The kid was back, clinging to his knees. "Again?" he complained.

Shammah begged, "Tell me what to do. Please?"

Benaiah opted for a simple strategy. *Make Josheb work for this one.* "I vote for … *run!*" Seizing Shammah, he tossed the skinny boy over his shoulder. Long legs flashed as Ben joggled and jounced his way toward the tower. "You scream like a girl!" he informed his squirming passenger.

"I hate you!"

That would've hurt more if you weren't trying not to laugh. Benaiah gruffly asked, "Is that any way to thank your savior?" Risking a glance over his other shoulder, Ben spotted Josheb. *Crud, he's fast.* Lengthening his stride, he added, "If a crazed guy with a spear catches up, you better cover for me."

"I will assist him in burying you," promised Shammah.

Benaiah laughed breathlessly. Even though he risked being squashed, he couldn't resist one last dig. "Save the threats for when you're big enough to carry them out."

Aleff laughs and teases.
He talks gibberish,
and he keeps his promises.
One of the reasons
I clung to him as a child
was his calm.
My keeper's face never
showed signs of fear,
worry, or doubt.
Until now.

25

Bad news travels fast.

He's not a kid?" Josheb's arms were folded over his chest, but his eyes sparkled with curiosity.

"Nope," Benaiah replied, matching the rider's stance. Shammah was hiding behind him, which was getting old.

Josheb said, "And you didn't mention this because …?"

"He wasn't ready to tell you."

Josheb accepted that with a nod.

Ben thanked him with a small smile. Not that the guy noticed. *He's more interested in Shammah than me right now.* Which was the best possible outcome. *He didn't take offense; he took interest.*

Leaning to one side in order to catch the boy's gaze, Josheb asked, "You ready now, runt?"

Shammah's death grip on Benaiah's leg tightened, but he replied, "Yes."

"Then show me."

The child shuffled backward and straightened, and he didn't

stop until he loomed over them. Josheb took a step back, then started to circle. "How come your clothes still fit?"

"I do not know."

"What kind of weapon do you use?" Josheb asked.

"I have none. I find them." Shammah's light voice held traces of menace. "My hands. My feet. Rocks. I used a tree once."

Josheb didn't criticize. "Versatile. Adaptable."

Benaiah declared, "Shammah the Giant will be a legend on the field of battle."

"We can list his name right after mine," Josheb said, smiling broadly.

Truce established, Ben was ready to move on to more important matters. "You hungry?"

With a disinterested wave, Josheb crossed to the brazier and tossed on a couple more logs. "Keep your flakes. I'd rather sleep."

A nap didn't sound too bad, but the pinch was back in Benaiah's gut. "What about you?"

Shammah was back at eye level, and he tentatively answered, "Yes?"

Not very convincing. Ben was almost positive the guy was giving the answer he hoped would please him. "Don't you eat?"

"Messengers deliver manna to the tower," Shammah replied in a vague way. "I am allotted a portion."

Benaiah groaned. "You, too? Am I the only one around here who eats solid food?"

"Nothing grows here." That thought was enough to

drop Shammah's size back to that of a child. With his brow furrowed, he wandered over to the fire and curled up opposite Josheb.

The Caretaker with no name returned, and Ben rounded on him. "What's up with the kid? He's wasting away!"

"Shammah can go for long periods without food," he replied, his gaze resting on the boy. "Perhaps he does not like to eat alone."

"If it's that simple, then why don't you sit with him?" Trying to keep his frustration in check, Benaiah muttered, "Can't you see how lonely he's been?"

The nameless angel answered patiently. "When Shammah becomes attached to someone, they are his everything. His soul is searching for God. I will not become a god so that he can have company." Nodding at the giant who looked like a child, he added, "Be wise in how you handle him. Do not let him worship you."

His warning was clear this time, and it rang true. "I think I get it. But he's still a scrawny thing. Can you get me something else to eat?"

"What do you require?"

"I don't know." Something to chew, swallow. Something to weigh down his complaining gut and quiet it for a while. "Anything's fine."

From within the full sleeve of his raiment, the Caretaker withdrew a handful of nuts. Dropping them into Ben's hand, he next produced small fruit with dark orange peels. "Will this suffice?"

Not meat, but I'm not complaining. He offered gruff thanks and aimed straight for Shammah. There was no way he wanted to be this kid's god. *Father can keep that part of his legacy.* But he wouldn't leave Shammah alone.

Dropping to the cushion beside the boy, Benaiah set to work peeling thick skin. The tang of citrus made his mouth water, but he pushed the first section into Shammah's mouth. The kid's eyes widened, but he chewed. *Maybe I should lace this stuff with manna.* "You need to eat better," he groused.

Suddenly, the door to the chamber swung wide, and Aleff breezed into the room, trailing copper hair and rich, meaty smells. All smiles, he exclaimed, "Who ordered take-out?"

Josheb scrambled to his feet, and Shammah burrowed. Ben lifted a hand as Othniel followed Aleff into the room. The burly warrior nodded politely to their nameless host before searching the room. Josheb and Benaiah received their nods, but he seemed puzzled. Drawing his sword, Othniel inspected its blade and called, "Shammah?"

The kid peeped out from behind Ben. "I am here."

Bushy red brows lifted. "Young."

"Looks can be deceiving," Aleff said, winking Shammah's way. "But first, who's hungry?"

Whatever his caretaker had brought eclipsed the nuts and

oranges, but Benaiah knew better than to waste a morsel. While Josheb stalked Aleff's assortment, Ben slipped over to the picnic basket and added his leftovers. Neri and Pazi blinked up at him from their little nest, and he whispered, "Aleff's back."

They brightened and blazed a trail across the chamber, looping in excited circles around their shepherd. Benaiah smirked. *He's their favorite. And they're his. Kinda makes me feel guilty for taking them away from him ... and him from them.*

Aleff's exclamations over the two tiny angels were standard, but Shammah's reaction startled Benaiah. He shot up, matching Aleff's height, and reached out with both hands. "I have heard of yahavim!"

"Didn't Benaiah introduce you to Neri and Pazi? What a dreadful oversight," Aleff replied, showing none of Othniel's surprise over Shammah's transformation. "Don't they keep a flock here?"

"I have never seen one," Shammah whispered.

Aleff shook his head. "Little boys are always pestering for pets. But now that you're older, maybe you're ready for the responsibility."

Shammah started and withdrew his hands. "You are a Caretaker."

"*Tsk.* Don't let that put a damper on things. I'm Aleff, and you are in for a treat!" Glancing around, he asked, "Did you bring your bottomless pit, Benaiah?"

"Yeah."

Aleff flung his arms around Benaiah, using a hug to cover his whisper. "Miss me less this time around, my gangling camel?"

Ben shook his head. He couldn't lie, not to Aleff. "I don't understand what Shammah needs. Can you help?"

"Yes and no."

Retreating into a scowl, Ben asked, "What's that supposed to mean?"

"Food first. And for pity's sake, stuff as much as you can down the baby bird's gullet. He's a twig!"

"That's what I said!"

Aleff messed up his turban. "Don't natter and fuss. He'll leave the nest long before you do."

Benaiah allowed his caretaker to shuffle him over to where Othniel and Josheb had taken seats. Once Shammah knelt beside Ben, Aleff closed the circle and uncovered dishes. There were three kinds of bird—skewered, stewed, and stuffed. Thick broths, different grains, and a variety of vegetables elevated the meal to a proper feast. Benaiah hadn't eaten so well since leaving David's home.

"What happened?" Josheb asked, pointing a stripped skewer at Othniel. "And don't give me the short version. Every strike! Every blow!"

The Guardian opened his mouth, hesitated, then closed it. When Othniel shot a pleading look Aleff's way, the Caretaker took over. "There's not much to tell, Josheb. They took the bait—hook, line, and sinker."

"Meaning?"

"Those who came to get a look at you won't be spreading rumors, but … our original captive is missing. We must assume that the secret of your existence *isn't*."

Josheb lapsed into a thoughtful silence, and Aleff turned to Benaiah. "The valley of horses. The storehouse of snow. These places are on the fringes of heaven, where the Fallen cannot enter. But …."

Bearing Aleff's instructions in mind, Ben had been dropping extra food into Shammah's bowl. Sneakily. When the Caretaker paused, he stopped worrying about fattening up his giant and met Aleff's gaze. "But …?" he echoed.

Aleff sighed. "I have reason to believe that the next boy won't be found in the heavenlies."

"Why? I mean, how would you know that?"

"That doesn't matter right now. But I'd feel better if I can confirm your next destination." Aleff searched Benaiah's face. "Are there any words on the wind today, Messenger?"

The lines came effortlessly to mind, and Ben's brows knit. He'd been going over Job's lessons ever since he realized that they might hold clues to his journey. *This one? Seriously?* There were lots of other sections that sounded more interesting, but he shrugged. "Yeah."

"Care to share?" Aleff prompted.

Sitting up a little taller, Benaiah quoted, "The hills bring him their produce, and all the wild animals play nearby. Under the lotus plants he lies, hidden among the reeds in the marsh. The lotuses conceal him in their shadow; the poplars by the stream surround him."

Aleff's expression clouded. "What a lovely muddle this will be."

"What?" demanded Josheb. "How come you're *saying* lovely when you *mean* awful."

The Caretaker traded a long look with Othniel. "You four will shortly be Sent to earth, where Time marches on. It's also where every Fallen was Cast, so you'll be thrust into enemy territory. All you can hope is that you'll be able to reach the next boy before … interested parties."

"Four?" Josheb asked sharply.

Othniel said, "I am going with you."

Shammah finally spoke up. "Who is waiting in the shadow of the lotus?"

Benaiah didn't look up from his food. Just answered. "Behemoth."

I couldn't shake the sense
that they were trying to
pack in what they could,
while they could.
One last lesson.
One last word of advice.
Long looks,
hurried explanations,
growing tension,
sinking feelings.
Something had changed.
And not for the better.

26

Some fears are justified.

Benaiah knew Aleff. "What's wrong?" he asked bluntly.

The Caretaker's brows arched. "Why would you assume something's wrong?"

"Something's wrong," he insisted. "Look at Neri and Pazi."

Aleff's beloved pets were crooning and patting the knuckles of his clenched fist. He immediately opened his hand so the sprites could climb between his fingers onto his upraised palm. Aleff sighed. "One thing's nagging at me. By any chance … did either of you name names while you were tangling with that Fallen?"

"We weren't there to chat," Ben replied, glancing at Josheb for confirmation.

The rider tugged at his narrow patch of whiskers. "But he was listening close, even when we weren't talking to him."

Aleff tensed. "How much did you say? How much did he learn?"

"Nothing, really. Oh." With a sinking feeling, Benaiah said, "I called Josheb by name."

Othniel interjected, "Yours?"

"Don't think so," Ben replied, startled when Aleff's shoulders sagged with relief.

Josheb shook his head but said, "The Fallen pegged his order though. Said he was built like a Messenger."

Aleff's flinch was barely there. Benaiah didn't call attention to it, but he stared hard at his caretaker. Scowling in frustration, Ben wished he could call him out. *No lies. Not with me.*

Brow's arching, Aleff silently replied, *Never.*

Benaiah blinked. Apparently, his Messenger make-up let him drill words through Aleff's thick skull. He glanced around self-consciously. Had everyone heard him? But Josheb was describing his mid-air spear-throwing session to Othniel. When Ben glanced back at Aleff, he was smiling wryly. Brows furrowing in concentration, Benaiah checked to see if he could do it on purpose. *What aren't you telling?*

Sadness saturated Aleff's soft, silent answer. *I wasn't certain before. Now I am. Benaiah, your father's back in the picture.*

Benaiah and Josheb had collapsed beside the fire to sleep off dinner. Being full felt good. Being lazy felt good. But shepherds rarely caught a break. *David never blamed his flock for interrupting his songs or losing their way. All part of the job. Shepherd, king, or captain.* When a small hand tugged at his sleeve, Ben asked, "Something the matter, kid?"

"Yes."

Maybe it was easier to be candid when you were small. Or maybe Shammah was afraid of what needed saying. *Shrinking from it.* Benaiah pushed back his drooping turban. A giant wasn't without his struggles. Maybe the Shammah before him wasn't the truest version, but right now, this Shammah was the one who needed to be heard. Budging over, Ben said, "Out with it."

"I am afraid."

Thought we covered this ground. But Shammah's gaze was steady. This wasn't the same as before. There was a purpose behind his words. Nodding, Ben asked, "What are you afraid of?"

"Falling."

"Sounds familiar. Me, too." Maybe that part was the same for all of them. "But isn't it simple? If you don't want to Fall, then don't."

Shammah scrunched the fabric of his sleeves with both hands. "But how can I know what is right? How can I be sure I am pleasing God?"

Those aren't heavenly worries. They're human ones. Benaiah relaxed into a smile. "Look, I didn't used to be able to hear God's voice. But even without it, I wasn't falling all over the place. Relax." He gave the boy's skinny shoulder a poke. "You're only partways angelic, Shammah. Some of you is human, and that means more than one choice. More than one chance."

The kid plucked at his sleeve again. "You hear God, but you could not always hear Him?"

"That's right. I sort of made a promise, and became one of the malakim. Even though I'm only half, I rank as an angel." Benaiah thought back. *Guess I never did explain that part.*

Shammah's whole aura shifted. Disbelief transformed into a shocking blaze of hope. And it was cold. *What the crud did he do?* The air around Benaiah was so frigid, his breath came in visible puffs. "Easy, easy," he soothed, suddenly faced with another mood-induced size change. Shammah was bursting, but the words weren't coming. "Out with it. Preferably before frostbite sets in."

"Will you tell me what to do?"

"Depends. Because I don't want to be your mother."

Shammah thumped Ben's pillow. "I am no child."

He held up his hands. "I can see that. So what do you want from me?"

"I am yours to direct. Josheb calls you our captain. If I obey you, it must please God," he reasoned. "You will be like God to me."

"Whoa, whoa, whoa! No!" Benaiah exclaimed, waving both hands. "No way am I anyone's god. That's messed up."

Shaking his head, Shammah tried again. "A spokesman of

God. His prophet."

"Oh. Well, that makes more sense. So long as we're clear on the whole fellow-servant thing."

"Or …." Shammah took a more cautious tone. "Some might consider us a kindred people."

Ben knew exactly what he meant. But it wasn't easy to say out loud. "You mean, like … brothers?"

"If you want."

He gruffly said, "Yeah. Sure. Sounds good."

Shammah solemnly offered one slim hand.

Benaiah took it and gave what reassurance he could. "God needs us. You and me and Josheb over there. We have a job to do, and we're going to do it. Finding each other's only the first part. You can trust me for the rest."

Bringing his other hand up to envelop Ben's, Shammah promised, "When you go, I will go with you. Where you lead, I will follow. Your king is my king."

"You'll like David." *Everyone does.* Pushing the cushions into a new arrangement, Benaiah said, "Get some sleep, little brother."

"I am older than you."

"Pulling rank already?" Ben complained, tossing a stray pillow at him.

Shammah settled nearby, closed his eyes, and shortly turned into a sleeping giant. Smiling to himself, Ben turned onto his side … and met Josheb's interested gaze. *An audience.* This was another thing he'd learned while shepherding with David. *Flocks give you zero privacy.*

Would Josheb accuse him of coddling? Make fun of him for pretending to be family?

But the rider simply held his gaze, nodded, and closed his eyes. Within minutes, Josheb was snoring again, but Benaiah was still reeling. Somehow, in gaining Shammah's trust, he'd earned a little more of Josheb's respect.

Aleff clapped his hands. "Before we get ahead of ourselves, let's review! What do each of you bring to the table?"

"Table?" mouthed Josheb.

Leave it to Aleff to clear things up by confusing everyone. Benaiah said, "There's no table."

"Figuratively speaking! Show your cards. Clear the air. Pass muster!"

Josheb muttered, "Translation?"

"I got nothing." Ben wiggled his fingers at Neri, and the little angel with wavy green hair zipped over. "Except I think he wants us to talk about ourselves."

Aleff said, "You need to know what's in your arsenal before traipsing off into enemy territory. Skills. Weapons. Abilities. How will you support one another?"

Josheb glanced at his companions. "There's three of us so far, and we're going after a fourth. We answer to the Messenger's brat with the doom glare." He thumped his chest and said, "A Protector's mongrel is our best chance at victory against any foe on any field of battle. And the offspring of a Caretaker hangs around to pretty up the place."

Demonstrating the doom glare, Benaiah blandly added, "Weapons are his spear, my two swords, and … big feet?"

Shammah blinked, then blanched.

Crud. Ben elbowed the guy and whispered, "Lame joke. Sorry."

The young man shook his head, and Aleff continued. "Nice gloss, but you're skin deep. And Josheb, while I'll admit you're *all that*, your teammates are something else. And you'd be wise to factor in their fire power."

Josheb tugged at his chin. "What can you do, Shammah?"

"Destroy things."

"Can you be more specific?"

"I am unstoppable." Shammah's delicate fingers knotted together. "Stopping is difficult."

"No offense, but I'm having trouble seeing that." Josheb shook his head. "You've refused every offer to spar. How do we know you can hold your own?"

Aleff stepped in. "Be glad he turned you down, Josheb. You wouldn't stand a chance."

"I'm not volunteering to be maimed or anything, but it's like you said. Weapons on the table. And I haven't seen his." Josheb turned to Othniel and asked, "Will you arm him? Train him?"

The big Guardian shook his head. "He needs no weapon; he *is* a weapon. Shammah could raze every man on a battlefield with his bare hands."

"Him?" Josheb asked, still disbelieving. "He doesn't look like a killer."

Aleff countered, "Do I?"

The rider hesitated. And evaded. "I still want to know what to expect."

Benaiah said, "When we met him, Shammah was a frightened child. It's hard to un-see that."

"Granted. And proof that this little chat needed to happen." Turning to the person in question, Aleff kindly asked, "Shammah, are you afraid to kill your enemies?"

"No."

"And who are your enemies?"

"The enemies of God."

The Caretaker inclined his head. "So you could enter a city and end the lives of every person within its walls—man, woman, and child—if that was heaven's judgment upon the city and its people."

"Yes."

A chill drifted across Benaiah's skin, and he glanced quickly at Shammah. The young man's demeanor had undergone a subtle transformation. Every line of his face had hardened with resolve. *He's dead serious.* When Shammah's gaze slanted to meet his, Ben shivered.

"No survivors? No mercy?" asked Josheb, interest keen in his eyes.

"Yes."

"I like your policy. Think I'll adopt it. But these are still only words."

Aleff rolled his eyes toward heaven and spread his hands wide. Everyone waited in silence until the nameless Caretaker with ropes of deep purple hair entered the room. Gesturing for them to follow, he said, "This way, please."

Benaiah walked beside Shammah, who refused to meet his gaze. *What could be so bad? Crud, I'm useless at this. What would David do for one of his lambs?*

Shammah's head snapped up. "What did you say?"

Josheb, who sauntered along behind them, drawled, "He called you a lamb."

Ben's face darkened with embarrassment. "I was only trying to …. Sorry."

From the front of the group, Aleff called, "Add Benaiah's brainwaves to the list of weapons at your disposal, boys. Communication is the key to deep, long-lasting relationships!"

"I can't *control* it."

"Practice makes perfect," Aleff cheerfully countered.

This time, it was Ben who refused to meet anyone's gaze, but Shammah touched his arm. "You are not useless. Thank you for your concern."

Josheb sighed impatiently. "Where are we going?"

Their host replied, "A place where broken things are kept."

Aleff chimed in. "Not all the storehouses are for innocuous things like hail. This is sure to be ghastly, so get a grip."

They entered the tower, which on closer inspection seemed to have been built from blocks of ice. Instead of climbing up, their guide led the way down. Wide stairs spiraled deep into the surrounding snow, toward a stone floor far below. Ben paused to gaze upward, fascinated that the light reached even here. The darkness and shadows associated with nighttime were only found in Shammah's cave.

Shortly before they reached bedrock, Josheb muttered, "Stink."

Benaiah caught a whiff and stopped walking. His eyes skipped everywhere around the room, searching for the source. "Aleff?" he called, his voice cracking.

"Not to worry," his caretaker replied. "They can't move, but they do leave a musty smell in the basement."

They finished their descent into the lower reaches and stared into hell. Josheb spoke first. "Are these demons?"

"We're overstocked with fallen Fallen!" Aleff made a shooing motion. "Feel free to browse. Let me know if you have any questions."

Ben approached the nearest of the stone blocks fanning out through the large, circular chamber. There was no mistaking the nature of the person stretched across the slab. *Demon. Or ... demon parts.* Holding his breath, he leaned in, tilting his head to one side. *I think someone scraped this guy up and put the pieces back mostly in order.*

Leaving the dismembered body behind, he let an increasingly morbid curiosity lead him through the rest of the chamber. The Fallen were like grotesque statues—twisted, misshapen, battered, and brutalized. Benaiah cataloged missing limbs, crumpled skulls, and one guy who looked as if half his body had been flattened under someone's heel. *Shammah did all this?*

Even though Benaiah had been on dozens of battlefields and witnessed the death masks of countless men, this was terrible enough to make him lightheaded. Everything was frozen in place—paroxysms of pain, snarls of rage, screams of fear. What made everything more horrible was knowing that none of them were dead. By some mercy, time stood still for them. Their wails would be waiting for them at the end of Time.

Aleff sidled up. "Did you have a question, young sir?"

"Why's this one have six fingers on his hands?"

"To match the six toes on his feet." In more serious tones, Aleff explained, "He was once a Weaver. Six digits come standard for members of his order."

"Okay. But why's he here? I don't see any wounds."

With a thin smile, Aleff replied, "Iced."

Benaiah checked on Shammah and spotted the young man sitting on the bottom stair, his face in his hands. *Bad memories? Crud, it could just be bad smells.*

Josheb worked his way through the room, circling each gruesome display without comment. Catching up to him, Ben reached the bottom of the stairs in time to hear Josheb say, "Shammah."

Their giant looked up. "Yes?"

"You're strong. I like that." Shammah squared his shoulders, but Josheb wasn't done. He offered his hand and said, "You and me, fighting together? That's going to be interesting."

Shammah pressed his palm to Josheb's.

Aleff smirked. "Locked and loaded."

Whatever that means. Benaiah was only too glad to follow his teammates out of the pit that stank of betrayal and fear.

I'd agreed to listen to God.
He could Send me, and I'd
have to go. But I was
starting to realize that
there was a whole lot of
wiggle room. This was the
right place, but it must
not've been the right time.
Because I didn't have
any idea where to go.
Not the best way to
impress someone with
your ability to lead.

27

Safe distance means long walk.

Aleff's bare feet made no sound on the floor as he paced. "Opening night jitters," he muttered distractedly. "Or would this be more like the first day of school. Oh, I don't even want to *think* of any of them being schooled. The rest of their training will be on-the-job, and there's no more safety net."

Ben sighed. "It's not time?"

His caretaker tossed up his hands. "One is not Sent until one is Sent."

"Are we late or something?" Thinking it over, Benaiah scowled. "Hang on. Wouldn't we arrive in the right place and time, no matter *when* we leave?"

"Sharpest tack in the box! I'm betting you were raised by a Caretaker."

The carefree remark didn't fool Ben. Aleff was worried, and chances were good that it had something to do with … *my father*. A fuzzy little thought drifted into Benaiah's mind, and with concentration, he brought it into focus. *Is Aleff in my flock? Or am I in his?*

'It is the same flock.'

As Aleff returned to pacing, Benaiah rubbed the palm of one hand with his thumb. *Yeah, I know. But just now ... didn't you ask me to take care of him?*

'What is Aleff to you?'

The fragment of a dream surfaced in his mind, and Ben whispered, "My one."

And that sounded like the answer. He'd always needed Aleff, but maybe Aleff needed him, too. *Because that's how it is.* With a scowl of concentration, Benaiah tried to catch the Caretaker's attention. *Who are you?*

Aleff jerked to a stop and turned. "Me?"

Rolling his eyes, he asked, "What do you do when you're not with me? When you're where David is?"

The confusion winked out in Aleff's brown eyes. "I'm widely known as a learned man—teacher, counselor, and diplomat. With a large dose of harmless busybody thrown in. Enough time has passed that my opinions are accepted. While the king doesn't know my face, I influence his influencers."

Benaiah's eyes widened. "Time's passed? How much time?"

"Ah. Maybe I shouldn't have mentioned that part," Aleff murmured. "In the grand scheme of things, you've been gone for ... let's see. Counting the early and latter rains, multiply by the moon festivals, subtract a Passover, carry the olive harvest, and ... two years, give or take."

"Y-years?" Ben's gut turned to stone. "It's been *weeks*, not years!"

"I know it seems that way, but these places are outside of Time-proper. And for the record, it can go both ways. Years could pass here with only minutes ticking by on mankind's earth. You have to stay flexible."

"But David must think I've abandoned him!"

"Do you really think yourself so forgettable?" Aleff asked, reaching up to tug his turban askew.

Benaiah batted his hands away. "We were only friends for one season."

Aleff soothed, "Your young king knows that I know you. He asks after you with shocking regularity."

"So David sits at the feet of Aleff the Wise?"

"More or less. Although he calls me Uncle."

"Uncle Aleff?" Benaiah snickered at the very idea.

The Caretaker smiled. "No. I'm living under an assumed name. Something commonplace that allows me to blend into the background."

"Yeah?" Aleff was playing coy, but Ben had connections now. And he was getting better at using them. With a casual tone to cover up his sly glance, he said, "So when I get back, I'll be Benaiah, son of Jehoiada."

Aleff eyebrows shot up. "Someone snitched on me. And bestowed a son."

"No one's gonna believe we're related."

"You're adopted. Didn't you know?"

Benaiah did his best to make himself heard without having

to say embarrassing stuff out loud. *Give me some credit. I know who my father is. His name's written on my hand.*

Aleff must not have believed him because he checked. And for once, he had nothing to say. The angel simply ran his fingertips over the letters that had appeared on Ben's callused palm. And smiled.

"Upon the hand. Over the heart. Onto your weapon," Othniel listed. "No matter where it appears, we say that their name has come under our hand. That person is under your watch-care."

Benaiah lightly scratched the letters on his palm. "Watch-care. Watch out for them. Take care of them."

The Guardian nodded and displayed the names engraved upon his sword. "This is usual for teachers, mentors, and captains."

With a sidelong glance at the others across the room, Ben said, "One name doesn't make me a captain."

"No. But before this is over, you will be."

Benaiah studied the redheaded warrior's rugged face. "Have you ever been a captain?"

"No. I am a Guardian, not a Protector."

"But I'm not either. Can a Messenger be a captain?"

Othniel considered the question, then gently grasped Ben's

shoulder. "It would be better to ask if Benaiah the First can be a captain."

Before he could think of a response, his Sending came. "Time to go."

Josheb jumped to his feet and crossed to the corner. Picking up packs and water skins, he crisscrossed their straps over his chest. "Coming, runt?"

Shammah stood just as Aleff was passing by. The Caretaker paused to scrutinize their giant. "May I ask a personal question?"

"Yes."

"Do you always match the height of the person you're speaking with?"

Benaiah noticed that Shammah was indeed the same height as Aleff. Meaning he'd dropped an entire hand from his height.

Aleff continued, "Let's break that bad habit. Match Josheb's height."

Shammah obeyed without question, and the copper-haired Caretaker nodded. "Yes, that's a good look for you. We'll make this your new default setting." Pointing to Josheb, Aleff firmly said, "He's your measure."

Ben checked on Neri and Pazi, shouldered his own bag, and hesitated. *Sandals or bare feet?* Frowning at Aleff, he asked, "Do you know what we're heading into?"

"The only fragment of history I caught wind of is similar to yours … yet nothing like it. So there's good news, and there's bad news."

Not what I meant, but crud ... what if I hadn't asked? Scowling at the angel, he said, "Anything you can tell us is good."

As the four of them gathered around, Aleff began, "The good news is that your counterpart's been hidden away for decades."

Decades? Benaiah glanced at Shammah. Were they going to find another guy who aged differently than normal people? Of course, he had no way of knowing if *he* aged normally. He and Aleff skipped around a lot.

"The bad news is … the one who hid him was his father."

Ben snapped to attention. "Not an angel?"

"I'm sure he was with one for starters, but something went amiss. His father found him, and they've been together ever since."

Josheb's grip on his spear tightened. "Willingly or unwillingly?"

"A good question. One I can't answer," said Aleff. "And to make things a smidge more dicey, we're not talking about some random, no-account Fallen."

Benaiah hadn't missed Aleff's remark. *A similar history. That can only mean one thing.* "His father's a god."

"Bingo!"

"Crud."

"For better or for worse, this would-be deity has been just as good as us about keeping the boy a secret. But it's safe to say his life has been nothing like yours. I don't know what you'll find when you reach him."

At that, Aleff opened a wide door. Othniel strode through

first, with Josheb right on his heels. Shammah stepped out of the storehouse of snow without a backward glance. But Ben paused, his fist tightening over the name under his hand. *We're all scattered. I have to bring everyone together. Then, they'll all be under my hand. Because that's how it's supposed to be.*

"Ready?" prompted the Caretaker.

"Don't feel ready," Ben admitted.

Aleff's eyebrows lifted. "Is it any wonder? Where are your shoes?"

Benaiah plowed headlong into air so thick with moisture, it felt like walking into water. The humidity clung uncomfortably to his skin. Such heavy heat was a shock to the system after spending time in a world of ice and snow. Lifting aside a broad leaf, Ben located the others. *They didn't get far. Couldn't have if they wanted to.* Lush greenery hemmed them in on every side, vibrant and teeming with life.

Josheb fanned at small flies already swarming. "Stinking bugs," he muttered. "Which way, Captain?"

It was disorienting, not being able to categorize any of the sounds and smells pressing in around him. Benaiah stared up, but the jungle closed off any glimpse of the sky. *All I can tell is that it's daytime.* "I don't know."

A sudden *whirr* of feathers exploded as birds with red plumage rushed away. Shammah's thin face held a rapt expression at the shrill of birds. "Parrots," he murmured. When hoots and groans rang overhead, recognition came again. "Monkeys."

Caretaker's clued in. Fine. Leaving the wildlife to Shammah, Benaiah waited for the bright sureness that had guided his steps in the past. *Which way?*

No answer came.

Josheb frowned. "How can you *not* know?"

Othniel calmly said, "Aleff set us a safe distance from our destination. He could have meant how close we are in steps … or hours."

"So we're early?" asked Josheb.

The seasoned warrior suggested, "Find water. Make camp. Wait."

Benaiah could already feel the trickle of sweat under his turban. "Fine with me, but I still don't have a clue which way to go."

Shammah pointed. "That way. There is a river."

"How do you know?" Ben asked.

"I can feel it."

"Useful," remarked Josheb. He held out a hand. "Lend me a sword, Captain."

A moment later, he was hacking his way through the undergrowth.

Benaiah lagged behind. *This is lame. I'm the leader, but I'm lost.*

'Are you?'

"I know I'm lost," he muttered under his breath.

'Are you in the lead?'

Ben flinched at the note of rebuke behind the question. *Sorry if I got the wrong idea, but ... the whole captain thing. Shouldn't I know what I'm doing?*

'I know what I am doing. Trust Me.'

He felt foolish, but he also felt much better. *Yeah. Got it. Lead on.*

Their canteens were nearly empty by the time they reached a wide river. Some kind of small deer skipped away when Josheb burst out of the jungle. He narrowed his eyes, marking its path. "There goes dinner."

Benaiah gazed critically at the thin ribbon of sky visible above the waterway. "Let's pick a spot. Start a fire."

Josheb snorted. "Cold?"

Ben was as wrung out as the rider. Swatting wearily at the hovering insects, he said, "Hungry. And thirsty. Which might be a problem. That stuff doesn't look too good." The muddy green river oozed along with barely a ripple. *I wouldn't wash in that, let alone guzzle it.*

Josheb eyed the water with distaste, but Shammah pulled up a handful in cupped palms. A swirl like snowflakes danced briefly in the humid air, and the young man drank. Josheb demanded, "What did you just do?"

"Cleaned it," replied Shammah, as if purifying water was an ordinary occurrence.

"Do it again." Josheb knelt beside him. "I'm thirsty."

Shammah repeated the trick, offering his cupped hands. Steadying them with his own, Josheb slurped. "This is cold!" he exclaimed.

"Yes. I prefer to drink cold water."

"And your skin is cold," Josheb accused.

"Yes. This heat is troublesome, so I adjusted." Shammah poked the center of Josheb's chest, and all the sweat on his skin iced over.

He grinned broadly. "Do that at regular intervals, and I'll refrain from making unkind remarks about your ears."

Shammah's brows drew together. "What is wrong with my ears?"

"Can't say. It'd be unkind."

With a dour look, Shammah clapped his hands over his ears.

Ben smirked. "Josheb'll be drinking mud for that." He tossed his water skin to their giant. "I like my water cold, too. Thanks."

"I will fill them all."

Josheb leaned on his spear. "And I think I'll track down another of those deer."

Just then, there was a rattle overhead. They all looked up, weapons ready, only to get a face full of water as the sky opened and warm water pounded around them. Rain soaked them to the skin and drenched their packs. *No chance of a hunt. No chance of a fire. No place to turn for shelter.* In a lame attempt to be cheerful, Benaiah said, "The bugs left."

Growing up, Aleff was my one,
my everything. And for
some crazy reason, I thought
it'd always be just the two of us.
It didn't occur to me that
I needed anyone else.
But God broadened my world.
My name was on Othniel's
blade for a good reason.
There were things I could
only learn from him.

28

They would make a captain of me.

hree teens sat in the mud under the shelter of Othniel's wings. The downpour sheeted off their luminous golden covering, but Benaiah was sick of watching endless waterfalls. Especially since they weren't the only ones who'd found shelter.

"Stinking bugs!" growled Josheb, slapping the side of his neck.

Benaiah wasn't used to thinking of others first, but weren't these "his" men? *What am I supposed to do?*

Othniel met his gaze.

Crud. Did I do it again?

The warrior's rugged features softened somewhat. Bushy red brows lifted inquiringly.

Ben tried to push a thought at him. *Advice?*

Othniel's gravely answer came effortlessly into his mind. *'Josheb endures. Shammah struggles.'*

He checked on their giant, whose wet hair clung to pale cheeks. The guy seemed to be zoning out, but if Othniel was concerned, Benaiah needed to act. After tossing out a bunch of idiotic ideas, inspiration flashed. It wasn't like a Sending, but it was a darn good idea. *Totally makes sense. Should've thought of it earlier.* Reaching over, he punched Shammah's shoulder. "Do me a favor?"

"Gladly."

Benaiah held out the basket where Neri and Pazi slept. "From what I've heard, keeping these guys happy is mostly left to Caretakers. Two isn't much of a flock, but it's a start."

Shammah took the basket with both hands, awe plain on his face. "You would entrust them to me?"

"Yeah. If you don't mind." Ben tried to keep it casual, but he was excited. This was the right thing to do. *They'll make a Caretaker of you.*

Opening the lid of the basket, Shammah murmured, "Will they accept me?"

Neri and Pazi peeped at him from their nest, then launched themselves at their new shepherd. As they wove circles around Shammah's head, Josheb grumbled, "More bugs."

"They are not!" Shammah defended, holding out a slim hand. The yahavim landed there and gazed up at him with bright expressions. Smiling back, he said, "They are God's provision."

Othniel grunted his agreement, and Josheb relented. "Guess their flakes will do in a pinch."

Shammah retaliated with a poke that turned Josheb's sheen of sweat into ice. As they jostled, Benaiah felt some of the tightness in his gut loosen. *Nothing much changed.*

Except the mood. But this is better.

Othniel was waiting for him to look up. The big Guardian's lips quirked as his thoughts reached Benaiah. *'These two are not much of a Flight, but they are a start. Captain.'*

The rain stopped as suddenly as it had started. Othniel shook out his wings and furled them. Picking himself up out of the mud, Benaiah noticed with envy that the Guardian's raiment shed muck. Shammah's blue robes were also mysteriously clean, but he and Josheb were plastered. Ben was still tugging at the legs of pants that clung uncomfortably to his skin when his head snapped up. "Well, crud. We go that way," he announced, pointing upstream.

"Finally," Josheb said, once more taking the lead.

The going was a little easier beside the river. *No more whacking through walls of vines and leaves.* Benaiah trudged along as the sun turned all the new moisture to steam. Bugs hummed. Birds made a racket. Sweat dripped. And shadows lengthened. Josheb seemed to be in a race against the sinking sun to reach whatever lay around the next bend.

Which always turns out to be another bend. But that's not stopping him.

The river meandered endlessly, and the scenery changed little. Once in a while, they had to slosh across a narrow stream joining the river from off to the side. Jutting roots and muddy patches made it important to watch your step. Josheb's boots squelched, and Ben's sandals became too caked with mud to do much good. *Shammah's barefoot, and his footing's fine.* "Hold up," Ben called, leaning against a tree to get rid of his shoes.

Josheb took a long drink while Shammah knelt by the river's edge to refill his water skin. To rinse off the mud before stuffing the shoes into his pack, Benaiah crouched next to him. Something pink caught his eye. Squinting against the sunlight glaring off the water, Ben asked, "What's that?"

Shammah made a soft noise of surprise. "There are more."

"What's with the flowers?" Josheb asked.

Pink and white flowers drifted with the lazy current, spinning slowly past. Shammah murmured, "Lotus."

Benaiah slowly straightened, saying, "That's not all."

Mixed in with the flowers were wooden blocks set with candles. The floats twinkled weakly in the sunlight, but whenever they hit a shadow, they sparked brightly. With a surge of certainly, Ben announced, "We need to cross to the other side."

"Here?" Josheb checked, eyeing the murky water suspiciously.

"Now." Ben waded out, and mud sucked at his feet. He grimaced as he sank in past his ankles. "The bottom's slimy."

Josheb wasn't about to be undone, and he was soon past his knees. "How deep will it get?"

"Not sure." Benaiah stiffened when something brushed

against his leg. "Uh, guys? There's something else in the water."

Plunging his spear sharply downward, Josheb hauled out an ugly fish with trailing whiskers. His impaled catch flopped helplessly. "Looks like I'll be eating more than flakes!"

Just fish. That's not so bad. But Benaiah's relief didn't last.

Shammah thrust his hand into the water, freezing a jutting section just as a huge reptile rammed up against it. A long snout with jagged teeth snapped at the air in front of Ben's face before it slipped back into the brown water.

"Crocodiles," Shammah said as he turned loose his barrier. "There are also snakes. And we should avoid the hippos."

Benaiah broke into a cold sweat as he watched the skimpy shield drift away. Obedience had just gotten a whole lot harder.

"This should be interesting," Josheb said, freeing his catch from his spear and readying it for bigger game.

As Josheb waded even deeper into the river, Ben frowned. "Can you swim?"

"No idea. Never tried."

That's when the bottom dropped out, and Josheb vanished. Othniel shouted, wings exploding outward, but Shammah was quicker. Leaving Benaiah's side, the young man grew as he waded downstream. When Josheb spluttered to the surface several lengths away, Shammah grabbed the back of his vest and flung him toward the opposite shore.

Landing in the shallows, Josheb staggered to his feet and leaned on his spear as he retched dank water. "No," he wheezed once he caught his breath. "Can't swim."

"May I?" offered Othniel.

Benaiah gratefully locked arms with the Guardian, who lofted him clear of danger within a few wingbeats. They reached the far shore at the same time as Shammah, who walked over to Josheb and thumped his back.

The rider growled, "Not sure if I should thank you or thrash you."

Shammah smiled wanly. "You are welcome."

More flowers and flickering lights bobbed along, and Benaiah pointed upstream. "That way."

The bedraggled team slogged around another bend and hit a wide place where the river split. The ground turned mushy, and sharp reeds scraped against Ben's arms. It took a moment to reorient himself. *Feels like we're standing on an island. The water's parting around us.* The flowers were coming from further upstream, the direction they needed to go.

"Most of the flowers are floating down that other branch," Shammah said. "What we saw were stragglers."

He's right. The water flowing off to their left was carpeted with blossoms. Their perfume hung in the air.

"What are they for?" Josheb asked, wading farther into the reeds to get a better look downstream. "Some kind of offering?"

Benaiah knew. "No. They're an invitation." Pointing past Josheb's shoulder to the opposite bank of the second branch, he quietly said, "*That's* the offering."

"Down," ordered Othniel.

Dropping to their knees in the tall grasses, they kept their eyes trained on the oncoming procession. A wavering line of torches snaked through the trees. Sounds came first—the jangle of metal rings, the chime of bells, the drone of chanting. As the group came opposite their hiding place, Ben caught glimpses of bright cloth—vermillion, russet, amber. A platform draped in more flowers rested on the shoulders of six men. In its center, two children knelt, girls with elaborate headdresses and painted faces.

"What is going on?" whispered Shammah.

"There must be a village down that way," Ben replied in a low voice. "And they're bringing gifts to their god. Poor kids."

"Something is wrong," Othniel said.

Benaiah gawked at the Guardian, who hadn't followed his own advice. Othniel stood firmly on the bank, plain to see with his luminous wings outstretched. *Oh. Right. Invisible to humans.* Shaking his head, Ben asked, "What's wrong?"

"Their Guardians are too far away. See there?"

Following Othniel's gaze, Benaiah saw what he meant. High overhead, angels flew in a wide circle. *Maybe they can't get any closer. But that makes no sense.* "I thought nothing could get between a guardian angel and his charge."

"That is how it should be," Othniel replied grimly. "But things are *not* as they should be."

In silence, they watched the long line of chanters turn upstream. "Well, Captain?" Josheb asked.

"We follow," Benaiah replied.

Smells can unlock memories.
I didn't need to see our
destination to know what
we'd find. I grew up in
a similar fog of incense.
But rich perfumes only
go so far. There had to be
a god in this temple.
I could smell him.

29

Incense never hides the stench.

et me guess," Josheb said, tipping his spear toward the enormous temple silhouetted against a coral sky. "He's in there."

"Yeah." Benaiah scowled at their next obstacle. Tier upon tier, weathered stone rose up over the surrounding jungle. Torches lined the entrance, and greeters in turquoise robes welcomed in the worshipers. "Doubt it's wise to go in the front way."

"Back door?" asked Josheb.

Ben nodded. "Worth a try."

Once the last of the procession disappeared inside, the four of them eased into the open and hurried around the building's perimeter. The first section they skirted was a featureless wall. *No way up. No way in.* But they had better luck farther back. In deep shadows, Ben found a narrow door warped by wet and weather. It creaked badly, then crumbled to pieces when he shoved.

Ducking through, he found himself in a short passage that

showed no signs of life. Othniel shouldered past him. His wings cast more light into a block of rooms that had fallen into disuse.

"Abandoned?" Benaiah asked.

The big warrior strode farther in and ran up against a tumble of stones. "Better," he replied. "Walled off."

"And mostly dry," Shammah said, peering into fusty corners where shriveled vines and dead leaves littered the floor.

Josheb stalked through every inch of the place, then asked, "Want to risk a fire?"

"Badly," Benaiah admitted. *If I can't be clean, at least let me be dry.*

Othniel nodded. "A small one."

"I'll hunt. You get crackling," said Josheb.

"Do not fall in the river, or we will eat your share of manna," Shammah said sweetly.

"Keep your flakes. I'm eating fish!" Josheb flicked the tip of their giant's pointy ear and sauntered out, boots still squelching.

Scraping together the burnable clutter on the floors didn't take long. *We need more than this. Which means the door's kindling.* While he broke the wood into smaller pieces, Shammah disappeared somewhere outside. Benaiah assumed he'd gone to relieve himself, but he returned with booty.

"Food," Shammah said, sounding pleased with himself. He'd collected fruit and vegetables in the front of his robes. Some of it was overripe and squishy, but it looked edible.

"Where did you find this?" Ben asked.

"Lying on the steps at the front of the building."

"These are offerings to the god of the temple."

"Yes." Shammah showed no trace of repentance. "There is a certain irony in sustaining ourselves on a demon's cast-offs."

Sleep didn't come easily. Benaiah missed the monster mound of cushions from Shammah's room. And in Josheb's valley, the winds would've swept away every last pesky insect. *At least my gut's full.* They'd toasted bits of raw fish on twigs over a miniscule fire and reduced Shammah's fruit to a pile of rinds, cores, and stems. He and Josheb huddled in opposite corners of the room, wrapped in damp blankets while their clothes "dried." Ben wasn't optimistic. *Looks like they're just soaking up smoke.*

Shammah sat next to the fire, feeding it scraps and turning Josheb's boots from time to time. And Othniel stood outside the door. *Guardian on guard.* Benaiah stretched out his legs, trying to get comfortable. *My butt's the only thing that's asleep.* Just then, Josheb's snores echoed off the low ceiling. *Okay, not just my butt.*

Benaiah scowled. Shammah smiled. Othniel ignored. And somehow, without warning, Benaiah was wrapped in a thickly-scented darkness. Hot and sickly sweet. Surrounded by whimpers. And a girl's low voice, singing snatches of a song. *This is a dream.* Ben could feel the echo of unreality all around him. *I'm seeing true things, but I'm not here. I'm asleep. Finally.*

Not that this sleep felt particularly restful. At the moment, Ben just wanted to know why he'd slipped into this vision. Following the noises, he poked his head though an opening in an embroidered curtain the color of a morning sky. The singer was washing heavy makeup off the little girls he'd spotted earlier. For an instant, he was reminded of his mother. *Nah, she's not the same. Except maybe for her hair.* The glossy black stuff hung almost to the floor. Plus, she was tiny. *Hardly more than a kid herself.*

She sang about the river, whose god was dark as night, and she sang about the day, with skies of beautiful blue. After a time, Benaiah realized that the song held a warning for the wide-eyed children. The river was cold, but the sky was warm. The darkness brought nightmares, but they could smile in daylight. "Hush now," she whispered, tucking the girls into a soft bed. "I'll be your angel until morning."

Ben blinked. "Angel?"

The girl whirled, dark eyes flashing dangerously as she reached for one of the jeweled rings that hung from her waist. Benaiah froze, but she looked straight through him. He held his breath while his mind whirled. *Aleff did say eight* boys. *She can't be the one. Right?*

But God didn't answer.

The next thing Benaiah knew, the toe of a boot was gouging into his bare ribs. "Move your butt. I'm tired of looking at it."

"You were wearing considerably less last night," Shammah pointed out in soft tones.

"Maybe because *my* babysitter never taught me to truss my …."

Ben lifted his head as a golden wing insert itself between him and the world. Othniel growled, "Do not belittle his modesty simply because you have none."

What do they care? It's too hot to wear much else. Benaiah stepped from behind the shelter of the Guardian's wing and glared at his teammates. "Don't you know how to tie a loincloth?"

Josheb waved the question aside. "I checked out the village this morning. Not much there."

"Meaning no horses," Othniel interjected.

"The farms prosper," Shammah said. "And this temple is quiet. Only a few men remained behind, tossing out the wilted flowers and fruit from last night. And swilling the liquor they are sleeping off now that the sun is high."

Benaiah checked his pants, which had been moved to a dappled sunspot on the floor. *Not dry, but good enough.* "You could have woken me sooner," he grumbled, pulling on his clothes.

"The bugs wouldn't let me," Josheb replied, curiosity alight in his eyes.

"Neri and Pazi," Shammah corrected, offering his fingertips to the sprites riding on his shoulder. "I wonder why?"

Benaiah hesitated. Josheb's wakeup call had interrupted something. *A dream. Mother? No.* Suddenly the memories piled into him. *The girl!*

Othniel said, "If you have any business outdoors, tend to it quickly. Rain is gathering."

Though it put his pants in peril of a fresh drenching, Benaiah headed outside. Josheb followed, and they skirted the temple together. Ben asked, "Only one way in?"

"No." Nodding toward the upper tiers, Josheb said, "There are openings all around the top. We can go in early. Watch from above."

"I like your plans. Simple."

The rider tugged at his chin, one eye on the sky. "Better bolt. Here comes the afternoon deluge."

They sprinted back to their hideaway with seconds to spare. Rain slammed into the earth, making it impossible to see the surrounding jungle from the open door. They waited out the weather in their stuffy, bug-ridden shelter. Josheb tried to get Shammah to teach Neri and Pazi to defend them against the flies. Shammah retaliated by flicking frozen water droplets at him.

Benaiah flaked dry mud off his pants with his thumbnail. Job's lessons repeated endlessly through his mind. *Look at the behemoth, which I made along with you and which feeds on grass like an ox. What strength he has in his loins, what power in the muscles of his belly....* He couldn't even imagine who they'd find inside. *Someone strong. And a girl with a bunch of scared kids.*

The rain stopped, and they slunk out of hiding. Clambering up the back of the temple, they caught up to Othniel at the top.

He reported, "No flowers. But the torch-bearers approach."

Tonight's procession was very different from the previous one. Less formal. Livelier. Raucous laughter burst from the group of men that rounded the bend. The brunt of their jokes seemed to be a young man leading a bull calf. Wreaths of flowers draped its neck, and ribbons fluttered from its short horns. "Looks like they brought dinner," said Josheb.

"Maybe," Benaiah replied, ducking lower.

Shammah quietly said, "That may be every man in the village."

The revelers spanned every generation, from white-haired men bent by many years to teens their own age. Loose pants and short vests were favored. Lotus flowers showed up everywhere, both the blooms themselves and the patterns stitched onto their colorful clothes.

"They paint their faces," Shammah noted.

Lines and dots, squiggles and swirls. Ben tried to make sense of them, but it was no use. *They're not letters or words. Just patterns.*

As the greeters stepped forward to accept the villagers' gifts, Josheb asked, "Well?"

"Inside." Benaiah traded a look with Othniel, then added, "Be careful. And quiet."

Josheb snickered at him. "I like your plans. Simple."

Ben's scowl tilted into a crooked smile. "Shut up."

They stole through gaps too narrow for Othniel. Their Guardian wasn't happy about being left behind, but neither of them had much choice. Benaiah needed to go. And

Othniel needed to stay.

Torchlight filled the temple's dark interior, where the men bowed before a statue on a platform against the back wall. Benaiah cringed at the wrongness of the scene—the grotesque idol, the droning instruments, and a strange, sweet smell that threatened to give him a headache.

"Today, it's cattle. Yesterday, it was children," Josheb said in a low voice. "What do you think they did with those kids?"

"My father was given many girls," Benaiah replied. "Not sure what happened to all of them. But they were frightened for good reasons."

Shammah pointed to the basins of flames on either side of the statue. The temple keepers were dropping in bundles of leaves and pouches that colored the flames. "Are you affected? I smell drugs."

Crud. No wonder my head's throbbing. Pulling free the end of his turban, he slopped water from his canteen over the cloth and pulled it across his nose.

Josheb held out his hand. "Don't be stingy, Captain. That stuff stinks to high heaven."

While Ben grudgingly undid his turban and untied a section for Josheb to use, Shammah declared, "It is an unholy stench. I could stop them."

Benaiah was certain the temperature dropped. Meeting their giant's cool gaze, he said, "Not this time. It's not why we're here."

The arch of Josheb's distinctive nose poked at the linen muffling his voice. "So where's our guy? Or the god for that matter?"

That sent a jolt down Ben's back. He looked more carefully at the room below. Now that his eyes were better adjusted, he could see different niches and arches leading off the main chamber. *I can smell it. It's faint, but it's there. And that means he's here. Or comes here regularly.* After another long look, Ben said, "I don't think there's a Fallen here right now."

Josheb grunted in surprise. "They're bringing out a girl."

A paunchy man with a forked beard escorted her to the platform on which the idol sat and made her to kneel on a plump cushion beside it. The excitement in the room doubled, and Benaiah frowned. *Doesn't feel dangerous. Good. She's not on the menu.* As this man flung his arms wide and began to speak, Ben sighed in relief.

"What?" Josheb asked, gaze sharp. "Can you understand what he's saying?"

"You can't?"

Rolling his eyes, he grumbled, "Out with the translation, Messenger's brat."

"Oh. Right." Benaiah gestured to the girl. "She's married to the statue."

Josheb's eyebrows buckled in bewilderment. "That blue chunk of rock with six arms? That makes no sense."

"It's some kind of formality." As the man brokering the marriage continued, Ben explained, "Now that guy is asking if any man among them is willing to give his heart to the wife of a god."

Shammah watched in stony silence, but Josheb asked,

"They're going to worship her now?"

"No. He's inviting the men to barter for her." Benaiah did his best to keep up with his fancy speech. "Only a man of strength and … uhh, stamina is good enough for a woman from the divine harem."

"Harem, huh? That's one busy statue," Josheb said.

The crowd of villagers pushed forward the young man who'd been leading the cow. Ben said, "That'd be the groom. At the cost of one bull calf and half his harvest."

"She seems happy enough with him." Josheb immediately lost interest. "But we're looking for a mongrel. *Something* should give him away. Pointed ears. Extra fingers. Wing marks. Funky hair or eye color."

"Who knows? I'll probably recognize him somehow."

Shammah said, "You will know his name."

"Yeah. That's how it'll be."

Josheb watched as the groom led his new bride off into one of the alcoves. The village men worked themselves into a fevered pitch, and cups made the rounds. "Once they're drunk, we should slip past and see what's behind those curtains. Besides old forked-beard's private harem."

"He said they're the god's wives," Ben corrected.

"Uh-huh," Josheb replied in pitying tones. "Let's get some air. This could take a while."

Hours passed in silence as they sprawled on the temple roof and listened to frogs. Othniel slowly wafted his wings, creating a light breeze. "Not as many bugs up here," Josheb remarked lazily.

"Could be the height. Could be the smoke," Ben replied, his eyes fixed on far-off stars.

Shammah, whose legs hung over the sheer drop that edged their narrow perch, softly called, "They are leaving."

Drunken men stumbled out of the temple, leaning on each other and laughing as they headed for their homes down-river. Josheb stood. "Now's our chance. Through the front door."

They quickly and quietly dropped down until they reached ground level, circling to the entrance. No sounds came from inside, so Josheb strode through, spear ready. Drawing his swords, Ben followed. Stone walls reflected the amber glow of Othniel's wings. Rustling mats gave way to thick rugs. A few torches still flickered, but the basins of fire in front of the idol had burned low.

"No one around," Josheb announced. Leaning against his spear, he stared at the statue. "It looks bigger from down here. But I was expecting something a little more interesting than a stone idol in orange britches."

Benaiah started to walk away, aiming for whatever rooms lay beyond the veils, but he jerked to a stop. Taking a step closer to the idol, his brows drew down. The temple god's vivid blue skin made a startling contrast to his silken pantaloons. *Crud, crud, crud. That's real cloth.* He could see the embroidery, and the light sparkled against beads.

Shammah tossed a handful of sticks into the nearest basin, sending sparks whirling upward. "Benaiah, look closer."

Can't be. Six arms fanned out against the wall at the idol's back. In the renewed light, Benaiah could see that the jeweled bracelets on each of its wrists were chained to the stone. *They worship a shackled god?*

Josheb hung back, but Shammah bent closer, his long hair sweeping against the idol's thigh. "Not stone. Not wood," he said. "He has been painted."

Benaiah stepped over a mound of striped melons and cucumbers and leaned in. The heavily-rimmed eyes that stared out from the god's broad face were actually painted on closed lids. "I think we found him."

Shammah reached out and poked the statue's cheek. It gave like flesh, and the god's eyes snapped open. Orange as flames. Ablaze with hatred.

Meeting one person
doesn't prepare you
to meet another one.
Josheb attacked me.
But I caught his interest.
Shammah hid from me.
But I won his trust.
I guess I figured
all of them would be
glad to meet me.
I was such an idiot.

30

Getting inside was the easy part.

Suddenly, Josheb pushed them both down. Something whirled over their heads to *clang* against Othniel's sword as he batted it aside. It landed with a muffled *thump* onto the carpet right next to Benaiah. The glittering circlet looked like some kind of child's toy, except it was studded by jewels. *Why's it look familiar?*

Ben reached for the metal ring, but Othniel kicked it aside with his boot. "The edges are sharp enough to cut. To kill."

Crud. That could've taken off an arm. Or my head.

Josheb was already moving toward their attacker, who had another ring twirling on the fingers of one hand. But Josheb pulled up short and lowered his spear. "It's a girl."

His hesitation could have cost him his life, but he used his spear to block her next throw. Benaiah immediately recognized the young woman from his dream. Her fancy pantaloons were embroidered with lotus flowers, and jewels glittered in her hair, at her throat, and on her forehead.

Josheb grumbled. "That bit into my haft. It'll need replacing."

"Better your weapon than you. Mongrels of your sort are hard to come by," Ben said, slowly rising. He stared intently at their slender attacker. "Careful. She has four more of those ring things."

Shammah spoke up. "Her face paint is like the idol's."

Blue paint made a wide band across her eyes, and her full lips had been dyed as red as the blood she seemed ready to spill. Anger sparked, and her voice was as sharp as her weapons. "Get away from him!"

"Don't hurt her!" Benaiah exclaimed, pushing forward.

Josheb shot him an injured look. "I'd no more hurt a filly than a foal, Captain."

They both ducked as another deadly circlet zinged past, and her voice grew more shrill. "Listen to me, or your lives are forfeit!"

"Peace, child," ordered Othniel. "We are not his enemies."

"Move away!" she snarled.

Benaiah grabbed the back of Josheb's vest and retreated. "We're between her and the one she's protecting. Let her get to her … god." She seemed determined to defend the one they'd come to find, but he wasn't sure about her motives. *Maybe she's his angel. Maybe she's his jailor.* But there was no questioning the ferocity in her eyes. Following his gut, Ben dropped to one knee and repeated Othniel's call for peace. "We won't hurt him. We're here to rescue him."

She hesitated, her gaze darting from face to face. "You're not men."

"Not exactly," Benaiah admitted, holding up empty hands. "Neither's he."

"Are you demons?" she asked bluntly.

Ben shook his head. "Only half right. Same as him. He's like us. Do you understand?"

The dazzling rings slowed to a stop, and she hooked them back onto her belt. "I'll spare you for now. Come this way. You'll need to hide until we're finished moving him."

"Thank you." Benaiah glanced back to make sure the other three were following. Josheb had picked up the two circlets she'd thrown and was testing an edge. Shammah's pensive gaze remained on the captive who'd slipped back into unconsciousness.

The young woman backed toward the curtained-off section, radiating distrust. She paused at the entrance into the temple's inner spaces. "If you touch any of the girls, I'll make eunuchs of you. I know how. I've done it before."

Benaiah held up both hands. "We won't touch, but I can't promise we won't frighten them."

Her full lips pressed into a thin line. "Don't underestimate our courage."

"Sorry," he muttered. "My bad. Let's go?"

While she led the way through a maze of passages, Josheb slipped up behind Ben and said, "Did you notice the blue guy?"

"Hard to miss."

"Did you happen to count his arms? Because he has *six*."

Ben nodded. "That's my tally, too."

"What does that *mean*?" Josheb pressed.

"It means … he has six arms," Benaiah replied with a shrug.

"Is that the best you can come up with?"

He shot a silent plea for help in God's direction. To his amazement, the answer came immediately. *Guess I should have been asking questions from the start.* Sheepishly scratching under the edge of his turban, Benaiah replied, "It means he's the son of a seraph. Seraphim have six wings, and that's how this guy's heritage bled through."

Josheb hummed in an interested way. "What's your David going to do when you show up with a guy with six arms?"

Nice that he assumes we'll succeed. With a half-smile, Ben replied, "Probably check to see if he can play three harps at once."

Josheb's gaze turned speculative. "Wonder if he can fight without tangling into knots. Make sure to ask him if he wants to spar."

Benaiah rolled his eyes. "All the stuff I gotta explain, and *that's* at the top of your list?"

"Why not? Though she's not far behind."

"Hang on. What do you mean by *that*?"

Josheb didn't have a chance to answer. The girl ushered them into a room with dozens of candles burning on narrow ledges. A huge bed draped in silk and mosquito netting took up most of the floor. Crossing to a recess in the corner, she pulled aside a filmy curtain and snapped, "Inside. And be silent. Or die. The choice is yours."

"Get in," Ben ordered. They shuffled into the alcove

already crammed with baskets and bolts of fabric. Not until Othniel joined the other three did she pull the drapery into place. After she vanished back the way they'd come, Benaiah glanced up at the big Guardian. "Is it just me, or can she see you?"

"She can."

"Is that …?"

"Unusual," Othniel finished for him.

A girl who calls herself an angel. A girl who can see angels. Benaiah begged for a little insight from on high, but all he received was an assurance that this was the right place and the right time. They waited for what felt like an eternity before voices approached. A man's. The girl's.

Josheb made a soft noise of surprise.

Ben's breath caught. *What did they* do *to him?*

They carried in the would-be god, the girl wedged under the lowest right arm, the temple leader bearing up under the topmost arm on the left. All the idol's paint and finery were gone. His black hair, which hung in four thick braids, dripped on the rugs beneath his feet. *No wonder they took so long. They must have stopped for a bath.*

They'd scoured away the blue veneer, exposing skin that made one thing clear. Six arms wasn't this guy's only inheritance. His skin tone didn't fall anywhere in the human range. *He looks like smoke. Or stone.* A short wrap at the waist kept the young man modest, but it exposed everything else. Wide bands of orange at each wrist stood out against deep gray skin. Ben leaned forward, trying for a better look.

Not bracelets. Definitely skin. Wings?

"I shouldn't need to do this," complained the fork-bearded man peevishly as they dragged the sagging deity to his bed.

"It's your own fault, drugging him like this," snapped the girl. "You don't need to. He would have cooperated. He gave you his word."

"Don't lay the blame at *my* feet." The man flipped his burden onto the enormous bed. "The longer he resists, the more I suffer."

She curled her lip. "Seek pity from your wives, but leave Ember in peace. And honor your agreement!"

"Tiresome girl. You'll pay for your sharp tongue."

"How can that be, since I am so richly favored by the gods?" Her voice hardened. "Now honor the agreement."

Her glare must have rivaled Ben's best scowl, because the man took a step backward.

She's a fighter. Was my mother this fierce?

The temple leader's smile was little more than the baring of teeth. "He's yours for three days, but no more. Otherwise, children may go hungry. Or have you forgotten where our bounty comes from?"

"Send the girls back to their mothers. Let their fathers see to their care. Leave this place to the river and its dark secrets."

"Would that I could, you ungrateful chit." With an impotent snarl, the man stormed out.

Josheb remarked, "She's not afraid of him."

Benaiah lifted aside the curtain. "That guy's more greed than guts, despite appearances."

"Not him," Josheb corrected, pointing to the person sprawled on the bed. "Him. The mongrel."

"So?"

"So she shouldn't be afraid of me. Right?"

Ben shot a look at the girl. "I don't think she's afraid of anything."

"Perfect!" Josheb strode out of hiding and offered his hand, palm up. "I'm Josheb. What's your name?"

They followed him out of hiding, and the four of them loomed over her. She dismissed three of them with a glance. Addressing herself to the one she shouldn't have been able to see, she asked, "You're a Guardian?"

Othniel replied, "I am."

"Mine is gone," she said. "Taken by the dark Hedge."

Dark Hedge? Ben wanted to know more about that, but Othniel latched on to something else.

The big warrior's brow furrowed. "You knew him?"

"Yes." Her chin lifted. "He was afraid for us, so he stepped in. Hafiz taught me to fight. He made sure Ember would have one angel."

"What are you called, child?"

"Tevy."

Inclining his head, Othniel said, "Your Guardian loved you greatly, Tevy."

Benaiah frowned. *Something's not right.* He caught the big warrior's gaze, but Othniel shook his head once. Questions would have to wait. And really, there were more important matters to consider. Like the son of a god.

While Othniel kept Tevy occupied with quiet questions, Ben leaned over the bed to get a better look at the person God was placing under his hand. The guy's ears were pierced, and metal clasps anchored the ends of each of his braids. There were rings on his fingers. *And that's a lot of fingers.* Judging by the muscle tone on his arms, their new recruit really could use all six. Once he woke from his drug-induced stupor.

He looks so helpless.

A hand lurched upward and closed around Benaiah's throat. Shammah and Josheb immediately jumped forward to restrain the guy. Shammah was shoved face-first into the mattress, and Josheb suffered three quick blows to the jaw that sent him to the floor.

Staring into eyes the color of flames, Ben rasped, "We're not enemies. Don't fight us."

Othniel stepped into view, and sternly said, "Fear not."

Ember's gaze roved over the warrior, lingering on his wings. In a deep voice, he named him. "Angel."

Benaiah scrabbled at the choke-hold and whispered, "Please, Eleazar."

The grip loosened slightly, but Ember didn't let him go. Emotions swirled in his eyes. Confusion. Distrust. And suddenly alarm. "What have you done with Tevy?"

"Done?" retorted the young woman, pushing past Othniel so Ember could see her. "Since they brought us an angel, I *allowed* them to live."

Ember released him, but Ben stayed right where he was.

"God Sent us to save you from all this."

Anger flashed in orange eyes, and he reached up again, grabbing a fistful of Benaiah's tunic. "Wrong. God has plunged you into hell. Now you're as damned as I."

"Nope." Maybe this guy couldn't see past the mess he was in, but Benaiah's perspective included David. Getting back to his king meant hauling Ember out of the tropics. *That's the way it's gonna be.*

An odd look passed across Ember's broad face. Maybe it was just the drugs. His eyes rolled back, but he blinked to refocus. Reaching up with one of his spare hands, he wrenched off Benaiah's turban. "Your mother was also blessed by the favors of a god."

Finally. He's catching on. Ben pushed lank hair out of his face. "Yeah. I was a temple brat."

"Does your father know you're here? He won't be pleased." Shaking his head, Ember grimly added, "But mine will be. His nightmares will consume you, body and soul."

Benaiah's heart began to hammer. "You know my father?"

Ember sneered and shoved him away. "You were made in his image, son of Sin."

Hatred and rejection were
normal enough parts of my life.
Men don't like the unlike, and
I was different. But the sneers
and slurs of strangers never
mattered much. I shrugged off
their ignorance. It was better
that they didn't know the truth.
But Eleazar not only knew
the truth, he knew more
than I did. And he held it
all against me.

31

He knew the truth.

Benaiah slowly straightened. "How did you know my father's name?"

"How did you learn mine?" returned Ember in harsh tones. "I told *no* one. Only my mother ever called me Eleazar. It was our secret."

"God knew. He told me."

Orange eyes narrowed. "And why would the ruler of heaven bother with a misbegotten son of a false god?"

"I'm His. And you're mine."

"You go too far," Ember replied, his deep voice a growl. "You assume too much."

Ben winced. *This isn't right. I said it all wrong, and he's furious. How can a Messenger botch a message so badly?*

God didn't answer, but Shammah spoke. "He does not speak of ownership. Merely leadership. And mutual belonging."

Josheb piped up. "Benaiah seems to be laboring under the

notion that we're his lambs."

Ember bristled. "That is demeaning."

"Isn't it?" Josheb agreed. "But watch him. I did. He proves true."

Benaiah could feel color creeping into his face. "Lay off, guys. He's not going to believe you since you're with me."

Othniel shook his head. "Eleazar is the son of a seraph. They know the truth. They speak the truth."

Josheb's eyebrows shot up. "Are you saying he can't lie?"

Ember's mouth thinned, but he didn't answer.

Leaning closer, Josheb asked, "And even *more* interesting, you can smell one?"

Stubborn silence.

"My favorite horse was a blood bay mare."

"Liar," muttered Eleazar.

Josheb winked, then said, "My mother's bread was the finest in our village."

"Liar."

"My captain sings pretty little lullabies."

Ember's gaze swung to Benaiah, who exclaimed, "Of *all* possible things, why the crud would you tell him …!"

Josheb wasn't finished. "And he's a proper angel. Ranked with the malakim. Not your average mongrel."

Clearing his throat, Ben grumbled, "I don't sing *every* night."

Ember rubbed his forehead, his attention wavering, and Tevy shoved them aside. "Stop plaguing him! Can't you see he needs rest?"

"Please," came a childish voice. "Let me help, Eleazar."

Ember turned his head to stare in confusion at the little boy who crawled onto the bed. The six-armed man didn't lash out, which left an opening. As Shammah's pale hand touched his forehead, Ember muttered, "Your fingers are cold."

"I know." The boy knelt right between two sets of arms. "Your head must ache. I will try to help, but I can make no promises."

Tevy confronted Benaiah. "What did he do? What did he say?"

"You heard him. He's trying to help."

She flashed an impatient look. "You talk sense. As does the Guardian. But the boy-man's words are a mystery."

Language difference. Josheb had complained about it earlier. "Sorry, Tevy. I didn't think. Shammah might be able to help Ember." Nodding to Josheb, Ben checked. "What about him?"

Her lips turned down. "He struts like a rooster, prowls like a tiger, and gibbers like an ape."

"Sorry," he repeated, though he wasn't sure what he was apologizing for. All of them were far from home.

Josheb stood before a rack on the far wall that held six daggers of unusual design. Their wide blades curved menacingly, and each jewel-encrusted hilt glittered in the candlelight. Flicking the heavy silken tassel knotted at the end of one of the weapons, Josheb caught Benaiah's eye. "If he can use all of them at once, that tops your twin swords, Captain."

Benaiah tapped the hilts at his waist. "Yeah. That's good."

Shammah's light voice interrupted. "He is not well."

At Tevy's sharp prod, Ben translated, "Ember's sick."

"The smoke does this to him," she said.

"She says it's the smoke."

Tevy continued, "We knew it would be bad, but Ember is strong. He won't let the river god get in."

Get in?

Before Benaiah could ask what she meant, Shammah said, "That is not the true problem. Not at all. Eleazar is weak. He is malnourished."

Josheb snorted. "Takes one to know one."

Shammah shook his head. "I am fine. He is not. He needs to eat. Tell the girl."

"Food," Benaiah relayed. "Tevy, can you bring food for Ember?"

For the first time, she looked frightened. "If they hadn't driven off his feeders, he would walk tall, dance well, and drive you out with fist and fury."

Which wasn't helping. Ben tried again. "If we feed him, he'll get his strength back. Can you bring some of those melons? Or meat would be …."

Tevy interrupted. "He cannot eat our food."

"The last of the feeders disappeared more than a week ago," Ember said dully.

"Mashed fruit and honey are the easiest for him to take," Tevy explained. "But what he really needs is the bread of angels."

Benaiah looked urgently at Shammah, but his expression was politely blank. *Crud, he didn't understand.* "Bring Neri and Pazi. Quick!"

Their diminutive giant slid off the bed and ducked past the curtain.

"Shy on flakes?" Josheb asked, strolling over to the bed and looming over Ember. "That should straighten things out fast. We have what you need. And that puts you in the Captain's power."

"I won't sell my soul for a mouthful of bread," Ember said in flat tones.

Josheb nodded. "Good policy. Think I'll adopt it."

Othniel startled everyone by drawing his sword. Eleazar struggled into a sitting position, his gaze darting to the weapon rack. But the Guardian held out his bared blade on open palms. "Eleazar, your name has come under my hand. Your safety is my responsibility. Tevy mentioned a dark Hedge. Why does she assume they took her guardian angel?"

"Hafiz," the girl quickly reminded. "All the other Guardians abandoned us, but Hafiz stayed. He was all alone."

Othniel inclined his head. "Where is Hafiz?"

"He goes off, but he always returns," Tevy said. "He will find a way. He always does."

"I see." Othniel took the two jeweled circlets looped over Josheb's forearm and returned them to the young woman. "Were these his idea?"

Tevy nodded. "We found them in the treasure room. They were the only weapon I could lift." She touched the chakram that bumped against her hips. "We practiced over and over until my arms were strong and my aim was true."

"Why did Hafiz do this?"

"I asked it." She glared defiantly. "Hafiz wants my happiness; he always bows to my wishes."

Othniel simply nodded again, then addressed Ember. "The dark Hedge?"

"Fallen Guardians who hold back the heavens."

Benaiah frowned. "We didn't see any demons on our way here."

"They let you through. And they'll keep you here."

Shammah returned then, still in the form of a child. Benaiah wondered if this was a sign of nerves on the half-Caretaker's part. *Maybe not. Eleazar's not fending him off. Is Shammah playing on his sympathies?* Curious, he asked, "Does a lie have to be spoken for you to recognize it?"

Ember looked from Benaiah to Shammah and back again. "This one acts in accordance with his nature. There is no lie."

Ben relaxed, but Eleazar grew more tense by the moment. *Crud, he must be starved.* "Turn them loose, Shammah."

The boy flipped up the basket's lid, saying, "See? I have a flock. They will supply your needs."

Eleazar looked stunned.

Josheb chuckled darkly. "All that leverage, and it never occurred to him to use it."

Shammah scooted closer. "You and I have something in common. Manna agrees with me better than human foodstuffs."

Ember lifted two hands in a silent plea, and Neri and Pazi zipped over. Only they bypassed his upraised palms. Instead, they latched onto the braids framing his broad face. Humming and cooing, they patted his cheeks, offering comfort. Ember's expression didn't change, but he released a shuddering breath, then rearranged his arms.

It's different than the shackled pose. Benaiah felt God's approval as the child of a seraph fanned out his limbs. One set stretched upward, palms beseeching. One set curved forward, hiding his feet from view. And as he bowed his head, Eleazar shielded his face with his last two hands. Within this graceful embrace, light intensified around Pazi as he made a wafer of manna and pressed it to Ember's lips. The young man accepted it and swallowed several times, dark lashes fluttering.

Tevy demanded, "Out!" She chased them through the door. "Out, out, *out*! He must eat. He must sleep!"

Benaiah allowed himself to be herded away, and one backward glance explained Tevy's haste. From behind Eleazar's outspread hands, tears fell.

I wasn't stupid.
God had told me
how brave a woman
could be. My mother
kept me safe, even if
it meant opposing a god.
This girl turned everything
upside down. To keep
a god safe, she opposed
the whole world.

32

Harems complicate things.

Shammah stayed with Eleazar, but Tevy hustled Benaiah and Josheb along a narrow passage lined with curtained alcoves. Cold stone kept the temple interior pleasantly cool. Rugs and cushions made it more comfortable. Lamps flickered within each draped chamber, but Benaiah kept his eyes straight ahead. Nothing stirred panic quicker than strange men in the women's quarters.

Josheb wasn't as willing to let things go. As soon as his curiosity got the better of him, he stopped to draw back a curtain and its accompanying netting. Ben was about to haul him back on track when Josheb whispered, "Not what I was expecting."

Benaiah gave in. Through the opening Josheb had made, he glimpsed a bed. But there was no woman in it. Only kids. Two little girls slept soundly. When Tevy backtracked to retrieve them, Ben quietly asked, "Is this them? The girls from yesterday?"

"Yes. They cried themselves to sleep again tonight." Shaking her head, she said, "Don't wake them and frighten them further."

She prodded them along and stashed them in another lavish alcove. While she lit the lamp, Benaiah asked, "Why is this one empty? It's not yours, is it?"

"The bride is gone. Her groom carried her away," Tevy replied. "Her parting gift, three days of peace."

"How did she manage that?"

"With smoke and chanting, gifts and guile, the village men stole away with one of the river god's wives. They dare not return for three days. Otherwise, the fickle god might change his mind and take her back."

So it's a wedding tradition. "Is that why Eleazar was chained up? For show?"

She hesitated. "Tonight, he went willingly into bondage so a bride could leave this place."

Benaiah thought he understood. "He usually refuses to play the part?"

"Always."

Once Tevy left them, Ben relayed her scant information.

Josheb asked, "What do you think of Ember?"

"I think … oh, I dunno. Obvious stuff. I think he'll have a

hard time fitting in. People will call him a monster."

Josheb dropped to a seat on the bed. "*I* think we have a problem. Don't let a chin wobble and a few teardrops get your hopes up. He has no intention of going along with our plans."

Ben slipped the swords from his belt. "What gave you that idea?"

"Silences are gonna be very important in dealing with someone who can't lie." Josheb shook his head. "We're not a godsend. We're an inconvenience."

That's a huge logical leap. Benaiah argued, "But he was sick. And starving. He was grateful. And at the very least, he likes Shammah. He let him stay."

"But *why*?" pushed Josheb. "You're making assumptions. Seeing what you hope to find."

Benaiah scowled, but the warning sent his mind racing. Sitting heavily on the other end of the bed, he asked, "You think he wants to use Shammah?"

"Could be."

"Shammah wouldn't turn against us."

"Not saying he will. But that doesn't mean Ember won't test the waters." Josheb stretched out on the too-short mattress and tucked his hands behind his neck. Gazing serenely at the ceiling, he said, "I doubt he's been sitting on his hands, waiting for us to rescue him. Three days, you said?"

"Yeah."

"A lot can happen in three days." Josheb frowned thoughtfully. "If it was me, I'd put myself three days' journey from this madness. Preferably on horseback. Right after making sure my stinking father couldn't follow. What do you think? Dismemberment?"

"Crud. You think he's planning to attack his father?" Lowering his voice, Ben pointed out, "That's drastic."

Josheb shrugged. "So's starving to death."

"But we fed him."

"That's bound to boost Ember's confidence. Daddy won't be expecting his boy to be at full strength. Speaking of which, you should sleep."

"I'm okay."

"Nope. You're not thinking clearly, and it shows." Benaiah bristled, but Josheb leaned closer. "For instance, where's Othniel."

I never even noticed he was missing. Groaning, he asked, "How long's he been gone?"

"*Long* time." Josheb crossed his ankles. "I'll keep watch while you sleep."

Ben reached for a pillow and tried to get comfortable. After some thought, he asked, "If Eleazar was planning to get out of here anyhow, why wouldn't he just leave with us?"

"If we could walk through one of Aleff's doors right now and go to David, would you ditch Shammah to do it?"

He rolled over enough to glare at Josheb. "*No.*"

"Then you should understand better than anyone."

Benaiah shivered as he peered around. He was getting quicker at recognizing when a vision had taken him. *But that doesn't mean this makes any sense.* The darkness had an oily quality. Everything smelled like mud and water … and death. Ben took a step back and kicked something on the damp ground. *Okay. That just makes this creepier.* Hadn't someone said something about nightmares? This had all the trappings.

Broken bones littered the floor. He could tell they were human, but probably not dinner scraps. *Someone wasn't eaten. They were torn apart.* There were enough bodies to explain the stink. *Except I know better. This is a special variety of reek. Demonic.*

Edging to the nearest wall, Benaiah pressed his hand against cool stone. The blocks were the same rock as the temple. *I'm probably still inside. Or under.* Heart thudding, Ben stepped carefully over slick stone and muddy patches, aiming for a still pool in the center of the chamber. *Not sure I want a closer look. But I need to be sure.* Everyone talked about the river god as if he was close. Not a scary bedtime story. Not a distant legend.

Glassy black water covered the center of the room. *Might be a pit. Probably filled with river water.* Except that the pool was clean and clear. As soon as he was close enough, Benaiah could see right down into its depths. *Definitely something there.* Despite the absence of light, Ben could make out every chilling detail.

At first, Benaiah was sure everything was magnified. *A trick of the water. That's the only explanation.* Except it wasn't. His helpful stash of new knowledge assured him that the seraphim were big. Even after they Fell, they were larger than life.

Arms wrapped around legs. Ribs standing out under taught gray skin. Knobbly spine. Stringy hairs clinging to a bowed head. Ben felt as if he was staring into a bleak womb, and he was sure that its inhabitant wasn't as lifeless as he appeared.

This was definitely Eleazar's father. The renowned river god. Bringer of nightmares. *Not good. More like ... bad. Lots of bad. Time to go!*

In the midst of a completely undignified scramble, Benaiah caught the sound of voices. They guided him to an exit that hadn't been there before. Letting the dream take its course, he stole closer. Light poured from an archway draped in the silk and mosquito netting that came standard in the temple. A man was speaking to someone. Benaiah listened in.

"You are weak. Easily bent."

"The elders called me *receptive*," came the weary reply. "That's why I was elevated from squalor to serve your needs."

"I need nothing."

There was a chuckle and a crunching sound. "But you *want* everything. Such appetite. Such thirst. Such plans."

"Insolence."

Ben craned his neck to see inside. Maybe this was like the other dream, and no one could see him. But maybe not. *Definitely playing it safe.* Nothing frightening awaited his first peek. Only the temple leader, sitting on a mountain of cushions. The low table at his elbow was heaped with bowls of food. And the crunching was fruit. Given the extra heft the man carried, Ben wasn't surprised. Except … he was alone. *Who the crud is he talking to?*

The man picked up a pot and checked under its lid. "There's honey. I took it from the villagers before the chit found it. Or don't you want its sweetness on my insolent tongue."

"You are not the one I want."

"By all means, leave me." He scooped honey onto one finger and stared fixedly at the golden strands drizzling back into the pot. In a softer voice, he muttered, "Leave me in peace."

Benaiah could hear two people talking, but only the fork-bearded man was speaking. The other voice echoed clearly in Ben's mind. It reminded him of when he could hear God speaking to Samuel on the day he sifted Jesse's sons. Only this wasn't God.

But it might be a god.

Whipping around, Benaiah stared at the black pool. Not a ripple marred its surface, but the conversation continued.

"The boy is weak."

"And heavy," complained the man, licking at the honey dribbling down his wrist before stuffing his finger into his mouth.

"I want him."

The temple leader simply rolled his eyes. Ben guessed that this was an old rant.

"My son is strong. He commands fear," growled the voice. "Youth and vigor. Power and passion."

"Yes, yes. Your pride and joy. Your prize."

When I consume his mind, I will taste with his mouth, touch with his hands, dance under the light of every moon. I will forge new immortality!"

"Except …" the temple leader dared to say, tapping his nose.

"He is weakening. I *will* have him."

"Don't blame me for his elusiveness. I followed your instructions. I allow you to come and go as you please."

"Like water through a broken vessel," the demon sneered. "Do not think too highly of yourself, little man."

Ben was surprised by the man's audacity. Was it courage? Or did he simply have nothing to lose?

"What next then?" the temple leader asked, a smile on his face.

The demand came haughtily. But it revealed a level of dependence. "Mingle honey with the wine."

While the man mixed his next drink, a soft scuffle sounded in the shadows behind Benaiah. He turned, reaching for his swords, but they weren't there. A figure slipped closer, edging into the circle of light. Ben knew his order at a glance. *Hadarim.* What was a solitary Guardian doing in this nightmare?

The stranger stared down at him, his face a mask of confusion. "You do not belong here."

"Yeah. Just passing through," Benaiah replied in a low voice.

An odd light gleamed in the newcomer's eyes. "Stay. Take his place."

A crash from the alcove dragged Ben's attention back to the temple leader.

He was staring straight at Benaiah. And his eyes burned orange.

He'd never pass for human.
Not on the outside.
Skin. Hair. Eyes. Limbs.
This man was born a monster.
But his humanity was impossible
to miss. And it yanked me
to full attention. Of all the Three,
Eleazar was the most like David.
Which is probably why
his hatred hurt. Him and me—
we were meant to be friends.

33

She held him captive.

enaiah woke with a garbled cry. Lurching upward, he grabbed at the person leaning over him and stared wildly into Othniel's eyes. Concern creased the big warrior's face as he said, "Fear not."

"I saw … I'm not sure what I saw. Crud." Ben held on tighter, if only to hide how much his hands were shaking. *He's down below. And he knows I'm here.* Despite a creeping sense of horror, Ben went over everything that had happened in the dark. "How long have I been dreaming?"

"Long enough."

Josheb stood next to the bed, tension radiating from his stance. "What does *receptive* mean?"

Ben blinked. "You heard?"

He shook his head. "You were muttering. I didn't like the sound of the stuff I could make out. By the look on your face, neither did you."

"Yeah. It was bad," Benaiah said. "There's a demon here,

and he's like my father."

"Self-proclaimed god, demands sacrifices, keeps a harem," Josheb listed.

"All that, but worse. My father could do this thing." The explanation came out in a jumble. "Get into someone's head. Mess with their mind. See what they saw. Speak with their voice. Take their place."

"Possession," Othniel said grimly. "Many outcast Messengers learned the trick of bending human minds."

Josheb was quick to point out, "Local deity's a seraph, not one of the malakim."

Benaiah nodded, but there was no mistaking what he'd seen. With a sudden rush, he realized two things. "He needs a mind that's weak or willing. That's what he meant by *receptive*. And ...."

"And?" prompted Josheb.

"Ember recognized me because I look like my father." Swallowing hard, Ben said, "He's probably the one who taught the river god how to possess minds. Tevy mentioned nightmares. The girls have nightmares."

Othniel said, "That is only part of it. The boy was right."

"What boy?"

"Eleazar." At Ben's skeptical glance, Othniel revealed, "He and Shammah are of an age, barely out of adolescence."

Crud. I didn't notice he was our age. He's so much bigger, and his voice is so deep. Loosening his grip on the big warrior, Ben asked, "What was he right about?"

"The enemy is deeply entrenched."

Josheb's expression soured. "You reconnoitered without me?"

Othniel straightened and stepped away. "The Fallen are holding back the angels we saw in the distance. Former Guardians forming a dark Hedge."

Benaiah shrugged. "All we have to do is hold out until Aleff comes for us."

Josheb snorted. "What makes you think you'd be safe if we stay put?"

Nothing. Actually, the complete opposite's true. Because if anyone's gonna be receptive to dreams, it's a Messenger. Or a half-Messenger. What did that guy say? "Stay. Take his place."

Josheb's eyes narrowed. "You said that, too. Right before Othniel snapped you out of it."

"There was a Guardian in the dream. He snuck up on me. That's what he said." Benaiah turned to Othniel. "Could he have been Tevy's guardian angel?"

"He Fell."

That struck a deep chord. Benaiah could hardly fathom the depths of sadness behind those two words. Hanging his head, he mumbled, "Thought so. Sorry."

Othniel replied, "You could not have prevented something that happened years ago."

Josheb leaned closer. "But why would her Guardian still be lurking here, years later?"

"Hafiz," Ben supplied. "She called him Hafiz."

"No," Othniel countered. "He is one of the Fallen, with no claim to his former name, rank, or glory."

Benaiah's uneasiness increased. "But she called him her angel."

"She doesn't know?" guessed Josheb. "But Eleazar would know. He has truth by the tail."

"We should talk to him about it," Ben said, swinging his legs over the side of the bed.

"If he'll talk." Josheb's tone held traces of the previous night's warning.

"For crud's sake, he's one of us. We came for him. We're here!"

"We came, but not quick enough." Josheb shook his head. "I was bored. I could forgive God a wait because it ended. This isn't that."

"What *is* this?"

Josheb stroked the hair on his chin, then sighed. "Something wild and wary. Be patient, or you'll drive him away, Captain."

Patient. Do we have time for patience? Benaiah pulled aside their alcove's curtain, startling two young girls who were passing by. After a stunned silence, they shrieked and ran back the way they'd come. Ben scowled. "She's gonna hold that against me."

Josheb yanked him back as a razor sharp circlet *clang*ed

against the stone. "That girl isn't normal."

"Are any of us?"

He smirked. "Unless her sire was a thundercloud, or her mother a wildfire, she doesn't have our excuse."

As soon as Tevy was close enough, Ben tried to apologize. "I didn't mean to …."

She cut him off with an upraised hand. "Last night, you said you were here for Ember's sake. You promised rescue."

"Yeah."

"But that was a lie," she said haughtily. "You are thieves. Ember told me."

"I'm not here to steal anything," Ben replied.

Tevy's eyes flashed dangerously. "What is your purpose?"

Benaiah searched for a simple explanation. "Eleazar has been chosen by God to serve the king of a land far from here. We'll fight together. We'll fight for David."

"Thief!" she snarled. "You want to steal Ember from us!"

From her perspective, I'm guilty as charged. He scratched uncertainly under the drooping edge of his turban. "I can't steal him, Tevy. It's no good unless he joins us willingly."

Her chin came up. "He won't leave us."

Bet that's what Josheb meant. Crud, this guy's got baggage. "Us. How many *us* are there?"

"Eighteen are his, and he is ours."

Benaiah wasn't sure he was following. "Do you mean like … he's your god?"

"Are you a fool?"

"Probably. Help me out here. What's Ember to the girls

here?" Ben pushed, "What's he to you?"

"Ask him," she retorted. "If he wants you to know, he will answer. If he doesn't want you to know, far be it from me to spill his secrets before presumptuous swine."

Josheb elbowed him, "Still can't understand a word she's saying. What's she on about?"

Ben shrugged. "She just called you a pig."

"Me?" Josheb eyed the young woman with a mixture of annoyance and fascination. "What did I do to deserve that?"

Thankfully, Shammah appeared at the end of the passage and called, "Eleazar's head is clearer this morning. Come, and let me introduce you properly."

To Tevy, Ben relayed, "Ember wants to talk. That's all. Talk."

She scooped up the circlet she'd thrown earlier and sashayed away without a word. Josheb glanced at Othniel and asked, "What do you make of her?"

"She lives in darkness, but she clings to the light."

Benaiah did his best not to flinch away from Eleazar's stare. *He hates me. Except he doesn't know me enough to hate me. So really, he hates my father. But so do I.* Not that Eleazar the Ember cared. His face was blank. His eyes were empty. His voice was flat. And it hurt more than it should have. *Why should I care?* Except he did. Ben could already feel

Eleazar's name, burning its way into his hand and his heart. *He's one of mine.*

At some point, Shammah had returned to Josheb's height. Which turned out to be the same as Eleazar's. That made Benaiah the shortest person in the room. The slim Caretaker touched his own chest and gravely said, "I am Shammah. My father is a Fallen Caretaker, and I am called the Giant."

"Yes," replied the six-armed young man.

Beckoning while he spoke, Shammah continued, "This is Josheb. His father is a Fallen Protector. He is called the Rider."

Ignoring Josheb's offered hand, Eleazar said, "Yes."

With a small crease of concern between his eyebrows, Shammah pressed on. "Benaiah the First is our captain. His fath–"

"Sin."

Ben couldn't stop the flinch this time. Or a scowl. "I'm one of the Faithful. And if you're any sort of seraph, you know I'm telling the truth."

Eleazar's empty stare gave way to a shimmer of anger.

Josheb whacked Ben's shoulder, and Shammah quickly interjected, "*All* our fathers Fell. We have no wish to follow them."

After a stony silence, Ember asked, "Will you fight them?"

Benaiah's stomach plunged. *Not my first choice. Not that I have much choice.* He shook his head. "From what I understand, we'll fight beside one man against other men. We'll be his strength. His guard." In a lower voice, he added, "His friends."

"Shammah called you a king-maker."

"Yeah, sort of. But not really. God's the one who chose David," Benaiah replied. "And He chose us to make sure David gets to the place he belongs. His throne."

"No."

Ben drew himself up. "I'm telling the truth."

"I was answering your next question," Ember replied. "Your king will have to do without me."

"But …!" Benaiah began, but the butt of Josheb's spear jabbed into his ribs, cutting him off.

The rider rolled his eyes, as good as calling him an idiot.

Fine. I get it. Be patient.

Othniel asserted himself. "How long has it been since the girl's Guardian Fell?"

For the first time, Ember lowered his gaze. "This is a place no angel could reach. But Hafiz found a way."

A terrible way. The fool became a demon to get to her side.

"She was born here?" asked Othniel.

Ember nodded. "The day I met him, he placed Tevy in my arms. She was barely weaned. Hafiz had stolen her from her mother. He saved Tevy's life, for she'd been marked for sacrifice."

"No wonder she's not afraid of you," Josheb remarked. "You raised her."

Othniel asked, "Has he tried to take her from you?"

"Several times," Ember replied. "When she refused to leave the other girls, he changed tactics. Taught her to fight."

"Why?" asked Shammah. "Why would a demon nurture

and protect a child?"

Ember answered stiffly. "He loves her."

"More than anything," agreed Othniel.

Shammah's face was a picture of puzzlement. "Why would you allow such a thing?"

"We were never in a position to be choosy about allies."

Josheb snorted. "You know how to skirt a lie."

Josheb was right about how careful Eleazar is at phrasing stuff. I need to pay closer attention to what he's not saying.

Shammah held out a hand. "We are your allies."

Ember set his jaw. Confirming nothing; denying nothing. Instead he retraced the thread of conversation. "I've always known what he is. As time passed, it grew difficult for him to hide the changes—dimming, thinning, withering. Hafiz rarely visits. I believe he's ashamed of what he's become."

"Is he still here?" Othniel asked.

"He's *always* here."

Josheb asked, "Trapped inside the Dark Hedge?"

"No," replied Ember, his voice cracking. "This temple isn't his prison. Tevy is."

Josheb's intuition could
slash through confusion,
straight to the heart of matters.
Already, I relied on him.
Trusted his opinions.
But Eleazar's insight
was something new.
The truth could be
right in front of us,
but we couldn't see it
until he spoke. I think he
enjoyed blindsiding us.

34

Conditional acceptance is better than refusal.

Tevy burst into the room and flung her arms around Ember's waist, hiding her face against the colorful silken scarves wrapped around his midriff. "He's back."

Ember grasped her shoulders with two hands, setting her back so he could cup her cheeks with two more. "Where?"

"My room."

Benaiah revised his opinion of Tevy. *She knows her angel is a demon in disguise. Why else would she be trembling?*

"He's not supposed to enter your chamber. Wait here. I'll find him and remind him of his promises. Stay with Othniel until I can bring h–"

"No." All eyes turned to Othniel, who said, "Hafiz would refuse to stand before me. Shammah will keep Tevy and your other wives safe. Take Benaiah and Josheb to meet him."

To Ben's surprise, Ember accepted the change in plans without hesitation. *Their safety is more important than his pride. And he trusts Shammah. That's good. That's a start.*

Josheb took long strides to catch up. "Wives!" he exclaimed. "Othniel said *wives*!"

"And?" Ember asked.

"I've *seen* your wives. They're too young to marry."

"That's why they're still here." Ember paused mid-stride. "You've been surveying the harems?"

"More like a few peeks," Josheb replied with an unrepentant grin. "Some are still in diapers."

Ember kept walking. "The littlest girls were born here."

"Where are their mothers?"

"There are women here."

Josheb's interest was piqued. "And what do they do?"

With a sidelong look, Ember brusquely replied, "It's better for the girls to marry back into the village. Wait here." Once he was certain Josheb and Benaiah were staying put, the six-armed man swept open the curtains covering one of the alcoves. "So you have returned, Hafiz."

"I promised," came the earnest reply. "I didn't go far. I couldn't leave. Not Tevy."

He sounds youngish. There was a slight hoarseness to the demon's words, as if Hafiz suffered from nothing more than a sore throat.

"You promised not to enter Tevy's room."

"Did I? Oh, I did." There was a shuffling sound, and the demon ventured, "Where is my girl?"

"She sent me to find you. By now, she'll have a table set with the things you like. Are you hungry, Hafiz?"

Something shifted in the voice. "You are the one who should be hungry. Why are you here instead of my Tevy?"

Josheb leaned close to whisper, "Tell Shammah to hide Neri and Pazi. Now."

Benaiah wasn't sure how far his thoughts could reach. After two abysmal efforts, Othniel's voice touched his mind. *"Trouble?"*

"All kinds. I fail at this talking inside people's heads thing."

"I can hear you."

"Yeah, and I'm grateful. Look, Josheb is a little riled about Hafiz. Wants Shammah to hide our yahavim."

"I will warn him."

Josheb's hand closed around Ben's arm, and he snapped to attention just as Ember backed out of the alcove, followed by Hafiz.

He looks ordinary enough. Not brutish and twisted, like the last demon we faced. His mind helpfully supplied the reason. *Newfallen.*

"Found you," Hafiz crooned, quickly closing in on Ben. With a soft laugh, he repeated, "Found you."

"I remember you," Benaiah replied, standing straighter. "You were in my dream."

"No," the demon countered in gently mocking tones. "I cannot dream. I was in the lower parts, where your visions carried you. But I knew you were there. And so did he."

Ember pushed his way between them. Glaring down at Ben, he growled, "I will need to hear more about this, but

Tevy is waiting."

Hafiz smiled, and eagerness glittered in his dark eyes. "Yes, please. I want to see my Tevy."

"You know the way."

"After you," countered Hafiz, his gaze darting suspiciously toward Josheb.

Ember said, "These men will not harm you."

The demon's lips quirked. "True."

Benaiah's stomach complained, but there was no way he was joining Shammah and Tevy, who were serving Hafiz honeyed tea and sweets. *His light is gone, and he smells bad.* It was also bothering him that Tevy treated the demon with so much kindness. *He disarmed her somehow. All her glares and threats are gone. She smiles and speaks softly, and he laps it up with hungry looks.*

Ember stepped into the path of a perfectly good scowl. Cornering Ben, he demanded, "Do you dream?"

"Yeah. Messenger's brat, remember?"

"Don't."

"Can't help it," Benaiah grumbled. "I need the sleep."

"Listen to me, son of Sin. You are in more danger than you realize." Pitching his voice low, Ember growled, "Do not listen to his whispers. Do not let his voice past your guard.

Build walls. Bar gates. Turn him away, or he will enter. And once inside, your hands are his hands; your feet are his feet. His appetite becomes your hunger, and his desires become your deeds. He will remake you in his image, and you will be nothing."

Ben's eyes glazed over. Eleazar's warning rang true. *Of course it does. He's part seraph.* With a mouth gone dry, he tried to explain his predicament. "I'm new at this. I don't know how to do … all those things you said to do."

"Then choose better footing for your fight. Tonight, before your eyes grow heavy."

"I didn't come here to fight. My Sending is to find you and take you to David."

Thick eyebrows lifted slightly, and Eleazar spoke what must be the truth. "There is only one way you will achieve your goal, son of Sin."

Not liking the new nickname. I'd rather go back to being compared to camels. Ben grabbed for patience. "Tell me."

"I must achieve mine."

"Which would be …?"

Ember shook his head. "We wait until tonight. After evensong."

"You observe evensong?"

"And?"

Benaiah only shrugged because Josheb sidled up. "Your little beauty is playing a dangerous game."

"True."

Josheb searched Ember's face. "Are there rules to this game?"

"Yes. Do not get between them unless he tries to take her."

"Which he will."

To Benaiah's dismay, Eleazar nodded. "When he offered her to me, Hafiz wanted me to protect Tevy from my father. But I think he knew I would need to protect her from him. The more she grows, the more his devotion twists."

"Glad you see it, too," Josheb said. "Be careful of her, or the next babe placed in your arms will be hers. And the number of mongrels in the world will change to nine."

Eleazar spoke slowly, as if explaining something to a youngster. "Before you declare this imaginary child a calamity, consider those you hope to sire. Half or quarter, they would all be mongrels."

Josheb was rendered speechless, and Benaiah's voice jumped an octave. "You want *kids*?"

Hafiz slipped back into the shadows as soon as Tevy mentioned evensong. Benaiah breathed a little easier without the doting demon stinking up the place. His appetite even perked up. *Someone's cooking somewhere.* With more than twenty people living inside the temple, that made sense. But maybe it was time for Josheb to hunt.

Before Ben could make up his mind, Shammah pulled him aside. "What are we going to do? Has God spoken? Is there anything you need?"

Since he wasn't sure about the answers to the first two, Ben focused on the third. "My head hurts, and my stomach's empty," he complained.

Shammah brightened. "Both are within my ability to change."

Cool hands framed Benaiah's face. In the very back of his mind, a whisper of fear set his heart to racing. Their giant could devastate a legion of demons with these same hands. *But this is Shammah. My brother.* With a sigh of relief, Ben leaned into the healing touch, letting his eyes slide shut. "Better."

"I have improved," Shammah said. "The more you are injured, the more I can practice."

Benaiah snorted. "Don't give Josheb any ideas. He might just run me through."

"No harm will come to you if I can prevent it."

"Likewise." Gripping Shammah's arm, Ben added a low, "Thanks."

From beside the doorway, Tevy announced, "You will join us for a meal. Frighten the girls, and Ember will drag you out so your beheading doesn't soil our carpets."

Josheb glanced over. "Translation?"

"Dinner," said Ben. "And behave."

Shammah's brows arched. "Her words were many; yours were few."

"I left out the gory parts. Just make sure he doesn't scare the kids."

"I shall do my part." In an instant, Shammah dropped to the size of a child. Slipping his hand into Josheb's, he said,

"This is necessary."

Hiding a smile by dragging his sleeve across his nose, Ben followed them along a set of torchlit passages and up a flight of stone stairs. The chamber they entered had high ceilings and narrow windows on two sides. Daylight angled through the smoky interior, adding sparkle to dust motes. Rugs and cushions scattered the floor, where food trays were arranged in two long rows. Before each one sat a wide-eyed girl.

Tevy called out, "These are the guests I told you about. They are tall like our Ember, but our Ember is stronger by far. I promise these men will respect our family. You have nothing to fear."

Josheb peered curiously at the members of the harem while Shammah tugged him across the carpet-strewn floor.

Ben almost laughed. Their placement had to be an insult. *Are we behind Eleazar because we're his inferiors? Or maybe it's reassuring to have him between us and them.* He didn't really care because the food trays were heaped with roasted vegetables and chunks of fish.

Benaiah hummed happily around his first mouthful. Josheb grunted his agreement. Shammah quietly slipped food from his tray onto theirs.

After every speck was cleared, Tevy brought a bowl of water and cloths. Wrinkling her nose she said, "Wash."

"Gladly," Benaiah replied, wishing once more for a proper bath. *I can't smell much better than a Fallen. What I wouldn't give for a lump of Aleff's soap.* Scraping stray gunk from under his fingernails, he made sure God knew how glad he'd be to see his caretaker again. Not until Josheb whacked him upside the head did he realize Tevy was impatiently tapping her beaded slipper. "Huh?"

"Tell them a story," she said in exasperation. "That is what travelers do."

"Oh. Yeah. Sure."

Ember beckoned for him to move to the center of the floor. The trays were being cleared, and little girls giggled and whispered as they formed a wide circle around him. Feeling ridiculously tall, Ben quickly sat and looked to Tevy. "What kind of stories do girls like?"

"It is nearly bedtime. If you bore us, no harm done."

A giggle rippled through the room, and Benaiah's ears began to burn. Help came from another quarter. *'Joseph's story.'*

Latching onto the heavenly directive, Ben took a deep breath and began. "Jacob, whose name became Israel, lived in a land where his father was a stranger. He had many wives, many sons, and many flocks. Now, when his son Joseph was seventeen years old ...." On and on, he recited the story as Aleff had taught it to him. A favored son. The bitterness of envy. A dark well. Years of imprisonment. Strange dreams. And a faith that never died.

Benaiah drew out the story the way Aleff used to, gesturing with his hands, adding inflections, losing himself in the telling. His audience showed no sign of boredom, except perhaps for the littlest among them.

Midway through his telling, Ben noticed a subtle migration. Bump and scootch. Creep and crawl. Small ones who must have been born in the temple were acting like David's lambs. Without fear, they crowded around their six-armed shepherd.

Eleazar doesn't even realize his arms are full. Throughout the telling, the young man's gaze never left Benaiah's face. *It's like the first time Josheb heard the old stories. But multiplied. Magnified. Is it because of his order? Yeah, that's probably it. My words are true. He craves the truth.*

The hour grew late by the time Joseph's story was all told. Older girls collected the little sleepyheads and carried them below to the harem. Some of the younger girls offered thanks for the story. One even begged for more.

"If I'm still around tomorrow, I'll tell you the next part of the story. About someone God chose to save His people." Finding Eleazar's gaze locked on him, Benaiah boldly said, "Right in the nick of time, he was lifted out of a river and sent to live in the house of a king."

The day God wrote
Aleff's name on my hand,
Othniel told me I would
have a Flight. Usually, that's
a team of angels.
But those under my hand
were as mixed up as
their captain. Some men.
Some mongrels. Some angels.
And before He was done,
God placed a woman's name there.
One whose name meant angel.

35

Give a little, get a little.

Since Eleazar seemed less guarded, Benaiah stuck close. *One story bought the girls' trust. Maybe he's warming up.* "Do you usually sing?" he asked. "I mean … *evensong*. That's what it means."

"Yes."

Ben wasn't sure if that was *yes*, that's what the word means, or *yes*, that's what we do. *Either way, the whole warming up thing isn't happening.* He closed his mouth. Even bit his tongue for good measure. *Since when am I the most talkative person in the room? Stuff has changed.* He had a sneaking suspicion Aleff would gloat. Or be proud. *Probably both.*

In the lower passages, Tevy flitted from alcove to niche. A few girls were her age, but most were young enough to want tucking in. And Josheb had been right. Some were in diapers. Benaiah had never seen Tevy smile so much or so softly. *Josheb was right about another thing. She's beautiful.*

Watching her made Ben a little homesick for the mother he barely remembered. Suddenly, he noticed something. "Why is she checking under their pillows?"

Eleazar ignored the question.

Which means it's important.

Benaiah trailed after Ember, who paused before each bed chamber. The young man was careful never to step into the rooms. From just beyond the threshold, he spoke softly to each little wife. Then he offered a prayer to the Most High God for peaceful sleep, for clear eyes, for hopeful hearts.

His words were simple enough, but they sounded good. *Like a song. Like a psalm.* When the last of the children were tended to, Ben was still pondering. *Is that what the seraphim were made to do? The same as David does when he composes?*

At once, God replied, *'My companions, My heralds, proclaimers of majesty, declaring the truth that sets them ablaze.'*

Benaiah wished Eleazar could see what a faithful seraph looked like. Their flames danced before his mind's eye, burning without ever being consumed. God's words flowed into him, and he gave them a voice. "Eleazar the Ember, the truth is ever on your lips."

Eleazar jerked to a halt and turned slowly.

"A coal has touched your lips," Ben continued. "You will uphold the glory of God by word and by deed."

The seraph's son closed the distance between them in no time at all. "Cease."

Which was silly, really. Ember had to know Ben couldn't stop. Not when God gave him a message. Slowly reaching out with one hand, he kept right on talking. "Burn with holy fire. Blaze upon the field of battle. Purify My holy mountain, the place I have chosen. Enter the throne room. Herald the king who loves My name as you do."

Ember's hands glided reflexively into position, fanning out over his head, low at each side, and before his face. Ben could tell. *He knows these are God's words.*

Orange eyes flew wide when Benaiah pressed his palm against the center of Eleazar's chest. Light bled around the wide bands of orange skin ringing his wrists. Glowing cracks raced outward, and it looked like lava seethed just below the surface of his gray skin.

"What are you doing?" Ember asked sharply. "What have you done?"

With a crackle and fizz, fire exploded around them. Except it wasn't hot. And they weren't surrounded by flames.

"Feathers," Benaiah whispered in awed tones. Six sets of wings clogged the passage with sun-burnished feathers, surrounding them with a thousand flames. At the thunderstruck expression on Eleazar's face, Ben asked, "Didn't anyone ever tell you that you have wings?"

Knocking Ben's hand aside, Ember backed away. "Stay away from me, Messenger."

Benaiah could have pulled his hair out in frustration, but he didn't argue. Just watched as the half-seraph pulled his glorious wings tightly around his body and fled. *Wasn't that a good thing? Crud, I'd give almost anything for a pair of wings, and he has three sets.* "If that didn't change his mind about me, I don't think anything will," Ben grumbled.

'He changed.'

While he wandered in the direction of his assigned niche, Benaiah replayed the whole encounter in his mind, looking for the tipping point. He stopped short and smiled ruefully. "I get it. *Messenger.*"

His allegiance with heaven had finally beaten out his lineage.

Benaiah rounded the corner in time to see a jeweled circlet crash into the wall opposite Tevy's alcove. Drawing his swords, he jogged over. "What happened? Is everything all … *oh.*" Tevy had two more of her signature weapons whirling on her fingers, and she looked mad enough to spit venom.

Rounding on Josheb, Ben asked, "What did you do?"

"She and I seem to be having a misunderstanding," Josheb replied with a grin.

Tevy's weapons lost momentum, and she held them in a white-knuckled grip. "I would be rid of this impudent fool! He stays when I want him gone! And he stares. Blankly."

"I can explain," Ben promised in soothing tones. "If he looks stupid, it's probably because he can't understand what you're saying."

Her voice lost some of its shrillness. "Then convey my disapproval. He won't leave me alone!"

Before Benaiah could translate, Josheb said, "She's alone. I don't trust that Hafiz character not to sneak back."

"Gotcha. But Tevy doesn't trust you. She wants you out."

Josheb didn't budge. "Explain it to her."

"Tell him!" Tevy insisted.

Great. Reduced to go-between in order to prevent war. *Can't we leave the diplomacy to Aleff?* Stifling a sigh, Benaiah started with Tevy. Spreading his hands in a plea for understanding, he began, "Josheb is half Protector, and that makes him … protective."

Her small chin tilted to a proud angle. "I can protect myself."

"Yeah. Totally true. But he can't help himself."

Tevy glared at the tall young man leaning on his spear. "I am Ember's. This one's approach is an insult. His gaze is full of desire."

Ben glanced at Josheb and groaned. *The guy's interested all right.*

Josheb pointed to the razor-edged circlets in her hands. "I want to try those. Ask her to teach me."

"I'm sorry. I'm really sorry. But he's not propositioning you as a woman. He's interested in you as a warrior."

Her dark eyes darted between the two young men towering over her. "Should I be … insulted?"

Benaiah was out of his depth. "He compliments you, lady. He respects your skill with a weapon he's never encountered before. What do you call those things?"

Tevy lifted her weapon. "Chakram."

"You gonna tell me what she's saying, Captain?" Josheb asked, reaching out to flick one of the circlets with a long finger.

"Just let me finish apologizing for your impudence," grumbled Ben.

Josheb chuckled. "*Impudent*. Is that a compliment?"

"Insult. Definitely an insult." Switching back to Tevy, Benaiah said, "He wants a truce with you so you can fight. Which sounds crazy, but that's the way it is with Josheb. He likes to spar. Is there someplace he could practice?"

"The armory, where Hafiz taught me to use the chakram."

"An armory is *perfect*. Can we go there?"

She hesitated for several moments, then whisked past them with a flutter of silk and sweep of hair. "This way."

Up one flight of stairs, Tevy led the way along a passage that took them in the opposite direction of the dining hall. She grappled a torch from its bracket before entering a large room with a high, domed ceiling. Weapons of all shapes and sizes hung from pegs or bristled like deadly bouquets in creaky old casks. Josheb immediately backtracked to get his own torch.

All the better for prowling. Ben figured they were somewhere over the abandoned rooms where they'd taken shelter on the day they arrived. In fact, parts of the walls here were damaged. Crossing to a tumble of stone dominating the far corner, he asked, "What happened here?"

"There was an earthquake. Long ago," Tevy leapt onto the base of the massive tree growing right up through the ceiling. Its roots sprawled across the floor and burrowed into the stone. Reaching up to touch its scarred trunk, she said, "This noble tree was my opponent. May he forgive my rough treatment."

They turned at a whistling of wind to see Josheb testing the weight of an ancient-looking sword. After an expert twirl, he set it respectfully back in its place. Plucking up another, he pulled it halfway out of its sheath to inspect its edge.

"Othniel needs to see this place," Josheb said distractedly. "Weapons master. Weapons. He'll like it here, right?"

"Yeah, probably." To Tevy, he said, "He wants to learn as much as he can, and your chakram are something new. That makes them—and you—interesting. Practice with him instead of your tree friend."

"How?"

"Throw them at him. Try to kill him all you want." With a small shrug, Benaiah added, "He'll figure out the rest. And he'll probably enjoy it."

Tevy thought that through, then whistled sharply for Josheb's attention.

He looked over in time to dodge her first throw. His surprise changed into a smirk, and he dropped into a defensive crouch. "Well done, Captain. We seem to have reached an understanding."

I was so focused
on getting stronger.
For David's sake.
For the sake of my men.
Back then, I had no clue
that my strengths might
expose me to my enemies.
And I didn't realize
what can happen when
you let someone see you
at your weakest.

36

Hearing voices is a bad sign.

nother dream? Benaiah's head bobbed, then snapped up. The insistent ring of weapons brought him around, and he grunted in annoyance. *Josheb might be able to do without, but some of us need sleep.*

Not that Tevy was suffering. She darted out of a shadow and flung three dazzling hoops in quick succession. *Zing. Clang. Whoop.* It hadn't taken long for Josheb to learn the trick of catching Tevy's chakram on his spear. And it was taking forever for them to tire of the game.

Benaiah let his head drop back against the wall and rubbed eyes that felt gritty. *I should go. It's not like they'll notice. And she's trying to kill him for fun now. That's an improvement.* Folding his hands across his chest, Ben let his mind drift. He should stay a little longer. Just in case Tevy lopped off the idiot's arm. David needed his men intact.

There it is again. Brow furrowing in concentration, Benaiah strained to hear. Was there a voice? Who was calling? Maybe it was Othniel. Or Eleazar. It was a deep voice. They had deep voices.

"Found you."

This time it was harder to shake the fuzziness. Ben opened his eyes, but they kept rolling back. Scowling and squinting, he managed to make out Hafiz's face.

"M'wake," Benaiah mumbled, fumbling for his weapons. Not easy, fending with your eyes shut. David would tease him for being so hopeless.

The whispering was louder now. Pleased. Delighted even. "Is he young?"

Hafiz answered, "Youth. Strength. Life. All yours."

Ben struggled against the voice. Why had he wanted to hear it? All he wanted now was to block it out.

"Receptive," gloated the voice.

And the whispers grew insistent. They put ideas into Benaiah's head. Terrible thoughts.

Three words cut through the clamor. *'Go to Eleazar.'*

The Sending had Benaiah on his feet and moving despite his stupor. He stumbled along the passage, but he couldn't escape the voice roaring in his head. *Voice? Voices.* The shouting hurt, and putting hands over his ears didn't help.

Lamplight shone behind the curtain to Eleazar's chamber, but Ben hesitated outside. *He won't be happy to see me.*

'He can protect you.'

With a whimper, Benaiah struggled to keep his sanity. *Or You could protect me.*

'Let him.'

Giving in, Ben stumbled through the drapery, landing on his knees.

Eleazar was gliding through some kind of dance. Or maybe it was an exercise. Because all six of his blades were in his hands, glittering dangerously in the firelight. His wings had refurled. He was alone. And annoyed. "Leave."

"Can't," Benaiah gasped. "Sent."

Eleazar's glare was terrible, but he sheathed two of his weapons and grabbed one of the lamps. Holding it high, he prowled closer. "I don't want you. I don't need you."

"Maybe. But I need you."

"Why?" he growled, grabbing Ben's chin and staring deep into his eyes. "What do you hear?"

"Whispers. Voices. Roaring." A tremor found its way into his voice as he admitted, "It hurts."

"I warned you not to sleep."

"Dozed off." Benaiah's hands found their way onto two of Eleazar's forearms. In his desperation, he flung his panic at the young man. *He's cruel. I'm such an idiot. Can't I do anything right? Don't let him in.*

"Get out of my head!" snapped Ember.

"N-no." Now that he could see the way to safety, Ben had to try. "Let me in. Hide me."

The half-seraph refused to answer.

To be reduced to begging, and to find no mercy. Benaiah tasted despair and found it bitter. But he couldn't blame Eleazar. Not if this roaring was the demon he'd faced every day of his long life.

Hands. Too many hands. They grabbed for him, and Ben's world tilted. Someone else was shouting at him, and his words were like fire, burning away the darkness. Then a door slammed shut, and silence echoed. It was dark. It was still. But it was also safe.

"Where am I?"

Don't. Talk.

That was Eleazar's voice—loud, clear, and angry. Benaiah risked his rescuer's wrath by whispering, "I don't understand."

That's when Ben opened his eyes. Except it wasn't him. Eleazar had opened his eyes, and Ben could see through them. And he was looking down at himself. A bedraggled, grimy Benaiah curled up on the bed. Looking a little too much like the slumbering horror in the temple's basement.

In a weak voice, Ben asked, "Possession?"

Sanctuary.

It had to be true, but it was still terrible. "You hate this."

Yes.

"I'm sorry," Benaiah whispered.

Don't. Talk.

So he shut up and tried to make himself small. It was the strangest thing he'd ever experienced, feeling sad and watching tears slide down his own face.

Long, deep, and dark—Benaiah hadn't slept so well since they left Shammah's cave. No humidity. No mosquitoes. He rather missed Josheb's snoring, though.

He lingered in that place between sleeping and waking. No hurry. Not hungry. But it was strange that he couldn't tell what was cushioning him. No bed. No blankets. For that matter, he couldn't feel his body.

Ben stirred, more awake now. The silence didn't alarm him. At least not personally. But someone else was upset. Someone beyond this peaceful pocket of unreality.

"Why won't you turn him loose? The danger's passed."

"He's unresponsive."

There was no doubt about who was talking. The first speaker had been Josheb, and Eleazar had answered. Shammah spoke next.

"Is he injured? Let me look."

Eleazar replied, "He's asleep."

"This long? It's been a whole day," said Josheb.

"Exhaustion," murmured Shammah. "He can't do without sleep for as long as us."

Josheb sounded interested. "Why would he turn to you, Ember?"

"He was Sent."

"And what have you learned from holding our Captain captive?"

"I'm not his jailor."

Josheb chuckled. "That's *not* what I asked."

After a lengthy pause, Eleazar said, "He trusts me."

"And is his trust misplaced?"

The question was asked lightly, but Ben detected a dangerous edge to Josheb's tone. Without really thinking it through, Benaiah said, "Doesn't matter. His name's on my hand."

There was a long silence, and Shammah asked, "Which hand? Can I see?"

"That wasn't *me*," growled Ember. "He's awake."

"Then open your eyes, already!" Josheb exclaimed. "I'm tired of staring at your eyelids."

And Benaiah opened his eyes. Except he was looking through Eleazar's eyes. Straight into Josheb's. "Is it like he said, Captain? You in there?"

"Yeah."

Don't. Talk.

"Crud. Sorry."

Josheb smirked. "As amusing as it might be to watch Ember argue with himself, you might want to get back where you belong, Captain. Shammah and his flock are fussing."

He—or was it *they*—glanced toward the bed where Benaiah still lay curled on his side. Hair-brushing was happening. And Tevy was helping. Ben's embarrassment stained the sleeping body's face, right to the tips of his ears. "That's … mine."

Tevy looked right into his eyes—no, Eleazar's eyes. Petting a lock of light brown hair, she asked, "Have you ever seen such a color? Isn't it pretty?"

Ember crossed to the girl, and with four of his hands, he gently freed Ben's hair. It was the strangest sensation, reaching out with limbs his mind didn't have room for. But Benaiah could feel the softness of his own hair. And Tevy's hands were small and cool against his skin. No, he could see that her hands were nestled against gray palms. Ember was holding her hands. But so was Ben.

With a small squeeze, Eleazar whispered, "You are embarrassing him."

Tevy pouted. "A man should not be ashamed if God has made him beautiful."

If Aleff ever heard about this …! Dropping Tevy's hands, Benaiah swiftly scanned the room and singled out Othniel. "Don't you *dare* translate that!"

The big warrior's grunt sounded amused. "Do you know how to return to yourself?"

"Crud."

Josheb was in his face again. "That sounds so wrong coming from you."

"It *isn't* coming from me." Ember knelt beside the bed, and one gray hand reached for Benaiah's limp one. Sliding his fingertips across Ben's, he coached, "This should come easily for you, Messenger. Wake from your dream."

And it *was* that easy. All at once, Benaiah was staring into Eleazar's eyes instead of through them. He tightened his fingers around the large hand in his grasp, but the half-seraph pushed it open. Checking. They found it at the same time. Eleazar's name was plainly written on the first finger of his right hand. Josheb's name was on the middle finger. And Shammah's name had been placed on his ring finger. The Three, side-by-side-by-side.

That's when Ben realized. *The whispers are gone.*

Eleazar's brow furrowed, and he pointedly replied out loud to Benaiah's thought. "You are a whisper."

Crud.

Orange eyes narrowed. "One I cannot close out."

Josheb leaned over and gripped Ben's shoulder. "Welcome back, Captain. How do you feel?"

That was easy. "Hungry."

Tevy slid off the bed. "I'll bring a tray."

Slowly sitting up, Benaiah self-consciously added, "And … cleaner."

Shammah offered him the linens that usually kept his hair hidden. "I practiced on you. Cleansing and healing are similar."

Benaiah still wanted a bath, but he didn't say as much. Twisting and knotting his hair, he rewrapped his turban. Glancing at his men, he asked, "Did I miss anything?"

Josheb said, "For a night and a day, Ember has demonstrated his godlike skills by sitting like a statue. We lost a day, waiting for you to wake up."

"But he needed sleep," reminded Shammah. "And we need our captain if we're going to do this."

"Do what?" asked Benaiah, looking from face to face.

Eleazar answered. "There's only one way you'll achieve your goal."

Ben remembered the last time he'd said it. And he knew what it meant. "We're going to fight."

Josheb grinned. "You woke up in time for a council of war."

Josheb's strategies
were deceptively simple.
But when he broke down
a battle to its basics, the
impossible sounded like
child's play. Which makes
total sense. For him, war
was a game. When it
came to claiming victories,
no one had more fun
than Josheb the Rider,
leader of the Three.

37

Having a plan guarantees nothing.

mber, you know *our* goal. Tell us yours." Josheb asked, "What's most important?"

"The girls."

For a moment, Benaiah was afraid that Eleazar wanted to bring his harem all the way to Bethlehem. The very idea made him cringe. And plead with God. *Please don't tell me there are eighteen girls under my hand.*

Ember said, "If I leave, the girls would be at my father's mercy. I want to send them back to their families. Let them beautify the village rather than this dank place."

Ben's tried not to show how relieved he was. Bashing their way through demonic battle lines was definitely preferable to being outnumbered by little girls.

"And if we do that?" pressed Josheb.

"I will accept your captain as my captain."

Benaiah knew this wasn't a compromise. All of them wanted the girls safe. This was their new teammate asking for help. *The rest of us left nothing behind. We had no reason to stay. But those girls depend on Eleazar to keep back the nightmares. He won't leave unless they're safe.*

"Decent trade-off," Josheb said. "Ember will fight our battles if we fight his first."

Ben was only too happy to agree. "Send them home. If that's what it takes, yeah. How long will it take the girls to be ready to leave?"

Tevy said, "We are ready. We have always been ready."

"Now," Benaiah translated. "Assuming we have a plan."

Josheb tugged at his chin. "Does it matter if we move them by day or by night?"

Othniel shook his head. "You will gain no advantage by waiting for darkness."

A slow smile spread across Josheb's face. "Advantages. That's the way to look at this! How long before the daily downpour?"

Rain sheeted onto a struggling line of runaways. Benaiah felt a little ridiculous, trudging along with a little girl in each arm. He was afraid to break them. *Which is stupid. I don't worry about Neri and Pazi. But ... this is different!*

"He's tall like a tree," whispered one.

Her best friend giggled and said, "Eyes green like leafs."

Tevy had been right. The girls were prepared to leave. Which meant Josheb had also been right on the mark. Eleazar had planned all along to get them out. Bundles containing clothing, dolls, food, candles, and smuggled coins had been stashed under every pillow. Blessings from their husband. Parting gifts.

They were making painfully slow progress along the river. Everyone carried big leaves over their heads, but it was tough to see. Ben could dimly make out Eleazar's orange pantaloons up ahead. That splash of color—and the muffled cries of the three little ones he carried—were all Benaiah had to guide him.

One of Benaiah's girls tugged at the trailing end of his turban. "Tell us a story?"

"Not right now, kid. We're being quiet."

They only giggled again. Ben doubted anyone could hear them over the rain, so he concentrated on not slipping. The last thing they needed was to have to pull someone out of the river. *Everyone's hands are full. Well ... except Shammah's.*

Their giant was with Othniel at the front, ready to implement Josheb's plan. Tear a hole through the enemy line. Tap into the reinforcements waiting on the other side. *We're going to reunite these girls with their guardian angels.*

A shout from somewhere ahead was their only warning. Othniel's voice barked an order in Benaiah's head just before Eleazar turned to relay it from down the line. "Into the trees!"

Off the muddy path. Into the thicket. They found a pocket

of space about the size of a temple alcove, and Ember knelt down. Tevy herded eight of the older girls over to the six-armed man, who held out his free hands to them. "Gather here," he called. "Close to me."

Benaiah set down his two girls, and pushed them into the safety of the crowd. Then he followed Tevy to find the ones still missing.

A bestial snarl put them both on edge, and Tevy eased closer to Benaiah. "Was that a tiger?"

"Worse." He swiped at his face with his sleeve, trying to clear his vision.

Othniel's golden wings blazed through the endless wet. The big Guardian seemed to be on the other side of the river. *Drawing attention away from us?* Dark shapes moved through the murk, and the stench was back. Rough shouts came from another direction, and Benaiah pulled Tevy back as a spray of thorny arrows slashed through the foliage.

"Stay down!" he snapped.

"Four more!" Tevy exclaimed, fighting to free her arm from his hold. "Where are they? They were right in front of me!"

"Relax. Josheb's got them." A colorful huddle broke cover just ahead, and Ben waved them over. "Here they come."

Josheb was bent low, half-running as he guided his batch of girls. Ben pointed the way to Eleazar, but Tevy did one better, grabbing the hand of the first girl and leading the way.

As they slipped into the jungle, Ben silently counted heads. *Fourteen ... fifteen ... sixteen ... seventeen ... eighteen. All safe. So far, so good.*

With a squelch of boots, Josheb returned to Benaiah's side and thumped his shoulder. "Stay back. Swords out. Help Ember."

"Yeah." It was strange, hanging back when it seemed like they should be fighting. "Are you sure Shammah can pull this off?"

A wail rent the air, and the river creaked, then snapped. When they went to check what was happening, a thin layer of ice shot across its surface, shattering under the downpour and spinning off with the current. Moments later, a frozen body splashed into the water. As it rolled, they glimpsed meaty fists clenched for a blow that would never connect. The river caught and carried the iced demon downstream.

Loosening the ties that held his spear, Josheb grinned. "All according to plan! I'll be between Shammah and you, in case anything slips by."

Hardly likely. But just then, something darted past.

They traded a look, then charged after it. Benaiah's thoughts raced. *What was it?*

"Trouble," Josheb shouted against the rain. "Loan me a sword."

Ben slapped the hilt of one of his weapons against his teammate's outstretched palm just as they reached the clearing where Ember waited with the children. His little harem crammed around him, preventing him from doing anything. Only Tevy stood apart, chakram spinning in both hands as she stared down the Fallen who'd found them.

Josheb didn't hesitate. His spear thudded wetly into the

ground between Tevy and her opponent, halting the demon's advance. An instant later, the rider blindsided the enemy, slamming him into a tree. Wicked spines lashed out as the demon bared rotted teeth, but Josheb's unfurled winglets deflected the blows.

While they grappled, Ember's girls whimpered.

They're too vulnerable. Even six arms couldn't offer enough shelter against such a terrible danger. "Wings!" Benaiah exclaimed.

When it was clear that Eleazar couldn't hear him, Ben pushed his thoughts at the half-seraph. *Wings work as a shield! Unfurl yours, and get them around as many kids as you can!*

Frantic eyes sought his, and Eleazar mouthed one word. *How?*

Coming! Benaiah darted forward, nearly tripping over his own feet in his rush. The demon noticed and lunged, and Ben clenched his jaw as pain sliced across his side. But Josheb rallied, and Benaiah made it by, sliding into the frightened huddle. Pushing up onto his knees, he yanked Tevy closer, then placed his muddy hand against Eleazar's chest. "Pay attention. You'll get the hang of it."

Light bloomed and burned, and the rainy world vanished in a swirl of flaming feathers. Silence reigned within the miraculous shelter. The girls peered around with astonished expressions. Eleazar kept his eyes downcast.

Tevy finally managed, "Ember, did you …?"

One of the little girls Benaiah had been carrying earlier whispered, "Birdie?"

Benaiah rubbed his nose on his sleeve, and Eleazar shot him a withering look.

Before any dignity could be lost, Josheb's voice came from outside. "Captain, you'll want to see this. We're surrounded."

Sometimes, things would
get strange. My orders
didn't make any sense.
But my men trusted me
because God could
speak to me.
They figured that
with direct access to
the divine, I couldn't
steer them wrong.
Except that's not
how it was.
Sometimes, I was
only guessing. Trusting
God to speak up
if I blew it.

38

Girls are a handful.

Benaiah eased out from under Eleazar's overlapping wings. *Rain's tapering. And yeah. Surrounded.* Josheb offered a hand, and even after he'd straightened to his full height, Ben had to look up. Taking a slow turn, he met each gaze as he silently counted. *Fourteen ... fifteen ... sixteen ... seventeen.*

"Ember's full of surprises," Josheb muttered. "Six wings?"

"That's my count, yeah."

"What happened to that Fallen?" Ben asked.

"Them."

Angels formed a double circle around the blazing mound of feathers where Eleazar's little wives were still hidden from view. Seventeen warriors stood shoulder to shoulder, facing inward. Seventeen more stood at their backs, with weapons pointed outward. Benaiah knew at once that they were Guardians. And this time, he realized something new.

Teams of two. Each guardian angel serves with a mentor.

Thinking back, Ben remembered the second Guardian hanging around with Rei.

Josheb handed back the borrowed sword for Ben to sheathe. Leaning on his spear, he said, "Maybe you should say something. Since we're standing between them and theirs. I hear Guardians are touchy about that."

"They're safe," Ben said, holding up his hands. "The girls are safe."

A single angel dropped down from overhead, landing directly in front of Benaiah. He said, "Reward their patience, Messenger."

"Who are you?"

The lean warrior mirrored Benaiah's peaceable gesture. "Eliel. Please. We've waited so long."

"Yeah. Hang on." Ben knelt in the mud and patted at the gleaming feathers. "Eleazar, it worked. They're through. Show them?"

Eleazar slowly swung back his wings.

Checking the warriors' faces for their reaction, Benaiah was a little surprised. *They're crying.*

Eliel said, "For several, this is our first meeting. Joy falls like rain."

Benaiah watched the children carefully, but they only had eyes for Ember. "The girls can't see you."

"No matter. That's how it should be."

"Except Tevy, of course," Ben added. The young woman's attention was mostly taken up by the little ones, but there were telltale glances.

"What do you mean?" asked Eliel in a hoarse undertone.

"She can see angels. Long story. Does it matter?"

Eliel nodded.

Benaiah took a longer look at the warrior before him—an archer with brown skin, old eyes, and two rings piercing his left ear. "Why?" Ben asked. "I know you're not her Guardian."

"What makes you so sure?"

Benaiah scowled. "I've met the guy."

"I see." Eliel unslung the bow from his shoulder and showed Benaiah the carvings on its grip, "Two names were placed under my hand. Although my apprentice's name has been banished, his charge remains under my watch-care."

Tevy's name. Touching the scrolling letters on Eliel's weapon, Ben whispered, "You were Hafiz's mentor."

Suddenly, the angels shifted, and weapons came up. Josheb was on the move. "Whoa, now! He's one of us. Let me through."

Benaiah followed, slipping between warriors who lifted their wings so he could pass. Shammah stood by himself outside the circle, and he looked terrible. Rain-wet hair clung darkly to pale cheeks, and mud smeared his bare feet. But that wasn't the bad part. *His eyes. Does he recognize us?* There was a distance in his gaze that spiked fear into his heart, but Ben hurried forward. "Shammah?"

Their giant frowned, and Josheb warned, "Careful, Captain."

But Benaiah grabbed Shammah by the arms and gave him a little shake. "Are you okay?"

Shammah focused on Ben's face. With a shuddering sigh, he whispered, "I am fine. It is done."

"Yeah, I noticed. Good job breaking through. These guys found the gap."

Othniel stepped up behind Shammah and gravely corrected, "This boy did not *break through* the dark Hedge. It is gone."

Ben tried to make sense of that. "But I thought you said there were *dozens* of …."

"There were," Othniel acknowledged. "Shammah reduced half of those Fallen to pulp and iced the rest. Caretakers are removing them to the deep places. This entire area has been emptied of enemies."

Josheb smirked. "That just leaves the local deity."

"You are injured," Shammah murmured, taking hold of Ben's sleeve.

Something about his tone put Benaiah on edge, and he searched their giant's face. "Good call. Anything you can do?"

Looking down at his slender hands, Shammah grimly replied, "I was made to tear and crush and kill, but Othniel was wrong when he called me a weapon. God granted me a mercy. I can heal."

"Go for it." Shammah found the rip in his bloodied robes and touched the shallow cut that burned across his ribs.

When Benaiah jerked away, Shammah gave him an injured look.

He rolled his eyes. "Your hands are *cold*."

By the time Benaiah turned back to the others, Eleazar

was on his feet. Despite their success, the half-seraph wasn't celebrating. *He looks sick and sad. And self-conscious about his wings.* Eleazar might be used to coordinating six arms, but his new plumage kept dragging in the mud.

Wading carefully through the harem, Ben said, "This is good. We can get your girls back into the village."

"*You* can." Eleazar lightly touched the heads of the children closest to him. "You and Josheb will lead them the rest of the way. My presence would cause confusion."

Ben pointed to himself. "I don't exactly fit in either."

"They will fear you, but they would worship me." His deep voice held regret. "See them safely home."

Josheb pushed forward. "Isn't this the part where I get to take down a god? Give me one good reason why I should keep babysitting. There are more than thirty Guardians here."

God's answer brought fresh color to Benaiah's face. "They're here to protect the girls. You're here to protect me."

Although he didn't argue, Josheb asked, "What from?"

"Not sure. But that's how it has to be."

He accepted the answer with a nod, shifted his hold on his spear and casually scanned the vicinity. "Start your goodbyes, Ember. And don't take all day."

Orange eyes were suspiciously bright as Tevy lined up the girls from youngest to oldest. Eleazar said their names, whispered a few words, kissed their foreheads, and told them goodbye. Except when he got to Tevy.

She warned him off with her head held high. "I am not leaving you."

"I gave my word. They'll be taking me far away."

Tevy rounded on Benaiah. "You can't take him without me! I won't let you!"

"Calm down, Tevy," Ben urged.

"No! Someone needs to watch out for him. Someone who *cares*."

Glancing at the others self-consciously, he said, "I do."

She was up on tiptoe as she argued. "I don't believe you!"

Benaiah held out his hand, thinking to show her the names written there. "God gave him to me."

If she could see the names engraved on his palm and fingers, she wasn't admitting it. "God gave Ember to me first. *Me*!"

"This is what God wants," Ben assured. "And I'm responsible …."

"You blind fool! Ember doesn't trust you. He doesn't like you." Tevy's outrage was beginning to frighten the littler girls. "I'm the only one who understands him, who knows what he's thinking!"

With a sidelong look at the young man in question, Benaiah replied, "If Eleazar wants me to know what's on his mind, all he has to do is tell me. I'll listen."

"Enough, Tevy," commanded Eleazar.

Tears spilled down her cheeks, and she loosed two of her chakram. "I belong to Ember! He belongs to me!"

Eliel stepped between them. "Peace, child."

Tevy didn't miss a beat. She glared up at this new obstacle and shouted, "You can't stop me either!"

Smiling faintly, Eliel said, "Your choices are your own, child. Make them wisely." Then he turned to Benaiah. "May I see your hands, Messenger?"

"Yeah." He spread them before the newcomer, all the while thanking God that women usually avoided him. *Why are they so dramatic?*

The archer's lips quirked. "Such a fuss, and all for naught." Eliel tweaked Benaiah's little finger and said, "God is God, and His ways are beyond understanding."

Ben stared at his right hand. *It's full. When did the other names show up?*

Josheb leaned over and asked, "Is this a good time to ask what Ember's little tempest is storming about?"

"Look," Ben replied, holding up his hand.

"Interesting," Josheb said. "Except I can't read any of it."

Shammah joined them, and Benaiah showed them both. Aleff's name was on his palm. Othniel's name was written upon his thumb. His first three fingers bore the names of the Three. And on his pinkie, God had placed Tevy's name. "She's one of us."

I'll never get used to
God's timing.
When I thought we
should rush in,
something forced us
to wait. And when
I would have liked
more time to prepare,
there was no choice
but to rush in.

39

Never dis a deity.

What's *her* name doing there? She's no mongrel," said Josheb.

Shammah's fingertips brushed across his own name. "Neither is Othniel, nor Aleff. God has given Benaiah charge of human, angel, and those who exist somewhere in between."

"Ember, come and see," Josheb called. "You can't leave behind one of your wives. God gave her to the Captain."

A moment later, Ben's hand was caught by four gray ones as Eleazar inspected the inscriptions. The seraph murmured, "Tevy's name was not here earlier."

"I'm as surprised as you are."

Eleazar whispered, "True."

"Tevy stays with us," Benaiah said. "Is that okay with you?"

"What fool argues with God?"

Josheb chuckled. "You're good at this. No lie, but no answer, either."

With a shake of his head, Eleazar said, "I'm grateful. I didn't like the idea of leaving her behind."

Elbowing their new teammate, Josheb asked, "Because she's your special favorite?"

He shook his head. "Because she's Hafiz's special favorite."

"Good point." Josheb glanced at Shammah. "Any chance you dismembered him earlier?"

"I do not remember details."

"Too bad. So … we need to tweak the second part of the plan. I'll stay with the Captain. Tevy goes with Ember, Shammah, and Othniel."

Ember hesitated. "I'd rather not bring her back into danger."

"It's the smart thing to do," Josheb said.

"Why?"

The rider's expression turned smug. "Because then you'll have Othniel *and* Eliel." Jerking his thumb at the second Guardian, he said, "Where she goes, the archer goes. And that's not a bad deal."

Benaiah quietly added, "Plus, she won't let you leave her behind."

"True," Eleazar sighed. "I have a question. If Benaiah is our captain, why does Josheb give the orders?"

That stumped Ben. *It feels like I'm in charge. But I don't mind following Josheb's lead. His plans work. Most of the time.*

Josheb held out both hands and said, "*I'm* not the one decorated with God's handwriting. And I've never met this king the Captain's pining for. But I make myself useful.

When Benaiah the First tells me what needs to be done, I figure out a way to make it happen."

"I see."

"And you're going to be just as useful to him," Josheb continued. "Keeping him honest."

Ben bristled. "I wouldn't lie."

Eleazar folded his middle set of arms over his chest. "He spoke in jest, implying that the opposite would be true."

Oh, I get it. Scratching under the edge of his turban, Ben said, "Others will try to lie to David. But we can set things straight."

"*If* he trusts your word above all others," said Eleazar.

Benaiah confidently replied, "That's the idea. So let's go."

The line of children winding up from the riverbank caused a stir as field workers spotted them. Many of the girls remembered their homes, and they talked excitedly. Some ran ahead. A few pulled at Benaiah's hands, begging him to hurry.

"What are they chattering on about?" asked Josheb.

"Girly stuff, mostly. And reminders that I owe them a story." With a bewildered glance at his bodyguard, Ben said, "I can't tell if they're more excited about their mothers or Moses."

Josheb's gaze locked onto the village men, several of whom carried farm implements. "Let's hope they put in a good word for you."

"Try not to look threatening."

"Impossible. Most of them are half our size." Still, Josheb shouldered his spear and let his hand rest limp over its haft.

Benaiah raised his voice. "Sorry for the intrusion. Don't be afraid." Looking from face to face, he tried to guess at their intentions. Clearing his throat, he added, "We brought back your daughters. You can keep them."

From hut doors, startled cries were soon followed by joyous calls. Mothers reclaimed their daughters with laughter and tears. The young woman Benaiah and Josheb had seen married a few days ago ran over, and the little girls quickly surrounded her. *Time to get out of here.*

'Wait.'

In the midst of the din, Ben caught mutterings about the river god's wrath. Fears for their future, their harvest, their homes. *Guess I gotta set them straight. But ... how?*

"You promised!" exclaimed a little girl he hadn't realized he was ignoring.

Ben looked down at the child tugging at his sleeve, then knelt. "Yeah, kid. I promised to get you home. And here you are."

"A story," she corrected. "More of the story about God and his man."

A nearby girl pleaded, "Tell us a story? Tevy said you would."

As more of Eleazar's little ones joined the call, an old man with a drooping moustache stepped forward. He seemed to be in charge. And he was definitely worried. "We have always honored our god. Have we displeased him?"

Obeying God's prompting, Ben asked, "Would you allow this traveler to speak? There's a story you all should hear."

They led him to the village center and made a bench for him under a spreading tree. The people left their fields and fires. Standing in small groups, they swapped worries.

Benaiah had heard it all before. Pale stranger. Queer eyes. Bad omen. But Eleazar's girls ignored the rumors and sat in a ring around him. And as Ben spoke, the story drew in more. By the time Moses was placed in a basket in the river, Benaiah had everyone's attention. Including Josheb's.

So Benaiah told them about a man who heard the voice of the one true God. When he talked about a bush that burned without being consumed, the little ones nodded wisely and whispered Ember's name. When Ben reached the plagues, the people gasped in awe. And when he reached the part about God leading His children home, men and women wept for joy.

Stopping there, Ben said, "I serve the one true God. I bring a message from Him. Don't go back to the temple. God has called down a plague upon the false god who lives there."

The girls nodded happily, but the elders worried. What kind of plague would God send? Frogs? Fleas? Darkness?

Benaiah stood and joined Josheb, who waited beside the path that would take them into battle. "Us," he answered. "God Sent us."

"The savior who tells stories," Josheb said as he jogged upstream.

"Actually, they think we're an unnatural disaster sent to take out a false god." Ben tried to change the subject. "Can't you go any faster?"

"Yes, but if you try to match my best speed, you'll be worthless once we get there. And I want you able to fight." With a backward glance, Josheb added, "At least you're outrunning the flies."

The storytelling had taken hours, and the women of the village had insisted on feeding them. *Felt like they were appeasing us in place of their old god. But that fish was good. Coulda eaten twice as much, but the day's almost gone.* Benaiah wiped his hands on his shirtfront and said, "Do you think they succeeded?"

"No. Othniel would have found us if it was over."

Josheb's plan for dealing with the river god was captivity.

He's sleeping in a pool of water. If Shammah can get close enough to freeze it, that'll hold him. At least until Aleff comes for us. Not the most detailed plan. But if it works, it'll save us a real headache.

All of the sudden, the earth shook. Josheb slammed on the brakes and shoved Benaiah behind him. "Swords out," he ordered.

Ben obeyed, but he whispered, "Didn't that come from the temple? We should get over there."

"Yes, but there's something between *there* and *here*." Filmy winglets spun away from Josheb's arms and back. "I thought Othniel said the jungle was emptied."

"Missed one?"

Two daggers flashed out of the shadows to collide with Josheb's green shielding. They fell harmlessly to the ground, and he scooped one up and flung it back. "Yes. One. Which means he's outnumbered."

Ben glimpsed the dark figure who dodged. "Crud. It had to be him."

Josheb immediately caught on. "Sly thing." Raising his voice, he called, "Where were you when the rest of the Fallen were taken out?"

"Safe." Hafiz glided into the open and smiled disarmingly. "Where are the little ones? I couldn't find them."

"Not with us," Josheb said, not taking his eyes from the demon as he crouched to pick up the second dagger. It was black and barbed. A nasty piece of workmanship.

Hafiz looked back the way they'd come. "Is my Tevy in the village?"

"No," Benaiah replied.

Her former guardian angel stepped closer. "Where have you hidden her?"

Ben scowled. "We didn't. She's with Eleazar."

"Where is he?"

Another huge crash rocked the ground underfoot. Birds screamed and scattered, leaving the jungle in silence. Josheb hurled the demon's dagger into the ground at his feet. "You're in our way."

Hafiz's brows drew down. "Why would you go back into

a God-forsaken hole where death awaits?"

"Sent," replied Benaiah.

The Fallen reclaimed and sheathed the dagger. He carried four altogether. "The sons rebel against their fathers?" Hafiz's voice sharpened. "Is that where she's gone? Into his darkness?"

Ben didn't need to answer. The demon knew, and knowing twisted his face with fury and fear. Without another word, he rushed off, leaping ahead of them along the riverside path.

Muttering an oath, Josheb snapped, "Run!"

Trust wasn't easy for me.
But not because anyone
had broken faith with me.
That would come later.
In the beginning, it was
simpler. I distrusted people
because they distrusted me.
Given and gotten.
Like for like.
It was a lonely way to live.

40

Leave no stone unturned.

While they tore along the path, Josheb demanded, "Why'd you answer him? Are malakim always honest?"

Okay, maybe it wasn't the smartest thing to just tell Hafiz where Tevy went. Benaiah scowled. "It's not my order. It's me. I won't be a liar."

"Even to protect someone with their name under your hand?"

"No," Ben replied stubbornly. *Words aren't meant for treachery. Where there are lies, trust withers and dies.*

Josheb asked, "Would you lie if David ordered you to?"

Benaiah's pace slackened. Was it possible for a situation to arise that would force him to choose between his God and his king? "I don't think I could."

"Good to know," Josheb said. "How about this? If you find yourself in a tricky position, you can delegate your lies to me."

A brief surge of relief quickly fizzled. "No. The Fallen are deceivers, and we're staying Faithful. No lies."

As the temple came into view around the last bend, Josheb asked, "Is that an order, Captain?"

"Yeah. Tell the truth."

"Can I be creative about how I say what needs to be said?" he pressed.

Ben slowed to a stop beside his teammate and braced his hands on his knees, winded from their fruitless chase. "Is honesty that much of a problem for you?" he asked in frustration.

"Think about it, Captain. Tact. Diplomacy. Keeping the secret of who sired us," Josheb said, holding his gaze. "Or are you planning to tell your king that we're demon spawn?"

"Didn't think of that," Benaiah admitted. *Is keeping a secret the same as telling a lie? Crud, I wish Aleff was here.* Shaking his head, he admitted, "I'm not sure what I'm supposed to do."

"Let's start with finding some light. Sun's setting, and thanks to us, nobody's home to spark the torches."

Except there's sounds coming from inside. Ben whispered, "Did you hear that?"

"Yes." Spear in hand, Josheb slunk up to the temple entrance. "Okay, not *nobody*. The priest's still here. And Ember mentioned women."

"How many?"

Josheb was on the move again. Thick shadows swallowed all but his answer. "Let's find out."

They didn't have far to go. Torchlight flickered faintly against passage walls leading into the central chamber with its shackled pedestal. Ben counted four torches in brackets, enough to give them a dim view. "Back there. By the curtains."

"I see them. And they see us." Josheb's eyes narrowed. "They're not much of a Hedge, but maybe they're all he has left to throw at us."

"Let's go. We need to get past them." Benaiah's gaze darted from face to face as they slowly approached this new obstacle. They were women. They were beautiful. And their eyes gleamed orange in the firelight. *The river god's possessing them. Or at the very least, using them as eyes and ears.* "He must have kept the girls who were most receptive. Are they armed?"

"Doesn't matter." Josheb took the time to strap his spear to his back. "I won't kill a woman because her will was weak. But be careful."

Without a word, Benaiah sheathed his blades.

The temple women swayed forward and danced around them. Catching at sleeves. Tugging on hands. Pressing close, they made their offers. "Stay with me. I could be yours."

Painted faces. Pouting lips. Ben had no idea how to deal with their overtures.

"You want me," they said in lilting voices. "Don't be shy!"

Clinging hands. Blank eyes. Close quarters. They were just as eager to waylay Josheb, and even with the language barrier, he knew what they must be saying. The half-cherub picked one woman up and set her aside, saying, "Sorry, pretty one, but this isn't the time."

"Hey, watch where you're putting your hands!" Benaiah bumped aside one woman and pushed through the gap made by her removal. No way was he holding still!

Josheb was making decent progress, chatting all the while. "You're a lovely lady! As much as I'd like to choose one of you, I have a job to do."

"Are you flirting?" Ben grumbled.

The rider kept right on sweet-talking the women he passed. "Delicate as a flower. And such soft hair! I'm busy at the moment, but keep me in mind."

Benaiah wasn't sure what else to do, so he apologized to the next woman he pushed aside. "Look, lady. I'm not interested. But try to shake loose from the bad stuff."

Josheb seized onto that and added similar urges to his running comments. "Don't listen to that voice, little one. He's trouble. And we're help."

"Sorry," Ben said over and again. "I'm not the one you want or need. Let us through."

Another earthquake sent them stumbling, and Josheb broke free. Grabbing one of the torches, he took off for the stairway at the end of the passage. "Coming?" he called.

Ben twisted past the last few women and jogged after Josheb, whose boots beat a sharp staccato down to the lower levels. They burst into the chamber from Benaiah's nightmare. He blinked several times before he realized that the cavernous space wasn't lit by torches. *Half the ceiling's gone.* Dust rose from collapsed stones at the far end of the sprawling room. Light from the rising moon glinted across the rippling pool at the center.

"What just happened?" Ben whispered.

Othniel's golden wings exploded into view as the Guardian charged across the rock-strewn floor, arms wide as he shouted, "Stay back!"

Benaiah drew his swords as Othniel's wings deflected a thrown chunk of masonry. From the deepest shadows beyond the destruction, Ben could hear breathing—harsh and heavy. Things hadn't gone according to plan.

A closer look at the pool in the center of the chamber confirmed it. *Water level's lower.* And what ice fringed the surface had shattered. Chunks and shards of it were strewn across the ground on the far side of the pool. Their enemy was on the loose. And even if he was only armed with rocks, there were plenty lying around.

"Who took out the ceiling?" asked Josheb.

Othniel replied, "The Fallen seraph grew tired of stooping."

"Big fella?"

Othniel grunted an affirmative as he took up a defensive stance.

Ben asked, "Where's Shammah?"

"Not far. And not well." With a small shake of his head, Othniel explained, "We have learned that he cannot heal himself."

"Eleazar? Tevy?" Benaiah checked, straining his senses. At the very least, he'd expected to spot Eliel's wings.

"I have not seen them since the collapse." Othniel's explanation was delivered in short bursts of information.

"There are several entrances. Passages honeycomb away from here. The architect was no fool. Escape routes abound. Tevy knows them all."

Stone scraped against stone, and another rock hurtled at them from the shadows. Josheb loosed his spear and unfurled his winglets, muttering, "Is it just me, or are you catching a draft?"

Pockets of chill air met their careful progress along the room's edge. Benaiah wished he could see where Shammah was, especially if he was hurt. But before they encountered their giant, a deep voice echoed through the darkness. "Part like water. Bend like reeds. Yield to me, ignorant boy, and I will teach you what it means to Fall."

Ben froze, his thoughts running in frantic circles. Was it possible for Eleazar's father to swarm into his head and possess him? *This was our trap. But it feels like* my *foot's in the snare.*

The planes of Othniel's face hardened. "Benaiah, leave. Get to Eleazar. *Now.*"

And he would have. But Ben's feet wouldn't budge. Rooted to the spot, he watched his foe loom out of the shadows. Dark skin sagged in waterlogged wrinkles from a giant's frame. This self-made god was easily as tall as Shammah's full height. There were hints that he might have been regal once. But now, this guy's most impressive feature was a nauseating stench.

With a strangled noise of disgust, Josheb pinched his nose. "Carrion walking."

For a few blessed moments, baleful orange eyes swiveled to the spearman. Benaiah gasped for air, glad to be out from under the weight of the demon's gaze. *He's powerful. And ugly.* But insults didn't change something important. Their enemy was pleased.

The river god's words resonated through Ben's numb mind. *"Fair as summer, cheerful as springtime. You will bring me even greater pleasures than your father."*

Fear curled in Ben's gut. *He knows.*

"I know who you are ... what you are." The gloating voice was hard and harsh. Impossible to ignore. *"You are the gift in my hand. And my fingers are closing around you."*

Josheb's slap knocked Ben off balance, but the rider grabbed him by the shoulder, steadying him. He snapped, "Shammah needs me. But I'm not going to him without you. Are you with me?"

"Not sure."

"Can you think straight?"

Benaiah hesitated, then shook his head.

Muttering a few choice words, the half-cherub switched gears. "If we can't bar the door, we have to hunt the beast." Catching Othniel's attention, Josheb said, "New plan. Bash its head in before it gets into the captain's."

The Guardian nodded once, then blazed across the room, bright as a star. Their enemy flinched away from the light, then dodged his attacker's sword. And with the break in his concentration, Benaiah's head cleared.

"Good?" demanded Josheb.

"Yeah."

"Then we're gone." Josheb raced in a wide arc to the other side of the room where Shammah stood, one arm hanging limp at his side.

I should follow. Stick together. Eyes on his men, Benaiah started walking. But his steps were sluggish. It was like trying to walk through soft sand. Or the frustrating slowness of running from the monsters that lurk in nightmares. *Is this a dream? I can't tell. That's bad. I should know my own mind.*

Josheb took hold of Shammah, who shouted in pain when his teammate popped a dislocated shoulder back into place.

Dragging steps finally caught up, and Benaiah reached out. Shammah's fingertips met his, and their ice zinged through him, finishing the work Josheb's slap had begun.

Ben asked, "You okay?"

Shammah rotated his arm, but quickly shrugged off his own aches and pains. Maybe because he couldn't do anything about them. Touching the side of Benaiah's face where reddened skin still stung, he stared hard at Josheb. "You struck him."

"I didn't like the color of his eyes."

Glancing from Benaiah to the demon, Shammah asked, "Possession?"

"Without Eleazar, the captain's vulnerable," Josheb confirmed.

Shammah drew himself up. "What do I do?"

"Distract it," Josheb replied, readying his spear. "If you can't get a hand on it, maybe drive it into that pond."

The temperature plunged around them, and Shammah

quietly said, "Step back."

As their giant rushed to his full height, Ben and Josheb hustled out from underfoot.

Robes flashing. Hair whipping. Gaze locked. Benaiah wondered if the river god knew he was marked for death. *Or the closest thing to it.* Judging by the cold fury rolling off Shammah, he was due for a very messy dismemberment.

I thought that
in order to be
a leader, someone
had to be the strongest,
wisest, and best.
But there I was,
proving myself weak,
stupid, and helpless.
The more I messed up,
the closer my men
watched me. So they
knew better than anyone
how often some
crazy miracle hauled us
out of trouble.
They trusted me.
But we relied on God.

41

Terrible things happen in the dark.

Shammah didn't rush his opponent. Even when the demon flung stones at him, he kept a steady pace. His calm in the face of fresh battle was a terrible thing. Confident. Contemptuous. And more intimidating than Benaiah wanted to admit. He didn't realize he was backing up until a wall put an end to his retreat. *Should I be afraid of my own men?*

Ben would have been more embarrassed if Josheb wasn't right there at his side. But the rider's expression hollered, "show me what you've got." And he looked ready to fly into the fray if his teammate needed backup.

He's happy. This is what he waited for. Craved. But me? Benaiah couldn't match Josheb's enthusiasm. The hand that held six names tightened around the hilt of his sword. *But I'll fight for him. Just like I'll fight for David. Even if I'm stained with blood. Even though I'll have to live with the scars.*

While Shammah's footfalls shook the ground, Ben

grappled with a sudden pressure inside his head. The river god's voice boomed through the chamber. "And the sons of God saw the daughters of men, that they were beautiful."

Benaiah automatically finished the sentence. *And they took wives for themselves of all whom they chose.*

The demon's fiery gaze drilled into Ben's head as he spoke. "You are not supposed to *be*. How many others harbored forbidden heirs?"

Josheb's warning look wasn't necessary. Benaiah bit his tongue. *You're getting nothing out of me.*

Again, the voice reverberated against his skull. A pleased chuckle, rich with approval. Possessive. *"Where did Sin cloister you, fair one? Are you harem-bred? Did he train you well?"*

Ben slammed his head against the wall behind him. Once. Twice. It didn't hurt as much as it might have. His turban cushioned the blow. But his struggle caught Josheb's attention.

"Othniel!" he roared. "The captain's in danger!"

"Get out, get out, get out," muttered Benaiah, dropping his swords in order to push his knuckles against his temples.

Josheb caught his hands and growled, "Braining yourself isn't helping. Where's Ember?"

Benaiah tried to focus on his teammate's face, but his eyes were crossing. His mouth was too dry to form words, but his soul cried out. *God? I can't ... I need ...* All he could think to ask for was Aleff, but his caretaker was worlds away.

"Which way? I'll carry you if I have to!"

He shook his head.

"Not Sent?" Josheb muttered. "What else is there?"

With a huge effort, he croaked out, "Hit me."

The slap took him by surprise. Josheb's pleased smirk didn't. His teammate cheerfully asked, "Again?"

When Ben hesitated, he earned a stinging crack across the other cheek. "Crud, that hurts! Enough already!"

"Just trying to help, Captain."

Benaiah touched his reddening cheek. *Guess I should be grateful he didn't use fists.*

The earth shivered underfoot, then bucked. Josheb used his spear to steady himself. In the lull that followed, he whispered, "Do you hear that?"

Benaiah's head had cleared enough to catch the slurp and gurgle of water. His gaze swung to the pool in the center of the chamber, which was brimming again. Water welled up and over its edges, spreading in every direction along the floor. Moonlight quivered across it surface, which rippled with a new tremor.

"The river?" Ben whispered.

Suddenly, one of Tevy's chakram glittered past, ricocheting off the ceiling with a ringing note.

Josheb craned his neck, then reported, "Eliel's with Tevy. I don't see Ember."

While Benaiah followed his gaze, he touched thumb to the tip of his little finger. The one that bore her name. *Even Tevy is scary.* But there, Ben's conscience twinged. She unsettled him for an entirely different reason than the other guys. A very human reason.

The young woman stood on the far side of the chamber, partially shielded from view by Eliel's wings, which were crimson, shot through with magenta filaments. While Tevy's weapons whirled, the lean archer loosed enough arrows to force their opponent to find cover. Othniel fell back, circling around to check on the influx of water.

From the shadows, the river god mocked. "Do you think to trap me here, in a refuge of my own making?"

Shammah didn't answer with words. He simply reached up with one hand and pushed. Stone crumbled around him, opening a wider gap in what was left of the ceiling. Cracks appeared in the floor, and water burst through with a roar.

Ben backed up. *At this rate, there won't be much of a refuge left.*

Someone tugged at his sleeve, and Benaiah jumped. An instant later, Hafiz was staring cross-eyed at the point of Josheb's spear. The demon tipped his head to one side and offered open palms. "Not so hasty, horseman. I want to help. I can take this boy to Ember."

Josheb's weapon didn't waver. "Why would you do that?"

Hafiz's gaze drifted toward Tevy. "My angel is impetuous. Protect her, and I will guard him." In an undertone, the demon added, "Two Guardians is better."

The tug of Sending made up Benaiah's mind for him. "Yeah." He turned to Josheb to explain, "That's the way it's gonna be."

Shouldering his spear, Josheb turned on his heel and strode away.

Wonder if that means he approves of the strategy. Or if he's sick of babysitting his captain.

Hafiz slid an arm around Benaiah's shoulder. "Away, before they notice."

"They *who*?" he countered, shrugging free and collecting his blades. "The god … or your mentor? Did you know Eliel is twice-pierced?"

"He was my friend. He is my enemy."

There was a hollowness to the Fallen Guardian's voice that Benaiah thought he could understand. *This guy doesn't fit in. He lost everything I gained. And he has to know that if he'd waited like all the other Guardians … crud. It's sad.*

Hafiz said, "Your pity is an opening through which a blade might slip."

Benaiah frowned at the warning. If this demon wanted to hurt him, why would he tell him not to drop his guard. Rolling his eyes, he said, "I'd trust you more if you stank less."

"Wise."

"You screwed up, but Tevy still matters to you." Ben eased further away from his guide, carefully sheathing his swords. "You'll leave me be for her sake."

Hafiz bared his teeth, and menace rang through his question. "You want her?"

"Not like that, idiot." Holding out his hand, Benaiah said, "Look."

The demon pawed at Ben's fingers until he found Tevy's name. His touch was light as a feather as he trailed one fingertip across the letters. "She was mine first. My Tevy, my angel, my life, my death." With mournful eyes, Hafiz whispered, "I died for her sake. Is that not love?"

"It was disobedience. Or didn't you notice that you Fell?"

Hafiz sneered.

"Like you said, two is better." Flexing his fingers, Ben said, "God made her my responsibility. Mine and Eliel's. We'll keep her safe for you. And from you."

With a hoarse chuckle, Hafiz said, "You can try."

Benaiah glanced back into the chamber, where Shammah stood in the middle of a churning whirlpool. His opponent had clambered out of reach, crouching on the upper stoneworks. The river god was a black shadow against the starry sky, breaking free more stones and pitching them into Shammah's maelstrom.

"He's going to bring down the building."

As if aware of Ben's remark, the big demon sought his gaze. A low laugh echoed through his thoughts, and the whispers began anew. Gloating over his victory. Reveling in the prospect of possession. Promising endless delights they would savor in tandem.

Benaiah swayed. Hafiz hissed blasphemies. The ground lurched anew, sloshing water around their ankles. And large hands clamped around Ben's shoulders.

How do you finish a battle
against an enemy
you can't kill?
Josheb was always quick
to quote our best options—
surrender, captivity, or
dismemberment. But the
real answer is ... you don't.
Because demons have
this nasty habit
of returning. Usually at
the worst possible moment.

42

Bad can lead straight to worse.

Hafiz ducked behind Benaiah. "We have an agreement! An alliance!"

With a wash of golden light, a wing cut between Hafiz and his half-human shield. Othniel corrected, "You are an enemy."

"Sent," Ben muttered. "He knows where Eleazar is."

"I am also Sent. We go together." To Hafiz, Othniel said, "Quickly."

Benaiah was grateful the Guardian didn't just pick him up, but the hand under his arm kept him from toppling over when the temple quaked around them.

Hafiz shuffled along backward, distrustful of Othniel's arsenal. "I meant no harm," he wheedled. "The boy trusted me."

Othniel's grunt sounded disapproving. "This *boy*'s name is under my hand. You know what that means."

"Too well." Turning, Hafiz sprang lightly up a flight of stairs.

They slogged after him. Ben was glad to be out of the rising water, which smelled of raw mud and rotting vegetation. His feet slipped on the stone stairs, but Othniel braced him until they reached the sections scattered with rugs. Hafiz ran without pause, forcing his companions to chase him all the way to the temple's front entrance. There, Benaiah finally caught sight of Eleazar, whose uppermost arm was raised in farewell.

Firelight on water. A procession of women, most carrying lamps or torches. *He must have emptied the temple leader's harem.*

At the sound of their approach, the six-armed man turned in time to catch his captain mid-sprawl. Too drained for more, Ben hung limply, leaving the explanations to Othniel. But Eleazar understood all too well. "You should have stayed away until my father's captivity was assured."

"Was worried about my own."

"True."

Eleazar hauled him upright and scrutinized his face. Benaiah wondered how two pairs of orange eyes could be so different. Which made him wonder if his eyes were different than his father's.

"Very," replied the half-seraph. "Now help me unfurl these stubborn wings."

Nodding, Ben rested his palm against the young man's bare chest. Flaming feathers closed around them. The oppressive shadow cast by Eleazar's father vanished. "This is better than possession. Thanks for sheltering me."

"It would be better for you to strengthen your mind." Displaying six empty hands, Eleazar pointed out, "You cower beneath my wings, preventing me from taking part in the battle."

"Yeah." Ben fiddled with the knots of his turban, tucking and tightening. "Yeah, this is lame. Can you teach me?"

"I'm no Messenger."

"And I'm not much of one." Benaiah scowled. "But I'm sick of being overrun by his filth."

From outside the barrier of feathers, Othniel called, "It is falling!"

Eleazar drew back his wings. They furled neatly against his skin, and they watched Othniel streak away. The temple's stones gleamed in the moonlight, as if coated in ice. A din came from somewhere below, and then the lofty tiers buckled inward. While Othniel swooped down, scarlet wings burst upward.

"Eliel has Tevy," reported Eleazar.

Othniel reappeared, rising slowly with powerful wingbeats. Once he was nearer, Benaiah was able to see what was weighing him down. The big warrior grasped Josheb's spear in both hands, and the rider hung from it. Shammah emerged last, scrabbling up over the rubble. Water trickled between upended stones, washing toward the river. The diminishing giant's bare feet sloshed through increasingly muddy tracts, but his clothes remained spotless. By the time Shammah reached them, his height matched Eleazar's.

And Josheb's. He dropped before Othniel landed, his boots

splattering mud in all directions. Benaiah wiped at his cheek with the back of his sleeve. "Did you dismember the guy?"

"Captivity," said Josheb. "The false god's half-iced. And now he's half-buried under rocks. And no, we shouldn't be doing things by halves. But Guardians are touchy about safety."

"He will only be delayed," Shammah warned.

"We have created an opening." Gripping Ben's arm, Josheb asked, "Any chance you can get a message to Aleff?"

Can I do that? Rubbing his thumb over the name emblazoned on his palm, Benaiah hoped for one of his caretaker's grand entrances.

Eliel stepped forward. "As it happens, *I* am Sent. Follow me."

"It happens that way?" Ben asked.

Othniel returned Josheb's spear, then drew his sword. "Yes. Any within a Flight might know the way."

Eliel furled his wings and touched Tevy's arm. The young woman started, and Eliel spoke gently. "Follow me, please. Upstream."

Benaiah grabbed Othniel's arm and quietly asked, "Does that mean Eliel's one of my men? Angels? Whatever."

Steering him toward the path the others were already hurrying along, the big warrior said, "Run now. Check your fingers and toes later."

They jogged along the riverbank. The moon offered some light, but heavenly things were much more useful for marking the trail. Luminous wings. Shining raiment. Recalling his littlest responsibilities, Benaiah asked, "Who has Neri and Pazi?"

Othniel strode along behind him, wings outstretched to shield their retreat. "With Eliel's help, Shammah spoke to Tevy. They have been hiding in her hair."

Sounds safe. Benaiah couldn't see the young woman up ahead. Their pace must have been set with her in mind. *It'd be quicker if Eliel carried her. Then again, we could probably travel faster if Othniel carried me. And there's no way.* Ben let God know how much it meant to have some scrap of his dignity still intact.

He tapped his little finger with his thumb. A girl. Why would God put Tevy into his hand? He didn't understand girls. *At least, not the way David does.* The future king of Israel was good at attracting female attention. Like Abi's. And Hino's. Ben scowled. Women complicated things. Would Tevy?

"Your thoughts linger on her. She can be our first conquest."

Benaiah stopped in his tracks.

Othniel drew up behind him. "What?"

"I heard ...." he began, but his voice trailed off as the dark murmurs gained strength. "We're being followed."

"Eleazar!" bellowed Othniel.

Everyone halted on the narrow trail between river and jungle, and Eleazar shouldered his way past Josheb and Shammah. His eyes caught the light from Othniel's wings so they seemed to flicker. With suspicion.

Eleazar guessed, "He has freed himself."

"Yeah," said Benaiah. "He's coming."

Eliel pointed confidently to the opposite bank. "Cross here."

Ben stared across the shining strip of water and the blackness of jungle beyond. He remembered what it was like, seeing the path bright before his eyes. Why wasn't the Sending *his* this time? *Not sure I like having someone else doing the seeing for me.* Benaiah found himself equally uneasy trusting someone else right when he was in the worst possible danger. *Can't I have a little more to go on?*

But his prayers met with silence from heaven. And hellish promises from their enemy.

While Eliel soared across the river with Tevy, Shammah resumed his full size. Dropping to one knee, he offered Josheb nested hands.

"You want to throw me over?" asked Josheb.

"Yes."

"I like the way you think!" He set one foot in their giant's hold, and Shammah straightened, flinging his teammate high into the night sky. Josheb whooped, and his laughter accompanied a lazy spiral to the spot where Eliel and Tevy waited. After his feet hit the ground, Josheb called, "We'll be practicing that move again, runt!"

Shammah waded into the flow but hesitated midstream. "Do you need me?" he asked, offering his hand to Benaiah.

"Go. Othniel can get me across."

Crashes came from the direction of the temple. Broken

limbs. Toppled trees. Othniel stood calmly, his head cocked to one side as he listened. Turning to Eleazar, the Guardian asked, "Are you running from your father?"

Eleazar shook his head. "I'm choosing a better path."

Othniel nodded. "And do you want to fight him here?"

"No."

Shaggy eyebrows lifted inquiringly. "Why not?"

Eleazar's vague gesture put all six of his hands into motion. "My father set himself against God, and he was banished from heaven's courts, never to see His face again. I've set myself against that god." With a grim shake of his head, he concluded, "I never want to see his face again."

Othniel eyed Benaiah. "What about you, Captain? Are you Sent to face this Fallen?"

"No."

"Neither am I," said Othniel. "You two cross over and keep moving. I am your rear guard."

"Fine by me," Benaiah replied, wading out after Eleazar.

They were hip deep in the lazy river when the six-armed man turned in place and drew four of his curved daggers. "Something swam past my leg."

"Big?" Ben whispered, senses taut for signs of danger.

Eleazar turned in place, lifting his voice. "Shammah, we need you!"

A gust of cold air sent a chill up and down Benaiah's spine, and the river exploded into foam. He had a fleeting glimpse of gaping jaws before they clamped down and pushed him under.

When you see someone's
second face for the first time,
it can be confusing. Do you
believe what they want to be,
or do you believe what they
try to hide? And when someone
knows their worst is exposed,
they're afraid of what you think.
Maybe that's why they
turn on you. Because
they can't face you.

43

Only a fool would Fall.

Water closed over Benaiah, filling his nose and ears. He pushed and pulled at the crocodile that was crushing the air from his lungs. The brute swam swiftly with the current. Deeper. Downstream. Away from the direction Eliel had been leading. Ben tried to fight, but the vice tightened around his chest, ripping into his flesh, creaking his bones. It hurt. Bad.

What happens to me if I die?

God answered immediately. *'You are Mine.'*

But if Ben died here, his promise to David would be broken. Had everything been for nothing?

'Do you trust Me?'

The crocodile began to roll, twisting around his prey. Dizzy and desperate for air, Benaiah couldn't figure out how to answer. *Stupid question. I gotta. No choice.*

'None?'

Ben was sort of offended. He'd rather die than Fall. The

last of the air left his lungs in a whine. *I don't understand. But I don't gotta. I'm yours. And I'm scared!* He grit his teeth and let his heart wail a wordless plea for rescue.

'Fear not, child of light. I am with you.'

Benaiah's lungs were on fire, and then the water turned to flames. Light dazzled him. Shadows reached for him. Pain seared across his chest. Once. Twice. The crocodile thrashed, wrenching Ben's sluggish limbs. His turban must have gone missing because hair swirled around his head. Through the confusion lanced another set of slashes. Between the teeth and the tugging, Ben was sure he'd be ripped to shreds.

The crocodile's hold slipped, and hands found purchase under Benaiah's arms, hauling him out of its maw. Ears ringing. Consciousness dwindling. Maybe he was too far gone to care. Why else would his fear have vanished?

And suddenly, the water was gone. Ben's head was too fuzzed to deal with the return of air, but the rest of him wanted to survive. He gurgled and choked, dragging in short gasps. Hands thumped his back, and he gagged, vomiting river water all over Eleazar's shoulder.

Limbs shaking. Eyes streaming. Hair plastered across his face. Ben was hacking too badly to say thanks or sorry. So he clung to Eleazar, trusting the half-seraph to see the miracle through. Flame-hued feathers dragged behind them in the water, which meant their Ember had figured out how to unfurl.

Ben mumbled, "On yer own."

"No one else can swim."

Josheb was shouting from somewhere nearby, but the words made no sense. Benaiah shivered and wondered why it was so cold. "I m-must look pit'ful t' you."

Eleazar's dragged him up onto the riverbank without answering. Instead, he asked, "Does my opinion matter?"

"Yeah. S'honest." Words turned to mush in Ben's mouth. "Me'n you's … truss. Frenz, m-maybe. F'want."

The other young man avoided his gaze. Pulling at Benaiah's robes, he lifted his wings high to shed more light. His expression was far from reassuring when he asked, "Does it hurt?"

"C-cold," Ben whispered, reaching for his rescuer. Eleazar caught his hand. His was so warm. Alive.

Josheb burst into his line of sight, and muttered an oath. "Still with us, Captain?"

Breathing hurt, but he *was* breathing. Ben confessed, "Can' swim … neither."

With a reassuring smirk, Josheb looked him over, then glanced up sharply. "You cut him?"

"Inadvertently." Eleazar shrugged and said, "He was between me and the creature."

"He's losing too much blood."

"Agreed."

Hands pressed over Benaiah's chest, and the creeping chill turned to molten pain. With a garbled cry of protest, Ben begged for mercy, but they didn't let up.

Josheb hollered, "Stop icing crocodiles and get over here, runt! He's bleeding out!"

Shammah sloshed over and hoisted Benaiah high into his arms. Ben struggled feebly, but his strength was at its end. The world was moving. He was being carried upstream. Back on course. Cradled against the giant's chest, he demanded, "S'this r'venge?" At Shammah's confused glance, he slurred, "M'not a child."

Understanding dawned, and Shammah offered a bemused headshake. "No, brother. This is not revenge. It is reunion."

Shammah's words made little sense to Benaiah's addled brain. *Reunion? Time to go back?* As much as he wanted to return to his friend, he didn't want David seeing him like this. *He'll think I still can't fend.* Shifting uneasily, he muttered, "S'gonna c-call me prey."

"Rest easy," Shammah said in low tones. "Your help has come. He arrived like a flash of lightning. Sent us after you."

"'Rived?" Benaiah echoed, wincing when the giant checked his stride.

"Done dredging the river?" called a familiar voice. "Did you fish out anything worth keeping?"

Aleff! More than anyone, Benaiah had wanted his *one*. Shammah sat on the riverbank, and Ben caught sight of raiment gleaming in the darkness. Not one, but two Caretakers stood ready to receive him. Aleff and the nameless angel with ropes of purple hair. "T-two?"

Gently lifting aside blood-sopped clothing, Aleff asked, "Seeing double?"

Benaiah meant to scowl, but a whisper slipped neatly into his mind. *"He cannot take you away. You are mine to pluck."*

The river god was still tracking them? *Where are Josheb … Eleazar … Tevy?* Ben snagged Aleff's sleeve and tried to explain that their Flight was in danger. But breathing hurt, and words were hard to form. "Liss'n," he begged.

Aleff's hands stilled, and his gaze locked with Benaiah's. "Hearing things?"

Ben pushed a bubble of panic at the angel who'd raised him. Jumbled explanations. Haunting words. Tangled histories. Lurking threats. Terrible plans.

All the laughter left Aleff's eyes, and he whispered, "Is that so? And my old friend taught him the trick of it?"

The nameless Caretaker inquired, "Are you Sent?"

"Like a fast ball over home plate. High and inside." Aleff pressed a kiss to Benaiah's forehead and said, "Root for the home team, and it'll be a cracker-jack finish."

Despite Aleff's usual joking tone, something was different. And frightening. The Caretaker's sleeve slipped from Ben's fingers, and he strode away, growing larger with every step. Aleff seemed to wade into the jungle, copper hair trailing through the trees behind him.

Shammah spoke to his former babysitter. "Why are you here?"

"To help keep you in check."

Surprise flickered across his thin face. "Is this my battle as well?"

"Yes."

With a sidelong look in Aleff's direction, Shammah said, "He is capable."

The Caretaker shook his head. "He will need you all the same."

Shammah nodded, then sought Ben's gaze. "May I go to Aleff?"

"G'wan." Ben tried for an offhand wave, but the limp flap couldn't have been very convincing.

"I will tend to your captain," offered the nameless angel. He matched Shammah's size in order to ease the transfer. At the half-Caretaker's hesitation, he added, "I will ease Benaiah's suffering. You will end his danger. Fight for him."

Without another word, the hand-off was made, and Shammah left. Ben stared into the face of the one who could save his life … or end it. *I didn't like this guy. I don't know this guy. But my life's in his hands.*

The purple-haired angel radiated calm. As he set to work, he sang a distractingly beautiful melody.

"Why're you here?" whispered Ben.

The Caretaker's glance was kind. His touch was balm. For an answer, he raised one finger to his lips, then returned to fussing with torn cloth and flesh. Benaiah made up his mind. *Don't matter if I know this guy or not. God Sent him.* And that was good enough. Maybe even great. Because Ben was warm and dry, and it no longer hurt to breathe.

In a matter of minutes, the ministering angel ebbed back to normal size and helped Benaiah sit up. There on the muddy riverbank, Ben lifted his arms so the Caretaker could bandage his chest. With fingers that no longer shook, he touched the shimmering gauze. *Glows like raiment.* The stuff of heaven, snugly wrapped around the ravages of earth.

Benaiah's thoughts formed without effort now, and they

made it past his lips intact. "Why are you holding out on Aleff?"

"Is that what you think?"

"Well, yeah. It's like you *know* what's going to happen to him," Ben accused. "Why he'll need Shammah."

"Not at all. The command was God's. The purposes are His. And I am awed by His foresight."

"Planning ahead?"

"We serve the all-knowing One." He brought together two ends of the bandages and knotted them as he continued, "Your need and God's supply have conspired to bring me here. This is my first taste of Time. And night."

Might be strange for someone used to heaven's light. Benaiah gingerly eased his arms back into the sleeves of his mended robes. "Are you scared of the dark?"

"I have been pondering that very thing," replied the Caretaker. "Because I often entered Shammah's cave to tend to his needs, I grew accustomed to darkness. Perhaps God was preparing me for this moment."

Josheb caught up. He skidded to a stop, but Eleazar ran straight past. "Ember will check on his lady and the archer. You're looking less mauled, Captain. How's your head?"

"I think these guys did something. No more voices."

"Something's stirring, though." Gazing off over the jungle, Josheb asked, "Are they fighting?"

"Yes," replied the Caretaker.

Benaiah had been trying *not* to hear things. But now that pain wasn't turning his attention inward, he caught a strange tension in the air. A sharp *pop* interrupted the jungle's deathly still. With a creak and groan, a tree thundered to the ground.

"That's five now." Josheb asked, "Is he pushing those trees over or stepping on them?"

The Caretaker beckoned. "Catch hold, and I will show you."

Once more, Benaiah was gathered up. But it wasn't half bad. Elation thrilled him down to his toes as the nameless angel's stature soared. The rush toward the stars reminded him of flight. Josheb's low laugh followed them, and Ben peered over the edge of the cupped palm supporting him. His teammate dangled just below the Caretaker's shoulder, his hand anchored in roped hair.

A swing, a stretch, and a scramble, and Josheb joined Benaiah in the giant's hand. Pointing at the other two colossal figures ranging through the dense jungle, Josheb said, "Not good."

As soon as Benaiah spotted Aleff and Shammah, he felt the tug of Sending. The nameless Caretaker must have received the same nudge because he started through the trees.

What the crud is going on? Pushing up onto his knees, Ben asked, "Is Shammah fighting Aleff?"

"And where's the river god?"

Benaiah shrank from the rising stench. The river god was close, but where? Shammah uprooted a tree, swinging the ungainly weapon in a dirt-scattering arc. It clipped Aleff's shoulder. When they came closer, Ben could hear Aleff's voice. Not the words exactly. But his tone was low and soothing. *He's holding Shammah back. Or trying to.*

Josheb shook his head. "Nevermind."

"What?"

He nodded downward. "Shouldn't be surprised that a Caretaker made quick work of his opponent."

"Eleazar's father?" Ben asked, dread coiling in his belly.

"What's left of him is underfoot."

A knot loosened somewhere deep down. Benaiah was almost ashamed of the wash of relief that left him limp. *Just like when I was little. Aleff comes rushing in when I cry out. And he makes the nightmares go away. What kind of captain waited to be rescued?*

This time, the God of heaven chose to answer. *'One who has learned to trust.'*

Was God asking him to trust his men more?

'Trust Me.'

Benaiah flinched inwardly. *Thought that's what I was doing. Am I messing things up?*

They came up behind Aleff, who'd matched the young giant's height, and Josheb prodded Ben's shoulder. "Remember what the runt said that time, about not wanting to fight because it's hard to stop? *Look* at him." Voice tight, Josheb said, "If his eyes were orange, I'd say he was possessed."

"Yeah. Not good."

Between the shimmer of raiment and the moon and stars, there was plenty of light to see by. Shammah's face twisted into a wrathful mask. This was different than the icy resolve he'd shown earlier. Something had snapped. A berserker's wildness consumed him, making Shammah a danger to friend as well as foe.

Benaiah tensed. "Can't Aleff stop him?"

"Not if the task is given to another," replied the Caretaker.

"Crud. That'd be me."

Josheb asked, "Got a plan, Captain?"

"I'm open to suggestions."

"If you're going in, make sure Aleff pins his hands. It might keep you from getting iced."

The chill that rippled up Benaiah's spine wasn't a figment of anyone's imagination. Shammah's eyes were dead cold, without a flicker of recognition. *Once he's stirred up, he loses himself, and stuff gets ugly.* This *is what Shammah fears.*

There was a shout from overhead as Othniel arrived on the scene. The big Guardian was forced to swerve when Shammah caught sight of him and threw his weapon. The uprooted tree spun crazily, and Othniel veered out of the way, pulling into a wary spiral that kept him at a safer distance.

"Not much he can do," Benaiah remarked. "He's outmatched, same as us."

"Look again," challenged Josheb. "Shammah's disarmed, and Aleff galloped through the opening Othniel made. You're good to go."

Sure enough. During Shammah's moment of distraction, Aleff had clamped his hands around the unruly young giant's wrists. Their ride eased closer, and Benaiah could hear Aleff trying to talk sense.

"Easy, young man. Let's take a time out. Give you a chance

to catch your breath, clear your head, rinse your feet …."

Benaiah called, "I'm here!"

"You shouldn't be," Aleff retorted, his voice still pitched in soothing tones. "You've barely recovered from your last brush with death."

"Tough. Sent."

"Thank heaven for small mercies." Aleff grunted when Shammah jerked to one side, trying to twist away. "Find your own way over. My hands are full."

"Don't let go," countered Benaiah, who staggered to his feet on the nameless Caretaker's hand.

Aleff increased in size until Shammah looked like a child by comparison. Several more trees groaned to the ground to make space for the up-sized Caretaker. But now, Aleff's hands were big enough to pin Shammah's arms to his sides.

"*Not* the best of times to dilly-dally." Aleff's brow quirked. "Alley-oop!"

Although the nameless Caretaker extended his hand, he didn't close the distance. *Well, crud. I'm gonna have to jump for it.*

"Need a push, Captain?" Josheb's smile was pure challenge. "Or will a boost do?"

Ben pointed down, and his teammate presented a foothold. A gulp of air. A gauge of distance. A fleeting prayer. The moment Benaiah's foot hit interlocked fingers, Josheb heaved upward, launching Ben at his goal. After a brief flail through uncertainty, he hit a curtain of glinting copper and grabbed hold.

Aleff chuckled. "Rapunzel, Rapunzel."

"Not in the mood for babble," grumbled Benaiah. But it wasn't really true. *If Aleff's smiling, everything's gonna to be okay. Somehow.* Hand over hand, Ben climbed up the swinging hair, finding footholds in gleaming raiment as he worked his way to Aleff's shoulder. "I feel about as big as Neri and Pazi."

"You make an adorable action figure."

Babble *and* gibberish. Grabbing hold of his Caretaker's ear to keep his balance, Benaiah asked, "So what happened?"

Aleff's jaw tightened. "This and that."

"A straight answer might speed things up."

"Words have power. And ugly ones found their way into Shammah's ears." Aleff's tones pleaded for understanding. "Don't think less of him for pitching a fit. He was provoked."

"Yeah. I get it. But what am I supposed to do?"

"Whatever you do, do it quickly!"

Just then, Shammah pulled an arm free and clawed at Aleff's hand. The half-Caretaker's power was staggering, but his attack didn't bother his captor. As Shammah's inarticulate rage met Aleff's infinite patience, Ben shook his head in amazement. *Maybe it's an angel thing. Dunno if I could be that kind to someone who was trying to gnaw off my thumb.*

Aleff turned his head slightly and begged, "Giddy-up, slowpoke."

"Oh. Right." For lack of a better plan, Benaiah simply obeyed the inner push to get to Shammah. Using Aleff's hair as a safety line, Ben rappelled down the angel's arm.

Transferring from Aleff to Shammah, he went from being bug-sized to kid-sized. *Still too small to do much. But my chances seem better.* Benaiah straddled Shammah's shoulders and reached forward, grabbing handfuls of brown hair to keep from being shrugged off. Leaning as close as he could to a pointed ear, he shouted, "Hey, it's me! Battle's over. You did good. Shammah? *Shammah!*"

The jerking and bucking didn't stop. In fact, it got a whole lot harder to hang on.

"Don't give up!" Aleff urged between clenched teeth.

Like I'd do that. There was no way Ben would bail on someone who'd waited for him, trusted him, then followed him into this insect-infested jungle. Words alone might not be enough, but Ben could give them strength by binding them to a melody. *Songs are sneaky. They can slip into stubborn places. It worked once before. Worth a try.*

What followed was probably the worst rendition of a psalm in the history of man or half-man. Benaiah's melody line broke whenever he panted for air, and his voice crackled with emotion. But he toughed it out. And the guy listened.

Shammah's resistance drained away. A shudder wracked his body, and when he turned his head, the crazy was gone from wide eyes. Instead, there was recognition, realization, and devastating regret. Shammah whispered, "Benaiah?"

"Right here."

An instant later, Benaiah plunged to the ground, landing on top of a shivering child.

Finding three warriors with
supernatural legacies—easy.
All I had to do was follow
God's lead. But introducing a
scruffy-winged spearman,
a six-armed swordsman,
and a giant to David—tricky.
It would take a miracle
for this to work.

44

Our time had come.

C rud. You okay?"

Pint-sized Shammah curled into a shaking ball. He whimpered, "Did I hurt you?"

Ben eased into a more comfortable position and tested his limbs. He'd cracked his elbow, and his pants had renewed their acquaintance with the local mud. But otherwise, no harm done. "Nope. I'm fine."

"What about Josheb?"

"You think he's foolish enough to get trampled?"

"Eleazar? Tevy?"

"They steered clear." Benaiah dragged the kid into his arms. "I had no choice except to be foolish. But it worked out."

"Are you angry?" Shammah asked in a small voice.

"Nope." Taking a page from Aleff's book, Ben pitched his voice to soothe. "You did good. Saved me from the bad guy. You were there for me in a big way."

A small fist thumped Benaiah's shoulder, and the kid

laughed shakily.

Someone cleared their throat, and Shammah stole a peek over Ben's shoulder. Aleff had returned to his usual stature, and the nameless Caretaker stepped out of the jungle. Both looked on with an expectancy that made Benaiah self-conscious. He lamely added, "Them, too."

Twisting his fingers into Ben's loose hair, the boy asked, "Are they angry?"

Benaiah rolled his eyes, then raised his voice. "You guys angry?"

"On several levels, but not with the shivering pup. Nor the raging beast," Aleff cheerfully replied. "Only you."

"Your captain reopened two wounds," the nameless Caretaker revealed.

Shammah scrambled off Ben's lap. In the next instant, a grave-faced young man was tugging at Benaiah's tunic. "You said you were not hurt, yet here is fresh blood!"

"Didn't notice." Ben grunted when fingers prodded a tender spot. They turned icy, and a piece of the pain vanished. Death and life had traded places again.

Gaze downcast, Shammah whispered, "Is God angry?"

Words could be weapons, but they could also heal. And it was a Messenger's privilege to speak for One whose words could bring light and life into the darkest void. Benaiah caught his brother's sleeve and gruffly replied, "Shammah, He's *pleased*. With both of us."

Aleff knelt beside Benaiah and folded his hands together. "Shammah the Giant, you don't need to shrink from the consequences of your deeds. Learn from them. Because that would-be god will not be the last demon you face in this world."

Ben came to Shammah's defense. "He iced hundreds of Fallen just this morning."

"Yet a well-placed lie was his undoing." Aleff sighed. "Benaiah the First, your quest is a qualified success. You found your warriors three, but your opposition hasn't just increased … it's multiplied."

The nameless Caretaker chose a seat at Ben's other shoulder, and he squirmed. *How come I feel surrounded?* A light touch on his back reinforced the notion, but Shammah distracted him by finding a bruised rib.

Aleff's lecture wasn't over. "The Fallen are trouble, but they don't have a corner on deceit. Shammah, trust your captain's voice above all others. He will not lead you astray. Benaiah, listen to this brother's insights. His innocence will be your refuge."

What the crud's that supposed to mean?

Shammah met his glance and shrugged.

Ben preferred advice that wasn't heavily laced with warnings. *Who'd try to lead Shammah astray? And why am I gonna need refuge?* He scowled when the long-winded Caretaker prodded his newly-healed rib.

"He's more seep than sieve, so that's enough patching," Aleff declared. "Today was a big day, and tomorrow's bigger."

"He needs sleep," decreed the Caretaker without a name.

"Hang on. Bigger … how?"

"Yes, I prescribe rest. Quick, Shammah," urged Aleff. "While we have him outnumbered."

Some message must have passed between the Caretakers, Shammah included. He reached out to touch Benaiah's cheek. "They are right. You should sleep."

"I don't wan–!"

The last thing Ben remembered was Shammah's faint smile and a whispered promise. "Refuge."

The first thing Benaiah heard upon stirring was impossible. Or wishful thinking. Reeds rattled faintly in a shushing breeze, and light touched his eyelids. Wings whirred, and a tiny hand brushed his cheek in a fleeting caress. *Home.*

Unwilling to let the good dream end, Ben kept his eyes shut as he searched his memory. They were actually in an insect-ridden jungle. Probably not far from a murky river where hippos and killer crocodiles lurked. No wonder he'd escaped into dreams. *This is more like it. Clean. Soft. Bright.*

His brow puckered as he tried to piece together what was happening outside the happy place inside his head. *Josheb. Shammah. Eleazar.* The last things he remembered were darkness, pain, and … *yeah, that's pretty much it. Oh. And being ganged up on by Caretakers.*

Even though Benaiah's mind was clearing, the dream

hadn't faded. In fact, details were sharpening. He could feel the weave of the sheets that swaddled him. The soothing hum of yahavim came from somewhere overhead. And he could smell Aleff's soap. Only a dry rustling sound off to one side didn't match his memories of the little hut hidden away in a sea of reeds.

Ben opened his eyes and blinked damp lashes. Swathes of linen in green, brown, and yellow hung near the ceiling. *Huldah's gift. My turban.* Neri and Pazi sat with four other yahavim on the makeshift clothesline, swinging their feet as they watched over him. It was all so normal.

A slim hand slipped under his, and Shammah leaned over his bed. "Are you in pain?"

Benaiah could feel a tear sneaking down his cheek. The little traitor. "Maybe a little," he hedged. "What's with the hat?"

Shammah helped him sit up, then pressed a cup of cold water into his hand. "A gift. I am told that the sun shines fiercely in our next destination. Josheb wished to protect me from it."

Following his gaze, Benaiah spotted a spear propped in the corner. Right next to a familiar pick, shovel, and pair of swords. *And Josheb.* His seated teammate looked strange in shimmering angel's raiment—loose calf-length pants and the sleeveless tunics favored by warrior classes. Barefoot, Josheb's crossed ankles partially obscured the pattern of green skin that swirled up his calves.

"Have a nice nap, Captain?"

"Restless?" countered Benaiah, indicating the heap of rushes.

Long fingers expertly twisted the raw material into an

endless rope. "Best way I know to mark time in a place that has none."

"How long have I been asleep?"

"The bugs have a new basket. We'll call that one day. I finished the runt's hat next. We'll call that another day and a half." Holding up the coil he was twisting, Josheb said, "This is another half day's work."

"Three days?" Benaiah ran his free hand over the bandages wrapping his chest. "What happened …?"

"Aleff happened," Josheb replied. "And he's *still* happening. But don't ask me what's going to happen next. I can't make sense of half of what he says. Or *any* of the stuff Tevy flings my way."

"She's here, too?"

"Your Flight is intact," assured Shammah, who still held Benaiah's hand. Turning it over, he tapped the little finger. "Eliel is pleased by his matched placement."

Ben held up his hands to study his palms. The scarlet-winged archer's name had appeared on the opposite pinkie from Tevy's. That put them side by side, smack dab in the middle of the others. Four more names would bring them to twelve, the traditional number for an angelic Flight. *Four more of us.* They were out there somewhere, awaiting their captain's call.

But that would still leave room for another name. *Will someone show up on my other palm?* Aleff's name was on the right. Maybe God would write David's on the other? That sounded right, considering how precious ….

"Ahem."

With a guilty start, Ben looked up and found Aleff's gaze resting on him. Warm. Welcoming. The Caretaker leaned against the door frame, as if waiting his turn. Now that he had everyone's attention, he said, "I need a second opinion. Preferably one that won't involve the near miss of razor-edged Frisbees."

Josheb leaned forward. "What did *you* do to rile Tevy?"

The Caretaker reached behind him and hauled another person into the little house. "What do you think? Will he pass for human?"

Benaiah stared blankly at a young man who only wore the pants part of his raiment. The creamy hue shone softly against ruddy brown skin. Long, loose, hair with reddish tendencies framed a broad face. And heavy brows drew down over dark eyes. Tall. Muscular. Silent. Ben couldn't imagine why Aleff would have brought a stranger here. *Hang on. Pass for human?*

Aleff laughed. Giving the stranger a shove, he said, "Man looks at the outside, but what's at the heart?"

The newcomer quickly caught his balance and moodily folded his arms over his chest. There were no clues to point to his angelic order, but a bizarre thought took shape in Ben's mind. *Give this guy a couple more sets of arms, gray skin, and eyes that can burn through your soul, and ....* The jaw-dropping reality broadsided Benaiah. "Eleazar!"

"Interesting," Josheb murmured, setting aside his handiwork and jumping to his feet. "Will you shorten

Shammah's ears next?"

"I'll let you hold him down for me!" Aleff replied.

I didn't recognize one of my own men. Which could only mean one thing. Radiating embarrassment, Benaiah admitted, "I never really looked past your eyes."

"That's a lie."

Ben stiffened at the accusation. "Orange eyes kinda overwhelm other details."

Aleff's smile had a knowing quality. "If you weren't studying the curve of Ember's cheek or the cut of his jaw, what tipped you off?"

"He moves like … I dunno. It's kind of graceful." Realizing that he was talking about Eleazar as if he wasn't standing right there, Ben met the young man's flat stare. "But mostly you sound the same as I remember."

"I didn't speak."

"Not out loud." Benaiah fumbled to explain. "What you *don't* say hasn't changed. You square your shoulders and cross your arms. And the way you look at me is … hard to miss."

Shammah arched his brows at Eleazar. "You do have expressive eyes."

"Windows to the soul," Aleff chimed in, smiling at the disguised half-seraph. "And from what I've heard, Benaiah has not only looked past your eyes, he's seen *through* them."

"True."

Ben wondered if Eleazar would ever forgive him for the intrusion.

Josheb weighed in. "The trappings are gone. You *do* pass

for human, Ember. Same skin tone as Tevy. And that hair color's common enough. Half your wives were sorrels."

"You're comparing women to horses?" Aleff's lips quirked, but his expression shifted. "*Wives*, Eleazar?"

"What did you do to his arms?" Josheb interrupted. "How am I supposed to test myself against a six-armed man if you rob him of his advantage?"

Suddenly, Josheb jerked forward with a sharp exclamation. Rubbing the back of his head, he scrutinized Eleazar. "You hit me!"

"It was more of a tap."

"Do it again!"

All Benaiah could see was Eleazar shifting his weight from one foot to the other, but Josheb's head snapped back. He swore and dragged the back of his hand across his split lip. "Six arms, but the enemy can only see two." With a particularly vicious grin, Josheb said, "Good news, Captain. Ember should be able to keep up."

Benaiah wasn't surprised when the next blow put Josheb flat on his back. But the gleam in Eleazar's eye when he helped Josheb back up caught Ben off guard. Especially when he understood what it meant … and why it hurt. *They're already friends.*

Aleff chased everyone else out before sitting on the edge of Benaiah's bed. "How's my favorite patient?" he asked lightly.

"I want a bar of soap. And food. In that order."

"Easily arranged. I'll even throw in the tub and bubbles. But first let me check your progress."

Benaiah submitted to unwinding, but his mind was elsewhere. It was strange, even surreal, having the other three here. *This is my home. Mine and Aleff's.* Having other people making themselves comfortable in his room was … unsettling. It was hardly an invasion, but boundaries were blurred. *If I'm uneasy over something as dumb as my pick and shovel, no wonder Eleazar hates me.*

"He doesn't hate you," soothed Aleff.

"Crud. Was I …?"

"Broadcasting teen angst on all channels? Yes. But I messed with your dials. Everyone else is hearing nothing but static."

"Thanks. I think." Ben sucked in a sharp breath and glanced down. The cuts made by Eleazar's swords still slashed across his chest, pink and puckered where they weren't still scabbed over. Nothing hurt, but it itched like crazy. "I thought you were going to fix this."

"God in His infinite wisdom decreed that these stay." Under Aleff's hands, the wounds healed over, becoming finer and white against Ben's pale skin. "Your king remembers scars. And they do lend you a certain scruffy charm."

"They kinda look like the old claw marks."

"And you'll be operating in a world where such imperfections are a badge of honor." Aleff cocked his head to one side to admire the final effect. "Scars tell a warrior's story for him."

"Mine all say, 'frequently in need of rescue.'"

"I'm sure that part will be lost in translation," Aleff grabbed Ben's chin and searched his eyes. "He *doesn't* hate you."

"But he doesn't like me."

"Many won't. Strike that. *Most* won't." With a sad smile Aleff added, "Young as you are, you already know the cost of standing out. That won't change."

Benaiah scowled. "I thought since we're mostly the same …."

Aleff took him by the shoulders and gave him a gentle shake. "You're a sheltered half-camel raised by an indulgent and demonstrative father-figure. He's a six-armed half-seraph isolated by a vile demon, kept in a drug-induced haze, threatened by imminent possession, burdened by the welfare of dozens of young girls …. Need I go on?"

But I want to be friends.

Aleff gently took his hand and uncurled Ben's fingers. Tapping the one on which Eleazar's name appeared, he advised, "Begin as his captain. He cannot deny your right to lead. The rest is in God's hands."

Ben managed a tiny nod.

"And if you don't mind a little unsolicited advice, watch for your chance to speak to Tevy."

"How come?"

"She's on the wrong side of a colossal language barrier.

I significantly altered the one familiar face she has left. And she's down to four chakram, which Josheb and Othniel agree has perversely affected her scariness."

Benaiah held up both hands. "I'm not so good with women. Girls. Either one."

"Then bless God for letting you practice with Tevy," Aleff replied. "This is a people skill you'll need. And soon."

"How soon?"

Aleff dropped a lump of soap onto Benaiah's palm. "That all depends on how long you dawdle in the tub."

Benaiah was still wet behind the ears when he stepped through one of Aleff's doors and into glaring daylight. Sandals tied. Turban knotted. Knees knocking. Ben glanced at the sun, then scanned the nearest hills to get his bearings. One corner of his mouth tugged upward. *Aleff cheats. We camped in the Valley of Elah more than once.*

Josheb propped his spear across his shoulders. "This the right place, Captain?"

"Yeah. We're in Judah." Knowing the lay of the land lent Ben some necessary confidence. Pointing the way, he said, "Aim for that rise. There's a valley beyond. He's there."

The four of them cut across dry, dusty ground, skirting prickly grasses and spiky weeds. Shammah squinted out from under the brim of his hat. "Those are carrion birds."

"Too high for the killing to have started," Josheb said. "But they're hopeful."

Benaiah followed their gaze, but he could barely pick out the birds. The sky wheeled with Flights of angels, their vivid wings creating a kaleidoscope over their destination. Heaven's attention was fixed on this time and place. *Something's gonna happen.*

'Watch and see what I will do.'

Lengthening his stride, Ben took the lead. "Hurry up. I want to be close enough to see."

They skirted a slope covered with so many goat trails, it looked ridged, then dropped into a rock-strewn wadi. During rainy seasons, the dry gully would fill with water, but for now it helped cover their approach.

"Listen," said Eleazar.

Everyone stopped and held their breaths, ears tuned to the murmur of many voices.

Josheb frowned. "That sounds more like a milling crowd than clashing armies."

"Perhaps they await our arrival," Shammah suggested.

Josheb chuckled darkly. "Nice of them to save first blood for us."

"That's not it," Ben muttered, dropping to his knees as he neared the brow of the hill. Suddenly, a roar filled the valley. Men shouted. Feet stomped. Spears beat against shields. Easing higher, Benaiah flicked a few goat droppings out of the way, then made himself comfortable. The others joined him in silent reconnoiter.

An empty battlefield spread between two low hills that were overrun by pitched tents and smoking cookfires. To the one side, idle soldiers stood in irregular clusters. Pikes bristled, and banners hung limp in the still air. The clamor came from the opposite slopes. Benaiah caught jeers and rough laughter. It didn't take long to piece together what was happening.

All eyes were on a soldier who sauntered out and struck a pose in no-man's land. He was a giant of a man clad in bronze armor. "Here we are again!" he boomed. "You line up for battle, yet day in and day out, you quail in your camp with your king. I'm *bored*! Send out your champion!"

Josheb assessed the two camps and pointed to the army arrayed behind the challenger. "Am I right in assuming that *they* are the enemy?"

Benaiah hummed an affirmative.

"Our guys are on the puny side."

"That's what I've been saying all along," Ben said gruffly. "David needs us."

"Goliath of Gath speaks boldly for the Philistine army! But your voices quaver like a dove's. No! Fear has stolen your voices! And defeat will claim your lives!" Brandishing a spear the size of a small tree, Goliath flung increasingly vulgar insults.

"Likes the sound of his own voice," muttered Josheb.

Shammah's indignation cooled the air. "He curses God in the name of a false god. I will not listen to blasphemy."

Ben grabbed their giant's shoulder and hauled him back down. "Wait. We're supposed to wait."

"King Saul, I defy you to give me a man." Goliath sneered. "Where's your best? Who will you send? Let him die in your place. He will lead you into servitude to the mighty Philistine people!"

"The threat is real. His confidence is justified," remarked Eleazar. "God's chosen people are small in stature."

Josheb grumbled, "Our giant is bigger. Me and Shammah could–"

"No," Ben interrupted. A ripple went through Israel's ranks as they parted for a single man—a boy among men. The teen skidded down the slope and jogged onto the battlefield. Benaiah immediately broke cover. "Oh, no, no, no," he groaned.

Eleazar's glance was sharp. "You know him."

Benaiah's thoughts were reeling, and his prayers held an edge of panic. *I'm here, but why? To watch? To prevent a tragedy? I have three strong warriors ready to go. Ready to make good on the promise You made through me. We could back him up. He shouldn't be alone!*

'Is he?'

The answer to that question settled the matter. Ben grimly said, "We wait our turn. God's got this one."

A buzz filled the valley as men on both sides gawked at Israel's so-called champion. Sarcasm twisted Goliath's tones as he asked, "Who is this twig of a boy? Did he wander onto the field by mistake? Or am I a dog, and you've tossed me a stick. By the gods, I'll snap him in two!"

Josheb stood as well, absently patting the dust from his clothes. "Who's the fool?"

Benaiah shook his head. "A reckless shepherd protecting his sheep."

Shammah found a more comfortable seat on a rock, his gaze fixed on the young man. "You were right. He *is* short."

"He's an insult." Josheb's gaze cut to the pavilion at the top of the hill. "Why would any king send an unarmed shepherd boy to the slaughter?"

Benaiah muttered, "Just because he doesn't have a fancy pokey-stick like yours doesn't mean he's unarmed."

"He has a sling," reported Shammah.

"And King Saul didn't choose him," said Ben. "God did."

Josheb blinked. "That little guy down there is our king?"

"David," Ben confirmed.

"Interesting." A sly smile spread across Josheb's face. "I like him already!"

This whole thing
started with David.
He was the friend
God gave me.
His side was where
I wanted to be.
But suddenly, I had
all these other names
under my hand,
dividing my attention.
So the moment
I saw David again, I had
two brand new worries.
Was I ready? Was he?

45

What kind of fool goes into battle without armor?

Benaiah stared fixedly at David, needing to find something familiar. His friend had a new tunic and coat. And his hair was trimmed differently. But things like that made sense. *How long's it been? Years for him. Weeks for me. Long enough for both of us to change inside and out.*

Finding Josheb. Training with Othniel. Gaining Shammah's trust. Searching for Eleazar. Big, strange, important stuff had happened. *But that's my friend. I'd know him anywhere.* And one thing definitely hadn't changed. Ben could feel the Sending that bound his future to David's. *I belong at his side. Let me go to him.*

But Benaiah's orders stood. So he stood there. And hated every second of suspense.

Goliath spread his arms wide and invited, "Come to me, boy! I'll feed your flesh to the carrion birds and toss your bones to the wild dogs!"

A sickly silence spread through Israel's camp, but David didn't share their dread. His voice rang clear and confident. "Come to me, Goliath of Gath, and bring your arsenal. I see your sword. And that's a fine spear. You even have a javelin, but you're ill-equipped. I come in the name of the Lord of hosts."

Ben took a quick step backward at the answering tumult and nearly fell.

Josheb grabbed his arm to steady him, asking, "Why are your eyes suddenly on the sky, Captain?"

"It's nothing. Nothing bad, anyhow." Ben tugged at his turban and explained, "Those *hosts* answered. The angels agree with David."

"This king of yours speaks the truth," said Eleazar. "He has courage."

"The guy's crazy!" Josheb was also zeroed in on David. "No one thinks he can win."

"He challenges the defiant," added Shammah. "He protects the name of God."

Benaiah almost laughed. *David still makes it look easy. But that's good. Makes my life easier.* In a matter of minutes, David had said and done everything necessary to impress three mongrels and send a cheer through the angelic ranks. *Keep it up. This is how it's supposed to be.*

The open field emphasized the differences between champions, in both size and preparation. Goliath was every cubit a hero. The pride of the Philistine army. Trained in the art of war. David looked young and naïve by comparison.

No one would mistake him for God's chosen king. But leading wasn't about having a title, crown, or throne. This situation showed exactly where David's heart was … and how deeply his trust ran. *He already thinks of God's people as his flock. Like a good shepherd, he's put himself between them and their enemies.*

Josheb asked, "If we're supposed to help that kid to the throne, who's sitting on it now?"

Benaiah pointed to an open tent at the top of the rise. "King Saul and his generals will be there."

"And all these soldiers are the same children of Israel from your stories. The ones chosen by God to worship Him."

"Yeah."

"Not sure I understand," Josheb muttered. "These guys know about that Flood, those plagues, the burning bush. About angels and the rest?"

"They're taught from childhood. Every man on the field knows his history, his ancestry, his duty."

"Then why are they afraid?" asked Shammah.

Eleazar pointed at Goliath. "He has deceived them with his challenge. Because no single man among them can match his strength, defeat becomes inevitable. For fear of failing, no one dares to try."

"God has turned his lie against him," Shammah said. "A single man *will* defeat him."

Josheb smirked. "In front of everyone."

David's shout pulled Ben's attention back to the field.

"You've defied the God of the armies of Israel! We are His

people. On this day, the flesh of every Philistine in your camp will fill the gullets of birds! Your entire army is dog meat!"

Josheb elbowed Ben. "Nice come-back, but can he pull it off?"

"Don't underestimate him because of what you see."

"But can he defend himself?"

Ben shook his head and pointed. "He's not thinking about defense. When there's a threat, David attacks."

David slipped his hand into the pouch at his waist. "On this day, everyone here will know that the Lord doesn't need swords or spears to save. God fights for us, and this battle is His!" Even before he was done speaking, his slingshot was a blur.

With a snarled oath, Goliath charged, spear poised for a killing blow. But David released the stone, and the giant stumbled.

"It hit!" cheered Josheb.

"No," Shammah gasped, "Can you see it? The stone clings to him."

Benaiah shielded his eyes as Goliath swayed. *He's right.* Just below the edge of the Philistine's helmet, a pale chunk of rock jutted out of his forehead. *It didn't just hit. It sank in.* Blood trickled down the Philistine champion's face like dark tears. He dropped to his knees, and it was quiet enough to hear the creak and scrape of Goliath's armor as he sagged to the ground.

"A mortal blow," said Eleazar, just as the Israelite army erupted.

And maybe the stone *would* have been enough to kill Goliath. But David didn't sit back and wait for death to claim his opponent. Running forward, he seized the hilt of Goliath's sword with both hands and dragged the weapon from its sheath.

"He won't be able to lift it," Josheb remarked. "Goliath's blade rivals Othniel's."

"This is no longer a fight." Eleazar rested his hands on the hilts of two of the six swords at his waist. "The boy doesn't need to swing that blade to claim his victory."

Angling the sword across the fallen warrior's throat, David ended Goliath's life with one ruthless thrust. A few more relieved the giant of his head. Dropping the weapon, David wrestled the helmet from the Philistine, grabbed his gory trophy by the hair, and lifted it high. From the midst of the Israelite encampment, the priests sounded their trumpets. Saul's army shouted as one man, and their enemy turned and fled.

"That's our cue." Spreading his arms to indicate the enemy's forces, Benaiah said, "From the nearest tents in the enemy's encampment to the farthest straggler … kill them all."

The four of them ran abreast, cutting across the Valley of Elah with long strides. Before they converged with the pursuing army, Benaiah handed down his first orders. "Shammah, don't just focus on stopping the enemy; save as many of David's flock as you can. Josheb, you're fast. Get ahead of the retreat. Make sure there are no ambushes out there. Eleazar, be thorough. Eliminate any Philistines who might be lingering in the tents, hoping to avenge their people."

After a quick round of acknowledgment, Josheb said, "One question."

"Yeah?"

"If I catch any horses, can I keep them?"

"They have horses?"

Josheb grinned. "A few that might be worth a second look."

"Guess that's okay," Ben conceded.

Once the rider angled off toward his quarry and Eleazar vanished in the direction of the encampment, Shammah caught Benaiah's sleeve and quietly begged, "Stay with me?"

Ben slowed to a stop. "You gonna have a problem keeping your head clear?"

Deep blue eyes flickered with a trace of amusement. "No. Aleff and Othniel made me promise."

"Oh. So it's not so much that I'm staying with you. You're watching out for me."

Shammah shrugged.

"If that's the way it's gonna be," Benaiah sighed.

"And if you will permit …?" Shammah began cautiously. "If I am to remain at this height, I will require a weapon."

"Plenty of cast-offs. Take your pick."

Shammah nodded and made an about-face, backtracking

to the place where Goliath's blood drenched the ground. From the headless corpse's fingers, he wrenched free the heavy spear.

"That thing's big as a beam." Benaiah glanced around and asked, "You sure that's the one you want?"

"Yes. God turned Goliath's threat against him. I will turn his weapon against his people." Shammah tested its balance and added half a hand to his height. "I am ready."

As they jogged across empty land, Benaiah said, "You would have liked making Goliath eat his words."

"Very much. But God's way was better."

They soon reached the first scattered bodies, and Ben drew his swords. "There's a whole army of Philistines ahead of us. Lots to do."

"Not if Josheb has his way," Shammah remarked blandly.

Benaiah followed his gaze and snorted. *Josheb's already found a mount big enough. And feisty enough.* The gleaming chestnut stallion bucked and wheeled, but his rider lay low over its neck. Flattened ears soon pricked, and the horse's pace evened into an uppity canter. Now in control, Josheb urged his mount out ahead of the troops. Ben could plainly see his winglets streaming, making the spearman impervious to the stray javelin and arrows that followed him.

They passed several pockets of Israelites, and Benaiah got good at shouting reassurances. "Peace! We're David's men!"

"You're strangers!" accused a seasoned veteran. "Where did you come from?"

"We fight for the one true God," Ben promised. "David

counts me as a friend."

"Wait!" exclaimed a younger man. "He's telling the truth. I'm a Bethlehemite, and I've seen this man in Jesse's household."

"Strange allies," grumbled the older man. "But I'll watch your back all the same."

Benaiah eyed the men, most of them old enough to have trouble keeping up. *Kind of like David's first flock. Hope they can teach me what I need to know.* "Form up behind me and Shammah. We'll cut through God's enemies together."

The soldiers they overtook fell in, and Benaiah was soon leading dozens. He spoke to each, offering assurances and introductions. David's name was well-known, and soon it was linked to that of Benaiah, son of Jehoiada. *No one wants a tall, eerie-eyed son of a camel ... unless he's standing between you and a Philistine horde.* Now all Ben had to do was reward their trust by keeping them alive.

Knowing the lay of the land helped tremendously. Benaiah scouted ahead and surprised a passel of Philistines lying in wait. As the desperate men attacked, Ben barked at the Israelites. "Stay back! Give Shammah room!"

Those who'd already seen the pale stranger in action obeyed immediately. Shammah swung Goliath's spear in a broad arc. It connected with the helmet of the first attacker, who dropped to the ground without a sound. Two more were clipped and howled in rage and pain. The blasphemy on their lips only served to spur Shammah on. His back-swing crunched a man's ribs, and the following blow swept four soldiers off their feet. When the last two men tried to escape,

Benaiah ended their lives.

"Where were you these last forty days?" asked one of the Israelites. "We needed a champion. And here are two!"

"Why wait for a champion? God is ever with you." Shammah planted the butt of his spear on the ground with a dull *thud*. "Have faith like that of David, and you may see even greater miracles."

Although several of the men looked annoyed, one old-timer guffawed and said, "May it be as you say, lad."

Benaiah led the way out of the wadi and picked a new heading. Men fanned out to check bodies, making sure none of their own were injured. And making sure fallen enemies were dead. Ben kept the pace easy, and more than once, he sent a couple of his group back to the encampment with a wounded comrade. But all of the corpses were Philistines. *David's triumph is complete.*

Out of the corner of his eye, Benaiah caught a furtive movement. "Hey!" he shouted, sprinting away from his crew. One of the Philistines was teetering on the edge of life, but he fumbled for a better grasp on his spear. The Israelite soldier crouched nearby had no idea there was danger behind him. He only had eyes for the oncoming foreigner. *Great. Wrong threat, idiot.* Ben hollered, "Eliab! Behind you!"

With no time left, Benaiah hurled one of his swords. It made an unpleasant sound as it sliced clean through the Philistine's leather breastplate.

Eliab finally had his spear up, but he didn't seem to know which direction it should be pointing. He glowered at the corpse before pinning Benaiah with a hard stare. Then, David's oldest brother tugged at his beard. "You're that stray David picked up. Samuel's servant."

"You remembered." Planting his foot on the dead man's chest, he reclaimed his blade. "The name's Benaiah."

"But why are you *here*?" With a glance at the men who hurried to join them, Eliab demanded, "Did you arrive with David?"

Ben was surprised to recognize several faces. A couple more brothers and several of David's nephews and cousins. "Nope. Haven't seen him. But I want to. Since I'm back," he rambled, feeling increasingly awkward. "Like I promised."

David's brothers traded a long look, and Eliab asked, "You plan to rejoin him?"

"I made a vow."

The heir to Jesse's household pulled Ben aside and lowered his voice. "Today, my insolent younger brother has put himself in a precarious place."

"But he was amazing," protested Benaiah.

"An opinion shared by every man here. Except one."

Ben didn't like this turn, even though it wasn't unexpected. "You make it sound like David's in danger."

"All of the time," growled Eliab.

Crud. Bet I know where this is headed. Still, he asked, "From who?"

"The king."

"But isn't David living in the king's household? I heard Saul keeps him close."

"Motives have their ulteriors. And this day has been both triumph and disaster." With a frustrated flutter of hands, Eliab complained, "That boy never considers the consequences!"

Benaiah scowled. "Isn't that kinda harsh? He never asked to be chosen by God. And you saw for yourself that God is with him."

Eliab's gaze sharpened, but he answered softly. "And *you* will be with him. Watch over him. *Try* to keep him from even greater folly."

Hours later, the Philistine army was no more. Benaiah was recapping his water skin when Rei appeared before him in a swirl of indigo wings.

"You have been taught," he said.

"Kinda. I learned some stuff. Seems to be working." Then the obvious hit him, and he scanned the milling soldiers. To Ben's embarrassment, his voice wobbled. "David's close?"

There was a trace of a smile on the big Guardian's face. "He has been hearing rumors, and he intends to find their source."

The battle was over, but there was still plenty of confusion. Pickers ranged through the valley. Flights filled the sky, but their war song had changed to one that promised comfort. Hundreds of Guardians dotted the surrounding hillsides, on their knees as they grieved for their charges.

Where ... is ... he ...?

Shammah's voice cut through the confusion. "Benaiah! Behind you!"

Benaiah whirled so fast, his feet tangled with one another. He didn't stand a chance.

With an almighty *whoop*, a blood-smeared, grinning tidal wave of triumph tackled him to the ground.

When you miss someone,
there are millions of things
you wish you could say.
What's on your mind.
What's going on.
Big stuff.
Little stuff.
Just stuff.
There was so much
I wanted to share
with David. But the sight
of him sealed my lips.

46

Bloody beheadings make lasting impressions.

These are new."

Benaiah's eyes slowly widened as he eased his blades away from David's throat. Letting the swords drop to the ground on either side, he said, "Sorry. Reflex."

"You not only carry two swords, you know how to use them?" his king asked. "I *might* be impressed!"

Ben was genuinely rattled, seeing how close those keen edges had come to the one he'd vowed to protect. It didn't help that Rei stood over them, glaring daggers. Swallowing hard, Benaiah muttered, "Says the giant-killer."

David's eyes sparkled. "You saw?"

"Everyone saw." Ben searched David's face and found hints of maturity. Less softness. Bristles along the jaw. *And so much blood.* Spatters and smears on his skin. Caked curls against his neck. Robes soiled beyond cleansing. Benaiah tentatively reached up and poked David's shoulder. "Next time you won't have to stand alone."

With a low chuckle, David said, "I'll hold you to that, but let's leave 'next time' for another day. Now, greet me properly."

"Can't move. You've gained weight."

"A little weight, little height, a little skill, a little learning." With a wink, David added, "And my pockets are full of rocks."

Conscious of the small crowd they were drawing, Ben grumbled, "And you still stink like sheep."

"And you're relieved to find me so little changed!"

"True," said a deep voice somewhere behind him.

Eleazar!

The half-seraph's voice echoed inside his mind. *This young king shows promise.*

Benaiah struggled up onto his elbows only to have David push him back down. "I knew it! You know him!" He gestured excitedly as he explained, "I ran into him earlier. Mistook him for a Philistine mercenary, but then he turned around and saved my life. We've been together since then, but we can't talk." David waved the silent warrior forward. "He doesn't understand my words. And I only recognize *one* of his. Your name."

"Saved your life?" Ben echoed. "Are you hurt anywhere?"

Patting his battle-grimed clothes, David scoffed. "This? Nope. Not a scratch on me. Pretty good for my first battle!" Then his eyes narrowed, and he tugged at the ties to Ben's clothes. "What about you? Is any of this blood yours?"

Before Benaiah could fend him off, David found the renewed scars on his chest and placed his hand over them.

"I'll never forget that day. You scared me half to death, going after that lioness with your bare hands."

Then we're even. Because I'll never forget today.

One of the men standing nearby asked, "You *know* this stranger, David?"

Benaiah scowled. *I'd have thought that was obvious.*

David laughed, then lifted his voice good and loud. "I not only know this man, I'm proud to call him my friend. This is Benaiah, son of Jehoiada."

A soldier joked, "Hardly a surprise. *Everyone* is David's friend."

"Born in Bethlehem, yet he knows the name of every man and maid in Gibeah," remarked another man in carrying tones.

"And my life's the richer for knowing you all!" David countered, all smiles for the crowd. But on a more serious note, he made himself clear. "But Benaiah and I have traded vows. We're lifelong friends."

Once more, Eleazar murmured, "True."

Ben unseated David and sat up. He was still in the dirt, but at least he wasn't on his back. Tightening the ties on his turban, he did a double-take. "Eleazar, you're …! Crud. Is that what I think it is?"

"He freed up my hands." David leapt up, crossing to Eleazar, who had Goliath's head tucked under one arm. He'd also propped the Philistine champion's enormous sword across his shoulders. Even with his more unusual features disguised, the half-seraph looked fearsome.

As soon as Benaiah straightened to his full height, those

who'd been giving Eleazar space took another step back. *Some things haven't changed.*

Murmurs stirred all around as soldiers swapped tales of the day's exploits. But David was more interested in Eleazar. "Introduce us!"

A thought occurred to Ben. "If you mistook Eleazar for an enemy, does that mean you attacked him?"

"Only a little bit."

Benaiah shot a questioning look at Eleazar, whose expression remained neutral. "Crud. I'm sorry. Even after Aleff reminded me, I forgot about the language gap. You have no idea what he's saying?"

With a small shrug, he said, "Please relay my greetings to your king."

To David, he said, "This is Eleazar, one of the three warriors I went to find. He offers greetings."

Easing closer, David asked, "Three?"

Explanations are happening all out of order. Ben wished they could have had a more private conversation, but the short version would have to do. "Yeah. I kept my promise. Your strength has increased threefold."

David looked ready to ask more questions, but he shook his head. With a smile for Eleazar, he asked, "How do people say *hi* in his homeland?"

Benaiah had to think hard. *I hardly notice when I switch between languages.* Plucking the simplest possible phrase from his mind, he coached his friend. David cheerfully botched it, but his efforts brought a faint smile to the half-seraph's face.

Offering a bow, Eleazar said, "Shammah is waiting his turn."

Ben snagged his king's arm and guided him in their giant's direction. David was quick to take in important details and elbowed Benaiah. "Please tell me you're going to introduce me to the man who carries Goliath's spear as if it were a trifle."

"That's the idea."

David's smile widened and he rushed up to the pale young man, who presented his hand palm-up. "I am Shammah. Benaiah speaks of you with great fondness."

From just over Ben's shoulder, Eleazar murmured, "True."

"Oh, yeah? What did he say about me?" demanded David.

"Words that betrayed the depths of his attachment. Songs that taught us to look forward to this day."

Even though Shammah was mercifully vague, color crept into Ben's cheeks.

"He sang my songs?"

"Benaiah taught us many of your psalms. Are there more?"

This time David looked embarrassed. "Dozens more. Would you like to hear them?"

Shammah gazed at his teammates over David's head and said, "Ever since Eleazar joined us, we have adopted one of his household's traditions. Evensong."

Ever since today. Benaiah checked to see if Eleazar minded, but his face betrayed nothing.

"You guys sing together?" David was up on tiptoe, his voice tight with excitement. "Am I invited? I'll bring my harp!"

"Yes, please," Shammah said warmly.

David's grin was acceptance, and Benaiah marveled at

Shammah's poise as he went on to ask about burial customs. Thinking back, Ben realized that the young man had been quick to gain Eleazar's trust as well. Given Josheb's kill-first attitude and Eleazar's grim silences, Shammah's polite manners were probably a godsend. *Thanks for that,* he offered heavenward.

Turning to Eleazar, Benaiah concentrated. *He told me you saved his life.*

Eleazar's gaze flicked to his, then to the gathering crowd. With a small nod, his voice reached back. *I was in a position to intervene.*

Benaiah blinked. *Were you Sent?*

No. I wanted to see this David for myself.

Eleazar's curiosity had probably saved the day just as much as David's crazy courage. Pushing as much gratitude into the thought as he could, Ben replied, *Thanks.*

Just then, the thunder of hooves rounded the neighboring rise. At the warning shouts, every head turned, and pickers lunged for their weapons.

He's a one-man stampede. Shaking his head, Benaiah said, "Good timing. Here comes Josheb."

David traded his sharp scrutiny for astonishment. "Your third?"

"We call him Josheb the Rider … for obvious reasons."

Benaiah shouted, and Shammah waved his hat. Raising his spear in acknowledgment, Josheb steered the horses their way. His hair was wild from riding, and fresh blood spattered his skin. Eight horses with their harnesses tethered to a familiar length of handmade rope slowed to a stop. Vaulting off the leader's back, Josheb worked his way through the line, speaking to each of the horses in turn. Confident caresses. Soft reassurances. By the time he was done, his new herd stood quietly.

Shouldering his spear, Josheb sauntered over. "It's done, Captain. Those who defied God are dead." His gaze switched to David's face, and he smirked. "Dog meat. As ordered."

Ben gave them to the count of ten to size each other up, then eased between them. "David, herder of sheep, meet Josheb, herder of horses."

"I finished what you started," Josheb boldly announced.

"Such a beginning requires a strong finish." Folding his arms over his chest, David's tone shifted to incredulity. "Can I be seeing straight? Are all *three* of you taller than Benaiah?"

With minimal jostling, David managed to line them up to compare. Ben blandly pointed out, "You asked me to find better men. They're superior in every way."

Shammah made a soft noise of displeasure and looked down into their king's face. "This very day you proved that our size is inconsequential. Look instead to our hearts, David of Judah. May you find us Faithful in every way."

"Where did Benaiah journey to find such men?" David looked them each in the eyes, then asked, "How is it that you're all strangers, yet you give honor to God?"

Ben was still searching for a way to answer when a runner arrived. Abinadab, David's second-oldest brother peered warily at the wall of warriors standing behind his sibling before delivering his message. "The king is calling for you. Eliab says to hurry, lest his mood turn."

David simply nodded. "Of course I'll come. I have gifts to place at King Saul's feet." Extending his hands to Eleazar, he first took back the Philistine champion's sword, which he passed on to Abinadab. Then he grappled Goliath's head into a comfortable position for carrying. Catching Benaiah's eye, he said, "I'll find you later. Where are you camped?"

"No place yet," Benaiah admitted. "But there's a cave not far from here. It would be a good spot to set up."

"Point the way for me," David urged, taking a step in the direction his duty called.

Ben quickly showed him which hill to aim for. There was no time for more, not even the proper welcome David had demanded earlier. So he bowed and begged, "Find me again."

David pitched his voice to soothe. "It's a promise."

Benaiah led his men to the priests, who set aside their astonishment long enough to guide three newbies through the steps that would make them clean again. Josheb found the entire process fascinating. Eleazar covered his face. And Shammah trembled with awe, then whispered his gratitude. They bypassed the free meal, and thanks to Josheb's spoils of war, they traded a long walk for an easy ride.

"Is there water near this cave of yours?" Josheb asked.

"Should be. Unless things have changed since the last time I was here."

Shammah pointed. "There is a spring. I can feel it."

"Yeah? Good." Benaiah looked out over the valley that had become a battlefield. *No diggers. Only pickers.* Since they'd chased the Philistines down, most of the bodies were far enough away that the stink wouldn't reach the Israelite encampment. *Or ours.*

"Othniel is here," Eleazar announced, nodding at the blaze of color high overhead.

Gold wings were soon joined by scarlet, and Josheb remarked, "If Eliel's here, so's Tevy."

"I see tents," Shammah said as they rounded the low hill.

Even better. Benaiah urged his horse forward. "I smell goat."

Aleff stood at the edge of an orderly campsite. Spitted meat sizzled over a fire. Stones had been pulled into a half-circle between their dinner and a cave. Its entrance was flanked by two tents. *Those look like the same kind God's armies use.* The draped cloth gleamed as brightly as Aleff's raiment.

"Welcome home, boys!" Aleff exclaimed. "Come aside, and refresh yourselves. "

"Thanks," Ben replied, swinging off his mount. "Wasn't expecting a private encampment."

"All the comforts of home," Aleff assured.

Tevy rushed out of one of the tents and caught the reins of

Eleazar's horse. "This absurd angel has created a bath inside the cave. You will tell me about the battle while you wash."

"Soon," he replied, reaching down to take her hand. "I appreciate your consideration, but the captain should bathe first."

"Why?" she asked, looking Benaiah up and down.

Eleazar hesitated, then shrugged. "He wants it most."

The young woman's dark eyes switched to Ben's face. He cringed inwardly, automatically checking to see if she was armed. But all Tevy said was, "Ember always knows."

Aleff cleared his throat and continued, "Little boys' tent to the right. Little girl's tent to the left. Aforementioned indoor plumbing falls under the *quaint* and *rustic* category. But Tevy's correct. You'll be able to bathe." Offering a lump of soap to Benaiah, Aleff added, "If you tip the attendant on your way in, he'll make sure the water's hot."

"Thanks," Ben repeated, suddenly weary. *Almost chewed in half. Nearly drowned. Jumped a rampaging giant. Chased down an entire army. Watched David walk away again.* Home and comfort sounded pretty good.

With a push in the right direction, Aleff murmured, "Out of the sun before you wilt."

Is that why I feel off? Too much sun? Guess so. Benaiah heard Eleazar offer to help Josheb with the horses before he made it inside. The cave was big enough for Shammah to sleep in, which didn't quite match his memory of the place. *Aleff must have enlarged it for him.*

In the far back, three squat lampstands illuminated the

promised bathing facilities. Ben snorted. *Aleff must have borrowed someone's cistern ... wine press ... dye vat ... thingie. I don't know where the crud he found it, but it'll work.* The oversized stone basin must have taken a giant's strength and a double door for Aleff to shift it here. And the water was hot. As promised.

Benaiah shed stained clothes and slipped in, cradling the soap to his chest. Even without scrubbing, the blood on his skin softened and slipped away, turning the water to rust. Ben stared at nothing for a long time. Until the soft scuff of footsteps came close. He started and turned to find Shammah standing there.

His brother lifted a plate and cup. "Aleff asked me to bring you these."

"Oh. Thanks."

Shammah knelt beside the tub and bluntly asked, "How many men did you kill today?"

Ben recoiled. "Lost count."

Setting aside the food and water, Shammah said, "I do not think you would."

"Not as many as you."

Their giant wasn't buying it. "How many, Benaiah?"

"Sixteen."

"Their deaths are the first on your hands."

Yeah. He's right. Ben glanced down at his hands. They were shaking. Something snapped inside, and his face crumpled. The glisten of tears in Shammah's eyes made it impossible to hold back his own. "Crud."

"Do you regret going to war?"

"It's not that. I obeyed God. Their lives were over. B–" Benaiah's voice broke. "But the angels were crying."

"I do not understand."

"Those Philistines might have cursed God, but God was watching out for them. They all had Guardians. And those angels cared enough to cry." Barely holding it together, Ben choked out, "I *killed* their charges."

"Will they blame you?"

"No. But I might."

Shammah sighed and wrapped his arms around Benaiah. Offering refuge. And Ben took full advantage, hiding his face against Shammah's shoulder to muffle his sobs.

When he finally shuddered to a stop, his throat hurt. His head ached. His eyes were swollen. And he felt stupid. But better.

Shammah dipped his fingertips into the lukewarm bathwater, cleansing away all traces of blood. And leaving a film of ice on the surface. Ben sucked in his breath and gasped, "Cold!"

"Stay a little longer. I will clean your clothes," Shammah calmly instructed before moving away.

Not until Benaiah splashed chilly water on his face did he realize how thorough the Caretaker's son had been. "You healed me," he mumbled, half accusing.

Shammah nodded. "You need your voice for evensong. David will be expecting you to sing."

Ben dragged his hands through his hair. "Today was David's first battle, too."

"Yes. He mentioned that."

"Do you think *he* …?"

"I would not be surprised," Shammah replied. "Ask him."

"If I get the chance," Ben mumbled.

With a sidelong glance, his brother said, "Fear not. Chances are given to all … and taken by those who dare."

I've often thought about
Aleff's words that day.
Not absolute triumph.
Not a clean victory.
He called my quest a
qualified success. A win
with strings attached.
Good mixed with bad.
Room for improvement.
Which meant my job was
far from over. And I
still had a purpose.

47

Some messages don't need words.

Subdued but refreshed, Benaiah followed his nose in the direction of dinner. The appetizer Aleff had sent in was good, but not nearly enough. *Josheb better have left some for ... huh.* Ben pulled up short and hovered just inside the cave's entrance.

The sun had nearly set, and shadows were lengthening. Someone had added torches to the edges of the campsite, probably to discourage critters attracted to the area by the abundance of fresh carrion. Eleazar was sitting close to the fire, his back to the cave, and he was speaking in low tones to Tevy. One of the half-seraph's big hands cupped her cheek, and she leaned into his palm. Benaiah couldn't tell what he was saying to the young woman. But there was enough tenderness in the scene to remind him that she was Eleazar's wife.

Benaiah quickly lowered his gaze, then jumped guiltily when Eleazar's voice touched his mind.

I know you're there.

Yeah. Sorry. Should I give you guys some privacy?

That's what I was doing.

Ben flinched. Had he broadcast his breakdown for everyone to hear? *Will I always be a wreck in front of this guy?*

Eleazar smoothly rose, telling Tevy, "I want to wash. Keep the captain company." On his way past, the half-seraph muttered, "Stop avoiding her."

Have I been? But it couldn't be a lie. Aleff had also told him to talk to the young woman God had placed under his hand. *It's been busy.* But the excuse was lame enough to limp away. *Guess I coulda made time.*

He stepped into the open and offered a tight little smile. It must have translated poorly because Tevy turned her back on him. *This is going well.* "Can we talk?"

"Why?"

"You seem …." Benaiah couldn't decide what word to put next. The ones that came immediately to mind would probably make her mad. Shuffling over to one of the stone seats, he finished, "… like you need someone to talk to."

Her eyes narrowed. "Is that what Ember said?"

"Not exactly. But he'd know."

She turned to look at the cave, then scrutinized him. Ben grew increasingly self-conscious. He always felt half-dressed without his turban on, but his hair needed more time to dry. And that's where her gaze lingered. *Crud.* He glanced wildly around. Josheb, Othniel, Aleff, Eliel—where *was* everyone?

"You are hungry," Tevy said briskly. "While you eat, I will brush your hair."

"No need to fuss."

"There is nothing else for me to do until Ember lets me braid his."

She pulled several skewers onto a small platter and added a cluster of grapes. There was even bread and some kind of soft cheese. Benaiah's stomach rumbled as she served him. He muttered thanks, then said, "There's this old lady. A weaver named Huldah. She always wants to brush my hair. Is it a girl thing?"

Tevy produced a small comb from within the complicated layers of her clothes. "No one would mistake you for a female."

Which wasn't what he meant at all. Ben hunched his shoulders but stayed put. She'd already started when he mumbled around a mouthful of meat. "Guess it's okay. It'll give us a chance to talk."

"Yes. We will talk, and I will understand your words. And you will understand mine."

Benaiah glanced over his shoulder. *I thought she was angry, but maybe she's missing the other girls? Or she could be scared about what's ahead. I dunno. Guessing is getting us nowhere.* "Sounds fair. You wanna start?"

Her lips formed a soft pout. "My complaints pile up, but there is no one to hear them."

"Tell me. Maybe there's something I can do to help."

She had a list.

"My angel has been traded for another. My Ember has been given a strange name. Then that shining one changed his face. And he says my clothes will draw criticism in your homeland. But the robes he offers are *ugly*. And Ember went to battle without me. I should have been by his side! But he says he must stand beside a new king, and I must wait in tents."

It's not just one thing. It's everything. And no wonder. "Crud, I'm sorry. We carried you off without explaining much. Let's start with the first one. Do you have a problem with Eliel?"

"Ember trusts him completely."

"And is that enough for you?" Benaiah checked.

Tevy's comb stopped mid-way through a stroke. "Ember's thoughts are not my thoughts. I know my own mind."

"So what do *you* think?"

"Eliel is everything that Hafiz is not," Tevy replied. "He watches me without imposing. He laughs at me without mockery. His kindness does not come at a cost."

Sounds like she already knows him better than I do. And she gets the difference between his love and Hafiz's. Moving on to the next issue, Benaiah asked, "Would it help if I called him Ember? Eleazar was the name God gave me for him, but I don't think it matters."

"I wish for Ember to be released from this charade!" she replied huffily, brushing with more force. "There is no shame in his form! Why does your king force him to pretend?"

Benaiah stuffed another chunk of meat into his mouth before asking, "Do I scare you?"

"To fear one so easily cornered?" she scoffed. "*No.*"

"But believe it or not, where we're going, people are gonna take one look and scream, scatter, or throw stones."

"Why? You are beautiful!" Tevy protested.

"No. I'm a *stranger*—too tall, too pale, too different. The only reason I have any place at all is because David's a little like you. He took one look and saw easy prey."

She hummed. "Then the man has eyes."

"Yeah. But David doesn't know everything. God wants the stuff about our fathers to stay a secret. And that means putting up with disguises. And being grateful for those few who know the whole truth."

Tevy brushed in silence, and Ben shoved more food into his mouth. *Was that it?* She hadn't exactly agreed with him, but he was still intact. Maybe they could be done now, and he wouldn't have to figure out what to say about the ugly clothes she didn't want to wear.

"Ember says God gave me to you."

Benaiah choked. "No! I mean, *yeah* … but that makes it sound like I gotta bring a bull calf and half my harvest!"

After a startled silence, Tevy giggled.

Breathing a sigh of relief, Ben set aside his food and said, "Come, look at my hands. Guess it's strange, but God's been putting names on them. These are the people He wants me to watch over."

She circled, then knelt for a closer look. "I see strange ciphers."

Prodding his fingers, he read off each one, ending with hers. "This is what Ember meant. God put your name on my hand. You're part of my Flight."

Tevy gently touched Eleazar's name, then her own. He showed her Eliel's placement on the matching finger of his other hand, and she demanded, "Tell me what it means."

"Not exactly sure about the *why* part. But I know it means you belong with us." Benaiah shrugged. "Maybe it's as simple as not breaking up your family. You still have Ember. He still has you."

"I can fight," she countered. "Are we not all warriors?"

"Yeah. God wouldn't overlook stuff like that."

Tevy set her small hand over his and looked up. "Can I learn to read such letters?"

"Not sure what good that'd do. This is heaven's language." Ben quickly added, "But learning the language of this land would be smart. You'll probably be here from now on."

Aleff strolled into view, and Tevy withdrew her hand. Standing, she haughtily said, "I will consider it."

She vanished into the tent Aleff had marked as hers. A moment later, Eliel's boots hit the ground in front of its entrance. Furling scarlet wings, the archer winked at him.

Dumping a few more skewers onto Benaiah's plate, Aleff said, "Less gawking. More chewing."

Ben wasn't about to argue. "Any more of that bread?"

"Compliments of the house." Adding another round to his pile, Aleff breezily asked, "How's Tevy?"

"Better, I think. She smiled. That's gotta be a good sign."

"Speaking of signs, you're blushing like the sky at morning!"

Benaiah didn't rise to the bait. Popping a grape into his

mouth, he said, "I thought Shammah healed everything. Fix it?"

The Caretaker's finger tapped his nose, banishing his sunburn. "Is there anything you want before I leave—take-out, toothbrush, teddy bear?"

"Do you have to go?" Which was a stupid question. *He's probably Sent.*

Aleff answered anyhow. "This is not the *me* your king can meet."

"David will be here? For sure?"

"Wild horses couldn't keep him away."

Hiding his smile behind an over-large bite of bread, Ben mumbled, "Where will you go?"

"I need to step back into Jehoiada's sandals." Gazing at the pale stars that were emerging one by one, he said, "Do whatever it takes to keep David here overnight. If possible, waylay him for a few days."

"Do you know why?"

"Yes." Arching his brows, Aleff replied, "If you don't, he'll die."

Shammah's soft smile was the giveaway.

Benaiah leapt to his feet and stalked out of the circle of firelight. Taking long strides up the hill they were camped against, he listened hard. The moon was bright enough to cast shadows in the Valley of Elah. *Can't see nothing. But ... that's him! He's singing!*

Josheb ambled over and leaned against his spear. "Even if the runt's ears aren't pointy anymore, they're plenty sharp."

As David got closer, his words carried. "The Lord is my light and my salvation—whom shall I fear? The Lord is the stronghold of my life—of whom shall I be afraid?"

"Catchy," remarked Josheb.

Shammah joined them and gave Benaiah's shoulder a poke. "Go meet him. We will wait here."

"Yeah. Be right back," he hastily agreed, taking off down the far slope.

Josheb's low chuckle followed him. Along with Shammah's parting words. "Take all the time you need."

Knowing this was his best chance, Benaiah lengthened his strides. David was easy to pick out, mostly because he walked between two angels. Rei and his mentor flanked the young man, their deep blue wings outspread. *It's kinda regal, like a heavenly train. A king, robed by angels' wings.*

When David caught sight of him, he left off singing and stretched his arms wide. "You leap like a gazelle! I almost mistook you for prey!"

Ben glanced between the two Guardians and fidgeted. Now that he was here, what was he supposed to say? *Wish I could just think stuff into David's head like I do with the others. So much simpler. Much less embarrassing.* Working up his courage, he gruffly said, "I missed you."

David wasn't half so shy about expressing himself. "Don't be so stingy. Your king demands a proper greeting."

"Gonna have to define that for me."

"Don't be foolish. The more you think about it, the more awkward it becomes." Grabbing Benaiah by the shoulders, David pulled him into a fierce hug. He laughed and said, "You must have grown. I *know* I grew, but I still barely reach your shoulder."

"Guess so," Ben replied, awkwardly returning the embrace.

"You sure you missed me? Because my brothers give better hugs, and I'm pretty sure they don't even like me!"

Benaiah muttered, "Picky."

"Not truly. But I want you close." In a softer voice, David said, "Too many people use an embrace to hide their dagger."

Mindful of Aleff's earlier warning, Ben wrapped his arms more snugly around David. Trading scowls with Rei, he demanded, "Did someone threaten you?"

With a soft sigh, David complained, "Today, I've been threatened with glorious fame, dubious wealth, a royal bride-to-be, too many cups of wine, several dark looks, and an unkind remark about my height."

"You *are* kinda short."

That earned him a jab.

"Only compared to you, the king, and the Three," David said, stepping back.

"*The Three.*" Ben pulled some of the baggage from his friend's back, shouldering a bulging pack and a canteen. "Sounds official. Ominous."

"After today, it is!" As they walked, David explained, "A wild man carried by twelve horses in order to avenge the twelve tribes. The pale fighter who stole Goliath's spear to turn it against God's enemies. A silent warrior with ropes of flame for hair. The stories are exaggerated further with each telling!"

"Not bad. They each made their mark."

"All the talk is about me … and the Three. You were overlooked somehow. Which is a shame. If it wasn't for you, the infamous Three wouldn't be here at all."

"I don't mind," Benaiah assured. "So long as you're safe."

David's steps slowed. "You sound like one of the king's bodyguards. They put his safety above everything else."

"Is that what you need?"

"Right now, all I really need is a green pasture by a slow-moving stream … and a sleepy flock to listen to the songs that are bottled up in my soul."

Ben pointed to the glow of firelight coming from just behind the hill. "I don't have any sheep, but Josheb might share his horses. And you promised Shammah music. He wouldn't let us start without you."

"I brought my harp," David said, his steps quickening. "Evensong sounds like heaven."

"Close. Real close."

Greetings turned to laughter. Promises became reality. Tuning gave way to song. And to David's boundless delight, his melodies expanded into harmonies.

He needed this like I needed to crash and cry. This must be how he deals with life's junk.

Eleazar's deep voice thrummed, and Shammah's tenor was sweet enough to raise the hair on Benaiah's arms. Josheb stuck to the melody line with David, and Benaiah messed with filling in chords. *Too bad he can't hear the Guardians.* All four sang along, blending their voices in David's psalm of praise.

> **Ascribe to the Lord, you heavenly beings,**
> **ascribe to the Lord glory and strength.**
> **Ascribe to the Lord the glory due His name;**
> **worship the Lord in the splendor of His holiness.**

With each passing verse, Ben learned things about David. *He must have traveled while working for Saul.* New places. Natural wonders. And as his world widened, the shepherd boy from Bethlehem had found more reasons to bless the Creator.

From inside her tent, partially hidden by its fluttering door covering, Tevy watched with eyes half-closed. She'd insisted on staying out of sight. Waiting to see if this new king was worthy to look upon her. Benaiah knew she couldn't understand a single word David had composed. But Eleazar's face was a picture of peace. So Tevy seemed favorably inclined to accept the young harpist.

> The Lord sits enthroned over the flood;
> the Lord is enthroned as King forever
> The Lord gives strength to His people;
> the Lord blesses His people with peace.

Floods. Thrones. Strength. Peace. The cries of David's heart neatly matched the stuff Benaiah kept hidden inside. *For his sake, I became one of those heavenly beings. Wonder if he'll ever know?*

As the last chord faded, David sighed his way into a smile. He drained his cup before remarking, "I remember when I met Benaiah. I asked him, 'Who would follow a boy like me?' The obvious answer was … *no one*."

"No one without courage," countered Josheb.

Shammah refilled David's cup and added, "No one without faith."

With a weary smile, David shook his head. "Captains and generals, priests and dignitaries—they don't pay any attention to the boy who crouches at the king's feet like a tame dog, plucking pretty melodies."

Benaiah silently translated for Eleazar, who inclined his head. "His answer has changed. Ask the question anew."

At David's inquiring look, Ben relayed, "Your answer's different now. He can tell."

"Yep. It's clear now that *you* would follow me. A boy can lead other boys." David looked from face to face and said, "We're close in age. All too young to be taken seriously. Yet we'll live in the king's house and learn the king's business.

It's as if God has hidden us in plain sight!"

Josheb elbowed Eleazar. "He just called us boys. Should I take offense?"

"You only want an excuse to spar with him," Shammah said mildly.

Ben was more amused by the *hidden* remark. But something else stuck out. *He's saying* we *a lot. Are we going to Gibeah?* How would King Saul feel about David bringing home four mongrels … and a girl.

Leaning forward, eyes bright with interest, Josheb asked, "After today, do you *really* think God wants you sitting back, watching, and waiting for the old king to dodder into his grave?"

"It's no use asking me. I don't know the mind of God." David rested his chin atop his harp. "Makes me wish I could talk to Samuel. But the prophet of God is no longer welcome in the king's city."

"Ramah isn't so far away," said Benaiah.

"Hey. Aren't you overlooking something?" Josheb demanded. "If God's chosen a new king, why keep the old one around?"

David shrugged. "King Saul is God's anointed."

"So are you," said Shammah.

"I won't raise my hand against him," David said firmly.

Josheb muttered, "*You* wouldn't have to."

Benaiah quickly pulled rank on Josheb. "*We* won't raise our hands against the king." With a pointed look at the surly spearman, he silently reinforced his order. *There's a difference between predecessor and enemy.*

The half-cherub held up his hands in surrender, but he mouthed something Benaiah didn't catch.

Shammah made another round, filling their cups. When Benaiah's was topped off, their giant whispered, "Josheb said, 'Tell that to our fathers.'"

Which was probably a good point. Ben accepted the reminder with a nod.

David set his fingers against his harp's strings, but his mood had taken a downturn. Confusion was plain on the young man's face, and his opening chord was melancholy.

Then Eleazar spoke. "David has been set apart from his youth. He belongs to God. The timing of his coronation also belongs to God. All that is required is all that ever was. Trust in the Lord. See what He will do."

As Benaiah translated, David's eyes widened. "Is Eleazar a prophet?"

"Nope. But I'd listen to him. Eleazar's always right."

David's last song told of messages that needed no words. Of the power of an unspoken testimony. Of a beauty David didn't take for granted.

> **The heavens declare the glory of God;**
> **the skies proclaim the work of His hands.**
>
> **Day after day they pour forth speech;**
> **night after night they reveal knowledge.**

> They have no speech, they use no words;
> no sound is heard from them.
>
> Yet their voice goes out into all the earth,
> their words to the ends of the world.

Day after day. Night after night. Far from the home where he stole the center of attention, David lived in service to the man he'd replace. So close to the throne God had promised to him. Yet overlooked by one and all. Taken for granted. *Until today.*

A shepherd boy had earned God's notice. Had he longed for more? The giant-slayer had earned fame. And all he wanted to do was return to his flocks. *But it's too late to turn back.*

At least he didn't have to go forward alone.

Into the quiet, Benaiah said, "When God made that sky and this earth, Job says that the morning stars sang together, and all the angels shouted for joy."

"I wish I could play all night, but my arms are as heavy as my eyelids."

Josheb smirked. "Must have slain one too many giants this morning."

With a soft chuckle, David carefully wrapped his harp in its coverings. "Loan me a stone for a pillow, and maybe I'll dream as Jacob once did. Angels from heaven can whisper new songs into my ears."

Ben signaled to his men, and they moved together. The four

of them knelt side-by-side between David and the fire. "We want to be clear. Say a few things outright," Benaiah said. "These are my men. They follow me, and I follow you."

David propped his chin on his hand and regarded them with traces of awe. "Yesterday, I was alone. Today, I'm surrounded by predators."

"We're as dangerous as we have to be," Ben acknowledged. "But you can rely on our loyalty."

"I'm flattered. I'm relieved. But I have to ask … why would your men be loyal to a song-twiddling shepherd boy like me?"

"If you will pardon the correction," Shammah said, "we are loyal to God."

"And that makes us the same as you," said Benaiah. "Faithful to His call. Ready to serve. Grateful for His gifts."

David rubbed at his nose and grinned. "You say the most embarrassing stuff."

"Only when you need to hear it."

Benaiah grabbed David's shoulders and steered him away from Tevy's tent. "Other one's ours. C'mon."

"What are you hiding in this one?"

"The fiercest warrior of the lot. Much too dangerous for the likes of you."

"Someone else is here? Why didn't you say so?" David craned his neck as he shuffled along. "Introduce me!"

"No. Bedtime."

David relented with a sigh. "Is it just me, or do your tents glow in the dark?"

They do, kinda. Ben figured they were woven from whatever was used to make raiment. *Same pearly sheen. Same soft shimmer.* But he tried to laugh it off. "What were you drinking?"

"Cold water."

"Well it must have gone to your head." Benaiah herded him through the entrance, saying, "Time to sleep it off."

David laughed and answered in a sing-song voice. "I long to dwell in your tent forever and take refuge in the shelter of your wings."

Benaiah's smile twisted ruefully. "You can stay as long as you like. Just make sure to leave room for me."

"What about your men?" David asked. "Aren't they coming?"

"They'll sleep when they need it. But for now, they'll stand guard. You're safe. Get the rest you need."

"I will lie down and sleep in peace, for you alone, O Lord, make me dwell in safety." David flopped onto the mats with a groan, and Benaiah shook out a couple of blankets. After making sure his friend would stay warm, he snagged a pillow. Shoving it under his head, he shut his eyes with a sigh. A moment later, a hand locked around his wrist.

"Yeah?" Ben whispered.

David answered in low tones. "I didn't know I needed you this much."

"God knew."

A long yawn. A sleepy hum. "Can you stay with me from now on?"

Benaiah wasn't sure. *Four more men to find. And who knows how far I'll have to go to get them.* But a silent inquiry left him with the answer he hoped for. "Yeah. That's the way it's gonna be."

Rolling onto his side, David stared at him with a solemn expression. When it warmed to a smile, Ben was certain he'd made up his mind to share something precious. *A promise? A vow? A secret?* He waited breathlessly to see what David would entrust.

"There's someone I want you to meet."

Benaiah blinked. *Oh, crud. Is this what Aleff meant when he said I needed to learn to deal with girls?*

David went right on talking. "You're my friend, my first follower, my most trusted captain. We'll be together *all* the time."

"Yeah. That'll be good," he cautiously agreed.

"That's why you need to meet Jonathan."

Uneasiness stirred in his soul. But Ben had to ask. "Who's he?"

The way David's gaze softened. The smile meant for another's eyes. They told a whole story before he ever said a word. Then just as surely as if he'd used his sling, David struck down a hope Benaiah hadn't realized he'd been holding close to his heart.

"Jonathan's my best friend."

EPILOGUE

**The Spirit of the Lord had departed
from Saul, and an evil spirit
from the Lord tormented him.
1 SAMUEL 16:14**

He waited in the darkened tent, knuckles white on the arms of his throne. A single oil lamp guttered on the ground at his feet, leaving him in shadow. Beyond these flimsy walls, his army still celebrated. Songs and drink. Laughter and boasts. Such a change from every other miserable night of this God-forsaken campaign. But the tides of war had turned. Victory belonged to God's people. All thanks to that boy.

"I told you he was trouble."

Saul turned his face, but there was no avoiding his tormentor.

"His praise is on their lips. His songs have stolen their hearts."

Counselors and healers assured Saul that he was sound and sane. As king, he bore the weight of the world on broad shoulders. If he heard the voice of his own doubts, it simply proved he was a man of conscience. Even so, Saul wanted to blot out the whispers. Just as earnestly as he wanted to wrest the psalms of David from the lips of every man, woman, and child in Gibeah. But apparently, a king's wants were nothing. And prayer was a waste of time. God had abandoned him on a teetering throne, with mockery for a crown.

"Send them away, and word will spread. Your soldiers will carry home the tale of David and Goliath."

Saul pinched the bridge of his nose and growled in frustration.

"Sir?" came a low voice.

The king grabbed his spear from its holder and stared hard at the man silhouetted against the half-open tent flap. With a grunt of recognition, he called, "I'm here. Come forward."

Immediate obedience. Confident stride. Saul dared to hope for good news. "Tell me it's done."

His soldier swayed as if struck.

"Orders like that only appeal to men with a death wish."

Saul's expression darkened as his most-trusted captain squared his shoulders and knelt before the lamp, placing himself at his king's mercy. Head bowed, the soldier asked, "Do I supply the lie you want? Or the truth you don't?"

Which could only mean one thing. Saul snapped, "He lives."

"He's *missing*," the man replied. "I cannot kill what I cannot catch."

"Then look for him!"

"I've been through the entire encampment twice."

Unthinkable. Surely the boy would stay to revel in his triumph. "Are his brothers hiding him?"

"The sons of Jesse are too far into their cups to be so clever. I checked their tents."

A fist pounded the arm of the throne. "He must be somewhere!"

"Certainly. But he isn't *here*. Even your son claims ignorance."

"Your son. Your heir. Your pride and joy. He'll betray you."

Saul's grip on his weapon tightened "A son should follow after his father!"

"We are of one mind. Fathers should rule over their sons. Can you reclaim yours?"

Rage seized Saul's heart, hot and heavy. He ground his teeth so hard, his jaw ached, and he tasted blood in his mouth. "You doubt me?"

"Sir?" The kneeling captain ventured. "Do you want Jonathan brought here?"

"He suspects."

Saul reared to his feet, head and shoulders taller than any man among them. Wasn't that why they made him king? Hadn't he the right to defend his throne?

Shock registered on the soldier's face. "S-sir, are you well? I thought I saw–"

"He's seen the truth in your eyes."

The king glowered as this captain of a thousand men sat back on his haunches. A loyal dog at his feet. One that would bite if he wasn't put down. Saul drew back his arm, adjusting his grip on his favorite weapon. "Do you mock me? Am I not king?"

"Of course! Forgive me! It was a trick of the light. I only imagined they were …. God have mercy, they're *green*." Pale-faced and panicked, the soldier scrambled backward, scuttling like a crab in his bid for escape. Shaking his head, he begged, "Please, sir! Anything! I'll d–"

With a single thrust, Saul drove his spear through the man's heart, pinning him to the floor.

"Decisive."

"Am I not king? And is not Jonathan my son?" Saul stepped over the body, muttering, "Nevermind. I'll find him myself."

THE STORY CONTINUES
FORSAKEN SONS, BOOK 2

The Thirty

CHRISTA KINDE

About the Author

Faith in a Father whose ways are mysterious. Hope in a Friend who's coming again. Love that bears fruit in far-off places. **Christa Kinde** believes in bright colors, good manners, crazy socks, word games, cat naps, and postage stamps. But most of all, she believes in God. She writes about her faith with studies, stories, and devotionals that bring truth into focus and give faith a practical spin.

Christa also publishes family-friendly fantasy under her maiden name. If you like magical master sculptors, shape-shifting brothers, stowaways with secrets, and mythical creatures, let your curiosity lead you to CJMilbrandt.com.

Forsaken Sons cast portraits, story art, outtakes, and postcards await you on Christa's website. Be sture to drop in for milestone parties, character Q&A sessions, and news about upcoming and ongoing stories.

ChristaKinde.com

Family Friendly Fantasy

Christa also publishes under her maiden name, C. J. Milbrandt.

Byways Books. Three brothers with a magical inheritance take sibling rivalry to new lengths as they race each other across their homeland. [A multi-book series for kids who are ready for chapter books.]

Book #1: *On Your Marks*: The Adventure Begins
Book #2: *Aboard the Train*: A Ewan Johns Adventure
Book #3: *Over the Bridge*: A Zane Johns Adventure
Book #4: *Up the Mountain*: A Ganix Johns Adventure
Book #5: *Inside the Tree*: A Ewan Johns Adventure
Book #6: *Into the Hills*: A Zane Johns Adventure
Book #7: *Across the Line*: A Ganix Johns Adventure
Book #8: *Down the Stairs*: A Ewan Johns Adventure
Book #9: *Through the Notches*: A Zane Johns Adventure
Book #10: *Back on Track*: A Ganix Johns Adventure
Book #11: *Beneath the Torch*: A Ewan Johns Adventure
Book #12: *In the Middle*: A Zane Johns Adventure
Book #13: *Among the Tents*: A Ganix Johns Adventure

Galleries of Stone. Of all the world's treasures, none are more valuable than stone from the Twelve. Children on all four continents are tested for affinity, for the mountains hold magic. But in the foothills of the Gray Mountain, no one remembers stone lore. The majestic Statuary is forgotten, as are the wonders that fill its galleries. Only rumors remain, and those are used to frighten children. For it's said that a monster lives in the heights.

Freydolf serves as the Gray Mountain's Keeper. Exiled. Feared. Unwelcome. But necessity drives him into a Flox village to hire a boy to fetch water and tend fires. Tupper Meadowsweet isn't the cleverest child, but he's brave enough to follow his new master up top. In the Statuary, Tupper finds hints of faraway lands, diverse races, long histories, unique customs, and danger.

Book One: *Meadowsweet*
Book Two: *Harrow*
Book Three: *Rakefang*